Cathy Williams ca— ———————— Boon books as a te———————————— hem she remains a ———————————— like creating roma———————————— each and every ———————————— ves in London. Her ———————— ue, Olivia and Emma—hav————— and continue to be, the greatest inspir———— in her life.

Canadian **Dani Collins** knew in high school that she wanted to write romance for a living. Twenty-five years later, after marrying her high school sweetheart, having two kids with him, working at several generic office jobs and submitting countless manuscripts, she got The Call. Her first Mills & Boon novel won the Reviewers' Choice Award for Best First in a Series from *RT Book Reviews*. She now works in her own office, writing romance.

Also by Cathy Williams

Emergency Engagement
Snowbound then Pregnant
Her Boss's Proposition
Billionaire's Reunion Bargain

Also by Dani Collins

Husband for the Holidays
His Highness's Hidden Heir
Maid to Marry
Hidden Heir, Italian Wife
The Greek's Wife Returns

Discover more at millsandboon.co.uk.

ONE NIGHT BEFORE CHRISTMAS...

CATHY WILLIAMS

DANI COLLINS

MILLS & BOON

All rights reserved including the right of reproduction in whole or in part in any form. This edition is published by arrangement with Harlequin Enterprises ULC.

This is a work of fiction. Names, characters, places, locations and incidents are purely fictional and bear no relationship to any real life individuals, living or dead, or to any actual places, business establishments, locations, events or incidents.
Any resemblance is entirely coincidental.

Without limiting the author's and publisher's exclusive rights, any unauthorised use of this publication to train generative artificial intelligence (AI) technologies is expressly prohibited. HarperCollins also exercise their rights under Article 4(3) of the Digital Single Market Directive 2019/790 and expressly reserve this publication from the text and data mining exception.

® and TM are trademarks owned and used by the trademark owner and/or its licensee. Trademarks marked with ® are registered with the United Kingdom Patent Office and/or the Office for Harmonisation in the Internal Market and in other countries.

First published in Great Britain 2025
by Mills & Boon, an imprint of HarperCollins*Publishers* Ltd,
1 London Bridge Street, London, SE1 9GF

www.harpercollins.co.uk

HarperCollins*Publishers*, Macken House, 39/40 Mayor Street Upper, Dublin 1, D01 C9W8, Ireland

One Night Before Christmas… © 2025 Harlequin Enterprises ULC

Heir for the Holidays © 2025 Cathy Williams

Boss's Christmas Baby Acquisition 2025 Dani Collins

ISBN: 978-0-263-34486-8

11/25

This book contains FSC™ certified paper
and other controlled sources to ensure responsible forest management.

For more information visit www.harpercollins.co.uk/green.

Printed and Bound in the UK using 100% Renewable Electricity
at CPI Group (UK) Ltd, Croydon, CR0 4YY

HEIR FOR THE HOLIDAYS

CATHY WILLIAMS

MILLS & BOON

CHAPTER ONE

'COME IN!'

Ella looked at her watch. It wasn't yet nine, which was disappointing, because she'd hoped he would be late—very late. Late enough for her to tell him that, sadly, he would no longer qualify to shadow her, because the one thing Ella categorically refused to indulge was lack of punctuality.

This was not what she needed on a Monday morning, with summer drawing to an end and all the work involved in changing the store fronts, doing the end of season inventories and working out the various temporary placements that were needed to cover the Christmas season.

What Ella wanted was to have her routine down pat, as she always did. She liked routine. She liked order. She'd had her whole week planned out until she'd opened her email at eight, when she'd arrived at Hailey's, only to find that she'd been tasked with taking a lad under her wing to show him the ropes for the next fortnight. Jose Rivero, there through personal recommendation by Sir Ron Brisk-Hailey, whose family had owned the department store on the outskirts of Dublin for nearly eighty years.

There was scant information on why this lad was interested in learning the ropes of a department store but, reading between the lines of Vera's brief email, she'd concluded that he was probably a friend of one of Sir Ron's kids—maybe on the last leg of work experience before hitting university. It didn't matter. What mattered was that she wasn't in the best of moods when she heard that knock on the door.

Half-standing, reluctant, resigned and still resentful, Ella was smiling grimly as the office door was pushed open. She looked up slowly, schooling her expression so that she gave the message that she was a busy woman and wouldn't tolerate anyone who wasn't willing to do as told.

She froze as the guy strolled into her office, paused, looked at her in silence for a couple of seconds and then shut the door behind him with a little nudge of his foot.

She knew that she was gaping. She couldn't help herself. This was so *unlike* her, so *out of keeping* with her usual calm, competent, unflappable, *serious* self. There was part of her that almost couldn't believe she was standing here, staring at this man as though she'd never set eyes on a guy before.

He was...*beautiful.* Sinfully, crazily, stupidly beautiful. He was tall and swarthy, with dark, dark hair that curled just a little at the collar of his black polo-shirt, and had eyes that were designed to demolish common sense, reason and sound judgement—three things on which she prided herself having in abundance.

'I... I think you've got the wrong room.' She was irritated by the breathlessness of her voice, so she cleared her throat and did her utmost to drag her eyes away from the guy who was still looking at her with his head tilted to one side.

'Have I?'

'Yes,' Ella said sharply. She hurriedly tried to find Vera's email, leaning over the computer, all too conscious of those dark eyes on her. Then she frantically scanned it for details that weren't there in the first place...so why on earth had she thought that they would suddenly materialise out of thin air?

'You're Ella Campbell?'

Ella looked at the man who was now walking towards her.

'I'm sorry but I was expecting... I wasn't expecting someone...'

Was he going to help her out with this? Evidently not. His amused silence was unnerving, and Ella was seldom unnerved. A serious child who had become a serious adult, she had only ever been unnerved once, when her heart had let her down. But everything makes one stronger, and she had toughened up. So to be here, now, with her thoughts all over the place and her heart beating like a sledgehammer, wasn't what she wanted. Not at all.

'Please,' she said curtly, 'Sit.'

Ella watched as he sat. He moved with the economic, elegant grace of a panther. He was sleek, powerful and, sitting in front of her desk, he seemed to dominate the space around him.

'I'm afraid I just found out this morning that you were showing up, Mr... Rivero.' She glanced again at her email, blinking at her screen because it saved her from having to look at his darkly beautiful face. 'Vera didn't send over many details about you and, like I said, I wasn't expecting someone...' She sighed and linked her fingers together on her desk. 'I thought you would be younger.'

'My apologies for disappointing you.'

'I see here that you were recommended by Sir Ron?'

'I was.'

'I presumed that you were perhaps one of his daughter's friends over here to do a little work experience before starting university in Dublin.'

'I *am* here for work experience, but I won't be heading off to university, and I'm a little old to be mixing with Sir Ron's daughters and their friends.'

'How do you know Sir Ron?'

'Is that relevant, would you say?'

Ella met his mild smile with pursed lips because somehow his response, though valid enough, was just a little too over-confident for her liking—borderline *insolent*.

A young lad she could deal with, even a young lad who wanted to fool around more than learn the ropes. She'd had two shadow her in the eighteen months since she'd been working at Hailey's. But this guy…?

She was flustered. 'Maybe you could tell me a little about yourself—your work experience and what you hope to get from being here for two weeks. Do you have any experience in retail?'

Their eyes tangled, and for a couple of seconds there was silence as Rocco thought about what he was going to tell her and what he wasn't.

Jose Rivero. Jose Rivero was the owner of a small outlet somewhere in Spain who had pulled one or two strings with the owner of this once-prestigious, now down-on-its-luck department store, ostensibly to see how a big store was run.

Maybe his home was in London and he was hoping to open somewhere there. How had he pulled those strings? What sort of place was he hoping to open? The details didn't matter. He was just an ordinary guy who would be temporarily staying at a one-bed rented flat somewhere close by. An ordinary guy, a minnow who wanted to get in with the big boys, grateful to have cadged a favour. Smart, ambitious but with a long road ahead of him.

Earlier, when Rocco had sat having his espresso in the café opposite Hailey's, he had felt oddly free at the thought of his modest, unassuming alter ego. He would have two weeks roaming through the store, under the guise of seeing how things were done, while casting his eye over everything and making sure that he knew just what would have to be done to the place when he bought it to convert into offices and high-end apartments.

For the first time in his life, in the guise of Jose Rivero, Rocco would cease to be the only heir to the great Mancini fortune. He would cease to be the billionaire who had grown up in a mansion, who owned multiple properties, a super-yacht and a fleet of eye-wateringly expensive cars.

It felt good. It felt good to be sitting opposite this small, sexy girl with the straight dark, shoulder-length hair with the big green eyes and skin that was as pale as milk and dusted with freckles. It felt even better to be with a woman who wasn't interested in making a favourable impression on him.

Rocco smiled. He liked the way she blushed and tried to hide it. She was in her twenties but trying hard to maintain the stern demeanour of someone older.

'Where to begin?' Rocco mused aloud, without any intention of telling her anything of significance. 'I'm just an ordinary guy who's been lucky enough to get some work experience here for a couple of weeks. To see how life in a big department store is lived.'

'You won't be seeing how life is *lived* here, Mr Rivero. You won't be getting involved in a set of a soap opera. The email I received doesn't specify a great deal but I'm presuming, from everything you've said, that you want to see how things are run?'

'Correct, but please, for the record, my friends call me Jose.'

'And please, for the record, I don't believe we're friends.'

'Perhaps not yet, but I've always maintained the importance of good working relationships in an office setting. So, let's start with my age. I'm thirty-two which, I gather from your reaction, wasn't what you expected.'

'The kids who come here are usually fresh out of school or earning money before they head off to university.'

'And how often are kids shown around the store?'

'I don't believe that's relevant, is it, Mr Rivero?'

'It could be if I plan on opening something more ambitious than I currently have.'

'Well, perhaps a handful a year. Summer time is popular and so is Christmas. We need the extra hands, and there are usually teenagers who want to earn a little money for the holidays.'

'Can I say that you look remarkably young to be in charge of running a department here? Because you are, aren't you?'

'I…'

'Not relevant. I know.' He held up his hands up in mock-surrender. 'Am I over-stepping my brief? I have a problem with that. So I've sometimes been told.'

'I… I'm twenty-eight.'

Ella licked her lips. The harder she tried to be composed, the faster she could feel this man getting to her, getting under her skin. He had walked through her office door, tall, dark and crazily *different*, bringing with him the enticing whiff of foreign shores and heady adventure. He'd reminded her of where she was—in a job she had never anticipated, living a life that had never been on her wish list.

A broken heart, her mother dying, her dad needing her…everything had fed all at once into bringing her here, back to Hailey's, where she had worked every summer as a teenager and then for several years between A-Levels and university.

Where were the years taking her? She liked what she did and she was good at it. But time was drifting by and her life was drifting by with it and now this man, showing up here…

She was only twenty-eight! Something about the way those dark, amused eyes rested on her made her feel conscious of her shortcomings. More than that, he made her conscious of her sexuality in a way she hadn't since she and Steve had crashed and burned. Since then, she had returned to the farm to help her dad and to process her own grief at the loss of her mother. That had happened shortly before she and Steve had broken up and put the sexual side of her into cold storage. The ice was beginning to melt just now and that was throwing her into a state of panicked confusion.

'Not,' she said in an over hearty voice, 'That my age has anything to do with…anything.'

'Of course not.'

'I…' She breathed deeply and wondered how possible it would be to dodge this job and hand him over to someone else. Vera had specified that she should show the man round because she knew so much about the store and because Pete, her boss, was off this week. But weren't rules meant to be broken? She'd never actually gone down that road but the thought of battling feelings that were suddenly at war inside her was a daunting prospect.

'I think you should fill me in on some basics if I'm going to assign you to the relevant department.'

'I would rather several relevant departments as opposed to just the one. The more I can see, the better.'

'Sadly, you don't get to decide where you go or don't go. Tell me what sort of shop you have and what areas are of interest to you.'

'A range of things, actually, although wine and everything to do with it is a large part of what I stock.'

'Really? Then why on earth would you want to look around a department store?'

'You stock food and wine?'

'Yes, of course, but that's a fraction of what we have in the store.'

'I would be interested in finding out what the profit margins are for that particular department in comparison to the others,' Rocco said smoothly. 'In a fast-moving age, it's good to find out what sells and what doesn't, wouldn't you agree?'

'Yes.' She was on more secure ground and relaxed. 'I think the white-goods department has suffered because of online shopping. It's so easy for people to flick through a website, find what they want and order it without having to trudge into a store to see what might not even be the full range of models on offer.'

'So true,' Rocco murmured.

She was preaching to the converted. He already knew the stats on which department was failing, and frankly not many in the store were succeeding, hence Ron finally agreeing to sell. Rocco had floated the idea two years previously. By then, his father had all but retired after suffering a stroke and, having been involved in his own extensive business concerns, Rocco had returned briefly to Spain to oversee certain changes he'd wanted to make for some time.

One had been to extend into eco-friendly, highly sustainable accommodation and office space. He had plans to be the leader in the field, and he'd met Hailey sufficiently often to have noted the decline in the department store which was in such a prime location close to Dublin city centre.

He'd made his move when he knew that the tipping point had been reached between holding on to the family legacy and letting it go because it was haemorrhaging money. He'd come here to make sure he wasn't being conned into paying over the odds and to work out floor plans.

He already knew everything else there was to know. In fact, as the woman stood up and beckoned him to follow so she could show him what he was actually not much interested in seeing, he realised that what he really wanted was to find out more about *her*.

'People can be lazy,' she said, walking ahead of him. 'Footfall in stores makes high streets thrive. Hailey's has been going for ever and it's the heart and soul of the community. The more people shop from home, the more a place like this loses its identity.'

'That's a very impassioned speech.' He caught up with her and fell into step. They had emerged into an open office space. Heads turned surreptitiously. She waved to a couple of people but didn't break pace.

'This is where all the paperwork gets done,' she said

without looking at him, but bee-lining for the lift. 'Accounts, sales co-ordinators...customer services section.'

'And you're in charge of everyone on the floor?'

She pinged for the lift and he lounged against the wall and stared at her, noting the creep of colour into her cheeks.

'Not everyone.'

'But most.'

'I handle the sales team, customer services and oversee one or two other areas as well.'

'Tough call. For someone so young.'

The lift came. Ella stepped in, aware of him behind her and the way her whole body was burning, conscious of unvoiced questions surfacing for the first time since she had returned home. What was going to happen next in her life? What lay around the corner? She enjoyed what she did here, but was she really happy or was she simply biding time? Was this it?

She stared at the panel, mouth dry as uncomfortable thoughts ricocheted around her head. The silence dragged until she felt compelled to break it as the doors opened onto the floor below, dedicated to the failing section selling white goods, a handful of computers and phones, and the much bigger toy section which always pulled up profits.

'I've had a lot of experience here at the store so when I...when I had to return I was fast-tracked to a managerial position.'

'Had to return from where?'

'Had to return from the place called *none of your business*, Mr Rivero.'

Their eyes met, Ella's appalled at her lapse in professionalism, Rocco's openly curious at how her hackles had risen. That was definitely disproportionate to his inoffensive question.

Rocco was accustomed to women making themselves available to him and one of the ways they did that was to present themselves as an open book. They were always keen to elicit his interest. They didn't set about shutting him down by being abrupt. This was new for him. But then, he mused, he wasn't Rocco Mancini to her, was he? He was Jose Rivero and effectively she was in charge of him. She was going to be his boss for two weeks! He had to suppress a grin.

'Point taken.'

'Sorry. My apologies... I...'

'I see what you mean about footfall.' He adroitly changed the subject, because trying to encourage her to talk would have the opposite effect, and his curiosity was growing by the second. 'It's very quiet on this floor.'

'It'll pick up as Christmas gets closer.'

Ella frowned and saw the store dispassionately, through an outsider's eyes, while knowing what this outsider wouldn't know. Profits were down and had been for a number of years. The annual financial reports didn't make for pleasant reading, but the general manager was always optimistic. Hailey's had been a presence in the town for so long that they were all convinced it would never be allowed to fall by the wayside. It was more than just a store. It was the heart of the community. It was only September, but they were already making plans for Christmas and the traditional events they hosted over the festive season.

That said, there was no doubt that the store needed

updating and that some departments were losing money hand over fist.

How much should she confide in a perfect stranger, though? Zero, she decided.

She pointed things out. She explained tricks they used to get footfall on the upper floors, which were always quieter. She was saying all the right, helpful things, while her mind was in freefall and her body responded to him in ways she didn't want.

She tightened her lips and fell silent as they toured the floor. She wondered whether she could palm Jose off on Hal in the white goods department. If he wasn't around her, he wouldn't get under her skin and she wouldn't think about the parts of her life that were so unsatisfying when held up to scrutiny.

'We seem to be covering ground at break-neck speed,' Rocco murmured next to her.

'There's a lot to get through before I decide what I do with you.' Ella flushed at the unintended innuendo.

'Do with me as you will. You have my word that you'll find me a very able and enthusiastic worker. Your wish will be my command while I'm here.'

'Great. We love able and enthusiastic little worker bees here at Hailey's.'

Rocco burst out laughing, and he felt that something again as her green glance slid across to him and held his amused gaze for a couple of seconds. A couple of seconds longer than was strictly necessary, his highly attuned sexual antenna told him. Something stirred inside him, the thrill of being in a completely novel situation for the first time in his life, he thought.

'Maybe we could take a breather for five minutes while I process everything you've told me.'

'You should have been taking notes.'

'No need. I have an excellent memory.'

Ella gazed at him, out of her depth with this lazy banter. She wanted to escape this yet she wanted to bask in it and enjoy the excited, light-hearted feeling it gave her. Neither option was the efficient, brisk response she knew she should give him.

'How many more floors have we to look around?'

'Three,' she said crisply. 'And don't tell me that you're exhausted. You don't look the sort who tires easily.' She cast a critical eye over him and reddened at the slow smile he shot her.

'What sort would you say I looked like?'

'Okay. The conference room is...' she nodded past the toy section to a bank of mahogany doors '...over there. If you like, we can recap on everything and then perhaps we could work out how best to put you to use?'

'Of course.'

He gave her a mock salute, which she ignored and walked towards the doors, stopping on the way to check out various displays that needed tweaking, aware of interested glances shot in their direction.

She would be composed and informative with him. She would work out where he could be placed—somewhere that wasn't in her immediate radius. In her own time, she would try and figure out why he had this effect on her and what it told her about herself.

Walking alongside her, Rocco had already taken in everything he needed regarding the state of the once-grand department store. He liked Ron, and had promised a fair deal, but it would be back to the drawing board on the price because he reckoned a full structural survey would reveal a lot more serious wear and tear than was on the surface. Probably more than Ron was aware of. He lived in Dubai and had left the running of the store to various board members—always a mistake.

She would normally have left the door to the conference room wide open. Stepping in behind her, Rocco half-closed it with his shoulder and then took the offered chair. He was amused to note that she made sure to sit in one that was broader and slightly higher than his.

Trying to assert her authority? Understandable. But there was an electric current zapping between them, making her skittish and on edge. He hadn't banked on any of this, but he was enjoying it. He felt a little skittish and on edge himself. Freedom from the responsibilities that came with wealth and power was liberating.

Rocco's life had always been propelled on a very specific trajectory. His family might not be of royal blood but they were wealthy enough always to have mixed with the most elevated of Spanish society. Theirs was old, inherited wealth going back generations. One smallholding had grown over the decades and spawned tentacles that reached into every business concern imaginable.

As an only child, Rocco had been brought up to realise the importance of carrying on the family tradition. An empire needed a guiding hand and he'd had no choice in the matter. He was clever and ambitious enough to have thrived on the pressure. Had he ever wanted to break free? No. Not because he lacked the imagination for it but because he had an unerring contempt for where that path led.

His uncle, older than his father and the natural heir to the Mancini empire, had gone off the rails. In the process he'd come close to ruining not just the family fortune but all the livelihoods that depended on the jobs the Mancini empire supported. He had found drink, drugs and women too irresistible, and the wealth at his disposal had made acquiring all three far too easy for an inherently weak man. Maybe he could have ridden that tide until he got too old to maintain it or ran out of steam, but he had made the mistake of marrying one of his hangers-on—an avaricious woman in her forties who had fleeced him for so much money that she had almost brought the company to its knees.

After less than two years of a volatile and desperate marriage, she had hired a clever lawyer who had done his utmost to slice off various arms of the company as part of the settlement. His uncle had also signed over part of his own holdings to her at some point, presumably when he was high on drugs. It had been a mess.

It had also been a learning curve for a teenager who had watched from the sidelines and taken it all in. Control had become Rocco's byword. His parents' marriage might have started life as a business arrangement, but it had worked perfectly. There had been no room for misunderstandings. His mother, from a similar background, had known from the start what duty and responsibility looked like. She had been the perfect wife. She had known how to entertain the clients and how to be supportive without expecting any reward.

Rocco found that he was curious about Ella's life. He'd always mixed in a circle that was small and reflected his own life. Had he been lazy in that respect? Maybe. But Jose Rivero, as he now was, was seeing a side to life he didn't have much experience of, and it had whetted his appetite to see a little more.

And a little bit more of the woman sitting opposite him, looking at him with narrowed eyes and a professional coolness that couldn't quite conceal an awareness of him that was pleasingly titillating.

'So...' Rocco drawled.

'So?' Her eyebrows arched upwards. 'I think it might be a good idea to set you on some of the little jobs that might seem boring but are crucial to the successful running of a company.'

'Tell me more. I'm eager to learn.'

'Filing.'

'You want *me* to do the filing?' Rocco couldn't hide his honest reaction to that suggestion.

'Yes. There's a lot of it waiting to be done.'

'Surely you don't still use those antiquated things called *filing cabinets*?'

'We're gradually transferring everything online.'

'When did you start doing that?'

'There's no need to sound so incredulous. Hailey's is an old-fashioned store. Perhaps it could have moved more quickly in that respect but as soon as I got here, and saw how archaic the IT systems were, I looked into an upgrade...'

Rocco considered her for a few seconds in stretching silence until she reddened and began to fidget under his unwavering stare.

She really was incredibly pretty, he thought. Sexy in a way that wasn't obvious. Sexy without wanting to be sexy.

Why was she still single? Or was she? Curiosity was in charge. He wasn't sure he liked that, because he was so accustomed to his head ruling everything, but this was a moment in time that would never come back, so why not enjoy it? He settled lower into the chair, crossed his legs and loosely linked his fingers together on his stomach.

Ella thought he looked totally relaxed. He looked like the guy calling the shots, which was ridiculous, because *she* was the one in charge here. She might not feel quite as in charge as she would have wished but she was still the boss.

But the way he was looking at her... Her mouth went dry, and for the life of her she couldn't drag disobedient eyes away from his face.

'So,' she said weakly. 'Back to the filing...'

'What did you study at university?'

'I beg your pardon?'

'I was just interested. Interested in knowing how you ended up working here, at this store. Did you study business? Accounting?'

'Geography,' Ella heard herself say abruptly.

'I guess that's a generic enough subject.'

Ella wanted to pull back from the conversation but something was urging her on. She hadn't much experience of this—of opening up, of straying out of her comfort zone... Her life had been on hold ever since she'd returned here. Maybe part of her life had always been on hold because she'd always played it safe.

She licked her lips and felt a slow fire inside her as those deep, dark eyes continued to look at her in silent appraisal.

'I didn't get the chance to finish my degree,' Ella confessed in a rushed undertone. 'I...my mother died. She'd been ill for a while—cancer. I was twelve at the time and I remember what that was like...but the cancer had gone into remission.'

'I'm sorry, Ella.'

The genuine sympathy in his voice opened up something inside her. Did she want that something to be opened up? Maybe not, but for the first time she wanted to confide.

'It returned in little baby steps,' she said, glancing down at her hands, which she then balled into fists. 'But then it seemed to snowball until she couldn't fight it any longer. When she died I came back here but...'

'But...?'

'But I guess this wasn't where my dreams lay.'

'Where did they lie, those dreams of yours?'

'I fancied getting involved in efforts to combat climate change.' Ella suddenly laughed. 'I was a big dreamer.'

'Sounds like a perfectly reasonable dream. But landing this job...it must have seemed like a stroke of luck. Like I've said, you're young to be in such a position of seniority.'

'I worked here over the holidays from the age of fourteen,' Ella confided. 'My mum worked in the haberdashery department and she pulled a few strings to get me temp jobs in the store so that I could have pocket money for the summer hols. After my Leaving Certificate, I came back and worked for a few years to save for my tuition fees at university. I didn't want to have a student loan outstanding.'

She cleared her throat and, when she yanked herself back to reality, she was appalled to consider how much she had revealed to a perfect stranger. Appalled and just a little bit...alarmed. What on earth was going on with her?

'Apologies. I went off-topic,' Ella said briskly. 'You're here for practical advice so, if you have any questions, please feel free to ask provided they pertain to the reason you're here.'

'Just the one.'

'What's that?'

'Can I shadow you for the duration of my stay here? I think I would learn a lot more with one dedicated mentor than if I flitted from department to department under the supervision of random people, picking up all the boring back-room jobs no one is interested in doing.'

'How do you know I won't lumber you with the same back-room jobs?'

'I don't, but I'm willing to take the chance.'

'I really can't promise that you can spend your time here under my sole supervision.' But her heart was thudding and she felt as though she needed to clear her head. Right now she wasn't in charge of her emotions. She was behaving unprofessionally and allowing him to get under her skin. If she didn't get some air, at the risk of appearing rude, then she was going to explode. No, worse—she was going to carry on waging war with common sense and that wouldn't do.

She thought of Steve and what he had put her through. She had been led astray by her emotions into ignoring red flags and handing her heart over to a guy who had never deserved it. Right now, the ground was shifting under her feet, and it was imperative that she didn't allow that to happen.

'Look at the time!' She stood up, leaving him no choice but to follow suit.

He stood up slowly and she followed that easy, graceful motion with fascinated attention.

He looked at his watch. 'Time flies when you're having fun,' he drawled and Ella felt that, yes, he couldn't have hit the nail on the head more accurately. She'd been having fun! It was crazy. She was supposed to give orders and do a job!

'I'm afraid I have some important chores to do in town

but I'll hand you over to one of my colleagues at the staff canteen and you can grab some lunch there.'

'And when you get back…?'

'When I return, I'll settle you in front of some…'

'Filing. I can transpose everything onto the system.'

'Would you know how to do that?'

'I can confidently tell you that it won't be a problem. And if I have more questions…?'

'Naturally, that's what I'm here for.' Ella's eyes locked with his and her heart picked up pace.

'I'm glad to hear that. And would you be prepared to answer them over dinner with me…?'

CHAPTER TWO

Over dinner with me?

What a nerve! He was there to shadow her, follow her instructions! Basically, when she thought about it, she was *his boss* for two weeks. He was on a par with Claire and Sharon, the eighteen-year-olds who constantly had to be told off for giggling and trying on make-up when no customers were waiting to be served.

Admittedly, there were some differences... Jose was thirty-two, wouldn't know how to giggle if he took a course on it and was a drop-dead-gorgeous, sex-on-legs guy. But she was *still his boss for two weeks!* Which was why she'd given him a cool, amused, derisory look four days ago when he'd voiced that outrageous suggestion.

Nevertheless, she'd felt a tingle of awareness race through her at the thought of having dinner with him, of seeing him outside the confines of the store. And, over the following few days, she'd been aware of him in ways that were scary and thrilling at the same time. She would park him at a desk and point out what she wanted him to do but, instead of getting on with her own workload, she'd find herself sliding little glances across at him while her imagination ran riot.

When she showed him around the various departments, she was aware of how every single person in the entire store looked at him with interest and curiosity.

Ella knew he was dangerous. At least, dangerous *for her*. Temptation happened on a daily basis: a murmured remark, a raised eyebrow, a slow smile... Little ripples in her previously calm existence bit by bit were waking her up to a general dissatisfaction about her life which she had successfully managed to ignore since she'd returned to the family home.

The breath of *something more out there* that he had brought with him on day one didn't fade as the days went by. It got stronger, stirring a restlessness inside her she couldn't control.

She was beginning to find excuses to come in a bit earlier than usual and to leave a bit later. Was it her imagination or was he doing the same?

Ella glanced at her phone. It was Friday and it was five-thirty. She could have clocked off at five.

At the desk next to her, Jose was doing something diligent in front of the computer. He was proving to be surprisingly efficient at pretty much everything she threw at him.

'Ahem.' Ella cleared her throat and swivelled her chair so that she faced him.

Today he wore a pale-blue polo shirt and black jeans. Her eyes drifted to the bulge of his muscled forearms and the taut pull of the jeans over his thighs.

He turned his chair to face her and leaned back, arms folded behind his head. 'Ahem?'

'It's okay for you to leave now, Jose. It's Friday, and I'm sure you have lots of things planned.'

'Why would you assume that when I'm new to the area? Takes time to make friends.'

'You don't seem to be doing too badly on that front.'

'Have you been keeping tabs on me, by any chance?'

He grinned, and Ella reddened. 'Of course not!'

'It *is* your job, though, now that I mention it. You wouldn't want me to accidentally delete something.'

'That wouldn't happen. There are back-up systems in place. I'm surprised you don't know that.'

Was this the sort of Big Retail Store Experience Jose had envisaged when he had wrangled his fortnight here? He never revealed anything. At first, she had vaguely wondered what he was doing here, when everything about him suggested a guy who could take on what life had to offer without anyone's help, but she had shrugged away her curiosity. He'd come via Sir Ron and it wasn't up to her to start playing detective just because he didn't look the part.

'Anyway…' She stood up and shuffled stuff on her desk, tidying things away and very much aware of his dark eyes on her. 'I should get going.'

'Big plans for the weekend?'

Did the cinema with a girlfriend on a Saturday count as 'big plans'? Ella wondered. 'Huge.'

'Well, spare a thought for me.' Rocco stood up, taking his time, flexing his muscles and not ungluing his eyes from her face.

'Why would I do that?'

'I'll be on my own on my last weekend here, watching television and eating a boxed meal for one.'

'I'm sure you could rustle up some company from the fan base you've made at the store,' Ella said politely. She hovered, unsettled by what he had said about this weekend being his last one here, which was a reminder that this strange excitement that filled her whenever he was around came with a deadline.

She considered her life beyond him with a sinking feeling of dread. Her heartbeat quickened and she licked her lips and continued to hover.

Rocco felt the blood rushing through his veins as he held her indecisive stare with lazy, shuttered intensity. He fancied her. He had no idea why he did, when that had happened or how he had managed to surrender his self-control, because he'd never thought coming here on a fortnight's recce would include this scenario. He didn't like complications and he especially didn't like complications when they involved women.

Reality had no room for sentiment, and sentiment was the enemy of control—just look at his uncle. That said, this was a different place, far removed from the usual concerns he would have in a situation like this. Jose Rivero didn't have an uncle who had squandered millions and nearly brought the family name to ruin. Jose Rivero was free of those constraints.

Right now, Ella was hovering, waiting, for...what? Waiting for their conversation to continue?

Rocco felt the sharp excitement of adrenaline race through him. 'I feel I should apologise,' he said huskily and then held her gaze when she frowned with confusion.

'Okay, feel free. Go right ahead, although I have no idea what you want to apologise about. Unless,' she said, eyebrows raised, 'You've done something wrong on the system and were too ashamed to tell me? I get the feeling that you don't like being wrong but we all make mistakes.'

'Thank you for being so magnanimous and understanding,' Rocco said humbly. 'But I don't make mistakes when it comes to tech.'

'Oh, really.'

'Generally speaking, hand on heart, I don't tend to make many mistakes.'

'Can I say that that's a very arrogant statement?'

'Of course you can.' He'd been spot-on with the body language interpretation, he decided. It was Friday, and the weekend lay ahead, but she wanted to be right here in a deserted office chatting with him. Where were her *huge* plans—awaiting postponement?

Dinner would be very satisfactory for both of them.

'So, what do you want to apologise for?'

'For asking you out to dinner a few days ago when I first met you.'

'Ah. Well…'

'You must have found that very offensive.' He began gathering his bits and pieces, such as they were, not looking at her but aware of her with every nerve in his body.

Eventually, when he did look at her, she was blushing and still indecisively hovering in the same spot.

'I…' she began.

'You must have thought me incredibly full of myself, which—and I'll freely admit this—I have occasionally been accused of. Didn't you just do that—accuse me of arrogance when I thought I was just being honest? I'm always mystified by other people's assumptions.'

'Naturally, it seemed…uh…a little surprising. Dinner…'

Rocco strolled towards the lift and was gratified when she fell into step with him. 'For starters, I never even asked whether you were involved with someone…' He looked down at her, at the way her shiny dark hair dropped in a straight sheet to her shoulders, at the economical grace of her movements as she walked and the swell of her breasts pushing against the pale-blue shirt primly buttoned up to her neck.

She was so *different*, so *composed*, so *cool*, so *reserved*... He got a kick every morning when he came in to find her there, in her starchy outfits that did nothing to conceal her innate sexiness. Now, his libido kicked into painful gear as he continued to stare at her. They hit the lift button and when the doors opened he stepped aside so that she could brush past him.

'Are you?' he asked, leaning against the mirrored wall and gazing at her with interest. 'Involved with someone?'

'That's none of your business.'

'It is, because I would really like to have dinner with you, but obviously if you have a partner then I'll back off. I've never been the sort of guy who treads on another man's toes. So, are you involved with someone? Because if not then I'd like to take you out to dinner.'

'Why?'

'Sorry?' Rocco was momentarily taken aback. He stepped out onto the ground floor and allowed her to precede him.

Here there were signs of life, although with only fifteen minutes till closing, there was the depressing atmosphere of the few customers there politely being ushered towards the exit. Half the staff appeared to have vanished, probably getting ready to join the Friday evening stampede out. Canned music added to the general air of a place just waiting for the axe to fall. He could have left after day one from what he'd seen, but he'd stayed put. He was beginning to see why.

'Why,' she repeated as they left the store, 'Do you want to take me out to dinner?'

'Because.'

'You're going to be here for another week. Like you

said, this is your last weekend, so it's not because you want to get to know me better.'

'You wanted to continue studying geography. You wanted a part in changing the world. You're serious about climate change. But you ended up here because your mother died and…was there no one else to save the day? What's wrong with wanting to find out a bit more about someone? So, tell me, was it all on your shoulders?'

'I didn't *save the day*. I came to help my dad out. He has a small farm. He needed someone to be there for him. He was…he wasn't functioning. Couldn't function. He was too wrapped up in grief.'

'What about siblings?'

'Honestly, I have no idea how we've drifted to this!'

'Because, like I said, I want to get to know you better. You aren't only interested in someone if they're going to become a permanent fixture in your life. Aside from all of that, I find you attractive.'

'Really.' Her voice was thick with scepticism.

'Yes, really. Tell me where this is coming from. You're very, very sexy—has no one ever told you that before?' He raised his eyebrows at her expression. 'Why are you looking at me with such a scathing expression? Doesn't make you any less sexy, if you want to know. We can explore that later. First, answer my question. Is there someone in your life? My gut tells me no, but only a fool obeys his gut.'

'No,' Ella said impatiently, 'I'm not involved with anyone.'

'Then have dinner with me. I know a good restaurant. I walk past it on my way to…where I'm renting. Nice atmosphere, always busy. Menu looks good…'

Ella could feel her heart thudding like a sledgehammer as she stared up at him.

It was busy outside the store. Everyone was out enjoying the dregs of summer before autumn and winter blew in, with jolly Christmas songs and cheerful reminders of what she was missing on the man front. The coffee shop opposite thronged with customers.

He found her attractive. He thought she was sexy. She should be wary of that, should have her guard up. Trusting a man wasn't on her radar.

And yet…and yet… Here she was, guard up, being careful, settling into a life where nothing exciting ever happened because she'd been hurt, because she was cautious. And here was this man, a stranger who would leave her life for ever in a week… A stranger who had made her look at her own life and see what it lacked.

Ella was suddenly filled with a sense of reckless adventure, a feeling that life was slipping past her and, if she didn't reach out to catch it, then by the time she woke up it might be too late.

'Okay. Yes.' She smiled hesitantly as their eyes tangled.

'Good.' Rocco drawled. 'Because I want to know all about Ella and why she was so surprised when I told her that I found her attractive.'

He began strolling away from the store and she kept pace. She knew where this was going and she wanted it to go there. She wanted to break out of the walls she had built around herself and see what a bit of adventure tasted like. It was almost too exciting to think about.

There was freedom in knowing he wouldn't be sticking around. She could do what she wanted, say what she wanted, they could have a good time for the next week and then he would be gone for ever. She was walking on air, barely aware of being shown to a table in the buzzy wine bar or wine being ordered.

'Talk to me, Ella,' he purred as soon as wine had been poured for them. 'And don't be shy. Or nervous, for that matter. You're not nervous, are you? I don't make you nervous, do I?'

Rocco enjoyed the way she blushed, the way the girl was so easy to entice out from behind the persona of the businesswoman—a persona that didn't fit nearly as snugly as she maybe imagined. At least, not to him. 'I just don't get why you're here, working at Hailey's. It's very pretty out here, but it's not exactly the centre of the universe for a young woman, especially one who had dreams of being somewhere else and doing something else.'

'I told you, I came because—'

'I know. There was no one else and you had to support your father.'

'My brother did come over but he could only stay for a very short while.'

'Why's that? Shouldn't it have been all hands to the pump?'

'Conor…he lives in Australia and he's married. He and his wife run a gym. He couldn't take more than a couple of weeks off. You know how it is, when you work for yourself.'

Ella felt something she seldom had before—a deep sense of unfairness. Was she being uncharitable? She felt tears prick the back of her eyes. She was just being human. Conor had come, and then in the blink of an eye he'd gone, and here she was all these months later, still picking up pieces, still being the dutiful daughter while Conor carried on…just being Conor.

'No. I don't.'

'What do you mean? Commitments…sometimes you can't spare the time when you might want to.'

'And did he want to? Because, from where I'm sitting, he sounds more than a little selfish. Surely he would have known that you would be putting your life on hold?'

And that was about the gist of it, wasn't it? A life put on hold—her life.

She didn't understand why she found it so easy to talk to this man. Was it because he was a stranger? Because he wouldn't be hanging around, so she would never have to face the consequences of anything said in confidence?

Or, deep down, had she simply been lonely after her mother died, and after the break-up that had been so painful? Did this guy just happen to have the key to open up a well of sadness she'd never properly acknowledged?

'I guess my kid brother's always been selfish.' Ella sighed. She propped her chin in the palm of her hand and looked at Rocco's beautiful, sympathetic face. Something inside her leapt, a thrill of succumbing to a feeling she wanted and was no longer going to resist, something that had been growing ever since she'd set eyes on him. 'My mum had cancer when we were both still at home and…well… I was always the serious one in the family, the dependable one. I was the good little girl and Conor was the one who got away with doing what he wanted.'

'I get it.'

'What? What do you get?'

Rocco didn't say anything for a couple of seconds. He'd never felt this engaged in a conversation with any woman in his life before but then, he reminded himself, he wasn't *Rocco*, he was *Jose*. Jose came with freedoms that Rocco had never had. Of course he would react in ways that were alien to the carefully controlled guy he'd always been!

'You never had your moment of rebellion because your

brother was the one who did that and, for as long as he was the rebel, you subconsciously strove to be the one who kept things on an even keel, especially if your mother was chronically ill.'

'How did you just do that?'

She smiled, and for a second Rocco's heart swelled with pleasure. He wasn't the billionaire who ran an empire and gave orders to people who jumped when he spoke. He was the kid who got the answer right in class in front of the girl he wanted to impress.

'Do what?'

'Get me to open up to you. I haven't said that to anyone but, yes, you're right. Conor was the rule breaker, and the more he broke the rules, the more I obeyed them. I suppose I thought that he could have stayed longer after mum died. He was helpful, and he arranged a lot of things while he was here, but then he was gone and here I am. I stayed.'

'But surely you didn't have to?'

'Why is this conversation all about me?' Ella glanced at the menu that seemed magically to appear in front of her and randomly chose something off it without really registering what she was ordering. She laughed but her laughter dried up at the depth of his dark gaze as it rested on her, questioning, thoughtful and breaking down yet more of those barriers she had erected.

'Maybe I fell into a rut.'

'Too much excitement out there? Easier to kick back and see where life decides to take you?'

But he was smiling when he said it, and she smiled shyly back at him.

'I needed to get away,' she said in a low, broken voice. 'I... I never thought I'd end up getting away for good. I always assumed I'd finish my geography degree, but then I came back here and day to day reality took over, and one day I realised that finishing my degree was no longer a priority. I guess... I fell into a rut of my own making.'

'You said that you needed to get away...'

'I... I'm boring you. I'm talking all about myself. You must think I'm crazy to be sobbing on your shoulder when I don't even know you.'

'Maybe that's why you find it so easy.'

'Tell me about yourself.'

Their food had arrived, as if mysteriously, because Ella was so oblivious to everything around her, including the waiter who had refilled their wine glasses and presumably made the usual noises to ask what they wanted.

'What do you want to know?'

'Do you have any family? Brothers? Sisters? Cousins? Annoying uncles and aunts you only see at Christmas? Do you miss living in Spain, running your store there? Actually, you haven't really told me where you live... Do you live over here?'

Rocco lowered his eyes. Her open honesty was discomforting, reminding him why he was here in the first place, and honesty didn't play a big part. He squashed his niggling conscience fast. What was happening here wasn't about his acquisition of the store. What was happening here was about the two of them and their unlikely attraction.

'No brothers or sisters. An uncle, yes—not in touch. He's the black sheep of the family.'

'That's a shame,' Ella said with sympathy. 'Family is so important, and it doesn't sound as though you have lots to go round.'

'Can't say I've shed tears over that.'

'But there's always a reason that a black sheep is a black sheep, don't you think?'

'Haven't really thought about it.'

'Sometimes it's the family dynamic, having to live up to a sibling who's cleverer or better-looking or the favourite…'

Rocco—who normally would have repelled that sort of mumbo jumbo—thought about what she'd said. He thought about his uncle and the steadiness of his own father—the cold confidence that had been in such stark contrast. They were rather like Ella and her brother, he thought, but so much more destructive with so much money and power at stake. There hadn't been room for a wild card, especially when the wild card had gone so far off the rails that he'd threatened to ruin the company.

'Maybe you're right, but hey, who needs the potted history?'

'I just gave you some of mine,' Ella pointed out.

'Far more interesting than mine. Tell me why you needed to get away, Ella. Your openness is sexy. I like it.'

Rocco relaxed. He was back on safe ground instead of uncomfortably skirting round the truth about who he was and why he was here.

'I fell in love,' Ella said simply. She laughed a little self-consciously. 'At university. I fell in love with a guy and I thought he'd fallen in love with me as well.' She raised her eyes to his and wiped her mouth on her serviette. What had she just eaten? It had been very tasty but she couldn't say. 'I don't know why I'm telling you all this stuff.'

'You know why. We're ships passing in the night. We can say whatever we want and do whatever we want because nothing will come back to bite us in the future.'

Also true. And this was why he felt so liberated, why he wasn't watchful with her, or keeping her at an emotional at arm's length.

'Tell me,' he said roughly.

'It's all history now, but I suppose it's why I stayed here. Deep down, maybe I was afraid to return to my course, afraid to bump into Steve. He was studying geography as well. We bonded over our passion about climate change. At least, that's what I thought at the time.'

'But instead...?'

She laughed, faltering. 'Instead, it turned out that he went out with me because he wanted to bond with my best friend. Actually, he wanted to do a lot more than bond with her. Or, rather, he *did* want to bond...in a very, *very* literal way. He used me to get to her, and she decided he was a better catch than the guy she was dating, who was messing her around. I was collateral damage and neither of them looked back.'

'Ella...'

'No need to feel too sorry for me,' she said lightly. 'Everybody has to have a little heartbreak in their life now and again, and I'm well and truly over him.'

Rocco felt a jolt of pain on her behalf. He felt submerged in her story in a way he would never have dreamed possible. Her sweet, heart-shaped face was a picture of the stiff upper lip as she recounted something that had clearly been shattering for her at a time when she'd been going through the grief of losing her mother.

'If that man was sitting here right now, I'd wring his neck.'

This time her laugh was genuine. 'You're sweet.'

'I'm the opposite of sweet,' Rocco growled.

'But you're not.' She reached across, gently touched

his hand and, when he linked his fingers with hers, she squeezed them and smiled. 'I thought you were the most arrogant guy I'd ever met when you waltzed into my office.'

'I'm extremely arrogant.'

'But underneath all that arrogance and self-confidence there's a really sweet guy who knows how to listen, and is genuine and honest.'

Rocco flushed darkly. 'I break hearts.'

'My heart isn't on the line here.'

'Good,' Rocco said in a low, driven voice. 'Because...'

'Because?'

'I want you, Ella. I want to take you to bed and make love to you until you're crying out for more. But I don't want to end up hurting you in the process.'

A thread of reckless abandon stole into her. She'd spent her entire life being careful and the oppressive weight of that was something she had always kept to herself. She had never really thought about it...until now.

Just when she'd least expected it, this stranger had come into her life and thrown everything into focus. He'd made her see things she might not have wanted to see, but she couldn't *un*-see them. She didn't like the trajectory of her life, didn't like the way she'd run away and then hadn't really stopped running, even though she could have a while back.

He was dangerous. She felt it. He was arrogant, self-confident, empathetic, strong: *a potent mix*. But did she care how dangerous he was? She could withstand that potent mix because she could never go for a guy like him; could never be sucked in to emotional involvement with someone who was so far out of her comfort zone.

She was too grounded, whatever temporary recklessness was possessing her.

'I… I've never done anything… I'm not the sort of girl… You're saying these things…'

'We both know why we're here, having dinner. This is foreplay, and we both want what comes next. You're still young, Ella,' Rocco said with cool, gentle persuasion in his voice. 'Give yourself permission to live a little, whatever heartbreak you've suffered. Or else the creep who broke your heart wins.'

'Yes, well…'

'Sometimes,' Rocco murmured, leaning forward and tugging her into him, 'It doesn't pay to be too careful. You spend so long dodging land mines that you forget there's a world out there where land mines don't exist. You forget how to live the life you have.'

Ella breathed, looking at the dark intent on his face. 'And sometimes you get out there and forget that you might just step on a land mine you hadn't expected because you got a little too complacent. And when that happens…it's all over.'

'Trust me—I won't be one of those annoying errant land mines, Ella.' He smiled slowly, flipped her hand over and traced tiny circles on the sensitive underside of her wrist. He held her gaze. 'You know what you're getting with me—no nasty surprises. What we'll have is fun for a week or so and then I'll disappear from your life.'

'No nasty surprises…'

'None. I'll leave. And when I do…' he smiled. '…you won't regret that I've been…'

CHAPTER THREE

WOULD SHE REGRET IT? Could she trust him? He'd smiled that slow, lazy, utterly charming smile and she'd blinked away all her doubts. She'd forgotten her vows to be careful after Steve. She'd relegated to oblivion all her resolutions about only letting any man into her life when she knew that he could be trusted.

'You should take a few days off,' he'd said, as they'd left the restaurant hand in hand, heading for the place he had rented on the outskirts of town. 'I want you to myself while I'm here and shadowing you is going to get in the way of that. Unless there are private cubby holes where we can hide…?'

'You can't do that!'

'Why not?'

'Because…you're here for a fortnight! You've signed up to work.'

'I'm not on a pay roll.' He'd shrugged. 'And I'm okay with trading some of my time here for more pleasurable pastimes. Live on the wild side, Ella—forget about duty for a minute.' He'd pulled her against him and kissed her, and that kiss had been devastating. He'd looked her in the eyes, sifting his fingers through her hair and cupping her face. 'And that means not finding excuses to be careful all the time. I'm not as poor as you think, even if I happen to be your slave for a fortnight.'

'Hardly a slave!'

'Don't knock it. I like the thought of you giving me orders. Take the rest of the week off. I'll book us somewhere—a cottage. We can play house until I leave next weekend.'

'Play house?'

'By that,' he'd clarified quickly, 'I mean lie in bed all day and only get up to shower or eat.'

He'd rented a cottage... *What had he expected?* He'd taken time out with women before—a five-star hotel somewhere in a bustling city. He travelled extensively and occasionally had a woman travel with him. If she disliked falling in line and taking second billing to his work commitments, then nothing had ever been said, because he'd lavished her with expensive gifts and taken her to classy restaurants. Money was always a great persuader.

Now, though... He'd had his EA find a suitably rustic cottage buried in the countryside. She'd emailed a picture of it and Rocco had given her the go-ahead. It was nothing Rocco Mancini would have contemplated in a million years, but as soon as they'd reached it, it had felt right.

Two days on, it still felt right. There were no expensive shops, no expensive restaurants, no expensive gifts bought. There was just a cottage in the middle of nowhere, nestled in rolling green hills.

'Need a hand?'

Rocco was sprawled on the deep, old-fashioned sofa watching as Ella busied herself in the kitchen. They were playing house. It wasn't something he'd done before in his life but he was doing it now and enjoying it. Outside, the fading sun was casting the last shadows over a garden bursting with wild flowers. Inside, the furnishings were cosy and worn, with lots of throws on the chairs and sofa, wooden beams on the ceiling and a central stone fireplace that dominated the living area.

Ella looked across at Rocco lying on the sofa, ankles loosely crossed and one hand behind his head, the other dangling to the side. It was a little after six and her body still tingled from when they had made love only a couple of hours before. She felt dampness spread between her legs and knew from the slow smile he shot her that he could read exactly what she was thinking.

I want you. Ella couldn't believe how far she'd come from the cautious girl who had resented having someone rearrange her work pattern by showing up without warning in her carefully ordered office to the girl she was now: open, free and trusting. She'd taken one look at the cottage he had rented for the week and had known that this was a guy who *got her*.

'What would you like to help me with?' she teased now, strolling towards him with a knife in one hand and an onion in the other.

'I can't have a conversation with you when you're approaching me with a knife. A man can get a little edgy around a woman with a knife.'

Ella burst out laughing. Yes, he got her. Got her in ways she had never expected. He made her laugh with his dry wit and listened to her with dark, pensive eyes that encouraged her to confide, confide, confide.

'Would you know how to cook a meal?' she smiled, moving to sit next to him and then curling into him as he adjusted his big body so that she could fit neatly into him.

'I can rustle up something edible if I have no choice.'

'Honestly, Jose, for a guy who lives on his own, I'm

shocked that you're not more proficient in front of a cooker. I guess you get women to cook for you?'

Now and again, Ella noted little things that made her think, like ripples quietly disturbing the calm surface of a lake. Such as the fact that she knew precious little about him aside from the basics. Of course, she reasoned, she didn't need someone's entire back story to know that they were right for her; that they were kind, good and fair. He'd told her to have an adventure, to live in the moment, and that was what she was doing. She was following his lead, stepping out of her comfort zone and enjoying it.

Except…time was moving on and now, nestled against him, feeling his heartbeat through his tee shirt, she wondered where things were going. Time felt in short supply and suddenly she had a pressing urge to find out more about him, to make the connection between them stronger.

Maybe to know whether there was room for them to develop what they'd started after he left…?

Her heart fluttered. She'd told herself that she was in control of a situation that brought her physical satisfaction without emotional entanglement, because her head told her he wasn't the sort of guy she was looking for. Not as a long-term proposition.

After Steve, she told herself she would be careful. She based her benchmark on her dad, who was quietly strong, reliable and kind, a man of few words who knew what it was like to devote his life to the woman he loved. He and her mother had adored one another. He'd been her rock and had been there for her through the many years of uncertain health.

That was what she was looking for. Not a guy who made her body sing, who took her to places she'd never imagined possible but who was also the essence of charm, easy wit and stunning self-assurance.

Yet…she couldn't quite imagine life without him in it, and that scared her. Was there a connection there for him as well? He wasn't taking a risk like she was. So was this just another every-day fling for him? Or more than that?

'I don't, actually.'

'So you cook for yourself? Tell me what you like to cook.'

'That's a lot of questions.'

'I want to find out more about you. You know so much about me. I've never confided in anyone the way I've confided in you, and I'm not even sure how you've managed to get me to tell you so much.'

'I'm a persuasive kind of guy,' Rocco murmured.

'I can't actually believe I'm here with you.'

'Yet how hard was it to tell your manager that you wanted a few days off? And I'm still not sure why you had to skirt around the reason for that by saying I'd had to cut short my stint there, and you needed a break to regroup from having your routine put out of sync by my unexpected presence.'

'People have a way of gossiping.'

'Does it matter what people think?'

'It does to me.'

'Why?'

'I suppose,' Ella said thoughtfully, 'That it's just the way I've always been. I've always been quite restrained. Like I've told you, Conor was the one who took up all the oxygen. He demanded attention and, the more he demanded, the more I retreated into myself. Especially with Mum—having to deal with health issues that cropped up time and again. I felt like the last thing my parents needed was the headache of two kids testing the boundaries.'

'Did you ever resent that?'

'Until I met you, it wasn't something I'd ever confronted. It was what it was. You're the only one who knows just how awful my experience with Steve was. I lost a future I thought I might have with him, but it was more than that. Because of what he did, I lost my friend as well.'

'People like that don't deserve your friendship or your love.'

Rocco could smell the sweet, floral scent of her hair and, as he breathed it in, he felt the tight, grim throb of rage when he thought about the guy who'd let her down, because she hadn't deserved that.

It wasn't jealousy. He didn't do jealousy. He never had. But, in a way, it was worse than jealousy, because it was a sort of possessiveness and that was alien to him. He almost wished he'd been around at the time to protect her from a guy who should have been kicked out of her life before he'd got his foot through the door.

What was *that* about? Why wasn't he more concerned at how intimate they had become in such a short time? He was a man who guarded his emotions, who never encouraged women to over-share and who was happy to have sex as the motivator behind relationships, safe in the knowledge that when the time came to take a wife he would only ever consider one who logically fitted the bill. Emotion would play no part in his choice.

But this unusual freedom…life in the guise of someone else, intimacy…didn't feel like a threat. He enjoyed her soft murmurings as she confided in him, told him things that were close to her heart. It made him want to talk to her as well.

'Have you ever lost your heart to someone?' he heard her ask.

'Not my style.'

'You're in your thirties and you've never lost your heart to anyone?'

'I...' Rocco hesitated, knowing that there was a limit to what he could tell her but also knowing that, within those limits, there was a lot he could confide, and it shocked him just how much he wanted to do that.

'Go on. I'm open with you.'

'You *are* very open,' he agreed. 'Sometimes, it feels as though you're from another planet.' He smiled when she laughed. 'In a good way. You tell me about yourself and you're not trying to impress me.'

'Women try to impress you? No, don't answer that. I can well imagine. Is that why you're so self-confident?'

'You can well imagine? I like that. Very good for my ego.' Rocco kissed the crown of her head and sifted his fingers through her hair, tilting her face to his and then very gently contouring her lips with his tongue so that she shivered against him and came a little closer.

He thought about his background: extreme wealth, extreme privilege, the very foundations of inbuilt self-confidence. He wondered how she would react if he were to come clean, but that wasn't an option, and if there was a twinge of unease at the thought of what he was obliged to keep to himself then he dismissed it because they were both in a bubble, far removed from reality. He would leave, she would return to being the person she was and it would be the same for him. Ships passing in the night.

'Maybe,' she mused, 'You're confident because you're

an only child, so you've never had to tailor your personality to adapt to a sibling, and you've never had to compete for your parents' attention. You must have been lavished with love.'

'Actually,' Rocco said pensively, 'I wouldn't say that I was very close to my parents at all.'

'Weren't you?'

She levered herself up and stared at him with undisguised curiosity, which made him smile again.

'They were very cold.'

'Why? Poor you.' She hugged him and held him tightly for a couple of seconds. 'You must have been lonely as an only child if your parents were distant. Were you?'

'I… I suppose,' Rocco said slowly, 'There were times when I was. Yes.'

'When?'

'You ask a lot of questions, don't you?' He breathed in deeply, and there it was again—a feeling of freedom that he knew he would treasure when life returned to normal and he resumed his responsibilities. 'Christmas.'

'Christmas?'

Rocco burst out laughing. 'For someone who's been through quite a bit, you're very soft-hearted. Yes, Christmas was never the highlight of my life.'

'My family was always very close. My brother may have been a little wild—' she smiled '—but there was never any question that we were there for one another. I feel for you when you tell me that you weren't close to your parents and were lonely at Christmas…that's a joyous time of the year. It's a big deal here and at Hailey's. We hold a lunch for people who are homeless and we arrange a Santa grotto for the kids. The store sponsors it all.'

Rocco didn't want to think about Hailey's because it reminded him of the fate that awaited it. It was also an unwelcome reminder that this liberated man wasn't him but someone else, someone on borrowed time, someone the real Rocco would look back on with affection and bemusement.

'Don't feel too sad for me,' he breathed, his body stirring into arousal as the feel of her against him became too much to bear. 'I got presents and there was a tree. It was just never celebrated with any warmth. What's happening with that food? Can it wait? Because I can't.'

He touched her, relaxing into the less challenging place where physical contact took precedence over touchy-feely conversation that was so unlike him.

'I like talking to you,' Ella murmured. 'You're nothing like what I expected when they told me that someone would be coming to shadow me for a fortnight.'

'And you're nothing like what I expected when I came here. I never thought that my boss would be a woman who drove me crazy with desire. Let's stop talking. I want to make love to you.'

Ella wound her arms round his neck and smiled when he hoisted her easily off the sofa and took her into the bedroom. She wasn't wearing a bra or any underwear. She'd quickly become accustomed to the way he wanted to touch her all the time, scooping down into her soft jogging bottoms to feel the wetness between her legs or pulling her towards him and pushing up her jumper so that he could caress her breasts. He'd told her that he'd quite like her to walk around completely naked in the cottage but, failing that, to dispense with the underwear. From the stern position of never making the mistake of yielding to any man, she had yielded to those demands with lightning speed.

Thoughts left her head in a hurry. She lay back on the bed and watched as he stripped off, as mesmerised by the muscled strength of his body as though she was seeing it for the first time. He was exquisite—broad-shouldered and narrow-hipped, muscular but athletic, as though he worked out, even though he'd told her in passing that he never went to a gym because he hated the thought of committing to a certain amount of exercise a week.

She tugged off her clothes, first the jogging bottoms and then the tee-shirt, and flung both on the floor. He strolled towards the bed and her legs parted of their own volition. She was so wet for him, so ready for him to settle over her.

The curtains weren't drawn and fading light filtered in, mellow and warm on the wood panelling and whitewashed stone. As soon as Ella had stepped into the cottage, she'd felt at home. It was warm and cosy, with timbered beams across low ceilings and faded rugs on the floor. There was an open fireplace in the bedroom and a basket of logs next to it, ready for winter. As Rocco caressed her, she idly wondered what it would be like if they were here in winter, snow falling and the feel of Christmas all around them.

She relaxed into that fantasy but that, too, flew from her head as he began a slow exploration of her body until all she wanted to do was writhe against those searching fingers. Years of her careful life were swept away in a torrent of explosive desire that was ripping her apart. She burned up as his hand moved from her small breasts to between her legs, rubbing the flat of his fingers against the swollen bud of her clitoris. Each stroke of those clever fingers ratcheted up the scorching heat of her responsive body.

His touch felt familiar but no less arousing, and she groaned, eyelids fluttering, her body moving as he caressed her between her sprawled legs. His nakedness was hot against her and she reached to circle his thick member with her hand so that she could stroke him, picking up the tempo, knowing exactly how he liked to be touched because he had been shockingly open about telling her.

She slowly bucked against his fingers, an orgasm building to sweep her away. It took all her willpower to fight it, to push his hand away so that she could devote herself to ministering to *him*, to pleasuring *him*. He was a generous lover, satisfying her before himself, taking his time when she knew that he was on the edge of exploding. He was the sort of lover who made her feel *loved*. Although, of course, this wasn't about *love*.

She angled her body and laughed when he tried to pin her down, but he was happy enough to lie back, to let her touch him, then lowering herself along his brown, hard body, down to his penis, which she licked and stroked before taking it into her mouth. She lost herself in the taste and the urgent throb of him as she sucked and felt the pump of blood in his veins, the pulsing response of a man who, like her, was lost in a world of sensory pleasure.

He detached from her with a low, guttural moan and fumbled blindly for the packet of condoms he had stashed in the drawer next to the bed. Not a guy to take chances. She was giddy with arousal. She wanted him to touch her again but knew that, if he did, she wouldn't be able to control the fevered urgency of her response and she didn't want to come against his hand. She wanted him inside her.

She closed her eyes and controlled her breathing, waiting for his body to merge with hers and for the yearning inside her to be sated. He thrust into her in one powerful motion that took her breath away and he began moving inside her, his rhythm deep and forceful until she could feel her whole body spiralling out of control in ways that were mind-blowing. She came on a cry of deep pleasure and flung back her head. Her mouth was open while her eyes were squeezed tightly shut. How was it possible to feel this depth of pure, joyful, satisfying, earth-shattering, wondrous pleasure?

She knew when he had come, his orgasm mirroring hers. She could feel him swell inside her, filling her up. She was oblivious to everything but the heat of her excited body as it slowly descended from the crescendo of her orgasm back down to planet Earth. She sagged against him and, for a few moments, neither of them said anything.

'I feel as though we've known one another for ever.' Ella broke the silence with a dreamy murmur. She held back the thought that followed: that she felt she knew this man after a few days so much better than she'd ever known Steve. Felt that he knew *her* a thousand times better than Steve had, and yet how was that possible? With Steve, she'd had hopes and plans for a future, yet it seemed restrained and limiting compared to the pure heady freedom she felt with this man, who was practically a stranger.

Wasn't he? Or was this what a *real connection* felt like—impossibly close, entwined, on the same wavelength? Was this what *true love* felt like? Love that wasn't a slow build but a rush of everything good all at once?

Her heart began a steady beat inside her. *He was going.* He hadn't said anything at all about prolonging his stay.

'How so?'

She warmed as he drew her closer. She rested her palm on his chest and felt his heartbeat, and a rush of love swept through her, leaving her weak, warm and giddy.

'I feel like a different person when I'm with you,' she confessed truthfully. 'I feel adventurous and I don't think I've ever felt adventurous in my whole life.'

'You've cocooned yourself here, and I understand. You were grieving for your mother, you were hurt from a broken love affair and it felt safe to be here where there's nothing to stretch you.'

'That's true, but it's more than that. I've always toed the line but this feels…different. You've brought out a side to me I never thought existed. Have I…have I done that for you as well?'

Rocco remained silent for a few seconds. He felt lazy and comfortable with her body against his, the smell and feel of her filling him. He shifted so that he was facing her, her breasts against his chest and his thigh tucked between her legs. He was Jose Rivero, here in this cottage with this woman in his arms. If the question might have felt intrusive in another life, in *this* life, the one where the weight of duty no longer existed, the answer was yes. He felt a different man.

For just a second, that fleeting thought was enough to send ripples of discomfort through him. But why should it, he asked himself, when he was going to be leaving in a matter of…?

A couple of days.

Rocco frowned at the tug somewhere deep inside him at the prospect of leaving. There'd been times when he'd almost forgotten why he was here in the first place! When he returned to reality, he would laugh at that and shake his head in disbelief.

'Brought out a side to me I never thought existed? Now, let me think about that. You've certainly brought out a sexual side to my nature I never thought could be so powerful.'

'You know what I mean. I'm not talking about the sex. When it comes to sex, well, that's a whole new conversation. I barely recognise the woman who's happy to walk around without any underwear and wants to be touched whenever and wherever.'

'You've led a sheltered life.' He grinned but actually found that he loathed thinking about her with the guy who'd later let her down. 'If I'd been around during your formative years, walking around without underwear would have been the least adventurous streak in you.' He thought of her as a young girl, quiet and thoughtful, making sure never to be the centre of attention. He would like to have been there for her, which was a crazy notion.

'You have such a big ego, Jose Rivero!'

Rocco winced at the mention of his alter ego. He heard himself say with rough sincerity, 'I've certainly never done anything like this before. A cottage in the middle of nowhere, with a woman walking around barefoot in the kitchen cooking meals for me while I pick apples from the trees in the garden.'

Rocco reflected on his relationships with women, casual and satisfying enough, but nothing like this. Women he courted, wined, dined and slept with, knowing that he would marry someone whom logic dictated would fit the bill: someone from his own class who understood what came with the job of being his wife.

'So I'm a first?'

'In many ways.'

Ella sighed with contentment as he stroked her back, his fingers tracing her spine light and ticklish. She liked the sound of him telling her she'd been a first. She wasn't going to say anything about how she felt; she was going to obey the invisible lines she thought were in place because, realistically, he hadn't once talked about a future.

Did he want more from them? He had worked a steady path into her heart but the residue of disillusionment from the way she and Steve had crashed and burned was still there. Yes, she had fallen straight into him, maybe against her better judgement, but part of Ella recognised the danger of letting go of all the barriers she had built up around herself.

But the thought of him walking out of her life in a matter of days made her blood run cold. For better or for worse, she had to find out where things stood between them. She had to know whether there was a chance he had feelings for her which he maybe hadn't even acknowledged, because it sure wouldn't have been part of his plan when he'd arrived at Hailey's.

'I can't think of any woman who's managed to distract me from work the way you have,' he said and Ella smiled against his chest.

'I don't believe you.'

'Work is part and parcel of who I am.'

'Yet here you are.'

'Yet here I am.'

'What happens to your store when you want to go on holiday? I know you've told me you have people who can take over, but surely you must relax now and again?'

'I play as hard as I work.'

'And yet you've never taken this sort of time out? Where do you go when you want to unwind? I understand how you've had to be focused on your job if you've had to build something from nothing. Working for yourself is always going to be a big ask—not much time to relax if you know that a week off might mean less money in the bank.'

'Times aren't quite that hard for me,' Rocco murmured uncomfortably. He flushed as the reality of who he was collided with the person she thought he was...and yet this wasn't game he was playing. For a moment in time, while he was here with her, he truly felt a different man—carefree and reckless, without the layers of control that, by definition, restricted a lot of his responses. It wasn't going to last, of course. Reality was something he could never ditch, not that he would ever want to do that.

'And when it comes to the sort of things I do to unwind...'

'No gym.'

'You remembered. No, that sort of regime doesn't suit me. I do get away now and again, but this is the first time I haven't been overly concerned about checking in to see what's happening at...er...work...'

Skirting around the truth heightened his discomfort, and instead he told her with surprising honesty, 'I've always been a very controlled person, even in my relationships with women. You...bring out a different side to me. Now, what's happening about food? We could venture out and eat somewhere.'

'I've already started doing something for us to eat.'

'Sure you don't want to be wined and dined?' Rocco thought about how satisfying that would be—to take her out somewhere fancy, to impress her. Was this the road his uncle had travelled, step by step, until he couldn't get off it? Had his problems started with an infantile desire to impress a woman unused to the seductive aphrodisiac of extreme wealth? This lack of self-control was so unlike him that he struggled to dismiss it as just a reaction to being in the unique position of a woman not knowing his worth.

His mind continued to play with the fantasy of her in his private jet, sitting in one of his many cars or being taken to one of his villas—one in Tuscany, one in the Bahamas and another on the outskirts of Madrid.

He looked around him at the quaint, rustic furnishings. The wooden beams on the ceiling matched the timber of the four-poster bed: old, weathered and gnarled. The windows were fiddly but, when they were open, the scent of the countryside poured into the bedroom, fragrant and heady.

There was no *en suite*. The one bathroom had an old-fashioned shower and a bath with clawed feet, as deep as a swimming pool. Filling it, which they had only done once, was a procedure that had to be commenced at least half an hour before they even thought about getting in.

This was a place the twenty-first century hadn't quite decided whether to visit or not. And now Rocco could say, hand on heart, that his enjoyment of it was every bit as complete as his enjoyment of any one of his splendid, eye-wateringly expensive places scattered across the globe.

He frowned as he quickly replayed the many confidences they had shared, bit by bit, and the way he had relaxed in her company, so that now she felt familiar to him. He barely recognised the man who had opened up in ways he'd never done before. She'd awakened in his arms in the morning, warm and smiling, and there had been dreamless times at night when they had made love, both half-asleep, their movements slow, languorous and incredibly sensual. Rocco was alarmed now at how natural everything seemed with her.

'This is perfect,' he heard her say, all the while trying to analyse the road he had travelled down so quickly it was shocking.

'Let's stop talking,' he growled, hand straying to part her thighs then cupping and rubbing the wetness between them until she was moaning softly and sighing, her body moving against his hand while she did some exploring of her own.

He slipped his finger inside her, then his hands and fingers caressed her until her soft moaning became the guttural groans of a woman on the point of orgasm.

'Not so fast,' he purred silkily when he knew she was on the verge of tipping over the edge.

'Please...'

'I love it when you beg, *querida*...but I need to be inside you...' He fumbled, found the packet of condoms and was vaguely startled by the quantity left when it felt as though they'd made love a thousand times over the past few days. He was losing his touch in a million different ways.

He cleared his head and found his sweet spot, the place where niggling thoughts ceased to exist, found the comfort of touch.

'We don't have much more time together.' The words had to be spoken; he knew that. Yet, they cut deep inside him. 'Let's make the most of it...'

CHAPTER FOUR

'THE BIG GUY—and I mean *Mr Big himself*—wants to see you right now, in the boardroom. And, before you ask, he's *specifically* asked for *you*.'

Ella was barely through the front doors of the department store, sodden, because she'd had to half-run from her car in lightly falling snow. She decided that her stress levels must surely have peaked with this.

'Why?'

'Believe me, I'm mystified as well—unplanned visit. I took a call from whatever assistant he's brought with him asking for you *by name*. Now he has free rein of the store, the lawyers have been in. He's been here since seven this morning. He's yet to be seen by any of us lesser mortals. Easier to spot a leprechaun.'

'Probably ashamed, turning the store into yet another office block and high-end apartments for yuppies who work in Dublin. And at Christmas too! What a time to tell everyone they're being laid off so enjoy earning money while they can.'

'It's awful.' Vera sighed. 'But there's nothing to be done and word has it that he's been more than fair with everyone working here. Generous redundancies or new jobs in what's going up, if they're qualified for the placement. We all knew, even if we didn't want to admit it, that things were going downhill. It's not such a shock.'

'So why does he want *me*? I'm not involved in the decision making. I'm not a lawyer or an accountant so what have I got to say to the man?'

Ella finally got her feet to move. She noticed how old and tired everything looked as she took off her waterproof and shook it out. None of this was Vera's fault, but once again hormones had taken over and directed her responses.

She was right. Once a proud bastion of high-end glamour and luxury, the store had been declining slowly over the years. There had been murmurings but nothing definite until, out of the blue, it was announced that the place had been taken over and would be restructured into a massive block of very expensive apartments, with the entire top floor given over to office space.

Maybe at any other time she could have dealt with it, but right now what Ella wanted more than anything else was continuity, and the store's imminent closure had hit her like a hammer blow.

Vera was looking at her through shrewd, narrowed eyes and Ella smiled and sighed. 'Okay, okay. I'm fine. I'll go and see him just as soon as I get my act together. I've barely had time to take a breath.'

'I know things are tough at the moment, Els...'

'I don't want to talk about it. You've been good enough already, listening to me on a loop.'

'It's what friends do.'

'Tell Mr Big that I'll be in the boardroom in fifteen minutes. And Vera...?' Ella grinned, for a moment the girl once again instead of the woman with the weight of the world on her shoulders. 'You don't have to worry.

I'll make sure the hormones are firmly under lock and key, whatever the man has to say.'

Three floors up, Rocco was seated at the sprawling conference table, gazing at nothing, with his thoughts all over the place. Yet somewhere deep inside, for the first time in months, he felt at peace.

The last time he'd been here, the sun had been shining and the skies were the milky blue of fading summer. Now, the onset of deep winter was making itself felt. It was bitterly cold, and through the bank of windows he could see the lazy flurry of snow, not quite sufficient to collect but enough to signal worse to come.

There was no need to be here. When he and Ella had parted company, it had been for good. They'd had a brief fling, nothing more. Towards the very end, he had felt the whisper of something just out of reach, emotions that could have led to an involvement that his practical side knew would never happen. She had looked at him and he had seen something that had set the alarm bells ringing.

More than that, he had sensed something inside himself, something that wasn't welcome, a pull that had begun to feel dangerously out of control. He had laid down his boundaries without hesitating, had reminded her that this was just a moment in time and then, on schedule, he had left.

By then, he'd known exactly what he would offer for the building and exactly how he would reconfigure it. He had seen the quality of the staff and acknowledged that he would be more than happy to offer alternative positions to some of them.

With everything nicely in motion, and planning permission smoothly progressing just as it should, there was absolutely no need for him to do anything more than sit back and oversee developments. His vast empire, with all the responsibilities that entailed, barely allowed him time to surface, far less make an unnecessary trip back to where…

Back to where he had left behind a piece of himself he had never known existed. That was the persistent thought that had nagged at him ever since he had left. Rocco had papered that over by telling himself that an uneasy conscience at withholding the truth from Ella was at the root of his restlessness since he'd returned to normal life. He'd get past it.

He hadn't. She'd played in his head like the refrain of a song he couldn't quite manage to forget. Why? He was always so adept when it came to women, always so controlled with what he gave and what he didn't. Emotions had never impacted on his behaviour but he'd found it impossible not to think about her.

So here he was. The chemistry between them had obviously been more powerful than he'd anticipated. What they'd shared hadn't burnt out and maybe it needed to be re-visited. It didn't mean there was anything serious between them. It just meant that an itch remained that needed to be scratched, and the choice was either to confront that by returning to face her or to pretend it didn't exist, which ran the risk of making the whole situation even more insupportable.

Reduced to the most basic level, Rocco reckoned that if something hadn't reached burnout, living in a state of denial wouldn't get it there any time soon. If he still felt this peculiar craving then chances were high that she did as well.

But he still felt ridiculously nervous as he waited for the knock on the door that would signal her arrival. And ridiculously excited at the prospect of how she would react when she saw him. Surprised? Dismayed? And, underneath whatever those initial reactions might be, excited at seeing him again? Bone-deep self-confidence settled on excitement.

He strolled towards the window, gazed down at the street below and then tensed as he heard the soft push of the door being opened.

Ella made it to the boardroom several minutes late but, frankly, she couldn't care. When she'd first been told about the sale of Hailey's she'd been more devastated than she'd thought possible. She'd known that the place needed an injection of cash, and that there had been chatter about it being sold for a while, but the reality of it had hit her for six. It was as if a tidal wave of memories and nostalgia had crashed into her with full force, sweeping her off her feet.

She'd wanted to confront whoever it was that had bought the store and tell him just how important it was for the town. But that outraged feeling hadn't lasted long because she'd known that whatever she had to say on the matter would fall on deaf ears. They'd been presented with a fait accompli and they would all have to live with it.

She pushed open the door and it took her a couple of seconds to focus on the figure standing with his back to her, staring out of the window in dark charcoal-grey trousers and white shirt cuffed to the elbows, and she noticed a jacket slung over the back of a chair.

He was very tall and dark-haired and, if something about him felt familiar, then she subconsciously dismissed the feeling because it was evident from the calibre of his clothing that this was the billionaire at the helm of the buyout. She was curious as to why he'd asked to see her but not nervous. Nothing the man said or did could possibly have any impact on her whatsoever.

'You asked to see me?'

Her voice echoed in the cavernous boardroom. She was standing by the door, focusing on the towering figure as he slowly turned to look at her.

Reality took a hundred years to catch up with disbelief and, even when her brain screamed that the guy now looking at her was the same guy who had disappeared without a trace, she still froze in shock, finding it impossible to believe.

It was impossible to believe because it just *couldn't* be happening.

'Ella...'

That voice...deep, dark and seductive...

Ella closed her eyes and every bone in her body went limp as she felt herself falling, falling, falling...in a desperate attempt to escape the reality she had just been confronted with.

She came to groggily, lying on the uncomfortable sofa against the wall with a cushion propped under her head.

'Here. Drink this. It should be something stronger,' that sexy, familiar voice said. 'My preference would be a shot of brandy but unfortunately this is all on offer.'

'No,' Ella whispered. 'This can't be happening.'

'You're in shock. Drink some water. You need a couple of seconds to gather your thoughts.'

'Who *are* you? Jose? I don't understand. What are you doing here? No. No, no, no...' She closed her eyes and heard her shallow breathing whilst feeling his gaze on her. He was still there when she opened her eyes a moment later.

'I'm Rocco Mancini. I'm going to pull a chair over. Don't try and stand; you'll probably fall over. You're still weak. There's some food on the sideboard, so I'll bring you something to eat.'

'You...you can't be. You...'

'Wait. Don't move a muscle.'

'I'm not hungry!'

'You need to get some strength up. Stay right there.'

Where the heck was she going to go? Fly through the window? Sprint out through the door to the nearest lift?

She was as weak as a kitten and all the weaker when she contemplated what was now in the process of unfolding. Her hand snaked down to her stomach with its barely-there bump, not at all noticeable under the layers of warm clothing, the vest, jumper, waterproof gilet and trousers with the helpful elasticated waist.

After nearly four months, Ella had become accustomed to the reality of her pregnancy. It had taken a while, even though she had known within a month of Jose leaving that she was pregnant. At first, she had just *missed* him. There had been a hole in her heart that was wrenchingly painful to endure. Any repercussions of their love-making hadn't registered at all and she'd barely noticed that her period was late. Then she had. About the same time as she'd realised that she'd gone off coffee and noticed that her breasts were tender.

And yet, when she'd done that pregnancy test, held that little stick and saw those two bright lines, she'd still been shocked. She had still felt the blood rush to her face and the race of her pulse.

God, she'd done her best to find him, but she'd had nothing to go on. She'd given him her mobile number, but it didn't take her long to realise that the favour hadn't been returned, and from there all her belief in what they'd had had collapsed like a house of cards. She'd done the unthinkable and fallen for a guy who had treated her in a way she'd hoped never to be treated again. He'd disappeared without a backward glance, making sure to leave no footprints in the sand behind him.

She poured her heart out to him and told him stuff she'd never told anyone in her life before.

She'd told him about Steve and his betrayal, and had felt all fuzzy and warm when she'd heard the anger in his sympathetic, horrified reaction. And what had he gone and done? Had he been any better? Steve had lied about his intentions. He had dropped her without looking back. She'd trusted him the way she'd trusted Steve and he had let her down exactly as Steve had.

Was *she* the common denominator? Was there something inside her that attracted the man who couldn't be trusted? Common decency had dictated that she try to locate the man who had fathered the baby she was carrying. However bitter she had felt at him and his vanishing act, however hurt she had been by the way she had been treated, the guy was still the father of their baby and deserved to know.

In the end, with no leads, she had given up the search and accepted that she would be a single mum. She'd concluded that, even if she managed to track him down, he wouldn't want anything to do with a baby he hadn't asked for with a woman he hadn't wanted in his life for more than a week and a half.

She gathered herself and wriggled upright into a sitting position just as he reached out with a glass of water, which she ignored.

'So Jose Rivero never existed. Why did you pretend

to be someone you weren't? Was it fun? Was it fun to string me along under a pseudonym? Were you laughing behind my back?'

In the heat of the moment, the horrifying business of the pregnancy faded into the background. Shock had quickly given way to a healthy dose of absolute burning rage at the curdled memory of the hurt she'd lived with for months.

'Ron Brisk-Hailey mentioned selling the department store some months ago. It was an off-the-cuff idea aired at a dinner party hosted by my parents at their place in Dubai, where Brisk-Hailey lives. The store has been losing money for years and he was propping it up with his personal fortune because it began life as a family concern. He confessed that it was a situation that couldn't continue indefinitely, and he couldn't see a way out, because the option to buy everything online, especially after the pandemic, had become overwhelming.'

'Carry on,' Ella said tightly. 'I'm beginning to see where this might be going but I'd like you to spell it out for me anyway. Just in case I miss any juicy bits out.'

'He could have put the place out to public tender, but he was sentimental about its heritage and wanted to make sure his employees were well-treated. In turn, I needed to assess just how much the physical building was worth, never mind the value of the plot it stood on. We agreed that there would be no point spooking anyone on the off chance I decided not to go ahead with the purchase. I was ninety-nine percent there but there was still a chance that the missing one percent might break the deal.'

'At what point did you decide that it would be fun to sleep with me? In your make-believe role of ordinary person having a look around?'

'It wasn't my intention to get involved with anyone while I was here. I came to see what I was getting myself into, establish whether it would be worth the investment—make sure I offered a fair deal but didn't pay over the odds—and then I was going to leave and let my guys conclude business if I chose to go ahead.'

'I don't even recognise you. You look the same, you sound the same, but you're a stranger in expensive clothes who thought it was okay to lie to me. Was that because you had so little respect for me—you thought I didn't deserve the truth?'

'My hands were tied.'

Ella noted with grim satisfaction the dull flush that stole into his aristocratic face, although who knew whether he had a conscience or not?

'Then you should have thought twice about getting involved with someone you felt you had to lie to.'

'It was a two-way street, Ella. We were attracted to one another.'

'I was attracted to Jose Rivero—who never existed, as it turns out. I wasn't attracted to Rocco Mancini, a billionaire who was here to spy on everyone.'

'You're upset. I get that.'

'Do you? That's very big of you.' Her hand stole to her stomach and she balled it into a clenched fist because right now she had to think about what she was going to do and how she was going to do it. She felt sick at the thought of what happened next in a situation she had never banked on. Telling Jose Rivero that she was pregnant had seemed daunting enough. Breaking the news to this stranger in front of her, a billionaire with an agenda that had never included her, was terrifying.

'I understand why you're angry with me, but in actual fact I didn't have to make this trip. I came because I wanted to see you. And, yes, I didn't reveal my true identity...what happened between us was one hundred percent genuine.'

'In the grip of a guilty conscience? Why?' She tried and failed to mesh the Jose she'd given her heart to, the carefree, sexy man who had held her in his arms, with this powerful, wealthy stranger, looking at her with his head tilted to one side, dark eyes revealing nothing.

It was hopeless.

'Do you feel guilty about pretending to be someone you weren't? Or because you knew what an awful upheaval it would be for the department store to be sold to the highest bidder only interested in making even more money for himself?'

'I know the place means a lot to you, Ella. I know you worked here as a teenager. I know your mother worked here. There's an affection for it.'

'I wish I'd never told you any of that.' *More confidences thrown back in her face—yet another reminder of how gullible she'd been.*

'But you did.' Rocco raked his fingers through his hair and sighed. He sat forward, leaning towards her. 'Look, I didn't come here to explain away the decision to replace this store with something that actually makes sense. You know as well as I do that the place is losing money hand over fist and has been for a long time. The edifice will remain the same and it will be renovated to the highest of sustainable environmental standards. It will be the gold standard for other properties I plan to develop. As someone who wanted to explore climate change and sustainable lifestyles, you should approve of what I'm doing here.'

'Please don't remind me of all the things I told you that I shouldn't have,' Ella retorted with ice in her voice. 'Vera said that you explicitly asked to see me. Why, if not to give me weasly excuses for what you did?'

'Weasly?' Rocco's dark eyes flashed with outrage and in return Ella shot him a sneering look.

'That's right.'

'No one's ever called me "weasly" before!'

'You're a billionaire,' she snapped scornfully. 'Everyone's probably scared stiff of you.'

'Except you.'

Ella bristled in silence at this rejoinder. Their eyes met and tangled, and she felt the slow burn of something unwanted and intrusive. The memory of how he'd touched her seared through her anger. It was debilitating and unwelcome because it flew in the face of her bitter disillusionment at how things had turned out. How could she possibly feel anything for this stranger? But there was still this jarring, disturbing pull. She hated it.

'You asked me why I came back here, came back to see you. I returned because I couldn't get you out of my mind. I don't have a guilty conscience about my plans for the store because it'll be the best thing that could happen to the town. It'll bring people in, and they will be a motor for reviving the shops that haven't been doing well over the years. Hailey's isn't the only place that's been failing for some time.'

That all made sense, which was infuriating. The man she'd known had been hot, charming and passionate. The one sitting here in this boardroom was cool, logical and controlled.

But here was the inescapable link: he said that he hadn't been able to get her out of his mind...

Had he returned to tell her that—that he'd been thinking of her? Or, more likely, had he come so that they could reconnect—continue what they'd shared even though he hadn't had a problem walking out on her four months ago?

Had it turned out to be more difficult than he'd thought to airbrush her out? He was a very physical man. Whether he was Jose or Rocco, he was still the guy with a red-hot libido. Ella killed dead the warm swoop of pleasure at the thought that he might have missed her. There was so much more at stake than a simple case of a fling that hadn't worked out. He had deceived her. A man who deliberately withheld the truth about who he really was didn't qualify to be a responsible father, did he? If she turned him away now, would he shrug and disappear, having given it a go?

Ella knew that she could withhold the truth of the situation from him, just as he had withheld the truth of who he really was from her, and she was tempted. But a child deserved the best of both parents, for better or worse. She had had that luxury while he…had not. She remembered what he had said about Christmas, about how little it had meant to him. Another lie? Her gut feeling was that he'd been telling the truth when he'd said there had been some genuine connection between them, even though listening to her gut feelings hadn't done much for her in the past.

She needed to respond now and not react. She needed to know if her gut feeling was right, if he was a decent guy. If he'd felt he'd truly had no option but to keep the truth of his identity to himself, even after they'd become lovers, then he could still be prepared to stay for a bit to see how the bombshell of his buyout would affect everyone in the store.

It was Christmas. Whether it made sense for the store to be turned into flats or not, it had still been a body blow to staff lower down the pecking order who hadn't seen it coming. They would be compensated, but they'd been left shaken. If there was nothing in it for him, would he still stick around to find out how the people whose lives would change because of him might be feeling? Was there a shred of real caring in him or had she utterly misjudged him?

It was a stupid test. Ella knew that, but she was clinging to something that might shine a light on the crossroads at which she now was, stuck and helpless. She desperately wanted him to prove himself because there was a baby inside her and she needed to know the measure of him.

'If you came here to see if you could get me back into bed, then you can forget it, *Señor Mancini*. I have better things to do than re-visit a relationship with someone who didn't care enough to tell me the truth about himself.' It was clear from the lowering of his eyes that she had struck the jackpot in correctly assessing why he'd suddenly felt a need to connect. 'But...'

'But?'

'If you're here to show me that there's a side to you that's actually *caring*...that you bear some sort of resemblance to the man I thought you were...' She drew in a swift breath because she felt herself weaken at her own foolishness in falling for him. 'Then you would show that you cared about the people here.'

'I intend to be very fair,' Rocco said quietly. 'I've made sure that the redundancy packages are generous and there will be roles to fill when the offices are functioning. The pay will be much better than they could hope to earn working for the store. I'll be laying out the details of the deals in the new year but I hope to put minds to rest by assuring everyone that they will be treated fairly.'

'You could stay for a while and let everyone enjoy their last Christmas here. We haven't even put up the usual tree in the foyer.'

'Yes, the Christmas tradition.' He flushed. 'You know how I feel about Christmas.'

'But this isn't *your* Christmas. This is the final Christmas spent here, at the store, and it should belong to everyone in the town before it disappears for ever.'

'I hear what you're saying, Ella.'

'You'll stay for at least a few days, be a presence here to stop jitters and ensure that everyone can leave this wonderful place with feelings of goodwill and optimism for what lies ahead?'

'It's good to see you,' Rocco murmured.

He smiled a slow, lazy smile, amused at the passion on her face, knowing that meeting her again had only re-awakened his libido, which had been dormant since he had left this slice of unreality behind. She was just as he remembered: outspoken and tough to impress. Even now, knowing he was a billionaire, she hadn't wanted to hop into bed with him, hadn't been tempted by his money.

He'd stay. Would he be able to persuade her back into a relationship or had he blown it for good because he hadn't told her who he was? He could understand that but, even so, when cold common sense told him there was no reason to remain here, that he *was* being incredibly generous in his final package, he wanted to stay.

Just entering the department store earlier that morning, just returning to this part of the world, Rocco had suddenly felt...*different*. He'd returned to the life he'd left behind. Two weeks had changed him in ways he couldn't figure out; it had made him curious, and he didn't understand why because he'd always known just how dangerous curiosity could be. His uncle had been curious about all the wrong things, and look where that had got him.

But the feeling when he'd returned... Yes, he'd stay.

'You're really not tempted to pick up where we left off now that you've found out who I am?'

'I prefer the straightforward guy who could only afford to rent a small cottage.'

'I might have billions, Ella, but I'm still the same guy who knew how much you'd like it there.'

He liked the thought of her not wanting him because of his money. He played with the idea of her softening, coming to him, walking back into his arms. He thought of a different relationship with everything out in the open, although still one that would never amount to anything more than a fling, even if the fling lasted longer.

His thoughts on marriage didn't involve the sort of love she would expect, nor was she a woman from the elevated background that would prepare her for the life she would have to lead as his wife. Control would be the very essence of his future, the sort of control that was counter-intuitive to who she was. That didn't mean that there wasn't this sizzle of chemistry between them. He looked at her with brooding interest, trying to prise beneath the surface to where her thoughts were hidden.

'There's something I think you need to know, Rocco.' Ella could feel him trying to get inside her head. He'd asked whether she was tempted by his money. He couldn't begin to understand just how much of a turn-off it was because the man who was the billionaire wasn't the man who'd listened to her, laughed with her and heard all her confidences. *He* was who she'd given her heart to and that guy hadn't been bolstered by money.

'I don't know how to tell you this, but I'll start by saying that I did my best to find you. I had no idea that you hadn't wanted to be found.' Her heart picked up pace and began to beat like a sledgehammer against her ribcage.

'We agreed that what we had wouldn't last for ever,' Rocco murmured. 'You told me that I brought out an adventurous side to you and… I'll admit that being someone else brought out something in me as well. I'm honest enough to admit that. I relaxed in a way I haven't done before, but I always knew that the end would come, which was why I walked away. And I meant to keep walking until…' he grimaced '…until I found that something inside me wouldn't let me carry on. I'm not saying anything I haven't already told you.'

'You hurt me.' She hated that admission but, even now and even in these circumstances, it was just too raw to keep to herself.

'I never meant to do that. Please believe me… I was born into responsibility. My family… I've been primed to take over vast business concerns. I could spend time explaining what that means in terms of my personal relationships but, in essence, the life you want and deserve would never be one I could give you.'

'I'm glad you said that.'

'Come again?'

'I'm glad you said that because you'll know, from the start, that I don't want anything from you when I tell you that I'm pregnant.'

CHAPTER FIVE

THE SILENCE WAS DEAFENING.

'Did you hear what I just said? Rocco, I'm pregnant. That's why I tried to find you after you walked away. It wasn't because I wanted to hunt you down so that I could try and revive anything.'

Restless, and fighting another surge of anger when she thought about how she'd been played, Ella pushed herself off the sofa and walked jerkily to the sideboard to pour herself a glass of water. Then she turned round and remained where she was, staring at him, eyes narrowed with hostility.

'You ask me whether I would consider re-starting where we left off now that I know how much money you have. Is that really the person you think I am? I... The man I went to bed with wasn't *you*. The man I ended up caring about isn't the person standing in front of me asking whether I'd consider sleeping with him because he's rich!'

'Slow down, Ella. Rewind!'

'Yes, you made me feel exciting and daring and...and *free*. And you say that I made you feel more relaxed, because with me you were someone else, but that someone else was a *lie*, Rocco! Did you come back here when you didn't have to because you wanted to take a little time out from being a big shot and you figured I would buy into that because you could pay me?'

'No!'

'I didn't have to tell you about this. I could have kept it to myself. When I found out that you didn't exist... Well, what sort of man *were* you?'

'I've already explained myself, Ella. Now is the time to move away from that and... I can't believe what you've just told me. You're *pregnant*?'

'If you'd told me that you couldn't be bothered to stay here, couldn't care about the fate of all the people here—some of whom have worked in this department store for decades—then I think I really would have turned my back on you and kept this thing to myself!'

Rocco stared at her.

Pregnant? This was the last thing he'd expected in a million years. Yes, maybe he'd come back to recapture some of that weird freedom he'd felt when he'd been with her. Maybe he'd wanted to test the ground, see whether the electricity that had surged between them was still there. Had he imagined that he could influence her in some way because now she would know what he was worth? Maybe. He'd never been short of women who were impressed by his vast reserves of wealth.

Was that belief so firmly embedded in him that he had simply tarred her with the same brush without bothering to dig a little deeper? To realise that she was not at all like any of the women he had dated or slept with in the past? He'd been a different man with her and maybe it wasn't because he'd had a new, assumed identity. He'd been a different man with her because she was a different woman.

Bit by bit, he realised that the issue of the pregnancy—which was still reverberating inside him like a bomb waiting to be fully detonated—would have to take a back seat to all her outpourings. She was carrying his baby. Not for a single moment did he not believe that fact.

She was also seething with bitterness and resentment. To get to the big thing that needed to be discussed, he would first have to find a way through her hostility.

'Say that again.'

'Which bit? The bit where I tell you that you're *nothing* like the guy I remember? The bit where I tell you that you did a good job camouflaging your *arrogance*, all the better to *seduce me*?'

'The bit where you tell me that you felt you had to put me to the test before letting me know that I'm going to be a father!'

Rocco raked his fingers through his hair and buried his head in his hands.

How? How the hell had this happened? He knew; of course he did. They'd made love like two people who had spent a lifetime starved of sex. He'd been careful but there had been times, at least two, when he had stirred in the middle of the night, reached out to feel her warm body next to him and hadn't been able to resist...

In that carefree bubble, he'd managed to make the ultimate mistake: he'd lost control. He'd spent his entire adult life reminding himself of the dangers of losing control and he'd fallen victim to the very thing he had preached about.

Playing any kind of blame game wasn't going to do, as he now faced the inescapable truth which was that every plan he'd ever made was dissolving in front of his very eyes. Blame games weren't going to work and arguing wasn't going to work.

Right now she was upset and furious with him. That was certainly the last thing he needed because the situation would have to be dealt with calmly and rationally. But he could understand where she was coming from and he wanted to hit something very hard in sheer frustration.

'Sometimes it's better for a child to just not know one parent rather than have a parent who doesn't take an interest. I was brought up in a very happy family unit. What would it have felt like if I'd thought that my dad had chosen not to have anything to do with me? If he'd known of my existence and then decided that I wasn't worth the effort? If you'd been prepared to walk away without a backward glance because you wouldn't be getting what you came here for, then you would have been that man. Maybe you still are. Maybe there *is* no Jose underneath the Rocco.'

'How the hell can you make a judgement like that?' But Rocco knew how. He'd set in chain a sequence of consequences and, whilst he knew that he wasn't to blame, he could see how she might view the situation through a different lens.

And yet, for him, there could be only one solution to the mess in which they now found themselves: marriage. The thought of any child of his being illegitimate was beyond acceptable.

'When you suddenly find that you're going to have a baby, your brain gets very sharp.'

'I can't have this conversation here, Ella.'

He moved to grab his coat, which he had slung over the back of a chair. It was black cashmere, as soft as butter.

'Would it make a difference where we have this conversation?'

'When this store opens, people will be coming and going. We'll be interrupted non-stop. We can't huddle in the corner talking about this...this...'

'Nightmare?'

'Don't put words into my mouth. What happened, happened, and resorting to sarcasm isn't going to change that. We are still where we are, and where we are demands a solution. This is a shock for me, so expect a shocked reaction.'

Dark, cool eyes collided with narrowed green ones. Ella scowled and looked away. He moved towards the door and she followed suit, first telling him that she had to fetch her coat.

'I'll meet you outside,' Rocco said. 'At this stage, maybe leaving together might raise one or two eyebrows. I don't care, but you might.'

'Sooner or later people will find out.'

'But you might appreciate the *later* option.' He held her gaze. 'You have a lot you want to say. I understand. I have quite a bit to say myself. The bridge between us will have to be crossed, even if you might think that I'm not the man you thought I was.'

Ella breathed in deeply.

He was right. Right that they were where they were, right that being on constant attack wouldn't change anything. A bomb had detonated in the very heart of his well-ordered life and he'd somehow taken it in his stride. It didn't matter how angry she was, how much his very presence made her realise the fool she'd been. She raged that he was acting like an adult and his cool, sensible response wasn't what she wanted, because what did she want—a declaration that he'd suddenly realised that she'd meant more to him than a fleeting romp between the sheets? She'd meant nothing to him when it came to any emotional bond. He'd come back to see if they could temporarily pick up where they'd left off and she loathed that that *hurt*.

Shame at her own weakness and determination to hang onto her pride stiffened her, and she pursed her lips tightly.

'If you tell me where we're going, I can meet you there once I've fetched my coat.'

'My hotel.'

'That's the last place I'm going,' Ella said with scathing dismissal.

'What's the problem with that?'

'Because *I don't want to*. Because I would rather we have this conversation on neutral territory.'

For a few seconds Rocco didn't say anything and then he shrugged. 'Ella, the hotel is in Dublin, half an hour away by taxi. There's a very big, very comfortable breakfast area where we can continue this conversation in complete privacy.'

Ella thought about all the people she knew in the store and in town. She hadn't kept her pregnancy a secret; what would have been the point? She'd vaguely said something and nothing about an affair that hadn't worked out, somehow making it sound as though she had been having a clandestine relationship for weeks, maybe months. No one knew the identity of the father. She'd never been an open book and everyone had been respectful of her reticence. Including her father, even though she had seen the disappointment and concern on his face when she'd broken the news to him.

The horror of ever confessing that she'd had a fling with a guy who had walked away without a backward glance and, worse, had done his utmost to make sure she didn't get in touch with him, hadn't borne thinking about. Did she want to be seen with Rocco in the local café where Sheila, the town gossip, would serve them tea and then promptly relay the sighting on the local grapevine? Dublin at least guaranteed anonymity and he was right: when it came to the world finding out, the *later* option held definite appeal.

'My driver will take me there and I'll pay for you to take a taxi. We can be assured of privacy without any curious looks or conclusions being formed, because I guess everyone knows that you're pregnant.'

'Not *everyone's* in the dark. I'm four months' pregnant. It's not something I can keep to myself for ever. It's just that no one knows who the father of my baby is.'

Rocco tilted his head to the side and looked at her in silence for a few seconds. He would have to tread carefully. Perhaps, for the first time in a life in which he was accustomed to having all orders obeyed and all needs immediately met, Rocco was discovering what it felt like to run headlong into an immovable roadblock.

The very thing that had beguiled him—her lack of awe of what he could bring to the table financially—was now the very thing that stood in the way of the most logical conclusion to this situation. She'd been positively insulted at the insinuation that she might be impressed by his wealth. She couldn't be swayed by any amount of money and, whatever they'd shared, her opinion of him now couldn't be lower. She barely liked him. She had spun him the story about the fate of the staff as a way of measuring his worth just to see whether she should even bother to tell him about the pregnancy. If he'd shut down the conversation without discussion, he uneasily suspected she would have withheld the news about the pregnancy, judging him to be the sort of guy a kid is better off without.

Maybe in due course, when their child had become old enough to be curious, she might have done something about that. He'd never considered fatherhood with any immediacy but, now that it had been thrust upon him, he was very clear on what he wanted. Doing the honourable thing was top of the list. He had been raised to value duty, after all, to value the virtue of responsibility. Right now, he was skating on thin ice when it came to achieving his goal.

He couldn't fault her hostility. She had been open and trusting with him, had confided in him and, in return, she had been repaid with what she would see as colossal betrayal. Rocco knew that if he were to suggest the honourable thing—marriage for the sake of their baby—she would recoil in horror. As she'd told him, he was the last person she would ever again want to be involved with.

But he was going to marry her. That was a given. He was going to give his flesh and blood the legacy he or she deserved, the legacy that was their natural birthright.

He told her the name of the hotel where he was staying, and watched the way she lowered her eyes. What would she be thinking? That this five star hotel was the last place she would have associated with the man she'd thought he was? The guy she'd trusted?

Rocco thought of the houses, the cars, his mansion in London...of the exalted background he had so carefully hidden from her.

It was what it was and he *was* going to get what he

wanted. He wasn't used to playing the long game but choices seemed thin on the ground at the moment.

'It must have been scary for you, Ella,' he murmured now, pausing by the door to look down at her with genuine sympathy. 'No, don't say anything. We can talk about all of this when we're at the hotel. I'll give you time to tell the boss that you won't be in today.'

'For a couple of hours, at any rate.'

'Let's not put a timeline on the discussion we're going to have to have. You…you don't look pregnant.'

'Don't you believe me?'

'Can you try to stop attacking me? That's not what I meant. I believe you. I wasn't as careful with protection as I should have been so, trust me, I not only believe you but I take full responsibility for…this situation.'

'I'm not blameless.' She looked at him mutinously, then lowered her eyes again. 'It's nearly four months,' she said. 'From everything I've read, you don't really show with a first pregnancy until later on.'

Rocco glanced at his watch. 'Let's say I meet you at twelve? Gives you quite some time here to do whatever urgent things you might have to do…'

'That would be dealing with the winding up of the store.'

'And we can have some lunch.'

'I…'

'Please don't tell me that you're not hungry because I've offered to buy lunch for you. You need to eat—you're pregnant. That much I do know without having read anything on the subject. Are you? Eating properly?'

'Of course I am. I'm more than capable of looking after myself.' She hesitated, then said in a semi-resentful rush, 'I've been for a scan and everything is fine with the baby.'

'Do you know...what we're having?'

Ella stared at him.

She could feel a slow burn inside her, something different from the anger, hurt and resentment. Over the months she had become accustomed to this being her baby, her situation, *her* responsibility. But now she saw that letting him in would unlock all sorts of other things. She would be opening the door to his presence in her life in ways that wouldn't be politely respectful if she decided she didn't want him to be there. He had a stake in what was going on inside her body and that scared her because she knew that she had feelings for him.

At least, for the man she'd thought she'd known. But Jose was Rocco and Rocco... For all the accusations she had thrown at him, he wasn't walking away, wasn't raging at her, wasn't blaming her for what had happened and wasn't telling her that he'd ruined his life even though he might think it.

'I don't want to know.'

'Right, I'll see you in a couple of hours, Ella.' He paused. 'And I should tell you that I won't be impressed if you decide to bail on me because you want to give me space to process. Or any other reason, for that matter.'

'Whether you're impressed by anything I do or don't do isn't my concern.'

'Listen to me. We're in this together, so you will have to be civil at some point. I can't keep explaining why I did what I did on an endless loop.'

'I know that. Can you get that it hurt when I found out that you'd lied? My ex lied to me because he wanted my flatmate, not me. Do you get that it felt like a very similar road I was walking down? And then you show up here, telling me that you're actually the guy who's bought the store… Do you get that it all feels *a little bloody overwhelming?*'

'Ella…'

'Forget it.'

She made to turn away and felt his hand circle her wrist, tugging her slightly towards him.

'It matters,' Rocco said gruffly. 'Believe it or not, I'm not that guy. I don't lie. Ever. What I did… Yes, I wasn't straight with you, but I really never meant to get involved and, once I had, I couldn't then tell you what was going on. I'm sorry.'

'Okay.' Ella pulled back but her heart was hammering and she could feel herself weakening at the sincerity in his voice and the gravity of his expression.

She wasn't going to weaken. He might be sincere but, even so, he could never be her type: a billionaire who could have his pick of women, who lived life in the fast lane, who had basically dallied with her for a bit of fun because of a passing attraction. Besides, whatever he said about being unable to be honest with her, he could have been. Everyone in life had a choice.

'Is it? Okay?'

'It's okay insofar as you're right,' Ella said coolly. 'We need to be civil with one another. Basically, what we had was more or less a one-night stand between two people who aren't compatible, who come from completely different worlds. I'll try to forget the past and just think about what happens next in this scenario.'

'We weren't *that* incompatible.'

'We were good in bed,' Ella said flatly. 'So, sure, in that sense we weren't incompatible, but I don't go for rich, powerful guys who go through life knowing that they can do exactly what they want.'

'Right. This rich guy will see you at midday.'

On the Tannoy system, Christmas music burst into life, tinny and joyful, and Rocco involuntarily grimaced. 'It's at least the season for goodwill,' he said. He waited a couple of seconds, got nothing by way of response, then he spun round, half-turned to give her a small salute and was gone, closing the door to the boardroom quietly behind him.

Ella stared at the closed door until the tangle of emotions racing through her began to settle.

Over the months, she'd been lulled into believing that she was going to have to make the best of her circumstances. She would be a single parent, would struggle to make ends meet but would have the love and support of her dad and her friends. She was grateful for living in a small, close-knit community.

Now, walking into that boardroom, seeing the man who had haunted her waking moments and her deepest dreams, sitting there... Even thinking about it made her shiver with a sense of unreality. She'd fainted. Something she'd never done before in her life. The shock... In a single instant, the life she'd come to terms with had been turned on its head.

She did a few things that couldn't wait, made some lame excuses to her colleagues, Vera and her boss and then, at exactly a quarter to twelve, she got a cab to the city centre.

The season of goodwill was in full swing outside the department store. The Christmas lights were on and the store fronts were bursting with giant bows and bunches of poppy-red holly. Outside Maccie's, the local butcher, a blow-up Santa bobbed, along with three reindeer. Over the past few days, the snow had been obliging when it came to creating just the right atmosphere and it was lightly falling now, as though dusting everything with icing sugar.

She felt furtive as she climbed into a taxi from the rank outside the one and only hotel in the town. She had time to think as the taxi purred towards Dublin centre. Did it help? Did it calm her? Nothing could stop the steady spiral of bewilderment and confusion that underplayed the biting disappointment, hurt and the sinking feeling that she had made the same mistake all over again.

They approached the city and the explosion of festive lights took her breath away. A giant Christmas tree dominated the square outside an enormous store, decorated with over-sized ornaments in shades of red, green and gold. People were everywhere, scurrying like ants, clutching bags and heavily bundled up in coats and scarves, their breath visible in the cold winter air as they breathed out. Light flurries of snow barely collected on the glistening pavements. There was a Christmas market on and she could smell the spiced aroma of mulled wine and mince pies.

Her stomach clenched with sudden tension as the taxi slowed in front of the hotel. Outside the lights were delicate, gossamer-thin lacy webs stretching elegantly across the façade. Two liveried men stood on either side of imposing glass doors and sprang into action as soon as she approached.

She breathed in sharply when she spotted Rocco sitting on one of the sofas at the back of the room. The gorgeous, lavish decorations, the elegant tree discreetly positioned by the bar, the massive vases stuffed with poinsettias, chrysanthemums and amaryllis all faded as her mouth went dry and her heart began to pound.

Jose and Rocco merged into one man, sinfully sexy... and breathtakingly beautiful.

She walked briskly towards him and it was only when she was standing in front of him that he looked up from what he was doing on his phone and stood to greet her.

'Ella.'

Rocco had sensed her but only looked up when she cast a shadow over him. Sprawled on the sofa, he'd sucked in a sharp breath as their eyes had tangled, and for a few seconds he'd been catapulted back to when they'd been lovers. To that taste of freedom, releasing part of him that had been completely authentic. He was too level-headed to be seduced into thinking that could have lasted for ever but it had still lodged inside him like a burr.

He'd gone past the shock. As he'd waited for her, his brain had begun to whirr along more practical lines. The end objective remained the same: marriage. With that in mind, he would feel out the lay of the land and, if she dug in her heels, then he would persuade her in whatever other ways it took. Getting lost in what had happened would have to be put on ice because where would it get either of them?

He had to break through her disillusionment. He would be businesslike in his approach. His views on marriage, on love, on the relevance of emotions, were so deeply ingrained that when he thought about marrying her it was exclusively on a no choice basis. He wasn't a man who fled in the face of responsibility. They'd had fun but she had never been on his radar for anything long term. Now that he was going to be in it for the long haul—even though she didn't know that yet—he felt it was important that he first got her on side and, second, clarified the parameters.

He would be a loyal husband and a dutiful father. He knew the value of responsibility. His uncle had set a terrible example of how to waste a life away. No flights of fancy or self-delusion for Rocco. As cold a parent as he was, his father had done what had to be done when it came to taking the mess his brother had left behind and dealing with it. He had been able to do that because he'd had the right woman by his side. A woman there through arrangement rather than love, brought up in a family in which duty also came first, who had allowed him the time to devote to work. Rocco could scarcely recall his father being around when he'd been growing up. Nor could he recall his equally cool mother ever complaining.

'A woman who's demanding is a woman who will drag you down. Look at your uncle. He liked women who wanted his undivided attention; it made him feel wanted. He was a weak man. Pay attention to where that got him.'

Rocco wouldn't pretend that there would be wild flights of love…although there would certainly be passion. Just thinking about touching her sent him into instant arousal. So, no problems on that front. It would be a better outcome than the icy coldness of his parents' marriage, even if it could never be what she might want. She thought he was a liar, which was an appellation he found distasteful, but he couldn't blame her.

As she sat down and faced him, Rocco tried to glean what she was thinking, but the green eyes staring back at him were veiled.

'Are you hungry?' he asked. 'I can order something for us to eat now or we can talk a bit first and eat afterwards.'

'I'll have some mince pies to start with.'

'Mince pies. Would you call that *food*?'

'My tastes have changed. I crave them.'

He ordered the mince pies and was amused at how enthusiastically she tucked into them when they came.

'You're hungry.'

'Only for mince pies right now. Aren't you going to have one?'

'Not my thing. I've had time to think,' he said seriously. 'It goes without saying that my preferred option here would be for us to marry.'

Ella's eyebrows shot up but, before she could push back at that, he smoothly continued. 'But, as you've already told me, I'm the last person you would go for.'

'Yes, because what I want is love. That's the glue that keeps a family bonded. I don't want someone to tell me that they'll put a ring on my finger because together we've made a mistake and now there's a baby on the way! Do you think I've lived my life dreaming of the day when I might become someone's burden? My parents had a wonderful, supportive, loving marriage and that's something I've dreamt of for myself. I see my brother in love with the woman he married, companions and best friends, there for one another. Now you tell me that marriage is the *preferred option* here! Well, that just sends a shiver of joy through me! I'm guessing you wouldn't even be sitting here if it weren't for the fact that you had to do your duty!'

'I don't *have* to do anything, Ella. I *choose* to be here—and, just for the record, *duty* isn't a dirty word.'

'And love? Does that get a look in?'

'Love isn't a sentiment I recognise.'

'That's awful.'

'I'm thinking about what would be best for our baby. If you find the thought of marriage to me unacceptable, then let's discuss the practicalities. Where are you living at the moment?'

'Currently with my dad, but naturally that won't be an ongoing situation. And I happen to be thinking about *our baby* as well, Rocco! A loveless marriage does nothing when it comes to providing what a child needs.'

'You've made your case, Ella. You don't have to drive the point home. Back to your living arrangements. I'll be buying you a house.'

'Hold on just a minute! Don't think you can swan in here and start telling me what I can and can't do!'

'No, Ella, *you* hold on. I didn't see this coming and neither did you. You might think it's acceptable for your pride to be in the driving seat, because what you'd really like is the fairy tale dream of happy-ever-after in a situation like this, but there's no room for pride here and you'd better start accepting that.'

'Or else what?'

'Or else I can safely say that your concerns revolve around yourself and have nothing to do with this baby, whatever you say to the contrary. I won't be able to relocate here, but I will buy a house close by for weekend use. This isn't about telling you what you can and can't do. This is about practicalities. I'm rich and I can afford it.'

'Where do you even live?' Ella suddenly asked 'Spain? Not Ireland, I'm sure. Isn't it going to be inconvenient for you traipsing up here all the time?'

'I have bases in a number of countries, and nothing's inconvenient when you have a private jet at your disposal. At any rate, I can personally oversee work on the store and remote work as needs be.'

'Private jet…'

'Additionally, I will set up an account for you. You'll

find that you'll have more than enough money to do whatever you want.'

'An account for *the baby*,' Ella corrected.

Rocco ignored that. With his end goal in sight, he intended to hammer home all the advantages that would come with being his wife. 'Of course, should you meet someone else, then...' He eloquently shrugged his shoulders and sat back, allowing her to register that possibility.

Out of the corner of his eye, he noted her taking stock of something she hadn't thought about.

'By which,' he hammered home, 'I mean some renegotiation would have to take place. I won't be paying for another guy's upkeep.'

'*Another guy's upkeep?* It's months before I even *have* the baby. At what point will this *other guy* come along, demanding to *be kept*? This is all moving way too fast!'

'I'm not a man who likes to take chances,' he said smoothly. 'You could say this is the outcome of taking a chance, or at any rate of losing sight of self-control. You ask when some guy might come along looking to be kept? You're going to be a very wealthy woman. You'll be surprised at how many men will start circling because of your money.'

'I really don't think we need to—'

'And naturally, there's me, while we're discussing probable scenarios.'

'I beg your pardon?'

'I would want a wife, and sooner rather than later. But, you're right, let's not get ahead of ourselves.' He waved that aside dismissively, shrewd enough to know that the idea would find a way into her head. 'To be discussed at a later date, no doubt. First on the agenda will be accommodation that's suitable for us and, after that, we can work on the details of finances and the rest. I'm assuming, at least for now, that lawyers need not be involved?'

'No!'

'Good.' Rocco nodded. 'Like it or not, we're in this together, Ella, so stop fighting me. Let's enjoy lunch and we can talk about…whatever you think needs doing at the department store as a final hurrah. And one more thing?'

'What's that? I don't think I'm up to dealing with much more at the moment.'

'Your father? I would like to meet him, and today seems as good a day as any to do that.'

CHAPTER SIX

A WIFE? SOONER rather than later?

What happened to the marriage proposal? He'd certainly accepted her refusal at the speed of light!

The bill was paid and as Ella was faffing, gathering her gloves and idly checking her phone for messages. She said casually, 'You would want a wife sooner rather than later, you say?'

She started sticking on the gloves and surreptitiously stared at Rocco from under her lashes. He didn't believe in love, and didn't think it was necessary for a healthy, happy marriage, so of course he wouldn't have a problem marrying a woman just to be a mother to their child, to provide the family unit he thought was important. A woman who would probably come from the same background as him. A rich, beautiful socialite who wouldn't make a nuisance of herself by demanding shows of love and affection.

She felt a dizzying tightness in her chest at the thought of that. It was fine waving aside a marriage proposal as unacceptable because it didn't meet her requirements. It was a little different when the marriage proposal was then airbrushed out of existence to give way to the possibility of another woman stepping in to fill the space.

'You have a problem with that?'

'I just think it's a bit early in the day to be putting it on the table.'

'Why?'

'Because…' She looked at him with consternation, hardly aware that he was wrapping her scarf round her neck and handing her the woolly hat that she had dumped on the table. She absently stuck it on and continued to gaze at him as she formulated something that resembled a reasonable explanation as to why she was so bothered at the thought of him with another woman.

'I believe that a child needs to have the benefit of a mother and a father.'

'So do I.'

'Ah, but key difference here—I won't be on an endless quest to find a suitable partner I'm in love with who can fit the bill. I don't believe that love is the be all and end all. In fact, when I think about it…' he slotted her arm into the crook of his and began ushering her out of the restaurant '…if you look at the divorce rate between people who declare undying love on their wedding day, only to relegate that to undying indifference or everlasting resentment a decade later, well, the statistics say it all.

'My driver is waiting. I think I'll get rid of him so we can drive together to your house and I can meet your father.'

'My parents were blissfully happy.'

'That's called the exception to the rule.'

'Your parents…?'

'Still together.'

'Which just shows…'

'Ella.' Rocco stopped and looked down at her, breaking contact and shoving his hands in the pockets of his coat. 'My parents' marriage was a business deal that brought together two important houses. They stayed together because they both understood how the world they inherited worked. They knew the rules.'

'You say stuff like that, Rocco, and I'm talking to a complete stranger.'

'Only when it comes to the details of my life,' Rocco said gruffly. 'One thing I do know is that, yes, I would want a wife by my side with a child in the equation.' He paused, giving her time to digest the scenario he was painting for her.

'A wife who comes from the same class as you? *Knows the rules*, like your mother did?'

'Preferably a wife who is the mother of my child but, failing that, then yes, quite possibly.'

Ella's mouth went dry. She felt jealousy, and she didn't know where that was coming from, because surely she should hate him? Hadn't he lied to her? Why would you be jealous of someone who'd lied to you, someone you justifiably hated? Yet if there was hatred there then it was well and truly swamped by the steady thump of possessiveness that coursed through her. Besides, the way he was now—the man willing to accept a situation he could never have banked on; the guy who still had that flare of fairness and consideration inside him—was no convenient cardboard cutout, easy for her to dismiss...

'I... I don't know anything about your parents. How do you think they'll react?' This to sidestep the rush of emotion inside her.

'That's something I haven't yet considered. I'm still in the process of trying to come to terms with the situation myself. Don't forget you've had a head start on me.'

'Not my fault I couldn't locate you!' This felt safer, and she broke eye contact, but her heart was still thudding as she clocked the sleek, black Range Rover idling on the other side of the road.

Rocco thought it best to steer her away from picking back up that line of attack. He'd given her food for thought. It was clear she didn't approve of the thought of another woman stepping into his life, and she certainly had a point when she'd said that it was a bit early to paint a future that involved other partners, but all was fair in love and war.

He wondered whether she was *jealous*, and then was surprised at the kick that gave him. The thought of her with another man didn't sit well with him. Was that jealousy or was it just that he was the sort of guy who could never like the thought of another man adopting a fatherly role to his offspring? He'd never had a jealous bone in his body but when he thought of Ella in the arms of someone else…

'Do you want to give your father some warning that I'll be coming along?'

'Maybe this isn't a good idea.'

'It's a very good idea.' He dismissed his driver and helped her into the passenger seat but held open the door, maintaining his calm. As far as Rocco was concerned, there were still a million practicalities to pin down, but he would let those wait for the time being.

A place for her to live? He would bide his time.

A car of her choice? In due course.

The details of maintenance? A bridge to be crossed.

At the back of his mind was the thought that those things would not have to be seriously addressed because she would come to him before that. She would recognise the advantages of marriage and would accept that sometimes flights of fancy when it came to fairy stories of love and romance get put to bed in the face of duties and responsibilities that would always take precedence. He would drop the subject of marriage and just let time do its thing.

'You're nervous about me meeting your father. Why? Is it because you told yourself that this situation would never arise? Because I was never going to show up in your life again?'

'Something like that.'

'And, now that I've shown up, you're nervous because…?'

'I'm not sure how my father is going to react to you,' Ella said bluntly.

'He's not going to think I'm a catch?' Rocco raised his eyebrows and grinned. 'Steady employment…good sense of responsibility…happy to put out the bins on a Monday…'

He watched pink creep into her cheeks and was gratified when she smiled at him, relaxing for the first time since he'd surprised her in the boardroom. This was the Ella he'd left in his wake and, if he could have turned back the hands of time, maybe he wouldn't have been so hasty in his departure.

It wasn't as though leaving that bubble behind had been a roaring success. He hadn't been able to relegate her to something fun that had happened one day. She'd preyed on his mind, which was why he had finally made his way back to her. Back to her and, vaguely, back to try and recapture something of that carefree man who had had a window in time during which he had broken free of what had always been expected of him.

Everything that subsequently happened had come as a shock. But to see her smile that sweet, hesitant smile suddenly made him feel ten feet tall.

'When I began looking for you, I was looking for an

ordinary guy,' she said truthfully. 'Someone I could relate to. Someone who shared the same worries and concerns that I did.'

'Tell me I'm not sharing the same worries and concerns right now that you're facing,' Rocco said.

The snow flurries pricked his face like needles. It was freezing, but no way was he going to abandon this conversation, because right now she wasn't attacking him and he was going to take that as a win of sorts. He understood her bitterness but he was determined to find a way through that because he had to. There was no choice.

'It's cold. You should get in the car.'

'I'm a big boy. I can withstand a little cold weather. Besides, I don't want you to clam up on me.'

'I'm not going to clam up on you.'

'And I don't want you to return to the comfort zone of attacking me for what happened. I want you to tell me what to expect when I meet your father. Will I be greeted with a shotgun and a pack of rabid dogs? What have you said to him?'

'I'm not talking to you until you're in the car. If you end up catching pneumonia, then I'll probably feel guilty, and you wouldn't deserve my guilt.'

'That's reasonable.'

He skirted around into the driver's seat and slammed the door behind him. He swivelled in his seat, leant against the door and looked at her in silence.

It was a feat of willpower for Ella to hold that dark, steady, unrevealing gaze and she half-wished she'd let him stand outside the car, shivering in the cold.

'Okay.' She sighed. 'My dad isn't going to know what to do with you. He's a straightforward guy and I don't think he's met anyone like you in his life before. Not only are you the guy who gets his daughter pregnant, but Rocco, you…you're…'

'Spit it out, Ella.'

'You're *from another planet*.'

'The money thing?'

'Yes, *the money thing*.'

'I never thought you were a snob.'

'Don't be ridiculous. I'm anything but a snob! I happen to have grown up in a very normal household. My dad has a small farm, my mum worked at Hailey's for years. How can I be a snob?'

'Aren't you pigeonholing me because of my background? Isn't that the definition of being a snob?'

'No.' But she flushed.

'Take the money out of the equation and I'm the same man you slept with three months ago.'

Ella opened her mouth to contradict him but she hesitated because, whilst she had initially been utterly unable to equate Jose with Rocco, the lines were becoming blurred. She had seen him in that boardroom and shock had catapulted her into a reaction that had been fast, spontaneous and unforgiving.

And then his outward sophistication—the expensive suit, the hand-made shoes, the priceless watch—meant he was no more the laid-back, charming guy but a cool, self-assured man with the confidence of someone accustomed to being obeyed.

Yet hadn't he been self-assured when she'd first met him? He'd strolled into her office and looked around him as though he owned the place.

'Not quite.'

'So I'm not what he's expecting on a number of fronts. What, exactly, have you told him about me?'

'I haven't said much…'

'Your idea of not saying much and my idea of not saying much are probably at opposite ends of the scale,' Rocco said truthfully.

'Maybe.'

Rocco slid a sideways glance at her. Outside, leaden, yellow sky was gathering snow. Christmas was all around them, in the lights everywhere and the excitement of shoppers stocking up.

He started the engine, the powerful motor roared into life then he edged out of the parking space.

'Can I say something, Ella?'

'You've already said quite a lot.'

'You must have been distraught when you couldn't locate me, when you realised that I'd given you a false name, but you were strong, and you still are, and I admire that. Whatever road this takes us, you can be guaranteed, always and for ever, of my complete support.'

For her, what had happened was as huge and as life-changing as it was for him, and she had dealt with it admirably even when she'd assumed that she'd be dealing with it on her own. Through all of that, she'd still had it in her to be concerned for the store that would for ever change the face of the town when it was converted into flats and offices.

'Do you get why the offices and apartments are going to work for the town? I'm going to be sticking around to answer any questions the staff might have, but I'd like to find out what exactly your thoughts are, bearing in mind that you're sentimentally attached to the place.'

'I was upset when the news first broke but…okay, yes. And I appreciate what you're doing…with trying to keep everything as sustainable as possible.'

'Think we might be making headway in breaking down some of the barriers between us?'

Ella shrugged.

'Because it's important, as we're going to be in one another's lives for a very long time, in one way or another.'

'One way or another?'

'Be it if I marry or if you do...'

Ella's lips thinned as she was forced to confront once again the idea that he would find someone else. She hated the thought of it. She wanted to ask him what his parents might think of her and then wondered whether he would even bother introducing her to them if she wasn't actively involved in his life. What would be the point? They probably lived in Spain. That would be where the family business was. A haughty, aristocratic couple, parents of a treasured only son who would meet a haughty, aristocratic wife who would be the sort of woman he would choose to marry.

Her imagination refused to be reined in. She feverishly imagined her child in this scenario and went cold inside. Having earlier scoffed at him for introducing a layer of complication that wasn't necessary because their baby hadn't even been born, Ella now found herself dwelling on all manner of unpleasant scenarios that somehow involved her being sidelined as a parent in the years to come.

She snapped back to the present. He'd programmed her address into the satnav but the going was slow because of the weather.

'So...'

His lazy drawl made her half-turn so that she could look at his sharp, aristocratic profile.

'You were going to give me the low down on what your father might be expecting.'

'Okay.' She sighed. 'I may have said that I had feelings for you.'

'Come again?'

'You heard me.'

'I think I need to hear you again so I can process what you said.'

'You don't actually have to hear it again to process anything because you can leave all the talking to me. You'll find out soon enough that my dad isn't very communicative. He'll really only feel comfortable talking to me, so you can take a back seat and go with the flow.'

'I'm not sure that works for me. No, I *know* that doesn't work for me. When you say you had feelings for me…?'

'I don't have feelings for you! I had to say something!' Ella shot him an exasperated sigh.

Everything was suddenly so complicated. Was he being deliberately obtuse? Couldn't he just accept what she was telling him and let her get on with it?

No, he couldn't. That wasn't his nature, and besides, he wasn't being obtuse. He was genuinely curious because, looked at through dispassionate, objective eyes, why wouldn't she simply have come out with the truth—that she'd had a quick fling and a mistake had been the unfortunate result?

'No one asked for lengthy explanations, if you really want to know. I've never been one to confide, as you well know, but I also would never normally hop into bed with some passing stranger. And when it comes to my dad, well, he knows me better than anyone, and I didn't want to break his heart even more than it was breaking already, so I said I'd fallen for a guy but the relationship hadn't worked out.'

'Because the guy had lied about who he was?'

'Because the guy and I decided it just wouldn't have been the right thing.'

'And the reason I stayed away for nearly four months?'

'I just said I had to come to terms with everything before... I involved someone who wouldn't have welcomed involvement. And, now that I've explained this to you, will you please trust me and let me do the talking?'

'What is this conversation going to look like? Can you give me a sample taster so I know what to expect?'

'The left turn to the farm's coming up, but you have to go really slowly or you'll miss it.'

'Well?'

'I don't know. I'll play it by ear.'

'I see.'

Ella looked at him narrowly because she had no idea what was going through Rocco's head. She'd said precious little about Rocco because, at the time, she'd known precious little about him aside from the fact that he'd appeared in her life and then vanished without trace, thereby proving himself to be just the sort of guy she should never have gone near.

Confessing to her beloved, quiet dad that she'd had a two-week liaison with a man who had never wanted any sort of relationship with her would have left him confused and saddened. So she'd told him that she'd lost her heart to a wonderful man and that they had parted company on the best of terms because they'd reached the same conclusion: that the relationship wouldn't work out.

And she had left it there. For the time being. Now, though...

The house appeared, emerging from the gathering gloom and the drizzle of snow, a two-storied building squatting in the middle of acres of land. The lights were on downstairs and she knew what she would find when she went in. Her father settled in the sitting room with the fire burning after a long day spent outside. There would be the smell of food cooking. He enjoyed cooking. He always had. He said it was relaxing after the gruelling physicality of tending to the land.

The car swung round in a perfect circle in front of the house and ground to a halt. When he'd killed the engine, Rocco turned to face her.

'I don't exactly know the details of what you told your father,' he said firmly. 'But the narrative from here on in will not be one in which I take a back seat. So go ahead and lead the conversation but I'm warning you to expect interruptions if I think it's going down that road.'

'How did I never notice how much you enjoy giving orders?'

But she minded less than she expected. In an uncertain place, was she somehow secretly relieved that someone was taking charge? What had happened to her feminist streak? When she thought of the reassurances he had given her earlier, she felt warm inside. When she thought about his strength, and the calm solidity of his presence, she imagined the marriage she had absolutely ruled out. Would it really be the hell on earth she had conjured up? He was a guy who had a strong moral compass and sense of responsibility. A guy who hadn't set out deliberately to lie to her but had found himself in a place where admitting the truth had not been feasible.

'I'll go inside ahead of you. My dad will have a heart

attack if I produce you from out of the blue, like a rabbit from a hat.'

'Don't worry,' Rocco said after a pause. 'It's going to be fine.'

'Really?'

'Look at it this way—you were going it solo and now you're not. If not for you, then for our baby, this is surely the best possible outcome?'

In the darkness of the car, Ella could make out the glitter of his dark eyes and she felt that thread of urgent, physical awareness wash over her, waking her up to the uncomfortable recognition of a desire that had not left her in the way she had hoped it might.

And beyond desire…something deeper and far more dangerous.

'I'll come out as soon as I can,' she said shortly. 'In the meantime, please just stay here.'

'Sure. Just as long as your interpretation of *as soon as* doesn't prove to be too long.' He half-smiled. 'We're in this together now, Ella. So, like I said, don't look so anxious. When faced with a problem, two will always be better than one at dealing with it.'

Ella's heart thudded, then he reached out and trailed the back of his hand against her cheek and she felt a tide of shameless response wash through her. It was almost too much to turn away and not keen towards that warm hand and lose herself in its comforting touch.

She exited the car at speed and then took a deep breath before she inserted her key into the lock and let herself through the front door.

Rocco watched as she vanished through the door and shut it firmly behind her. Around him, the snow continued to fall gently, insistently. Away from the glittering Christmas lights strung from lamp post to lamp post in the town, out here felt quiet and remote. The house was a stone structure, sprawling in a U-shape that enfolded the courtyard where he was parked. Around it, open fields stretched through the gathering twilight in magnificent isolation.

Comfort zones had long been left behind. He was dealing with a situation for which nothing had prepared him but in truth, looking back, he felt that comfort zones had been dumped the minute he had met her. It was a relief that her explanations to her father had been perfunctory. That said, facing her father was something he would be able to deal with. *She* was the one who made his stomach twist with nerves because he didn't know where he stood with her. Because, for the first time in his life, getting what he wanted wasn't going to be a straightforward exercise and the stakes were the highest he could ever have imagined. His parents would have to be told immediately and there could be no question that he wouldn't marry the mother of his child.

He was absently staring at the door when it opened and there she was, framed in the doorway. For a few seconds, the breath was sucked out of him. She was so small, so slender, and yet right now she was singularly the most powerful person in his world.

He leapt out of the car and strode towards her. 'Ready?' he murmured, looking down at her.

She flashed him a look that was a mixture of defiance and anxiety and he recalled the sensation of her soft skin under his fingers when he had touched her cheek. The surge of physical awareness that had jolted through him.

He also recalled the fleeting but powerful acknowledgement that she had responded to that touch in a way she might not have found entirely unwelcome. He'd felt her body come alive, just for a moment, had felt the sudden softness in her and had known, on some level, that she wanted him. Desire was a difficult beast to control.

He looked at her with lazy speculation.

'Just don't say much. I've told him that you got in touch and...'

'And? Since he's under the impression that you're crazy about me, are we on course for a grand, romantic reunion?'

'No.'

'Why not?'

'Because anything between us is over and done with. You know why. I don't have to keep going into it.'

'So the part I play is...?'

'We're friends.'

'Lovers to friends,' Rocco mused. 'I always thought it went in the opposite direction—friends to lovers.'

'Not this time.'

She uneasily remembered what she had told her father—that she'd fallen for a guy before acknowledging that they lived in different worlds, worlds that would never be destined to meet. She hoped nothing she had said would come back to bite her. Fortunately for her, her dad wasn't the sort to launch into animated conversation about anything. He would eye Rocco suspiciously, would be tight-lipped and unwelcoming and she would lead the way in dispelling any notion that Rocco was anything but someone who would have no place in her future aside from fulfilling the duties of fatherhood. All Rocco had to do was go along with everything she said and keep contributions to the conversation to a minimum.

She could only hope that he wouldn't be a wild card.

As Rocco looked around him with curious eyes, what he saw was an old house, unrenovated but sturdy, built of concrete and stone, with thick walls and furnishings that were old and tired. Scott Campbell, weathered from a life spent outdoors, was proud and silent, in his mid-sixties at most, who looked much older than his years.

Rocco liked him on sight. He could deal with this man. He would enjoy it, in fact.

His handshake, as he was introduced, matched his host's in firmness. He smiled a warm, engaging, encouraging smile. At the same time, he paid utterly no attention to Ella's slight body suddenly stiffening by his side.

'Mr Campbell. I can't tell you how honoured I am to meet you and how pleased.' He lowered his voice and bent the few inches that brought him face to face with the bright blue, narrowed eyes focused on him. By the end of the evening, he intended to wipe out every scrap of wariness and suspicion. He might be cast in the role of lover turned friend but, by hook or by crook, the distinction would soon become pleasantly blurry.

He clasped the leathery hand warmly between both of his and smiled. 'Circumstances may have taken me away prematurely from your enchanting daughter, sir, but I assure you that I will not fail when it comes to fulfilling my duties supporting her in these…unexpected but very happy times…'

He sensed rather than saw the wiry body relax. Not much, but enough to encourage him. 'But I'm sure there will be ample time to discuss everything with you on that subject, to reassure you that your daughter will be supported one hundred percent by me. In the meantime… I've always had an interest in farming. I would consider myself privileged to hear everything about your farm. Who knows?' He chuckled. 'I might find there's a farmer lurking inside me somewhere...'

Rocco was invited to stay the night. Separate rooms, of course, as they were now just *friends*, but still...

Several hours later, Ella was still reeling from Rocco's charm offensive. He'd laid it on thick. Her taciturn father, known to happily spend an evening without uttering much more than a couple of sentences, had been downright loquacious.

Did Rocco actually know anything about farm equipment? Differences between agricultural tractors and regular tractors? What fertilizers were best for different crops? Weather patterns and harvesting? It seemed that he did and, what he didn't, he'd been keen to find out with the sort of phoney zeal that made her head spin.

He'd politely refused the offer of a bed but not until her father had been one hundred percent won over. When she'd made the mistake of yawning, her father had actually told her that she should go get some rest and that he'd see Rocco out!

On the spur of the moment, Ella dialled the mobile number that she now had, the very number she had previously been denied when she'd been the disposable woman he'd had a fling with.

'What do you think you're playing at?'

'Ella?'

'Of course it's me! Who else is it going to be? Do you have women ringing you all hours? And what were you doing earlier? Didn't I tell you to leave all the talking to me?'

Dressed in thick flannel pyjamas she'd had since

she'd been a teenager, Ella slid off the bed, scowling, and strolled towards the chair by the window. When she parted the curtains, she peered out into a dark wilderness with a light dusting of snow covering the fields that stretched out into infinity. Christmas was everywhere… except here. It hadn't really been here since her mother had died, even though some effort had been made for the past two Christmases. The back should have been ablaze with lights, and downstairs the tree should have been up and the stockings hung.

She let the curtain drop and tucked her knees up to her chest.

'I don't encourage women to ring me all hours, now that you mention it, and definitely not now that I'm a taken man.'

'You're not *a taken man*. I told you not to do any talking.'

'I really like your father. Clever man. We had an informative chat after you left about how he could think of diversifying to make the most of his land. Apologies if I didn't use the playbook you laid out.'

'You're not sorry at all.'

'You're right. I'm beginning to admire how well you read me.'

'As long as you left it with us just being friends.'

'As opposed to what?'

'As opposed to…to…'

'I won't lie when I tell you that marriage is the best option for us, Ella. Especially meeting your father… Family life on both sides, although it's fair to say my experience of family is wildly different to yours. He misses your mother.'

It took a couple of seconds for Ella to register the change of topic.

'Sorry?'

'Louise—your mother. He misses her every day. Especially at this time of year.'

'What are you talking about? Did he tell you that?'

'He did. Just before I left.'

Ella didn't say anything. Her father had never shared his sorrow with her after her mother had died so suddenly. He had been stalwart and silent and she hadn't quite known how to break through that barrier of quiet stoicism.

'What...what did he say?' she asked eventually. 'He... he never talked to me about that. He was there for me but I was never sure if I was ever there for him in the same way.'

Rocco's voice was a thoughtful murmur. 'I think he's a very protective dad. He didn't want to burden you with his own feelings at such a sad time. He's a strong, silent man who is perhaps a little hesitant when it comes to freely expressing emotion.'

Ella's voice was ragged and distressed. 'It's a little upsetting to think that he shared stuff with you he felt he couldn't share with me.'

'Ella, you really mustn't think that way. You must think that you're very lucky to have a father who loves you so much and whose driving desire is to always do what he thinks is best for you.'

'Thanks for saying that, Rocco,' she said gruffly, because his words helped that sudden, jarring unhappiness.

'It's the truth. He said that this Christmas is going to be very different, special, because of...our situation. I got the feeling that this baby on the way has struck him deeply.'

'Yes, I think so.'

'Which is why I'll be round first thing tomorrow morning.'

'Sorry?'

'He feels that this Christmas he would like to celebrate with a real tree instead of the silver make-do one you've used since your mother died—and maybe a party.'

'What?'

'New beginnings and all that.'

'Rocco, you weren't supposed to be talking about *new beginnings and all that*.'

'The subject of how life will change with a baby was going to arise and I had no intention of hiding from it. At any rate, like I said, I like your father. I like the fact that he doesn't talk much, but what he says is worth hearing. Makes a change from most of the population. So, if a request for a Christmas tree was made, then I'm not going to suddenly play coy and tell him that I'm not interested, because we're supposed to be just good friends, and as such my role is to hide in a cupboard of your choosing when you point to it. So the upshot is, I'll be back first thing tomorrow morning and we can go and choose a tree.'

'Wait, don't you hate Christmas?'

'"Hate" is a strong word.'

'But you're willing to go tree hunting for my dad?'

'I'm not the ogre you think I am and more than that…'

She heard the smile in his voice but the undertone remained deadly serious. 'What…?'

'More than that, I'm willing to go beyond the extra mile because this is a situation that demands it. Think about that, Ella. Can you say the same for yourself?'

CHAPTER SEVEN

'Have you forgiven me?'

Leaning against the doorframe, Rocco looked at Ella as the front door was pulled open and she shuffled her way out into the cold.

'More to the point, don't I get a cup of coffee?'

'I thought it best that we get the tree-buying done and dusted. Dad's out inspecting some fences…and forgive you for what?'

Ella had been up since six. She'd made her dad his usual pot of coffee and inwardly winced when he'd said, in his usual direct, vaguely sheepish way, 'Liked the man.'

'He's…er…' She'd struggled to find the right words to talk about friendship and reliability whilst avoiding the thorny issue of what happened next. 'A nice guy.'

'Guess that's why you fell in love with him.' Her father had looked at her in silence, his flask of coffee in one hand.

'About that, Dad…'

'Good men are hard to find. The man seems a good one to me.'

So much for her down-to-earth father having no time for a richer-than-rich billionaire, Ella had thought. Instead, she had realised uncomfortably, he had managed to do the one thing she was finding so difficult to do—he had accepted Rocco Mancini for the man he was instead of judging him because he was attached to a big bank balance.

The truth was that Rocco's parting shot had given her food for thought. He was prepared to go the extra mile. Buying a Christmas tree might be a small thing but what it represented was much bigger—a willingness to put himself out because the situation demanded it, as he'd said.

He'd asked her to marry him. She'd immediately seen that as unacceptable, because it clashed with the dreams and hopes she'd had for herself of being in a relationship where she was treasured and loved. She had made it all about her, but there was a baby inside her that they shared and, tough though it was to admit it, wasn't her immediate refusal of that marriage offer tied up with the fact that he didn't love her the way she knew, deep down, she loved him?

That was the sobering thought that had kept her awake for a lot of the night. She could rant and rave about Rocco not being the man she had given her heart to—and for sure, when she had first set eyes on him, the sophisticated billionaire with the cool, self-assured attitude hadn't matched the easy-going charmer she remembered—but now... The qualities she'd fallen for were still there.

'Penny for them.'

'Sorry?'

'Your thoughts. You're a million miles away.'

'Sorry.' She shut the door firmly behind her, pushed it to make sure it was properly closed and then half-ran against the persisting snow to the black Range Rover.

'Forgive you for what?' was the first thing she asked as soon as Rocco was in the car, starting the engine.

'For not obeying orders yesterday.'

Ella sighed. 'You got along with my dad when I didn't think you would. I thought I could control the situation but maybe that was just wishful thinking. Everything's a muddle, and I thought it would be slightly less complicated if we kept a dividing line between you and my dad.'

She sat back and watched the dull, grey winter landscape go by as he manoeuvred the car away from the house and into the narrow lanes, taking it very, very slowly. She didn't expect him to reach out and give her hand a reassuring squeeze.

She slid her glance sideways to see that he was staring ahead, focusing on the road. When he returned his hand to the steering wheel, her heart thumped, and she still wanted those warm fingers to be clasped with hers, steady and reassuring, smoothing away all the turmoil in her head.

'He likes you,' she added.

'And that's not a good thing?'

'I suppose it's…okay.'

Rocco burst out laughing and when he cast a dark glance in her direction, she blushed, taken back to the times they'd had when laughter had been in plentiful supply.

'Just okay? Think about it, Ella, isn't it a good thing that your father has been reassured that I'm the sort of guy who isn't going to disappear in the face of the responsibilities that have come his way?'

'You honestly didn't have to pass the test with so many flying colours.'

'I've never been a guy to do things by half-measures.'

'You've met my dad now. What happens when I meet

your parents, Rocco? What are they going to make of this situation? Or will you keep them in the dark from it?'

'Keep them in the dark? That would be impossible.'

'How are they going to react to the fact that we won't be getting married, when they married because it made sense?'

Rocco's mouth thinned. How would his parents react? He already knew how, because he had already had that conversation. There had been no point delaying the inevitable, but it wasn't a conversation he had looked forward to, and it had gone as expected: a cold reception followed by an icy reminder of his uncle and what had happened when he had found himself trapped by a gold-digger.

'And that was *without* the complication of a child!' his mother had said in one of the few truly explosive reactions Rocco had ever heard.

Their cold fury had fired up a possessiveness inside him towards Ella which he had known was there without knowing just how powerful it was. Nothing about her could ever be described as greedy for money. Everything she said and did only confirmed that.

He felt her eyes on him and, for a split second, his heart opened up and warmed at feelings that lazily swirled inside him, defying logic. Logic said he wasn't built for the highs and lows of love. Logic said that his uncle had been the benchmark of how a loss of control could ruin lives. Logic told him that to marry and yet keep a distance was the way the marriage would work and, better than that, would thrive. He wouldn't pretend emotions that would never be there, and so she would never be disappointed because she couldn't access them. But she would be satisfied on every other front.

'I guess they would have expected you to get married to someone from the same social standing as you?'

'I'm sure that's exactly what they expected, but in life things don't always go according to plan.'

'They'll be bitterly disappointed that not only will you not be marrying the right type of girl but that that wrong type of girl is pregnant with your baby.'

'My parents' opinion belongs to them,' Rocco said, voice cooling as he thought about his parents. 'I hope I can change it but, if I can't, then I won't let it affect me or how I behave in this situation.'

'Really?'

'I don't have the same relationship you have with your father,' Rocco said quietly. 'I've looked at the interaction between the two of you. There's no hiding the deep love that's there, and I'm guessing your entire family unit was like this?'

'It was,' Ella agreed with a smile in her voice. 'Conor may have been as wild as anything sometimes, and Mum may have been dogged with health issues, but there was so much love there. When you say you don't have the same relationship…'

'I think I may have given some hints on that particular topic when we…were together.'

'Maybe.'

'The details may have been omitted but all the necessary bits were there.'

'I know you told me that you don't like Christmas. You can fill in the gaps now. It's not as though we aren't on a long journey together, for better or for worse.'

In the silence of the car, Ella found that she was intensely curious to hear more about him. The black and white picture was fading and in its place was the colour of a rounded, three-dimensional man.

'Fill in the gaps... I suppose you could say that Christmas in my family's palatial house wasn't all you might think it was cracked up to be.'

'No festive tree?'

'Several. All huge and all decorated by an outside company who always did an excellent job when it came to making them worthy of a magazine cover. There was never a time when we ever went out to physically buy a Christmas tree.'

'Even when you were a kid?'

'Never. Nor was there ever any excited opening of presents on Christmas morning. I always had one present given to me at breakfast on Christmas day, and I was allowed to open it once the dishes had been removed by staff. It was always expensive, and elaborate, and as soon as I opened my gift it was expected that I would go upstairs to play with it so that my parents could get on with the rest of the day.'

'What was the rest of their day?'

'There was always a lavish buffet luncheon open to the usual great and good. Sometimes, they would bring their kids over and I would have company.'

'Am I allowed to feel sorry for you?'

Lulled into the ease of conversation which she remembered from when they were lovers, Ella settled into something that felt familiar and exciting at the same time.

'If that makes you happy. Does it?'

'I can't imagine what that must have been like.' Would he compare the experience he was going to have putting up a tree for her father to his experiences as a child? Would that serve to underline the differences between them? He said that he would never let his parents influence how he dealt with this sudden bombshell dropped into his well-ordered life, but could the kid who had grown up in a mansion be completely immune to his past experience?

He talked of marriage, but could he sidestep prejudices that must have been in place from birth really to accept someone like her? Or was she being judgemental, allowing her own personal fears to cloud the issue?

She wondered why those thoughts were playing in her mind at all when she'd decided not to marry him, when everything he said now confirmed *why* they could never be suited. But there was enough doubt about that decision forming in the back of her mind to keep the thoughts churning as the car pulled into the packed car park that serviced the garden centre.

'We're really worlds apart, aren't we?' she murmured as he opened the passenger door for her, automatically reaching to help her out of the car.

Squirming round to fetch her backpack by her feet, she straightened to find that he had stilled and was looking at her with brooding intensity.

'Yes, we are.'

'What on earth did you ever see in me in the first place?' The thread of hurt forced its way back to the surface. 'Was I just a novelty toy you got to play with for a couple of weeks?'

The to-ing and fro-ing of people, kids, voices, laughter and, in the distance, the tinned sound of Christmas carols faded away. Ella could feel the burn of his dark eyes on her and it hit her that this man would be around for their child while she got on with her own life—except how easy would that be when she was emotionally involved with him?

'Never that, although...'

'No, don't say it.' She forced a laugh. 'I sense what you're going to say next isn't going to be one of those compliments that has me fainting with joy.'

'You made me laugh and you still do,' he murmured with a slow smile.

'I hope the festive spirit here doesn't give you too much of a headache. You'll find that when it comes to Christmas we do things in style in this part of the world.'

She made to clamber out but his hand kept her in place.

'Although, like I said before, you brought out something in me that I hadn't realised was there. For a while I was someone else, someone without the responsibilities that have always come with my upbringing, and I liked that *someone else*. I told you that I didn't have to come back here, Ella and that was the truth. I didn't. Maybe I came back to be re-introduced to that *someone else* I found when we were together.'

'But I was never going to be a permanent part of your life, Rocco. You might have wanted to feel free again for a while, but you were always going to go away in the end.'

Their eyes tangled and she was the first to look away. He neither confirmed nor denied that statement. Of course he would never have hung around to have a proper relationship with her second time round. The guy wasn't into love and had been brought up on a diet of duty, with a suitable wife somewhere along the line, someone from the right background who knew how things worked in that rarified life of his.

But could she be wrong? Impatient even to think along those lines, Ella snapped out of her temporary trance and hopped out of the car.

'You honestly don't have to help me out of a car, Rocco. I'm not an invalid.' But she tempered that with a smile because the gesture was really quite appealing. 'Now, let's go find a tree. I'm warning you that, if you're not a fan of Christmas, you might find the overload of decorations a little alarming...and watch out for errant elves.'

She swept through revolving doors into the garden centre, which was awash with fairy lights. The smell of pine in the air was heady and aromatic and, of course, carols blared from loud speakers dotted here and there.

In the cold, dull winter light Rocco was a sight to behold, so tall, lean and sexy. People walking around him slanted curious glances in his direction because he stood out, his long black coat the last word in expensive elegance, and his tan a sharp contrast to the pale faces all around them.

'Don't you think it's incredible that we will have a child who will be able to enjoy the meeting of two very different cultures—Irish and Spanish?' he murmured, tucking her hand in the crook of his arm and covering it with his own.

'I hadn't thought of it like that.'

The remark was casual but there was an intimacy there that reminded her, again, of the tantalising thought of what it would feel like to be married to him. She'd been so sure of herself but now...this felt a lot less clear-cut.

She wondered whether that also had something to do with the way he had engaged with her taciturn father. It occurred to her that her dad would have hated Steve, with his easy smile, his ready charm and that habit he'd had of pushing his blond hair out of his eyes. Steve would also have been at a loss with her father because there wouldn't have been a single meeting point between the two and she doubted that her ex would have bothered to make much of an effort.

Which brought comparisons to mind as she glanced sideways at Rocco's commanding figure next to her. He was so much the superior person in every single respect. Truths concealed seemed less relevant. It made her wince to think how readily she had buried herself back here, recovering from the loss of her mother and from a heart broken by a guy she could barely remember because next to Rocco, he barely registered now on her radar.

'I don't think I've ever been anywhere like this before,' Rocco said, and she glanced up at his handsome face and smiled.

'More firsts for you?'

'They seem to come with the territory where you're concerned.' He smiled back down at her.

Her heart lurched in what felt like a perfect moment. To the left, a group of tiny schoolchildren, who were maybe five or six years old, were bunched in a choir belting out a Christmas carol with tuneless enthusiasm. Rocco paused, looked at them and slowly strolled in their direction, taking Ella with him, and she could feel the tightening of his body next to hers. Ella glanced up at his riveted expression. He was shorn of his sophisticated, self-assured charm and the cool, lazy, tough veneer that made people jump to attention.

Right now, as he stood silently watching the children sing, there was a naked curiosity on his face that made her pause and her heart constrict. He reached into his pocket, found some notes and put them into the brightly wrapped box in front of the choir, then he turned to her.

'Tree?'

'I'm surprised that cash is still accepted,' she said. 'I half-expected a card machine.'

'Is that a tradition here? The kids singing?'

'I told you we do things in style around here. I used to go to the same school as those kids. And, yes, it's a tradition, like the Christmas tree in the store and the festive meal for the people who have nowhere to go over Christmas. I know you've already chatted to Vera, and told her that your door is open to anyone who wants to talk to you about what's going to happen, and you've also decided to go overboard and make the store as festive as possible. Thank you for that.'

The kids were still heartily singing as she drew him towards the back of the garden centre where the trees stood upright in their containers, waiting for approval.

Here, it was relatively quiet. The cold pinched her face. The flakes of the past few days hadn't materialised into full-throttle snowfall but still hung in the air with the promise of it.

The feeling of Christmas was all around them: the sound of the children's voices; the busy laughter; the lights and feeling of good cheer. An impressive display of Santa, his sled and team of reindeer adorned the entrance to the centre.

'What do you think of that tree?' She pointed to one in the corner and went to inspect it.

'Seems small.'

'Maybe compared to twenty-foot statement pieces where you lived,' Ella said wryly. 'We never had a big one at home. It was all about the decorations. And the lights, of course.'

'Will it be the same without your brother here?'

'We'll do a video call on Christmas Day. I guess you'll

be with your parents on Christmas day? You haven't said…'

'All in due course. Now, will they deliver this, or do I organise a driver to take it to the house?'

Ella burst out laughing. 'Don't be ridiculous. When you're in Rome, you have to do as the Romans do, and these Romans don't get drivers to deliver Christmas trees. It will be delivered to the house some time later this evening.'

'I think maybe a little sooner than that. I enjoy stricter timelines.'

He offered them a bumper donation to the Christmas choir fund and was duly rewarded with a tree that would arrive within the hour.

'Shall I tell you something? This is the first time I've ever felt any sort of Christmas spirit.'

Ella's breath hitched. He reached to stroke her face. She wanted him to kiss her so much it hurt, but he didn't, and it was all she could do not to pull him against her and kiss the living daylights out of him.

She didn't want his kindness and respect. She wanted passion. Should she give this a chance? Should she take what he was offering? He'd said that friends turned into lovers and not the other way round, but could they do a full circle? Could lovers become friends and then friends become lovers once again, but with the depth, commitment and love of two people destined for one another?

He said things that came straight from the heart and she knew, deep inside, that what he said was only for her and nothing to do with the fact that she was pregnant. She was sure of it! She didn't think that he even realised that. Maybe that was why she'd felt that powerful connection the very first time they'd really started talking to one another.

That was why his departure and the deceit she'd uncovered had been so devastating. It was also why she continued to be pulled towards him, yearning to go against what her head was telling her about lessons learnt.

The way he said that hadn't been just a statement of fact. Yes, he'd explained why Christmas meant so little to him, but there had been something achingly poignant when he'd told her that this was his first taste of real Christmas spirit.

'Sure you want to do the whole tree decorating thing with me and my dad?' she asked softly, resting her small hand on his arm.

'Why wouldn't I?'

'Because it's really not necessary,' she hedged awkwardly. 'Also…'

'Also?'

'Also if you're uncomfortable…' She laughed hesitantly.

'You're very sensitive, aren't you? Do you think I'm going to burst into tears in a moment of rare sentimentality?'

'I'd love to see that. But really, Rocco, you must have had a lonely childhood.'

Primed to react according to instinct, to put barriers into place, Rocco found that he couldn't because the usual safeguards weren't there. For a few seconds, he felt as though he was freefalling, then he regained control sufficiently to smile at her with wry self-deprecation.

'I coped, so don't feel too sorry for me. Now, shall we get some coffee? Breakfast? I noticed a café by the desk over there. Have you eaten?'

'I'm fine. There's no need to fuss.'

'I find it seems to come naturally with you being pregnant.'

'You sound surprised by that.'

'Who'd have thought?' Rocco half-murmured to himself. 'Okay, let's get back. Snow looks like it's beginning to get serious. We'll get the tree sorted and when that's done… I suppose we need to sit down and have a conversation about the details of our arrangement if marriage is not on the cards.'

As if she'd been doused by a bucket of cold water, Ella suddenly felt the sharp pang of fear at the prospect of not having this man in her life. Of seeing him disappear into the arms of some appropriate woman who would… what? Provide the sort of cold example of part-time surrogate motherhood that his own mother had, from the sounds of it? How did she feel about that? How did she feel about him no longer fussing around her or being in her life aside from slowly becoming a stranger whose only link would be the child they shared?

Did she want him moving on without her?

By the time they made it back, the tree was already at the house, and her father had positioned it in the usual place in the sitting room, by the front window. He bustled them out of the cold and hugged her and Ella hugged him back hard. Hugged him for the grief he had lovingly protected her from seeing when her mother had died, and for the hope and joy inside her because she knew that she was going to accept Rocco's marriage proposal.

Rocco watched this show of love with mixed feelings. Who was this man standing here, torn because all his ingrained and deeply embedded principles felt shadowy and ineffectual as he witnessed their open affection for one another? He'd found some other side of himself when he'd started his affair with Ella and it was still there, illogically defying a lifetime of indoctrination that had pointed him down the rigid path he had always been expected to follow. The path he had willingly *accepted* was the right one to follow.

He'd dropped all talk of marriage, but was discomforted when he thought about losing this link to someone he had grown to like, someone without the constraints that had ruled his life.

'Here, help with these.'

Rocco shrugged off uncomfortable thoughts and found a bundle of lights in his hands. 'What's this?'

'It's an absolute pig's ear of tangled Christmas tree lights! That's what happens when you don't pull them out for a year! Your job is to do your best to get them up and running. And don't tell me you've never done anything like that in your life before. You can see it as one of the festive season's little challenges!'

Rocco looked at the clear green eyes gazing at him with amusement and he smiled. The urge to touch her was overwhelming. The flare of panic he felt at her not accepting his marriage proposal was suddenly equally overwhelming.

'Now, a good challenge is something I've never been able to resist.'

Her eyes lingered on him just a little bit longer than necessary and the pink that infused her cheeks kick-started a rush of physical desire, which was something he understood and could deal with. Easier than troublesome, introspective thoughts.

The air was sucked out of Ella as she gazed back at him, on some subconscious level tuning in to what he was feeling, which mirrored her own response—hot desire, a need to touch and be touched. Her breasts were suddenly heavier than normal, her nipples, darker and bigger in pregnancy, even more sensitive than they'd been.

Freed from the restraints of having to convince herself that Rocco was unsuitable for her, a liar who didn't deserve much of a second chance, was her body now reacting to the freedom that had come with her change of heart? Her breathing slowed.

'What about you?' he murmured into the electric silence. 'How are *you* with challenges?'

'G-good, thanks,' she stuttered.

'Shall I get on with the lights? You're distracting me.'

Ella blinked like an owl when he raised his hand and dangled the ball of Christmas lights in front of her, although his dark eyes never left her face for a second, not until they dipped to linger on her mouth.

The rest of the morning passed in a blur as they strung the lights and hung the decorations, and it was nearly one by the time her father decided to call it a day, because crops had no respect for Christmas traditions.

'But stay for dinner, young man,' he said over his shoulder before he left. 'Always plenty in this house when it comes to food.'

'I'll have to ask your daughter for permission.' Rocco turned to Ella.

'So…' he drawled, when her father had left. 'Think the tree was the right choice?'

'Amazing, and thanks for the lights.'

He moved to stand next to her so that they were both gazing at the tree, and again he felt that peculiar hollowness inside him.

'The decorations...' he murmured.

'I know. Most of them are ancient, relics from childhood for me and Conor.'

He listened as she went through them, picking some of them out, smiling and reminiscing about times past and showing him a world he hadn't known existed because it was one he'd never encountered. The decorations were spread wide, dating back to childish paintings on cardboard with makeshift holes for hanging.

'So, do you say *yes*, Ella?'

Rocco looked down at her upturned face.

They had somehow drifted over to the deep, comfortable sofa by the fireplace. From here, Rocco could see unbroken greyness through the window and the stubborn flurries of light snow slanting in the thin afternoon light.

Ella didn't bother pretending to misunderstand his question.

'Yes. I'll marry you,' she told him quietly. Free to get physically close, she rested the palm of her hand on his chest, as if trying to gauge his heartbeat. 'I know...it comes with certain terms and conditions...' She waited a heartbeat for an interruption which didn't come. 'No love or romance or any of that other stuff...but you were right. This isn't just about the two of us now. This is bigger and it's something that calls for some sacrifice. And besides...'

'You're not making a mistake.'

Wasn't she? Ella couldn't have said but what she did know was that between a rock and a hard place a choice had to be made, and with this choice came the opportunity for her love to infect him, because they would be around one another, filling the spaces between them with laughter and affection. Those things were only a heartbeat away from love. If she held his hand for long enough, she could surely lead him there?

'I hope not.'

Rocco stayed the night.

He didn't know how he managed to make it through the remainder of the evening. He knew that the meal her dad prepared for them had tasted great. He knew that the snow had gathered momentum. He appreciated the Christmas tree, ablaze with light and the dozens of decorations that sat by the window, advertising a spirit of celebration and love that his family's grand tree never had. And, naturally, he knew that they had talked about marriage, and had been aware of her father's quiet approval.

He had ached to get to that bedroom, and when they made it there, after what had felt like hours of talking and eating, and eating and talking, he took his time.

No hurried sex with clothes being ripped off and strewn on the floor because desire overwhelmed finesse. He'd undressed her very slowly, removing each layer of clothing with solicitous, painstaking care.

Her body was ripe with their child. Her nipples were bigger and darker, her belly just beginning to show the soft roundness of pregnancy. He had buried himself in the soft down between her thighs, had sucked on her breasts and had caressed every part of her until, when neither of them could take any more, he had come in her.

He hadn't pushed back against her refusal to marry him. He'd waited. For a man who preferred the immediacy of action, the wait had proved fruitful.

Today, he thought much later, as he lay in bed with her head against his shoulder, had been a good one.

CHAPTER EIGHT

ELLA WOULD HAVE liked the honeymoon period to last for more than five and a half minutes but she had to admit to herself that that was never likely to happen.

They weren't leads in a romcom where eleventh-hour revelations occurred and love was shouted from the rooftops. He might be attracted to her—and her body burned when she remembered just how heatedly he had proven that—but this was a practical matter for him. After the night they'd spent together at her house, he'd almost immediately reminded her that things would have to be set in motion.

And, since then, Rocco had been true to his word. He had stayed for the night and the following morning he told her he would have to return to London.

'Come with me,' he urged quietly, his dark eyes intent and serious. 'Because we need to pin down timings and details of what happens next. Life for both of us is about to dramatically change, and I'm not a man to approach big changes in life without due diligence being done beforehand.'

He was standing fully dressed by the side of the bed at the crazily early hour of half-past six in the morning. It was still pitch-black outside. It could have been midnight. Ella was lying naked under the thick winter duvet, barely awake and still pleasurably indulging in drowsy thoughts of Rocco slowly beginning to love her the way she loved him. After the most wonderful and loving experience with him the night before, she was inclined to optimism.

She snapped out of that in a hurry.

'London?'

'I have a place there as well offices.'

Which brought home to her just how different his alter ego had been—the one with a small business concern in Madrid and an eye to elevating his position in life. The one who had rented a one-bed cottage to give her the illusion that that had been the most he could afford.

She knew it was stupid to dwell on those differences because the outward trappings didn't reflect the inner man who was one and the same. At least, they didn't most of the time. Right then, as he stood restlessly next to the bed, she could almost believe that man was morphing back into the autocratic businessman she had first encountered in that boardroom.

'Before we marry—and incidentally I feel that marriage should be as soon as possible—documents will have to be signed, preparations put in place. The usual paraphernalia of two people getting hitched.'

'Documents?'

She watched him hesitate, but only briefly. 'Financial stipulations. A pre-nup being top of the agenda.'

'A pre-nup? I wouldn't call that "the usual paraphernalia of two people getting hitched".'

'It is in my world. Would you be...amenable to signing one?'

'Of course.' But the atmosphere had changed subtly, even though she acknowledged that this was no different from what anyone with his kind of wealth would have suggested.

Especially bearing in mind that she didn't come from the same place as him; didn't share the same social standing. The rules of the game were completely different.

He hadn't dwelled on those differences. When he was with her, he was relaxed, as at home in her dad's house and with her dad as anyone could be, but those differences existed. She just had to think back to when he had described the sort of woman his parents would expect him to marry.

Love, though, overcame everything.

'Rocco, I wouldn't dream of trying to get money out of you if…if for some reason… *No.* I'm just not that kind of person.'

'I'm not doubting you but…'

'But rules are rules?' She shrugged, choosing to give him the benefit of the doubt. 'I get it. Just about. It's a weird world you live in, but I suppose you always have to be on high alert for gold-diggers. Also, yes, I'll come to London. When? And where do you want to meet?'

'I thought you could come to my place.' He moved towards her, leant over and kissed her gently on the forehead before pushing her hair back. 'I'm looking forward to marrying you,' he murmured. 'I'm really glad you changed your mind. You're doing the right thing—I know that—and so am I. The right thing for our baby. I realise you feel you're making a sacrifice, perhaps in ways that I'm not, and don't imagine that I don't appreciate that. I do.'

Beautiful words. Her heart softened.

'Okay. I'll sort a train out.'

At which Rocco had looked at her with amusement. 'Consider public transport a thing of the past,' he said with surprise in his voice. 'Too uncomfortable in your condition.'

'Really?' Ella smiled. 'Maybe you should try telling that to the thousands of them heading here, there and everywhere on buses and trains and tubes.'

'I could arrange for my helicopter to get you. A driver can collect you from here and—'

'No!' Her voice was terser than intended because she had a sudden vision of letting go of the sort of life she'd always had, floundering in a new world order in which she didn't belong. 'I'd die of fright in a helicopter.'

'I also have a private jet at my disposal.'

'Rocco, a commercial flight will suit me just fine.'

It had felt like a small win for her world over his. But, she fleetingly thought, how long would that last?

It had taken a little longer than the original twenty-four hours planned for Ella to head to London. Important meetings had demanded Rocco's absence from the country, so it was five days after they had agreed the visit, at a little after six in the evening, that Ella stood in front of an impressive Regency house, one of about twenty that formed an imposing crescent that curved in a semi-circle around a private, gated park manicured to within an inch of its life.

The houses were fronted with perfectly symmetrical cream columns. Even the lamp posts outside every three houses appeared to stand to attention, respectful of their grand surroundings. There wasn't a Christmas tree in sight, and certainly no inflatable Santas on sleds gaily announcing from the tops of the buildings that it was the festive season. There *were* wreaths on the doors, however, with lush foliage and just the right shades of metallic accents to contrast nicely against the highly polished black front doors.

It was hard to marry the man who had joked around with her dad and been intrigued at the kids singing carols with the man who lived behind that imposing door. It was deathly quiet. The cars parked outside were eye-wateringly high-end—cars that belonged to people who also had private jets and helicopters at their disposal.

Ella pressed the doorbell and, before she could remove her finger from the buzzer, the door opened and there he was, standing in front of her, and her heart leapt.

It was freezing outside but he was in a pair of loose, black jogging bottoms and a tee-shirt. Apparently it was summer in Belgravia, even if it was the middle of December everywhere else.

'Ella…'

Rocco smiled and stood aside so that she could brush past him, pulling a small case on wheels behind her. She smelled of a fragrant scent which, he suspected, was nothing more than the smell of her shampoo. He was ridiculously pleased to see her because, even though it had only been a matter of days since he'd returned to London, only to jet off immediately to New York, she'd been on his mind. He'd missed her and he put that down to the fact that they were on a completely different footing now. Naturally she would be on his mind because their relationship had undergone a seismic change. Plus, their love-making had been…sensational.

'I still think you should have let my driver bring you to London,' he said without preamble as she moved gracefully into his house and looked around her with an expression he couldn't quite read.

'This is an amazing place.' She turned full-circle and then crooked her head at one of his paintings. 'Is that a real Hockney on the wall?'

'All the artwork in here is the real deal.'

Rocco went to relieve her of her coat and noticed she was wearing a million layers underneath. He itched to get them all off. However, he'd had time to think, and he was going to play it cool. Attraction or no attraction, this was first and foremost an arrangement that made sense and not a searing tale of high romance. He didn't want her getting the wrong impression. He didn't want her expectations to be built to levels he wouldn't be able to meet.

He didn't want her falling in love with him.

Of course, she wouldn't do that, not when she was coming from a place of mistrust because of the circumstances under which they had met. Not when he'd had to convince her to marry him. Not when she had been through disillusionment with a partner and was wary of emotional involvement with the wrong guy.

But still… Right now she was independent, and wanted nothing from him beyond what he had put on the table, but that was *right now*. He didn't want her investing in him emotionally as time moved on. He didn't want her to become the sort of clingy, demanding wife who expected shows of devotion and was disappointed if they failed to materialise. He didn't have it in him to be that sort of man, even if he could fill in the blanks in all the other areas that mattered, and he knew it would be a fine line between disappointment and eventually filing for divorce.

So he would play it cool. Even though, right now, as he looked at her turn full circle in his vast hallway, he was anything but cool. In fact, he had never felt hotter.

'You should shed the layers, Ella. I keep this place well heated in winter.'

'So I notice. I never asked, but you must have been freezing when you stayed the night. There's always been a strict policy at home of layering up in winter because only namby-pambies rely on central heating twenty-four seven to keep warm.'

'I incline to the policy that there's no point freezing to death to prove a point. By the way, I hope you don't think I'm a *namby-pamby...*'

Ella reddened. 'You *should* be,' she said truthfully and reddened a little more when he strolled towards her with a wolfish, curling smile.

'I'm one of a kind,' he murmured, sliding his fingers into her hair and cupping her face. 'Haven't you realised that by now?'

Desire surged and memories of how she had felt against him, pregnant and naked, filled him up until he was drowning in the need to bury himself in her. He breathed in deeply and pulled back to a place of self-control.

'Want me to give you the guided tour? Or can that wait? You must be tired after your journey.'

'I guess the guided tour can wait and I'm not tired. The train was very comfortable. It's a novelty to travel first class.'

'You make me want to show you all the things that money can buy,' he confessed in a roughened undertone and she burst out laughing.

'You're so shallow, Rocco Mancini. How did you ever cope with being Jose Rivero?'

'Women are impressed with what money can buy.'

'Well, to parrot what you've just said, *I'm one of a kind.*'

She was, and he was pleased and satisfied that maybe the gap between the man he was and the man he'd pretended to be was closing. She was smiling at him, and for a few seconds he was deprived of speech. 'I've ordered in food—French. I hope that's fine with you?'

'Lovely.'

'And you've been eating, haven't you?'

'I've been eating. I know you're fully engaged with the pregnancy but you don't have to caretake me. You've phoned a thousand times since you left Ireland.'

Rocco flushed. 'What's surprising about that? You're having my baby. I'm concerned for your well-being. Naturally, I'm going to phone to find out how you are.'

'Yes, it's very sweet.'

'I'm not a sweet person. Anyone would tell you that.' Sweet? Never a description that had been applied to him. 'Have you missed me?' he asked in a husky, lazy voice which matched the look he shot her from under his lashes. 'Because I've missed you.'

'It hasn't been very long... How was New York?'

'My libido doesn't keep tabs on time, and New York was New York.'

He stroked the side of her face and smiled when her eyelids fluttered and her lips parted. Their kiss was soft and sweetly captivating. Sliding gently between his lips, her tongue was a lingering caress that did amazing things to his body.

He tugged her closer so that he could feel her against him and he knew that she could feel his stiff erection pushing through the jogging pants he was wearing. 'Want to take this further?' he growled. He guided her hand to his erection and encouraged her to massage it.

'Rocco...' she breathed.

'I like it when you say my name. Your accent...turns me on.'

'Just my accent?'

'Everything about you turns me on. Why do you think this is going to work so well? This thing between us...

this chemistry...makes what we have more than just an arrangement because you're pregnant.'

But, Ella suddenly thought, that was it, wasn't it? It was just an arrangement in which the added bonus was sex. She now had so much more of a complete picture of the man he was, the man with the background that had shaped his beliefs, who was quietly convinced that to love and to be vulnerable in love was something he could never do. This would be a marriage on his terms and, if she hoped that she could reach inside and slowly guide him to a place where he would give without thought the love he now felt he couldn't give, then she would have to be wary of losing herself in the process.

She might have put Steve into perspective, downplayed the heartbreak she had felt because he had been so insignificant compared to Rocco, but the disappointment in that relationship, in the why and the how it had failed, was very real. He had let her down, and she had to protect herself against being let down by Rocco.

Yes, there was a sincerity about him that Steve had never possessed underneath the glib charm, but there was a lot of road to be travelled before she could fully trust him.

He had concealed the truth from her once, whatever genuine excuses he had made about that.

But how she was tempted to toss in the towel and go for broke on the trust front...

'We have time for...you know...all of that. And, actually, I'm quite hungry.'

'Yes. Dinner.'

'You shouldn't have gone to all this trouble,' was the first thing she said when she was confronted with the elaborate French meal that had been prepared by one of Rocco's favourite chefs of a Michelin-starred restaurant a stone's throw away.

'What trouble? Everything was delivered in heat-proof containers, ready for the oven. I didn't have to do anything.' He shrugged. 'Jean Claude is a personal friend and, whenever I want something, he's always happy to help out.'

'*The* Jean Claude?'

'The very same.' Rocco nodded at his granite-topped table and watched as she warily sat down, looking around her all the while.

He suddenly realised that he was so accustomed to the very pinnacle of luxury that he rarely noticed his surroundings. Now, though, he looked at his own house through her eyes: a sprawling London townhouse in one of the most expensive postcodes in the capital. Close to eight-thousand square feet of prime real estate. He had originally bought it because it was conveniently located for his offices, and because it was light and airy, and that reminded him of Spain.

Every room had soaring ceilings. The artwork was priceless, the sort of artwork many people might keep locked away for insurance purposes, but for him, what was the point of that? The furnishings were pale and minimalist, every single piece bespoke, and had been chosen and sourced globally by the most expensive interior design team in the city.

When he remembered her father's cosy place—the Christmas tree with the hand-made decorations; the old, comfortable sofas; the weathered kitchen table and the feel of *love* imbued into everything—Rocco felt something pierce him deep inside. Ella would be entering his highly refined, wealthy orbit. It was a world to which he was wedded and she would be as well. The comparison to the one she inhabited now, the one she had grown up around, and his own could not have been more stark.

Another reason to make sure that they didn't start this very important next step with her harbouring any romantic illusions that he would ever become the sort of cosy, homey guy she had probably been brought up to seek out as a mate. He couldn't change his destiny, and experience had taught him that it was best served with rigorous discipline and control. He was who he was and she would, essentially, have to fall in line.

He served the food, waving down her offers of help. Then, when they were facing one another at the table, he said, gently but in a businesslike voice, 'To recap what we briefly touched on before, Ella—documents have to be signed. I can make an appointment for us to see lawyers first thing tomorrow so we can get the ball rolling on the financial front.'

'I've only just got here!' She dived into the food and glanced up at him from under her lashes. 'What's happened to the guided tour?'

'The paperwork comes first, I'm afraid.'

'You could always just bring whatever it is I have to sign here and I'll sign it.' She shrugged. 'We don't need to get lawyers involved, do we? Didn't we say it would all be a little less formal?'

'We very much do. And besides, in my world, lawyers are *always* involved.' He looked at her as she continued eating and wondered whether he could detect a certain stiffening of her shoulders. 'It's not just about the pre-nup. It's what happens with the child in the event of a break-up of any kind, from separation to divorce. Financial arrangements need to be put in place along with something that is legally binding on custody.'

'Rocco, I just can't think that far ahead! Our baby isn't even born yet!' But she couldn't help but see the pattern of someone who left nothing to chance—except, as it turned out, contraception. Whether he liked it or not, control was something that could end up very slippery.

'They're just precautionary measures.' Rocco flushed. 'There's no avoiding them.'

'I'm happy to sign whatever you want me to sign if it's to do with money, because I don't care about the money. But I'm not signing away rights to my own child in the event that something happens somewhere along the line and we don't end up together. I'm just not prepared to do that.'

Rocco paused. He lowered his eyes. 'Like I said, it's just a precaution. My background dictates certain measures be taken.'

'Or else what? Is the world going to stop turning if you don't take those measures?'

'Hardly, but—'

'I won't do it, Rocco.'

Rocco sighed, flung both hands in the air and shot her a frustrated glance from under his lashes. 'Why are you so stubborn?'

'I just can't plan every single detail, and besides, I have to stand up for myself, Rocco. Look around you—all this privilege and wealth. I can't afford to let you dominate the narrative. I can't afford to be overwhelmed by all of this.'

'But we have to find a way past arguing about things that have already been accepted. We're going to be married.'

'That doesn't mean that I don't have to protect myself,' Ella said evasively.

She was skating on thin ice. Yes, they were going to be married, and she wanted the marriage to work, and not just because it made sense. Lots of things in life *made sense* but that didn't mean that one was compelled to take those roads.

She wanted to hope a piece of his heart was willing to open up, and she knew that all it would take would be a chink, but to show how she felt now... How would he react? He thought he knew all the answers and, what he didn't know, he could somehow predict and so control.

How would he react if he knew how she felt about him? Would the marriage proposal come off the table? Now that she had accepted it, she couldn't face the thought of not being married to him. She'd come full circle. From bitterness and scepticism, he had managed to prove himself to her and, his having done that, she had let hope creep in. But hope and complete idiocy were two different things and she still had to have some safeguards in place.

'What are you protecting yourself from?'

'From landing up in a place where I don't know the rules of the game and there's no one to show them to me.'

'Where do you think I'm going to be during all of this? Haven't I proved to you that you can count on me?'

'You don't understand. It was easy for you to slide into my life, to charm my dad. But what I'm facing is completely different. I mean, have you even told your parents about...about everything?'

'I'm going to break the glad tidings to them later tonight,' Rocco said, rising to his feet and doing a half-hearted job of tidying the table.

He could feel the sudden tension in his shoulders because this was a blatant lie. Or at least, a very creative way of dealing with the truth. But he decided, without analysing it too deeply, it would be better to give her the final reassurance she needed that she hadn't been manoeuvred into a marriage she hadn't originally wanted.

And he hadn't *manoeuvred her*, he told himself, without a shred of inner doubt. He'd just allowed her to see that he could be counted on. He'd allowed her to be persuaded by all the advantages she and their baby would have if she tied the knot with him.

If he'd presented the situation to his parents earlier as a fait accompli, then likewise he'd been smoothing the path for them. All told, it was the best way of handling everything, and he was accustomed to handling things in the most efficient way possible.

'There's dessert.' He changed the subject as he fetched some bowls from the cupboard. When he turned round, he released a short sigh of relief, because her face had softened.

'Sometimes I see life in black and white,' he admitted. 'A lot of people imagine that to be born into a life of privilege must be pretty amazing—holidays to far-flung places, the best of everything life has to offer—but in my case it was a rigid life without much scope for…moving too far outside the box. The very gilded box.'

'And that's why you felt so free when you didn't have to be the person other people expected things from… when we met.'

'We worked for one another, Ella. We just didn't see this coming. All I'm doing is dealing with it in the only way I know how.'

'Which doesn't mean that I don't have concerns. I mean…is there a timeline for going to see your parents? If they don't know anything just yet, do they expect that you'll be spending Christmas with them?'

'I'll arrange for us to see them before Christmas. I'm guessing you'll want to spend Christmas with your dad and, if I'm honest, so would I.' He shot her a crooked smile. 'Now I've had a little bit of what Christmas should feel like, I'm hungry for more.'

Ella smiled and relaxed. 'Just think of how much fun it'll be when there's three of us.' She accepted the chocolate gâteau and fork that he handed her on a small plate.

Doubts eased away. 'I could get used to all this fussing even though, naturally, it's not necessary, and on principle I object.'

'I admire a woman of principle.'

Ella could feel her whole body react to his proximity as he dragged a chair over and waited until she'd finished the cake before dabbing some stray chocolate from the side of her mouth. She sucked in her breath and had to resist the temptation to wrap her arms around him and bury her head against him.

'Okay, guided tour...' he growled against her neck and she started with dismay.

'What *now*?'

'To my bedroom. First and only stop will be my bed.' He scooped her off the chair and ignored her half-hearted protest. He walked and kissed her at the same time, fired up by her tiny, little whimpers of pleasure.

Ella lost herself in her body's urgent, driving needs. She was on fire by the time they made it to the bedroom. He laid her on the mattress, stepped back to look at her and she basked under his hungry gaze and was ready as he pushed up the top. She wasn't wearing a bra. She quivered as she clamped his mouth onto her nipple and sucked, his tongue rasping on the stiffened bud, driving her crazy with pleasure. She was barely aware of him undressing her, not completely, but enough. Enough to trace her no longer flat stomach with his hand, to ease off the loose trousers she was wearing, followed by her panties. She was so wet for him. She flung back her head, closed her eyes and groaned with the anticipation of being pleasured, opening her legs to accommodate the mouth she knew would find the throbbing bud of her clitoris. Her body ached and yearned for him.

His tongue found the perfect spot and she moaned as he flicked it against her clitoris, over and over until she could feel the steady build of an orgasm. She couldn't hold back. She wanted him deep in her, but she couldn't resist his demanding tongue, and she moaned and shuddered against his mouth as she came.

Shaken, satisfied and drowsy as desire slowly ebbed away Ella blinked like an owl and then sighed. 'Rocco...'

She shot him a hooded glance as he straightened, still staring at her with a little smile, and in that smile she could read all sorts of very acceptable levels of appreciation. Ella shuffled herself back into something resembling a state of dress and yawned as exhaustion began creeping in.

'You're tired.'

'I... I'm okay.'

'You need a nice hot bath.'

'You're fussing again.'

'You like it,' he teased and she thought, a little uncomfortably, *yes, far too much...*

He scooped her up and took her directly to an *en suite* bathroom that was as big as a football field and very, very modern. There was no glass door concealing a shower cubicle but a huge wet room, a massive bath...and even a comfortable chair against the wall big enough for two.

He sat her on the chair while he ran the bath and tested the water. She thought, *if, in a fortnight, you could find part of yourself you'd never accessed before, then over time, with a child uniting us, is it really so much to think that I could bring out the person I know you are?*

She could have lost herself in that daydream for ever. Turning it into reality felt like a tiny heartbeat away.

'You relax here for a bit,' he said, pushing her hair back and helping her into the warm, deep, foamy water. 'I'll bring your bag up and then I have a couple of work calls to make. Climb into bed. I won't be long.'

He was gone before she could reply and she did as told. She enjoyed a long, lazy bath. Like the rest of the house, the enormous bathroom was in pale marble, only broken by a granite square defining the wet room. The towels were big, fluffy white ones and beautifully warm from the heated towel rail. She felt like a special guest in a very expensive five-star hotel.

When she'd had her bath, she clambered into bed and was nodding off when Rocco eventually returned.

'Sorry I took a little longer than I expected. One of the calls I made was to my parents.'

'Ah. How did it go? How did they take the news? They must have been shocked. Did they ask a lot of questions about us?'

'Some, as to be expected. I've arranged for us to go and pay them a visit. It will be a fleeting one.'

'You've actually arranged a date? Already?'

'There's no point delaying the inevitable,' Rocco said wryly.

'Why not? We could delay it for a bit longer. Let them get used to the idea of their one and only son getting married to the unsuitable girl he got pregnant.'

'Getting used to that might take them a while.'

'That's not very reassuring for me.'

'You have nothing to worry about. We'll be there two days and, while we're there, you can count on me to shield you from any awkward interaction.'

'Awkward interaction?' Ella laughed nervously.

'Nothing that can't be dealt with,' Rocco soothed. 'But you have to understand that they're very traditional and they've had set ideas about the direction of my life. Including the sort of woman who might eventually wear my ring.'

'And you've never led them to think that you might ever want to follow a different route…'

'Like I said, my life was set in stone from a very young age.'

'So when is this visit going to take place?'

'Tomorrow late-afternoon. My private jet is on standby.'

Private jet? Standby? Just for a second Ella had a fleeting and vaguely uneasy vision of the life she had signed up to. It wasn't going to be anything like the one she was accustomed to living. She'd known that, of course, but she'd been lulled into a sense of security because he'd been on her turf and in her territory. Now, she would be entering a different world, and she had to fight the chasms between them opening up around the seeds of hope that had taken root.

He would be by her side. He'd assured her that everything would be okay. And she believed him because he had proved that he was the man she'd thought he was.

CHAPTER NINE

ELLA HAD HER first taste of how the uber-rich lived first thing the following morning.

She was swept into a world of personal shopping, where the normal trudge from store to crowded store was exchanged for the emptiness of the high-end boutique and the fawning subservience of assistants bending over backwards to show her the latest pieces. There were no price tags on any of the clothing.

'I have enough clothes to last two days,' Ella had pointed out.

'My parents are aficionados of formal attire,' Rocco had told her. 'I've never seen either of them in a pair of jeans.'

Ella had immediately got the message: cargo pants, dungarees, baggy jumpers and her capacious winter coat weren't going to do. She ended up with several outfits, shoes for the evening and a bag, only escaping a trip to a beauty salon because they'd been running out of time. She wasn't sure whether she'd enjoyed the experience or whether she'd felt manipulated into a spending spree she wasn't altogether comfortable with—even though she belatedly realised that this sort of spree, so ridiculously uncustomary for her, would probably become the norm.

Now, as they sat waiting for Rocco's private jet to take off, Ella glanced down at the beautiful pale-grey cashmere trouser outfit she wore and the black designer coat casually slung over the cream leather seat on the other side of the aisle. She felt a little faint when she took in the rich wood veneer of the private jet, the plush seating arranged in little clusters for maximum comfort and the large windows with electronic shades, everything the last word in luxury.

Next to her, Rocco was scrolling through his phone, catching up on emails.

'I feel like an imposter,' she said, turning to him.

Rocco stopped what he was doing and swivelled to look at her.

'Why?' Of course, he knew why. It had been impossible not to notice her bemusement underneath the quiet compliance as she'd been shown outfit after outfit in the sort of exclusive shops in which he doubted she'd ever set foot before in her life. And now she was sitting next to him on his private jet.

She'd wanted to look at the windows of the big department stores, which were dressed lavishly for Christmas, but they hadn't had time and he'd felt like Scrooge as he'd firmly guided her back to his waiting chauffeur.

He'd thought of the department store where she worked and how proud she'd been of the Christmas tree and the effort the staff had poured into decorating it, knowing it would be the last one to grace the foyer. He'd recalled her own Christmas tree and the warmth and love between her father and her as they had pulled out the decorations and taken a trip down memory lane with each and every one. He'd watched her gaze up at the lights in Knightsbridge as they'd been driven through the congested streets, where throngs of shoppers flanked the slow-moving traffic.

'I don't belong in this world,' she said bluntly.

'It's the same world as yours,' Rocco returned. 'You're only wearing slightly different clothing.'

'The closest I've ever got to a private jet is when I've seen one in a movie.'

'Aren't you enjoying the experience?' He said this as it taxied and then roared upwards. He raised his voice and continued to look at her, easing her gently towards an understanding of the life she was going to occupy.

'I guess there are no crowds at a packed terminal. Have you ever endured a winding queue at a terminal anywhere?'

'No.'

'What's it like to live your life, Rocco?'

'Very, very good now that you're in it and pregnant with my baby.' He reached out to cover her hand with his and smiled, a soothing, reassuring smile.

Ella closed her eyes and relaxed in her seat, with his hand still covering hers. She'd been so hesitant about accepting this marriage proposal but he'd waited patiently for her to make her mind up, and had taken his time to show her all the sides of his personality so that she could see what a dependable husband he would make—and a dependable husband would become the devoted dad.

And with both of those...well...who knew where things might eventually end when the beginnings were auspicious? What had started in deception, the thing that had so devastated her, had ended in this happy place. She would meet his parents and, if they were a little reserved to start with, she was sure they would eventually warm to her. Or at least accept her. Surely? Besides, he would be by her side and they wouldn't be staying for long. How objectionable could they be when they'd only have a very small dose of her to deal with?

'I hope your parents like me, even if it's eventually.' She voiced her thoughts aloud as the jet sped towards their destination.

Rocco squeezed her hand. Personally, his thoughts were more in the direction of 'all in the fullness of time' but his parents were far too well-bred to openly voice any disapproval.

'They will.' His voice was reassuringly persuasive.

'What if they don't?'

'I've never seen the point in dealing with hypothetical situations. Always best to wait until something happens and then deal with it, rather than creating a range of possible scenarios and getting worked up.'

'That's rich coming from the guy who was happy to project to a future where we had other partners,' Ella said absently, chewing her lip and frowning.

She briefly conjured up one of those hypothetical scenarios he had talked about. What if she'd dug her heels in and refused to marry Rocco, the son and heir to the family fortune that needed protecting? Would she have made this trip out to Spain now? Or would they have tried to convince their son to walk away from a child he had accidentally fathered, one who would have remained illegitimate? They were clearly traditionalists to the bone. Was she only going out to see them because she had agreed to marry their son at long last?

There was fertile ground here for all sorts of wild imaginings, but she shut the door to it, because she was now on a road and there was no turning back.

'We still have to discuss all the details of our marriage.' She turned to him and met his dark gaze steadily. 'Whatever you say, your world couldn't be more different than mine. It's not just a simple case of things being different superficially but the same deep down. You've seen where I come from, seen the life I've been accustomed to.'

'I admit some changes might be on the horizon.'

'I can't live a life of spending money and being pampered,' she told him bluntly. 'You asked me whether I'd enjoyed the day. As a one off, it was an experience, but I wouldn't want that to be my entire life.'

'What are you proposing?'

'I want to carry on working.'

'Ella, maybe we could postpone this discussion for later, when I'm not having to shout over the roar of a plane engine?'

'I feel like I'm on a roller coaster,' Ella returned with a frown. 'Yes, I'm really happy that you're taking an interest in this pregnancy...that was never something you expected or asked for...'

'This feels like well-trodden ground.'

'Now we're on our way to see your parents and that feels like I'm just a little bit higher on the roller coaster. If I'm not careful I'll be at the top, I'll have lost sight of the ground beneath me and, by the time I come hurtling back down, planet Earth won't bear any resemblance to the place I left behind. And Rocco...? That scares me.'

'That's very descriptive, Ella,' Rocco said thoughtfully. 'But, okay. I understand where you're coming from. Do you think holding down a job is worth the effort? Whatever you earn will be a pittance in the grand scheme of things. Also, I would want you to devote time to our child. I...'

'Yes?' There was sudden insistence in her voice.

'I know how sidelining a child to the safekeeping of strangers can have an effect,' Rocco said roughly. 'I wouldn't want to see...that outcome for any child of mine.'

There was an electric silence during which Ella looked

at him, taking in the dark stain on his cheekbones, the sudden tightening of his well-shaped mouth and an air of vulnerability that was so rarely apparent in him.

Her heart constricted as once again she was exposed to a past that had doubtless been lonely for a small child, however much money had been thrown at him. It was another glimpse that made her feel so connected to him. She impulsively reached out to link her fingers through his, half-expecting him to make some deflecting, jokey remark about not wanting her to feel sorry for him, but he just squeezed her hand in response and gazed at her with a shuttered expression.

'Can I tell you something, Rocco?'

'Depends.'

'On what?'

'On whether you think I'll like what you want to tell me.'

He grinned but his dark eyes were wary and she smiled back. 'I'm being serious,' she said.

'That sounds ominous but go ahead.'

'First of all, when I say I want to work, the money would have nothing to do with it. It would be about mental stimulation. I would be very happy to get involved with some kind of volunteer work. And it would never be a full-time occupation. I would always put our child first and foremost. I know that there would be a nanny of sorts and, as long as I get to say who that nanny is and what their duties are, then that's fine.'

'That sounds reasonable enough,' Rocco murmured.

'Something else. Can I ask what sort of woman you envisaged yourself marrying? Or rather, let me rephrase that, was there already someone lined up for you in true "marriage of convenience" style?'

The silence stretched and Ella's mouth tightened because that silence spoke volumes. 'Forget I asked that.'

'What do you want me to say? I never imagined I would end up with an Ella but, while we're going down this road, not that there's a point to it, did *you* think you would end up with a guy like me? Someone who made you feel as though you were on a roller-coaster ride?'

'I guess not.' But Ella thought that roller-coaster rides, however terrifying, could also be exhilarating. And addictive. And all sorts of things when one got used to it and started concluding that life without the roller-coaster ride was unthinkable.

She wished she hadn't asked the question of him because she wouldn't want to hear it confirmed in stark terms that someone like her would never have been on his wish list. She didn't like to be reminded why, exactly, she was sitting on a private jet next to him because, cravenly, she wanted to hold onto the belief that they were destined to be together.

She'd invested in her dreams and her hopes and she stubbornly refused to let go. Was she being a blind fool? Was her optimism misplaced? But no. He hadn't tried to force her hand. He'd respected her decision to turn down his marriage proposal and had allowed her the space to make up her mind. He'd been the decent guy who had more than compensated for the cardboard cut-out creep she'd thought he was when she'd discovered the truth about him.

'I guess we can fine-tune the details,' she said, voice raised over the sound of the jet engine, 'In the next few days. Meanwhile, tell me about your house. What can I expect?' She hid her frown under a smile and banished unwelcome thoughts.

* * *

Nothing could have prepared Ella for what confronted her when Rocco's chauffeur finally pulled through a pair of imposing wrought-iron gates that led into sprawling gardens with manicured lawns, fountains and statues. The sort of place where a person could be forgiven for getting out their purse because they might have to pay to get inside and look around.

When she lost count of the windows, she decided it was no longer a house, it was a palace—which she should have expected, given everything he'd said, but which she discovered she really hadn't at all.

Tall arches and a series of marble columns were emblazoned with intricate stone carvings, and everything drew the eye to the magnificent double-door entrance. The grand windows were fronted with iron balconies, all as intricate as the stone carvings, lacy in their details. There were rows and rows of them, perfectly proportioned and as precise as an architectural drawing.

She stopped and stared. Her heart was beating fast and her mouth was dry. She was glad for the steadying grasp of Rocco's hand as he linked his fingers through hers.

'Don't worry,' he said with more hope than expectation. 'It's going to be fine.'

'Have you described me to your parents?'

'Why would I have done that?'

'They might be in for a shock.'

'They'll handle it.' Rocco shrugged. 'They've dealt with shocks before.' But he could feel the nervous shakiness of her hand in his. What could he say? It was a necessary hurdle and they wouldn't be there for very long.

'How can you be so cool and collected at a time like this?'

Rocco didn't say anything. Instead, he pressed the doorbell and heard it reverberate. One of the many servants, who did everything from clean to cook to tend the vast acreage of maintained lawns, would answer the door. Sure enough, his favourite, Jorge, did so and bowed deferentially.

His parents were in the casual sitting room having drinks, he was told, and would expect them both to join them at seven sharp. Only then, message delivered, did Jorge smile broadly at Rocco, ushering him in, and then greeting Ella with even more deference when she was introduced.

When Rocco glanced at Ella, he could see that she was shocked at the lack of ebullient welcome.

'My parents,' he murmured, leaning into her, 'Are slightly different to your father.'

'Are they excited to have you here for a couple of days at Christmas?'

'Come on,' was his non-committal response. 'I'll be in my usual suite of rooms. We can freshen up and then join them for pre-dinner drinks.'

If the boutiques with the fawning saleswomen, the chauffeur-driven cars and the private jet told a tale of wealth, then this *palace* and non-appearing parents told an even starker story of the differences between Rocco and her.

She gazed around her as he ushered her away from the front door. The hall was vast, with high ceilings and a massive chandelier that cast a mellow glow over highly polished marble floors. It should have been breathtaking but it felt like a mausoleum.

Ahead was a sweeping double staircase and, to the side, an over-sized Christmas tree, professionally decorated and there to impress. It was as coldly beautiful as the rest of what she saw. The perfect tree, branches dense and full, stretched up, up, up towards the ornate ceiling and decorated in a thousand delicate, hand-blown glass baubles in shades of red, gold and ivory. The thousands of golden lights twined around the tree reflected off the polished floors and crystal chandeliers above.

'I can't believe you grew up here,' she whispered.

'In between boarding school and trips abroad.'

'I'm beginning to understand what you meant when you said your parents liked formal attire. Jeans would look out of place here.'

Ella wanted him to talk, wanted to hear his voice, because it might have distracted her from the nerves gripping her now like a vice. She half-listened as he described the dining room, the ballroom used for highly formal occasions, the original stained glass on the first floor and the gold-leafed ceilings that dated back over a hundred years. There was a library stocked with first-edition classics and a private study that overlooked the manicured lawns at the back. As a boy, he had used it to work in it, he told her.

'There were peacocks back then,' he said with a certain amount of wistfulness. 'Sadly, no more. Still, the black swans on the private lake remain.'

As they walked up the impressive staircase, her eyes strayed to classic Spanish paintings and tapestries. They emerged onto the broad corridor of the first floor, and she gasped at the stretch of wall comprised entirely of a hand-painted mural depicting some era in Spanish history: horses, men in armour and stylised trees and castles.

She suspected a legion of servants tended to the mansion and its grounds, yet a ghostly silence hung over the exquisite palace. Aside from the terrifyingly huge Christmas tree in the hall, anyone would think that the festive season had bypassed the palace completely.

Rocco's suite was as big as her dad's entire house.

'I'll leave you to get ready,' he said. He glanced at his watch, then back at her. She looked lost. 'One of the housekeepers will knock in an hour and take you down to join my parents. I'll be there. Is that all right with you? I expect I should have a little down time with them before you join us.'

Ella smiled and walked towards him. He was so tall, so commanding, and had seemed so curiously distant towards his parents, but wanting to see them without her made sense, at least for a bit. She could more easily relate to this person.

'Of course you want to see your parents without me! You don't have to feel awkward about that.'

'I wouldn't say I felt awkward.'

'An hour will be more than enough. As long as I don't have to find my way through this place.' She smiled a watery smile. 'Then I'll be fine to join you later. If I have to locate whatever drawing room you're in, then there isn't a satnav on earth that's going to work. I'll be wandering the corridors for the rest of my life.'

'That would be the last thing I'd want.'

Ella's breath hitched in her throat as his dark eyes roamed over her with warm appreciation, reminding her of just how much she loved this guy. She thought of a lifetime of nights together and that gave her just the right amount of backbone she needed.

'Okay,' she said a little breathlessly. 'I'll see you downstairs.'

It was going to be fine. Everything was in place and

she was happy that it was. Her doubts had been banished, replaced with trust. Of course she would occasionally have doubts. This wasn't the future she had had in mind for herself, but Rocco had stepped up to the plate, proved himself worthy of her love, and she was determined to hang onto that.

The suite in which she now stood was lavish. She stepped into a small hall, adorned with an imposing tapestry on the wall, and from it she could see several doors opening out from a spacious living area to various rooms. The most eye-catching, however, was the bedroom, to which she quickly walked. She would like to have taken time to appreciate the splendour of the massive fireplace, the velvet drapes and the canopied bed with its sultry, deep-purple spread. A quick jump onto it wouldn't have gone amiss but, conscious of the time, she instead headed straight to the bathroom.

It was all marble. What else? There was a hot tub, deep bath, rainfall shower and, most impressive of all, floor-to-ceiling windows that overlooked the landscaped gardens at the back. Ella showered quickly. It took time to figure out the controls but she felt refreshed afterwards, although suddenly exhausted.

She dressed in one of the over-priced new outfits she had bought, a navy-blue cashmere dress that clung and showed off the beginnings of her bump in a way none of her baggy outfits did. She stared at her reflection in the long, freestanding mirror and was overwhelmed by a feeling of unreality.

Who was this person in a dress that cost more than her monthly salary, with shoes of the finest leather, staring out at manicured lawns that housed its own private chapel? And about to be married to a billionaire who had been brought up amidst this unbelievable grandeur.

She'd made a stand about continuing to work when the baby was born but was that just a laughable notion? What was her life going to look like once she was married to Rocco? She was handing him her heart and putting all her trust in him. *Was that a wise decision?*

She felt the baby stir, a fluttering, butterfly feeling deep inside. She placed her hand on her tummy, took a deep breath and was relieved when a knock on the door told her that her escort had arrived—twenty minutes earlier than expected, so thank heavens she was ready and waiting. Make a late appearance and who knew? She didn't want to deal with thoughts that kept trying to surface, because there was no backing out now. But, with each deathly silent step towards whatever room Rocco was ensconced in with his parents, she could feel the drum beat of her heart getting louder with tension.

The door to a room on the ground floor was pushed open by the man who had led the way in silence. Ella blinked at the polished dark-wooden floor, the inlaid marble, the Persian rugs the original mouldings on the walls and the frescoed panels...all accented by the warm glow from the chandelier, with its fine crystal beads.

She noticed, with a flare of panic, that there was no sign of Rocco. Instead, there was just his parents, who both rose to their feet, which she could instantly see was a token gesture of welcome, because their faces were cold and unsmiling. They both had the same darkly striking beauty of their son but Ella's eyes were drawn to his mother, with her raven-black hair pulled back tightly into a chignon.

'Sit, please.'

'Where's Rocco?' Ella asked nervously.

'I have asked Rocco to deal with an urgent work-related issue but he will be here shortly. We thought we might get you here a little earlier so that we could acquaint ourselves with the woman who is suddenly to be our daughter-in-law.'

His father spread one arm towards an upright chair sandwiched between two long sofas and Ella obediently sat down and clasped her hands on her lap. She could have done with some water, because the glass would have given her something to fiddle with, but obviously whatever they wanted to say was more important than the ritual of offering drinks.

'We do not,' his mother said coldly, perching on the sofa to the left, while her husband mirrored her position on the opposite sofa, 'Have to tell you how shocked we both were when our son informed us that he was to be a father.'

'Naturally this was the last thing either of us expected.'

Sideswiped by what felt like a full-frontal attack without the courtesy of a preamble, Ella felt her body stiffen with tension. 'It was the last thing *I* expected, Señor and Señora Mancini. Believe it or not, my plans at this stage in my life didn't involve getting pregnant. But it's happened, and Rocco and I are both finding a way of dealing with it.'

'Our experience of women like you,' his mother said, 'Has been unfortunate, and you will excuse us if we are blunt on this matter.'

'Women like me?' Ella's head swivelled from left to right as she was besieged on both sides by the couple.

'Of course it is to be expected that our son would be targeted for his money. That has always been our fear.'

'I didn't *target* your son for his money! I didn't even know who Rocco was when I met him!' She looked at the door in desperation.

They were worried, she told herself, and that was to be expected. Yes, they came from stupid wealth; and yes, they would be on guard for people wanting to get a foot through the door so that they could get some of that money for themselves. They were naturally scared that she might be a gold-digger. It made perfect sense, really, when she thought about it. They didn't know just how much she loved their son, and they didn't know that he loved her as well, whether he could admit it or not. They were primed to be suspicious. Rocco had told her about his uncle. How else could they be expected to react to her except with suspicion and fear?

She took a few deep breaths to calm the rising tide of her anger. 'You don't have to fear that I'm after your son for his money,' she said coolly. She looked around at the lavish, funereal surroundings. 'I'm much more at home in simpler surroundings. I wouldn't dream of wanting any of this.'

'But this is where my son belongs,' his mother said with a stiff smile. 'You will be entering a great family house. You may say you are not interested in everything that comes with the Mancini name, but you will still have to do your duty as my son's wife, as you will likewise have to raise his heir to be the man who carries on the family name. I trust that all pre-nuptial agreements are signed and in order?'

'I think it's best if we move on from this, Señor and Señora Mancini. I can't say any more than I already have. You'll just have to trust that I'm not out to fleece your son and I haven't contrived to get pregnant so that I could pin him down.'

'In which case, arrangements for the wedding will have to be discussed.'

Rocco's father finally stood to offer her something to drink and rang a bell to summon one of their staff when she opted for a glass of water.

'I realise you've only just found out… You probably haven't had time to think of anything…er…' Ella stumbled over her words while wondering whether Rocco intended to show up any time soon. Having said she could rely on him to be a protective wall between his parents and her, he had instead thrown her to the wolves and left her to fend for herself.

'I have already, naturally, been in touch with various people and given basic instructions on the sort of ceremony we have in mind.'

'You have?'

'This will be an illustrious event. Naturally, the sooner plans are put in motion, the better. What we cannot change, we must unfortunately accept. Rocco told us a week or so ago that he would be marrying. It does not afford us much time with a baby on the way so I have already begun to put things in place. At the very least, I have made a list of attendees. I would calculate that in the region of *quinientos invitados*…five hundred guests…'

'You've made a list…?'

The ground seemed to be opening up under her feet as she did the maths. His mother had known that they would be getting married a week ago? That was when Rocco had shown up out of the blue, when she had first broken the news to him. Yet he'd given her the impression that he had only just told his parents, as they were packing their bags to leave for Spain. Which meant…

Solid ground began to turn to quicksand and she licked her lips while her mind went blank, fighting against the very obvious conclusion that she had been deceived by Rocco yet again. She'd thought that he'd taken his time to win her over, to prove to her that he could be the man she wanted, even if he wasn't in love with her. That, whatever the outcome, he would respect her decision.

But he hadn't, had he? He'd gone right ahead and assumed that she would marry him, and had been so confident that he would get exactly what he wanted that he'd briefed his parents from the start. Had all that thoughtful, caring stuff just been an act to get her where he wanted her?

She felt sick at the thought of it, at the thought that she'd let stupid feelings, disingenuous love, hope and optimism get in the way of the common sense that had guided her at the very start.

There was no way on earth she would marry him now. She spun away and muttered that she was suddenly feeling queasy. Maybe the trip over…stress…perhaps she hadn't eaten enough…a ragtag jumble of nonsense… She left eyes down, not wanting to see those cold, disapproving faces for a second longer.

Tears blurred her eyes and every muscle in her body was rigid with tension as she moved stiffly towards the door, that was pulled open before she could get to it. And there he was, taking a few seconds to register that something was wrong, then glancing behind her to his parents before returning his dark gaze to her stricken face.

'What the hell is going on here?'

CHAPTER TEN

'I ASKED WHAT'S going on.'

The atmosphere was electric with tension. Instinct told Rocco that Ella was desperate to leave the room but he stayed her with one hand because he wanted to find out what the hell had just happened. No one was going to run away until he found out, and that included his parents, who had risen to their feet and were looking at him with thin lipped defiance.

His parents were punctual to the point of pathological. His father had dispatched him to check over something with one of the subsidiary companies, but he had made sure to head straight to the sitting room so that she didn't end up facing his parents without his reassuring presence.

He ushered Ella back into the room and dismissed the man who had appeared with a jug of water and a glass.

'What have you said to Ella?' He addressed his mother but included his father in his grim, unsmiling, narrow-eyed stare.

'We simply made it clear, Rocco, that we are not people to be taken in by anyone entering this family who might wish us harm.'

'You accused *my wife to be* of what, exactly? Of being a *gold-digger*?'

'We have enough experience of those sorts to be on guard.'

'Those sorts?' Rocco left that derogatory judgement simmering in the air between them for a few seconds.

'Is this all that was said?' He turned to Ella and felt something pierce deep inside him at the hurt and dismay on her pretty face. A surge of possessiveness, a driving urge to protect her, washed through him and he dimly recognised that it had nothing to do with the fact that she was carrying his child. He didn't need her to answer because he could take a pretty good shot at guessing just what had happened.

'You sent me off on a wild goose chase about something and nothing so that you could corner my fiancée and cause her distress?' he asked coldly.

His parents had the grace to flush and exchanged a quick look.

'We thought, Rocco, that…'

'I don't want to hear any of your excuses. You've upset Ella and, in my books, that is unforgivable. Let me make one thing absolutely straight.' He took a step towards his parents and outstared them. 'If you want anything to do with our child, then you will never say anything to Ella again that might upset her. Do I make myself clear?'

'There are duties that must be fulfilled. This is how you were raised, Rocco.'

'And rest assured what has to be done will always be done. In my way and on my terms. Now, I'm going to head upstairs with Ella and, when we return for dinner, no more will be said on this matter. I expect my fiancée to be treated as a welcome member of the Mancini family.'

Fine words, Ella thought. Yes, they'd warmed to her. It was nice that he'd stuck up for her, because she had been lost and out of her depth in the face of his icily disapproving parents. But no amount of warm sentiments could erase the bitterness of knowing that, in his mind, marrying her had been a fait accompli the second he'd known about the pregnancy.

Ella waited until they were in the bedroom before she turned to him, schooling her expression. How could he stand there, so beautiful, so sophisticated, so unfairly sexy, so ready to say what he knew she'd want to hear and knowing just how to deliver the words to the best possible effect?

'Thank you for having my back in there, Rocco.'

'I apologise for my parents. I'm afraid, this is who they are. I had, however, expected better from them. At the very least, a show of polite good will. It seems they dispatched me so that they could see you on your own and…well…again, I apologise on their behalf.'

'I understand their concerns. Maybe they thought you'd inherited your uncle's predisposition for ending up with someone out for his money.'

'You're upset. I get that. Do you want to skip the dinner they've had prepared? It might be better to face them, and I can assure you there won't be a repeat of what happened down there. You have my word.'

'Your word. Now, *that's* interesting, isn't it, Rocco?' Her words were cool and precise but her body still yearned for him in a way that made her feel angry, distraught and hopeless.

'What are you talking about?'

'You lied to me, didn't you?'

'I lied to you?' He stilled as wariness replaced the warm reassurances of moments ago.

'You made your mind up that we were going to get

married from the very second I told you I was pregnant.' The heat coming from him was too much. He was too close to her. She couldn't think straight when she could breathe him in the way she could now. She watched in alarmed fascination as he strolled towards the window. He looked out for a couple of seconds then turned to look at her. She absolutely loathed the shudder of sexual awareness that rippled through her, alive and alert, despite the emotions raging through her.

'Ella, please...' He nodded to the velvet sofa by the window. 'Sit down and let's talk about this. You're pregnant. Getting stressed the way you are now isn't good for your blood pressure. You've already been stressed out enough by my parents.'

Ella stared at him expressionlessly for a few seconds and then heeded his advice, because her legs were wobbly, and she knew that he was right insofar as stress on her body wasn't a good idea.

'You were never going to take *no* for an answer, were you?' she said quietly. 'When I told you that I was pregnant, when you proposed marriage, I wasn't in favour of it. It was never where I saw my life going. It was never what I wanted. I wanted to be loved, to love someone, to know that there would be a strong bond between me and the father of my child—a bond glued together with all the love that came when two people *wanted* to spend their lives together. Not when two people felt they had no choice *but* to spend their lives together.

'You didn't love me, Rocco, and you were never going to love me. Not in the way you knew I wanted. But you didn't want an illegitimate child.' She looked around at the grand bedroom, the decades and decades of family wealth wrapped up in suffocating, restrictive traditionalism.

He was conditioned for this extraordinarily high level of obligation and duty. Maybe there had been that window of letting his hair down when they had first met, but he'd always known that that window was going to close. She understood him, and yet could never forgive what she now saw as a calculating attempt to win her over by pretending to be someone he wasn't.

'I can't deny that the thought of sharing custody of my own flesh and blood was abhorrent to me, Ella,' he admitted.

'Was it all a game for you?'

'What do you mean?'

'The way you set about proving to me that you could be the perfect father and the perfect husband. The way you strung me along, wearing me down a little at a time, having already spoken to your parents as though everything was a done deal.'

'You think I was acting out some part?'

'Haven't you done that before?' she asked tersely 'You were a certain *Jose Rivero* when we met, or have you forgotten that?'

'I thought we'd put that one to rest. Ella, I'll admit that I wasn't going to give up on the notion of marrying you so that our child could get the very best life had to offer. And I don't mean all of this—' he waved a hand at their surroundings '—although *all of this* is substantial. I mean I was, and remain, convinced that becoming husband and wife is the right thing to do and always will be. Whether I informed my parents that this would be the case earlier than you thought doesn't change that fact.'

'It does for me.'

'What are you trying to say?'

'I want out. I can't go through with this.'

'What...?'

Ella steeled herself against the urgency in his voice which struck to the very core of her. Should she tell him honestly how she felt? Yes, she would do that and take the consequences. There had already been far too much deceit, concealment and dishonesty.

'It took a lot for me to trust you, Rocco. I was devastated when I discovered that you had lied to me about who you really were and I was even more shocked when you turned up out of the blue and admitted that you were the guy who was going to buy the department store.'

'I know that. You've already told me that.'

She swept past his interruption, 'I understood the reasoning behind the takeover, of course I did, but you still lied to me and it still left a sour taste in my mouth.'

'I had no choice. I thought we'd gone over all this.'

'Well, here we are, going over it again. After you showed back up, after you took the pregnancy so well, after you set out to prove to me that you were marriageable material even if marrying for the sake of a child had never been my life's ambition... Well, Rocco, I really began to believe you. More than that.'

'Yes?'

'I began to hope that what you felt might be more than just a sense of duty and obligation.' Hope, optimism and time would give her the outcome she'd wanted... How naïve she'd been.

'Love, Ella—it's not in my repertoire. I never led you to believe that it was. Did I?'

'No. No, I can see now that it was just me reading all sorts of stuff into some of the things you said and the confidences you shared with me.'

'Of course we shared things, Ella,' he said roughly,

raking his fingers through his hair. 'It would have been unnatural, given the circumstances, if we hadn't.'

Ella could sense his discomfort. How tempting it would be to pull herself away from the brink. She knew that if she mumbled something, *anything*, about hormones, exhaustion or not being quite herself, if she laughed this earnest conversation off, he would happily sweep it all under the carpet and continue as though nothing had changed. He would be able to do that because on an emotional level he wasn't involved.

'Rocco, I didn't want to, but I fell in love with you. And I hoped that, in time, you would see that you'd fallen in love with me as well. But that's not going to happen. I thought you had emotions that were just never there. You knew you were going to marry me, you knew that was what you wanted, and nothing was going to get in the way of that. You did what it took but I can't marry a guy like you. I can't marry you and have my heart broken over and over again, every single day, because I would never stop wanting more than you could ever give me.'

She took a deep breath. 'Could you do that, Rocco? Give me what I want?'

Rocco felt the world come to a grinding halt.

In his fiercely controlled life, there was no room for the heady romanticism of love, and he had always projected the sort of demeanour that repelled women from going there. When the time came, he would take a wife, and it would be a sensible arrangement.

Hadn't he made it clear from day one that love with all its complications wasn't for him? She could hardly say that he had encouraged her to think that he would suddenly, against everything in his nature, fall in love with her. Hand over all his self-control into the safekeeping of someone else.

Because that was what love entailed, wasn't it? Yes, the pregnancy had generated a marriage proposal, and it was a proposal that made perfect sense. She, herself, had come round to that conclusion so why was she now braking to a halt because of the small issue of timing? The enormity of her decision rammed into him with brutal force.

'You want me to promise you something you know I can't do?' He thought of her walking away from him with wrenching pain. This was about the child they shared. He felt dizzy and panicked. All of this, simply because he had happened to tell his parents about the pregnancy and had naturally assured them that they would marry. He hadn't thought twice. He'd been confident because that was just the way he was.

And now… It was all slipping away but the thought of promising love, of her asking that of him…

'I thought you'd say that. It's going to be very difficult for me to remain here with this happening, Rocco.'

'I can't believe this.'

'I wanted to be completely honest with you, Rocco. I love you and you…you broke my heart, not once but twice. But I'll get over it because I know I deserve more than a man who breaks hearts. Nothing will change when it comes to the baby.'

Rocco looked at her. Was it his imagination or could he already see the shutters coming down? Her soul was turning to ice, sealing him off, because that was what happened when love was turned on its head.

He gazed down when she reached across to cover his hand with hers.

'We can still sign the documents and I will never, ever

get in the way of you having access to your own flesh and blood. And, yes, I can see that this legacy belongs to your offspring.'

'Yes.'

'I realise that one day you'll meet someone, and I will as well, because we both deserve that. I'll meet someone who loves me, who would never lie to me, who appreciates me for who I am, for all the right reasons. And you'll meet someone…who makes sense, I guess. And, when that happens, it'll be a bridge we'll just have to cross. In the meantime… I don't want to stay here a minute longer. You're a billionaire, Rocco. You can do anything with the click of a finger. Could you maybe take me away from here by clicking your fingers? I just want this whole thing to be over now.'

Ella gazed out at a landscape of softly falling snow. She was back at home. She had been for nearly a week, ever since she had fled Rocco's palatial mansion and ran away from the love she'd set her heart on which would never materialise.

She'd told him that she couldn't stay a minute longer and he'd arranged everything with the ease of a man who could dial two numbers and get whatever he wanted. He'd begged her to stay the night—it was late and she would be mentally and physically exhausted. He would ensure she left first thing in the morning, unnoticed and without the trauma of having to socialise with his parents. He would explain the situation to them. They would accept it because they would have no choice. Just as she had left him with none.

Every single decent word that had passed his beautiful mouth had reminded her of all the foolish reasons she had seen more in their relationship than really existed. He didn't love her. He was just a fair-minded, honourable guy who would never give his heart to her, or maybe never *could*. What he had seen as a foregone conclusion—about which he had made assumptions about a future in which the concept of her not marrying him had never crossed his radar—she had seen as betrayal. And those were fundamental differences between them that could never be breached.

The reach of his privilege, of growing up with such immense wealth, had made him imperious, and it didn't matter whether he was honourable or not. He would always presume that his way was the best. He would, and never could, be the vulnerable man who would be able to meet her halfway.

Maybe he could only really fall in love with someone from his own class. She'd met his parents and it was easy to understand that he'd been raised to accept a certain type of woman as the ideal match. Nothing else was ever really going to do. He said he didn't believe in love but he probably just hadn't met the right woman who ticked all the boxes. When it came to anything emotional, Rocco would always view the world in black and white. But life wasn't black and white; the time would come when he would find that out but not with her.

Having a baby ticked an important box for him but he would come to thank her for walking away because, just as for her, all those other boxes also needed to be ticked beyond the one that came under the heading of 'duty'.

A driver had whisked her away from his family palace before half-past eight the following morning, and she had avoided seeing his parents, so had been spared any follow-up accusations.

And since then…

Her poor dad, silent, awkward and bursting with love and sympathy, had had to deal with her long face and bouts of tears. He handed her tissues and patted her on the back, trying hard to find the right words to comfort her, but there was part of her that was inconsolable.

Now, he was in the kitchen cooking dinner for them. She gazed around her at the wonderful, warm Christmas scene that had been filled with such hope and joy when, little more than two weeks ago, she and Rocco together had put up the Christmas tree and hung all the decorations.

Since she'd returned, she'd done her best to banish negative thoughts by going all out on the decorations, reminding herself that there was a lot to be grateful for, not least the little baby growing and kicking, having fun inside her. Above the stone fireplace, with its roaring fire keeping the winter cold at bay, evergreen garlands were threaded with red berries and pinecones, which she herself had fetched from the garden. She had hung the stocking she'd had since she'd been a kid and a new one for the baby inside her, which she would fill with little soft play treats.

Outside the snow was falling, as it had done for the past three days, lightly but persistently, blanketing the countryside and turning everything magical. She had put Christmas carols on the CD player her dad insisted on keeping, even though she'd tried to introduce him to some more advanced technology for listening to music. He'd had none of it. The background music was soothing and, staring out through the windows, stretched out on the large, comfy sofa with a soft throw over her, she almost felt at peace.

The sharp bang on the front door made her jolt upright.

'Dad?' she called out. 'Are you expecting anyone?'

Her dad bustled out of the kitchen, apron still round his waist, and looked between her and the door. 'Not in this weather, and not on Christmas Eve, love. Don't budge. I'll get the door.'

'Don't be silly.' Ella smiled at him and stifled a yawn. It wasn't yet seven in the evening, but she could have slept for England. 'It's much more important for you to make sure the cooking gets done and all the prep for tomorrow. This pregnant lady needs to be spoiled, and I'm just quoting you on that. I'll get it.'

She slipped off the sofa, pleased to see her dad grin, a happy sort of 'my girl's back' grin. She pulled open the door, because in this part of the world that was what people did, and there he was—the guy whose image had haunted her every waking moment and most of the sleeping ones.

Ella was so shocked that for a few seconds she couldn't breathe. Yes, he'd contacted her, made sure she was okay. Just the dark timbre of his voice down the end of the phone had made her grit her teeth in frustration because he'd sounded so *normal*, while she was breaking up inside. He'd steered clear of conversation that might release any more emotional outpourings. One lot had clearly been quite enough, thank you very much. So she'd been left nursing her broken heart, not quite knowing what to do with it.

He'd set up an account for her and had transferred so much money that she'd protested.

'A house,' he'd said without bothering to allow her a protest vote. 'A car, living expenses... Accept it, Ella. There will be a lot more where that came from.'

He'd transferred her enough money to buy whatever house she wanted and the sort of ridiculously high-end car he was accustomed to owning. What had been the point of being coy?

She hadn't asked him how his parents had taken the marriage being called off. She'd taken her cue from him and not mentioned anything at all that wasn't purely practical. It had been agony. He'd been so...*nice*. The nicer he'd been, the more she'd wanted him to show *something*. Anything.

Now, he stood in front of her in all his glory, and she couldn't manage to get a word out. The snow was settling on his dark, woollen coat and patent leather shoes. He had his hands shoved in his pockets as he stared at her. She felt a whoosh of pure love because she could recall every line and groove in his beautiful face.

'What are you doing here?'

'I've come to see you.'

This was right, coming here, stifling doubts that had been bred over a lifetime, doubts about trusting instinct and emotion and not being scared of them. Rocco sucked in a deep breath and stared at her. Even after she'd gone, he still hadn't quite believed it. He would have blamed his parents, but that would have been the easy way out, because he knew his parents for what they were. They were manacled to a belief system that he had always taken for granted, a belief system that might have worked for them but didn't work for him.

Had he ever thought for himself when it came to love and giving himself to someone else without restraint and with trust? No. Never. In every other area of his life, he had been high performing, brutally ambitious and fiercely proactive. But with his emotional life he had been lazy, and only when she'd walked away from him had he faced the truth about himself.

He'd met her and she had kick-started a process of self-discovery that had changed him. Maybe he'd just learned how to access what had always been there. She'd given him the chance to take off the clothes he had worn all his life, an outer shell wrapped up in duty, formality and the acceptance that throwing caution to the wind and loving someone utterly and completely wasn't for him.

He'd assumed that the lesson had been a two-week anomaly, but then she'd left him, and slowly he'd realised just how much he'd changed and just how much he'd found the way to love.

He needed to tell her all that but the green eyes inspecting him were narrowed and suspicious. As soon as he was in, and before he could divest himself of his coat, she stood back to the wall, her hands pressed together in front of her.

Ella knew that, however devastated she was by his rejection of her, she still had to communicate with him and accept the situation without bitterness or regret. She'd chosen to speak her mind and it wouldn't be fair to make him pay the price for not being on the same page as her.

Her father appeared in the doorway and Rocco turned round.

'Mind if I have a few words with your daughter, sir?'

'Nothing you couldn't say to her by post, young man?'

'No one uses the post any more, Dad.'

Ella couldn't manage to raise a smile when her father made a snort of disapproval under his breath but then he vanished back into the kitchen.

'If you need me to sign more stuff, then you could have let me know by email.'

'Can we sit down to have this conversation? Please?'

Rocco hesitated, for once not daring to presume that he wouldn't be thrown out by her.

'Why? What have you got to say? If it's not about practicalities, then it's because you want to try and convince me to marry you and to forget everything that went before.'

'I wouldn't do that, and that's not why I came.'

'You'd better come through and say your piece, Rocco. And I can tell you that the only reason I'm being hospitable is because we're going to be in one another's lives and we have to be able to communicate.'

'Understood.' He followed her into the sitting room and then looked around him at the familiar sight that had struck such a chord in him. 'Being here feels more like home than my own home did.'

'It's not going to work, Rocco. You can't just waltz in here and start playing more games to try and win me over.'

'The only thing I'm here to do is to ask you to listen to me. No game playing, Ella, not that I ever thought I played games with you.'

'What would you call "stringing me along"? Making me believe that you were Mr Perfect, when in fact you were just Mr Doing All He Can To Get Exactly What He Wants?'

'Will you listen to me? I won't be long but there are things I finally realise I need to say to you. Things I never thought about until I found I couldn't stop thinking about them.'

Ella stared at him narrowly. Her heart was still beating fast and her pulse was racing. She wanted him out of the house, and yet she couldn't bear the thought of him leaving now that he was here, because his presence fed her love and that feeling was consuming.

Plus she wanted to hear what he had to say. He looked tired and hesitant, two things she'd never associated with him. If this was going to be another ploy to get her back to the place she'd walked away from, then who wouldn't be curious to find out what his tactics were going to be?

But no tea or coffee. No getting comfy. No feet under the table. She didn't care how long it would have taken him to get here in poor weather.

'You have fifteen minutes,' she said flatly.

It was lovely and warm from the fire crackling in the stone hearth and the only light came from two table lamps and the standing lamp by the door. The air was scented by the Christmas tree, a fragrant pine smell that was all about the festive season. It made her think of when he'd last been here, when they'd decorated the tree together, when all her hopes had begun to bloom.

'When we met, Ella...that first time when you thought I was someone else... How do I explain this?' He leant forward, elbows resting on his thighs and his fingers clasped loosely together. 'I've spent the past week sifting through everything in my head, trying to work out how it was that I never realised...'

'Never realised *what*?' As her curiosity grew with dangerous speed, so did the sharpness of her voice, because she was determined to deny any more entries by him into her heart.

'That the man you made me feel like that first time—a man who was free and unweighted, and for the first time happy, really happy, in an unencumbered type of way—wasn't a flash in the pan because I was pretending to be someone else. That man was who I was always supposed to be. You unlocked the potential for joy inside me and left me wanting more.'

'Don't start spinning stories, Rocco. Is this just another twist on a ploy to get what you want? Does marriage and tradition mean that much to you?'

'That's what I'm saying now, Ella, my darling. Marriage and tradition count for nothing in the grand scheme of things.'

Darling... Ella shivered and clenched her fists in an effort to ward off the softening inside her at that term of endearment, spoken with such depth of feeling.

'I've lived my entire life so grounded in thinking that I knew exactly what I wanted from life that, when the unexpected came along in the form of you, I still carried on thinking that I could extinguish all the weird and wonderful things happening inside me. That I could explain it all away until...until I find that I can't.'

He looked around him. 'This is what I want and all I want—the peace and simplicity of what love brings because it doesn't have to be chaotic and ruinous. It doesn't have to be the emotional freefall of my uncle, or the acrimony of the divorced people I've met, or the stiff formality of my parents. Everyone's different and I want us to be the ones who succeed. I want us to be like your parents. I want to take the chance.'

'Rocco...'

'I know you don't want to believe a word I'm saying, because you think I've deceived you in the past, but Ella... I'm asking you to marry me for all the right reasons. I'm asking you to marry me because I've fallen in love with you and because I can't see a life without you in it by my side. I want you and need you but... I get it.'

Their eyes tangled, and in that moment Ella knew

that every word he spoke came from the heart. She had a euphoric surge of sheer joy as dreams she thought had been shattered now settled into place. Dreams she knew were going to come true.

'I love you, my darling, but know this—if you don't want to marry me, if it's too little, too late, then there will never be another woman for me. I will remain yours for ever.'

He reached into his pocket and, just like that, without ceremony—although she noted that his hand was shaking ever so slightly—he opened the small, black velvet box. Nestled inside was the most beautiful engagement ring she could have imagined. No adolescent daydream could ever have conjured up something so perfect—the round, flawless diamond took centre stage on the sleek, simple band of platinum.

'I'm offering this to you with love in my heart, Ella. Please, my darling, tell me that you'll be mine for ever.'

'Oh Rocco,' Ella breathed, finally allowing herself to feel all the love she had been so desperately trying to stifle. 'I want to marry you with all my heart…and for all the reasons you want to marry me.'

She watched him slip the ring on her finger and felt tears prick the back of her eyes. She looked at him, then glanced through the window at the steadily falling snow, then around the room where so many memories had been made of wonderful Christmases celebrated with family.

The door was opening to more Christmases spent with love and contentment as a family and, wherever they were, Ella knew that they would always be exactly the sort of Christmases she'd always dreamed of.

EPILOGUE

Ella had one last look at the Christmas tree in front of her, the tree she and Rocco had chosen and put up the week before. She closed her eyes and smiled, reliving the memory of them decorating it while baby Louisa Isabella had watched with lively interest from the baby bouncer, her pudgy legs kicking merrily away, mesmerised by the lights on the tree.

How could life possibly get more perfect? She was married to the man she adored, a guy who never tired of showing her just how much he adored her right back. They had married before their daughter was born, without fuss on a fine spring day. First in the church in the village where she had grown up, and then a blessing in a rather more formal ceremony in Madrid, a ceremony worthy of a Mancini. Like adversaries learning to circle one another, she and Rocco's parents had begun the journey towards communication without resentment.

The house they had chosen to live in was close enough to London for Rocco to comfortably commute but sufficiently far out for a garden big enough for fruit trees, a vegetable corner and enough space for all the equipment Rocco was looking forward to buying.

She heard her name being called and she hurried off to the kitchen where the smells of Christmas lunch made her stomach churn. She knew what she would find and she was already smiling at the thought of it.

And sure enough, as she entered the kitchen, there they all were—her beloved family. Rocco and her dad were busily cooking together, which was a terrific achievement, because his original plan had been to have the entire meal catered by a top chef and delivered in style to the house. He laughed when she'd shot that idea down in flames and had told her he hadn't thought for a minute that she'd agree.

Baby Louisa was sleeping peacefully through the chaos, her baby bouncer on the kitchen table. Ella thought she was probably worn out at having to witness her dad and granddad getting in each other's way in the kitchen although, it had to be said, the outcome looked excellent.

She and Rocco had invited his parents, but they had declined, although without rancour. Ella had thought she'd seen the older woman actually stifle a smile of resignation at the formal luncheon they would be obliged to host, as they had done for decades.

In three days, they would fly to Madrid and celebrate on a much smaller scale. The wedding had thawed them but it was the arrival of their granddaughter that had really done the trick and now, a year later… Yes, there was definite light at the end of the tunnel.

Throw another baby into the mix and who knew? BFFs was her hopeful thought, not least because she could see how much Rocco's relationship with them was changing as they came to accept how much their son loved her.

Another baby…

Ella smiled and thought of the night that lay ahead and decided, *tonight looks like a good night to conceive…*

* * * * *

BOSS'S CHRISTMAS BABY ACQUISITION

DANI COLLINS

MILLS & BOON

A big thank-you to Allie, a lovely fan who suggested I revisit the Sauveterre siblings. I hope you enjoy this little catch-up with all of them.

CHAPTER ONE

SIOBHAN UPTON HIT the call button for the elevator then tapped to check her phone.

Ugh. Her sister was asking about Christmas. Again.

Siobhan was the youngest of four girls. Both her middle sisters had invited her to stay in America for Thanksgiving, a holiday they'd both adopted since moving here from London. Their mother was flying to Miami to stay with them and swore she wasn't leaving until winter was over back home.

Meanwhile, Siobhan's eldest sister, Cinnia, was pressuring her to spend Christmas with her and her family in Spain. Cinnia was hosting all her in-laws for the first time in years. Siobhan knew them well and genuinely loved them, especially the children, but she hadn't been able to enjoy Christmas since her bat guano of an ex-boyfriend had ruined that time of year for her five years ago.

She was dodging all of it by claiming to be focused on finding a job and a place to live. Which was true. She had these interviews in San Francisco then needed to get back to Sydney to pack up her flat, not sure where she would end up—

Wait.

She gasped with excitement as she saw the email from the placement agency.

Pleased to inform you... Employment contract will be forwarded... Expect you in Madrid on Monday December first...

"Yes!" That was only ten days away, but Siobhan punched the air and nearly leaped out of her borrowed Jimmy Choo heels.

"Are you going up?" The deep male voice held a hint of a Spanish accent.

She glanced up to see a man inside the elevator, holding the door for her.

Her heart took a swerve. Wow. He was really hot.

"Yes." She swallowed. "Thanks."

She stepped in beside him, blood fizzing for another reason. She tried not to stare, but he was kind of dazzling. He was thirty-ish and had an aura of dark sexiness with his thick black hair swept back from his forehead, and irises that were such a dark brown they seemed black. His cheeks were long and clean-shaven, his jaw well-defined. His nose was blade-sharp and his upper lip distinctly peaked.

As a uni student, Siobhan had fallen into wearing off-the-rack hoodies and other casual wear that helped her blend in, but she'd been around enough haute couture to recognize that navy suit was bespoke. It sat perfectly against his upper body, accentuating his broad shoulders and extremely fit physique.

Was he an actor? This was San Francisco, not LA, but he could be here on movie business. He certainly looked as though he financed blockbuster productions. Or starred in steamy thrillers as a morally gray character.

One thick black brow quirked, polite but patronizing. "Floor?"

"Oh, um…" Good grief, she was behaving like an idiot. As she tried to open the app, she watched him use his phone on the reader, then touch P. "That works for me. Thanks. I got the job I wanted." She wiggled her own phone as the doors closed. "I'm not usually such a scatterbrain."

"Congratulations."

"On not being a scatterbrain? Thanks."

The corner of his mouth twitched. "Australian?" he guessed.

"English. But I've been in Sydney long enough to adopt their accent." The better to blend in and not have her past follow her.

He was looking at her as though trying to make up his mind about something.

She warmed under his study, wondering when she'd last felt this level of instant attraction. Had she ever?

The doors opened to the foyer of the elite level. In front of her was a frosted door labeled Concierge. A fountain trickled a soothing rhythm next to a courtesy bench.

"Have a nice evening." Siobhan flashed a smile. She felt awkward as she turned away, as though she'd forgotten how to walk.

"Are you going to celebrate?" he asked behind her.

"I should, shouldn't I?" She experienced a rush of relief and pivoted to face him, then tilted her head as she considered it. "I have another interview tomorrow, but now that I've got the job I want, that's just for practice. Maybe I'll order champagne. My sister's paying for the room. Why not?" she added with a cheeky grin.

"No one to celebrate with? I'll buy you a drink." He nodded toward the private lounge reserved for guests on this floor.

Her inner defenses reflexively ran through her mental house, bolting and locking all the doors and windows. It was a PTSD response, not because she feared men. She was more than capable of taking care of herself on a physical level, but she didn't want to be used and betrayed again.

Even if he knew who she was, he didn't look like someone who needed her connections, though. *Did* he know who she was?

"You're not single?" He misinterpreted her hesitation. The hint of warmth in his expression turned to cool dismissal. "Perhaps another time."

"No, I am. I just..." *Never hook up.*

Not that she was thinking about *that*. She barely dated or even went out with friends. Her mates at school had been her age, but infinitely less mature and jaded. They had partied as often as they studied while Siobhan had focused on keeping a low profile and finally completing her degree. Her social life was mostly confined to family and conducted out of the public eye. Her trust in strangers was very low.

This particular stranger was exceedingly compelling, however. And she didn't want to drink her champagne in a hotel room while talking to her mother over the tablet. She wanted a few more minutes with him.

"I was just surprised," she said with a smile that felt unsteady.

"That a man offered to buy you a drink?" His black brows lifted in skepticism.

"No." A man at LaGuardia had offered to buy her a drink and there'd been a whole convention of men at the hotel in Miami trying to hit on her. "That I want to accept."

"Ah." His eyes narrowed slightly. She suspected that was as close as he got to a smile.

He was ringless, but she cocked her head to ask, "Are *you* single?"

"*Sí.* Joaquin." He offered his hand.

"Siobhan." She shook his hand and felt the tingle all the way up her arm.

Breathless, she walked into the empty lounge and excused herself to the powder room where she washed her hands and touched up her makeup, smoothing her brunette hair back into its chignon.

When she returned, Joaquin was at a table by the windows. He rose to help her with her chair. "The wind might break up the clouds and give us a sunset."

"It's a nice view either way." It was overcast and spitting rain, but the Golden Gate Bridge stood reddish-orange against the mist.

"Have you been here before?" he asked.

"No. And I leave after my interview in the morning so I won't have time to explore." She was looking for a menu, but the server arrived with an ice bucket and showed Joaquin a bottle of Cristal. He nodded for it to be opened.

"You're spoiling me," Siobhan said. "I would have ordered a split of the California bubbly."

"My family has vineyards. I'm a snob."

"Is that what brings you here? Are they here?"

"No, I had meetings. I'm in tech, heading to Asia tomorrow."

She suspected that was a deliberate detail to let her know this was a very casual encounter, barely a date, not the beginning of anything serious.

"Where do you live?" she asked curiously.

"These days? On my plane," he said ironically.

The cork popped. Joaquin smelled and tasted, then nodded his approval.

The server poured into a crystal flute rimmed in gold and offered it to her.

The pale amber sparkled with fine bubbles. Siobhan lifted it and closed her eyes as she inhaled the aroma of sea air and lime zest.

When the server walked away away, Joaquin said, *"Salud,"* and offered his glass.

"Cheers. And thank you." She touched her glass to his, then sipped. The delicate effervescence coated her tongue with a silky mousse-like texture. Buttery flavors of crushed nuts and yeasty sourdough melted in her mouth, followed by saline and citrus and a lengthy floral finish.

"You're also a snob," he accused lightly.

She opened her eyes to realize he'd watched her savor her first taste. Her heart hiccupped and her gaze got all tangled up in his intense stare. She licked her lips and his attention dropped to her mouth, making her pulse swerve again.

"I'm lucky enough to have been around the finer things in life." She lifted the glass. "I make the most of it when I can."

His brows went up in a prompt for more information.

"I'm not an escort," she blurted, suddenly fearing that was why he'd offered to buy her this drink.

"I didn't think you were." He was definitely laughing at her behind that impassive expression. "Tell me about your new job."

"I would, but then I'd have to kill you."

His dark gaze flickered to her shoulders and the slender wrist holding the delicate glass. "You could try."

"Don't be fooled. I've taken self-defense. I'm actually very dangerous."

"That, I believe." His expression was relaxed and she had his full attention. It was heady. A glow of enjoyment spread through her chest.

"I'm trying to sound more exciting than I am," she admitted. "The truth is I recently finished my BBA. I want to go into contract law, so I'm gaining experience in that field."

"How old does that make you?" His brows lowered into a frown.

"Relax. I'm twenty-four. Old enough to drink." And do other things. She bit back a smirk.

He made a noise of contemplation, and his gaze traveled over her short jacket and the dark hair gathered into the roll at her nape. "I couldn't tell. You look young, but you seem very self-possessed."

"Mature for my age?" she asked drily. "I've been told that all my life. Forty at fourteen."

"Are you still speaking to the people who said that?"

"Ha. Yes. Because they weren't wrong." She shrugged. "I was in such a hurry to grow up, I finished my A levels at sixteen by home study. Regular school was too slow and boring." And she had been helping Cinnia with her twins.

"Then what? You moved to Australia? Took a gap year?" His brows came together in calculation. "Or three?"

"I actually had most of a language degree completed by nineteen, but my education was interrupted." Thanks to that absolute turd weasel, Gilbert. She washed away the bitterness on her tongue. "I started over when I moved to Australia. Transferring the credits wasn't an option, but I still managed to finish early. I would have preferred to be further ahead by now, but..." She had needed to lick her wounds. Be someone else. Someone who didn't make stupid mistakes.

"Is this new job articling?"

"No. That's what I should be doing, but I'm sick of school." She rolled the stem of her glass between her finger and thumb. "This is just a maternity cover as an EA, but it's a good opportunity and puts me back into the real world. Plus, I'll be closer to my sister and her children. They're growing fast—" She stopped herself from prattling. "This is the real reason I didn't want to tell you about it. It makes me sound very dull."

"It could all be a lie to disguise the fact you're really an assassin." The corner of his mouth dug in before he hid the faint smile behind his glass.

"True. Siobhan isn't even my real name." She waved a dismissive hand. "That's both a joke and the truth. Siobhan is my second name."

"What's your first name?"

She wrinkled her nose in reluctance. "I don't share it. Not because I don't like it. I was named for my great-grandmother and I don't mind keeping her alive in that small way."

Her name was Doreena. Siobhan had grown up as Dorry. Her family still called her that, but hearing it was something she both loved and hated. It made her feel connected to them, but it was an uncomfortable reminder of that silly girl who had screwed up so badly.

"I just prefer Siobhan." Siobhan had her act together. Siobhan didn't make dangerous mistakes.

"Here I thought you were going to admit to hiding from the law."

"I love that you think I'm that interesting. No, the bald truth is I'm related by marriage to some very rich people." She watched him, looking for signs he already knew, but only saw mild curiosity in his expression. "That's how I can tell Cristal from Dom." She tilted her glass. "I was stung by someone who used me to get close to them so I changed my name to distance myself."

That was a very watered-down version. It was also a warning that she wouldn't allow it to happen again.

Anyone else would have asked: *Who are they?*

Joaquin gave an impassive blink. "Why contract law?"

"Are you suffering insomnia and need something to put you to sleep? Why are we still talking about *me*?"

"I'm interested."

Was he? He was listening attentively, but his motives were impossible to read. He was most likely trying to get lucky. Perhaps he was lonely. Maybe *he* was an assassin trying to blend in by having a drink with a stranger.

She really wanted to take him at his word, though. She was feeling a deep pull of attraction and yearned for it to be mutual.

"It's another deeply unsexy answer," she warned. "When I was young, our family went through some hard times. One of my sisters got into estate law to pay the bills. Probate and such."

"Not the direction desperate women usually take," he noted with a twitch of his lips.

"Right?" Siobhan grinned, but the truth was Cinnia had also been the girlfriend of a very rich man and had taken flack for it, even though that wasn't how she'd kept their family afloat. "She always said there was good money in doing the tedious work no one else wants to do. I have a good memory and I read fast. I'm detail-oriented and I can be cutthroat when necessary. I love the idea of achieving something difficult by wielding fine print."

"This is the sister who paid for your room?"

"No. I have three. The one who booked the room is married to a pro athlete. She travels with her husband and collects tons of points so she didn't technically pay for it. This—" Siobhan indicated the designer jacket she wore over a snug cashmere sweater and pleated trousers "—I stole from another sister's closet. She works in fashion. I take what fits and hope she doesn't notice."

"Ah. You're not hiding from the law. You're hiding from *her*," he accused.

"Truth. She's vicious when crossed."

"Are they all in Australia?"

"No, we're sprinkled everywhere." This was getting too personal so she turned it around. "What about you? Siblings? Any crimes against them you'd like to confess?"

His expression lost all its ease. His gaze dropped to the glass he was pinching.

"I had a brother. He passed eighteen months ago."

"I'm so sorry."

"You didn't know." He took a hefty gulp of champagne. "We'd grown apart. Things were complicated." His expression shuttered and he looked out the window. "I feel strongly that I let him down so yes, in that way I committed a crime of negligence that I'm trying to make up for with his children."

Oh. She understood that need to self-flagellate far too well. She couldn't help reaching across to set her hand on his hard wrist, offering what little compassion she could.

"It's so easy to believe there will be ample time later,

isn't it? You don't have to talk about him if you don't want to, but you can. I understand *complicated* very well."

His gaze came up from where she touched his wrist. For a few seconds, she saw into his soul, where regret and glimmering coals of self-directed anger lived.

She felt the walls within her shift. They didn't fall open, but they angled as though adjusting to nest against his. It became a shared beveled wall. It was the sensation of sitting back-to-back with someone. Not aligned, exactly, but occupying the same space.

He is *lonely*.

His hand shifted to take hold of hers and the mood altered again. Excitement flared within her, shocking in its intensity. There was a reciprocal flash in his eyes, one that made her skin burn where his thumb stroked across the backs of her knuckles.

"Let's talk about something else," he said.

"Something simple?" she suggested shakily, not moving her hand but very, very aware of how her fingers twitched in his loose grip. "Quantum mechanics, perhaps? Or fate versus free will?"

His mouth pulled sideways. "I lean heavily toward free will. You wouldn't have got the job you wanted if you hadn't applied. You wouldn't be having a drink with me if I hadn't invited you. You sat down because you wanted to." His thumb skimmed across her skin again, short-circuiting her brain.

"But you wouldn't have asked if we hadn't wound up in the same elevator," she challenged shakily. "Perhaps that was kismet."

"Please," he scoffed in that sinfully sexy accent of his. "I took one look at the attractive woman beside me and made a deliberate decision to shirk the calls I ought to be making."

"Say more." She was trying to hide that she was barely able to breathe under the lazy way he scanned her features. "I'm the mousy one so I'm usually overlooked."

"Who are you comparing yourself to? Your sisters?" He shook his head in refutation, fingers shifting to twine with hers in a way that felt very intimate. Now his thumb stroked at the base of her thumb into her inner wrist. It was deeply distracting. Arousing.

"How...um... How would you know?" Her suspicions reared. "Have you met them?"

"No." There was no subterfuge in his expression as he continued making love to her hand with his innocuous touch, sending signals into her chest that made her breasts tingle. "But I can't imagine there's any way to improve on perfection."

A bubble of incredulous laughter escaped her. She flushed with pleasure, though. "Your efforts to seduce me are working."

"I prefer to think of it as an invitation. It's up to you whether you accept. Free will and all that." He shifted his glass aside so he could use his other hand to reach across and brush a loose tendril of hair behind her ear. His fingertip caressed her ear and the edge of her jaw. "Would you like to order something to eat? Before we get drunk on champagne?"

"And each other?" It was a corny thing to say, but in her case, it was becoming all too true. She was losing her appetite for food and was no longer thirsty for champagne. She was falling into lust for the first time in her life.

"Mmm," he agreed in a rumble. "You're certainly intoxicating." He brought her hand to his mouth and nuzzled his lips into her palm.

Every bone in her body melted.

This wasn't the adolescent inquisitiveness that had driven her to kiss boys who were nothing but bravado and hormones. It wasn't the romantic infatuation that had drawn her into the bed of a dishonest man. This was something exciting and enthralling. A pull that was filled with promise. With *need*.

She had agreed to have a drink in a seize-the-day impulse. It was another step toward coming out of her self-imposed exile. She had already been high on being chosen for her merit, not her connections. This was another octave of that. He knew nothing about her except what she'd told him. It felt good to be desired purely for herself.

It felt good to *feel*. For the first time in a long time, the numbness of betrayal was falling away. She felt feminine and desirable and brimming with her own sexual power. She felt like indulging herself.

"Why don't we take the champagne to your room?" Her voice thickened with a mixture of shyness and the eroticism that was taking her over. "We can order food later."

"That is an act of free will I can get behind." He kept her hand as he rose and drew her from her chair.

CHAPTER TWO

Joaquin Valezquez didn't make a habit of picking up women. Which wasn't to say it had never happened, but he was a busy man who couldn't afford distractions, especially today.

Thirty minutes ago, word of yet another one of his father's financial overextensions had reached him. Joaquin had left his team finishing out his presentation to a tech mogul and called his father on his way to the hotel. Just hearing Lorenzo's voice made his skin crawl. Trying to work *with* him was like trying to reason with a swarm of murder hornets. Every time Joaquin swatted at one damaging sting, another threatened from a new direction. Nothing about it was pain-free.

Brooding on the fact he had to find a more permanent way to keep his father from destroying the legacy that belonged to his brother's children, Joaquin had stepped into the elevator that opened as he arrived in front of it.

His mind had been on the calls he had to make. The plans that needed hammering out. There had been rumbles among the board of LV Global that they would be willing to vote Lorenzo out if Joaquin stepped in as CEO.

Joaquin would rather go back to scrubbing toilets for drunk tourists than take over LVG, but someone had to. He needed to call a headhunter and his sister-in-law. Others.

Despite his preoccupation, his libido had absolutely noticed the woman who seemed to be waiting for the elevator. She was well dressed in a casually tasteful way. Her smart jacket and designer trousers made the most of her figure without being blatant about it. She struck him as a sophisticated woman who was establishing herself in a professional field. Her dark brown hair was in a tidy roll at her nape. Her profile was a graceful line that belonged on the kind of pink brooch his grandmother had once worn.

When a huge smile arrived on her face, she was incandescent.

His cloud of distemper had lifted. He asked if she was going up.

She met his gaze and his breath stopped. She was genuinely beautiful. Her makeup enhanced a wide mouth and high cheekbones and long brows that delivered an impression of intelligence and directness. Confidence.

As she looked at him, her bright blue eyes took on a gleam of interest that was deeply gratifying when he was in such a foul mood.

She'd said something funny as she joined him. He'd already forgotten what it was because she seemed to offer a lot of throwaway remarks that kept him on his toes.

Siobhan. Her name was as charming as the rest of her. She seemed both open and closed, playful yet careful. Empathetic without offering pity. She was lovely to look at and sensual in the way she appreciated her first taste of wine. When he took her hand, her pulse skipped under his touch.

That had been as enticing as a flick of a ribbon to the desire prowling like a jungle cat inside him. He was wound up and longing for a chase and a capture and a wrestle.

As he opened the door of his suite for her, she carried

their half-full glasses inside, offering him a whiff of vanilla and oranges from her hair as she passed.

He let the door fall closed and set the ice bucket on the coffee table, then dropped his phone beside it. He joined her at the window and took back his glass.

"Have you ever been to Alcatraz?" She nodded at the view through the shroud of the curtain and the mist on the water.

Metaphorically, he'd grown up there. "No."

She slid a sideways look at him and seemed to grow skittish, putting a few steps between them. "I want you to know that I never do this."

The loping animal in him slowed his pace. "When you say *never*..."

Her chin dipped coyly. "I'm not a virgin. I mean I don't jump into bed with strangers."

Her cheeks flushed pink. She was trying to be bold, but she was shy at heart. Fascinating.

"I'm not making judgments. Or assumptions." After a beat, he magnanimously added, "We don't have to use the bed. Lady's choice."

Her throaty laughter was as much a turn-on as the rest of her, filling the room with her presence. "Good to know. That helps my nerves a lot. Thanks."

"This is you nervous?" She had invited herself in here! "God help the man who encounters you when you're feeling confident."

Her mouth pulled wide in a satisfied show of her teeth. "Thank you for that. I actually hate feeling less than five thousand percent confident. But you've got all of this going on..." She motioned at him in an encompassing way. "It's intimidating."

"I think there might be a compliment buried in there,"

he said drily. "But to be clear, I like five thousand percent consent. If you're here because you feel intimidated, or you think I expect sex because I bought you a glass of champagne, then we need a longer conversation before we do anything else."

"That's not what I think. I'm very comfortable saying no when I need to. I've made a habit of it for a while now." Her mouth twisted with irony. "More often than I needed to. It's the saying yes that makes me feel out of my depth. I'm out of practice."

"Like saying yes to a drink?"

"Exactly. I don't know how to be spontaneous anymore, but I'd like to be. If you're getting mixed signals, that's why."

"You use truth to disarm," he replied, studying that contradiction of squared shoulders and a high chin with the pink that sat in her cheeks and the way her lashes kept screening her thoughts. "You only reveal a sliver of the truth, though. It's a clever sleight of hand."

"Is that a compliment?" Her brows went up to a haughty level as she mocked him with his own words. "Because you've buried it."

"I believe you're nervous." Even though she was disguising it well. "I'm observing how well you counteract it by calling it out. The way you're confiding in me sounds like a sign of trust, but it also lets me know I can't take advantage of you. Not if we're being honest with each other."

"You're making it sound like I came in here to screw with your mind not your body. I assure you it's the latter."

"Please continue with both. As foreplay goes, I'm enjoying it." He swirled the final mouthful of champagne in the bottom of his glass before swallowing it, meeting her gaze over the disc of the stem.

Her blue eyes glittered with amusement.

Dios, she was marvelous. He hadn't even kissed her yet and he wanted weeks and months and years to saturate himself in her.

That thought brought him up short. He had a few hours. The night at best. The slow-motion train wreck in Madrid needed mitigating. Dealing with his father required all of his concentration and a matching level of ruthlessness.

Joaquin loathed the idea of being anything like his father. It made him sick to contemplate it so he brushed that disturbing prospect aside. He set down his glass and ambled toward Siobhan, watching her eyes widen.

"There's no rush," he assured her. "No signed contract to fulfill. Leave anytime. But I'm dying to kiss you." He cupped the side of her neck and gave her a beat to decide.

Her gaze held his until her pupils expanded, then her lashes swept down. Her attention dropped to his mouth and her lips parted in tremulous invitation.

"I want that, too." She leaned into him, mouth uptilted in offering.

He sealed his lips over hers and desire exploded within him.

Yes. Here was the portal to escape he'd been looking for.

Siobhan hadn't realized what a sense of heightened anticipation she'd been in until his mouth covered hers and relief arced through her.

There were still nervous crackles in the back of her mind. What if he was an accomplished liar? What if it wasn't *her* he wanted, but *them*?

All of that receded behind the avalanche of more immediate signals—the lingering taste of champagne on his tongue, the subtle notes of aftershave applied hours ago against skin that was warm with the musk of his own personal scent. The lightest scuff on his chin where his five o'clock stubble was coming in. The seductive play of his fingertips against her neck, masterful as a pianist teasing a love song from his keys.

A moan of need left her. She flowed into him, arms lifting to twine around his neck.

His arm twitched and there was a delicate ping and shatter of crystal against tile.

He broke their kiss and they both looked down at the glass she'd dropped.

In the next second, his arms slid around her. He lifted her off her feet and pivoted her out of the broken shards. As he set her back down, his mouth captured hers again, eclipsing all but the heavenly feel of him firmly surrounding her. Strong, restless hands slid under the back of her jacket, pressing her closer. He angled his head to kiss her deeper. She tightened her arms around his neck to arch herself into the bow of his towering frame.

All she knew was the erratic pulse in her ears, the sear of sexual heat in her blood, the edgy hunger that wanted to *devour* him. She slid her hands into his hair and lightly scraped her nails against his scalp.

The sound he made was regressive and thrilling. In a powerful move, he swept her up into the cradle of his arms. His gaze tracked over her with possessive satisfaction before coming back to meet hers, flashing with demand.

She was still trying to catch her breath. A fine tremble weakened her muscles. She suddenly had a new appreciation for how powerful he was. How unknown. Nerves accosted her again. Apprehension paired with a thrill of excitement.

"Say yes," he commanded.

Oddly, his stern demand was the reassurance she needed. He wouldn't do anything she didn't want. But she did want. Her desire for him was profound.

Holding his intent stare, she toed off one shoe, letting it thud to the floor. Then the other. Her sister would kill her for treating them so poorly, but the way his nostrils flared was worth it.

"Quit being a brat."

She curled her arms around his neck and pressed her smile into his throat, then licked the salty skin near his Adam's apple. "*Sí*. Take me to your bed, Joaquin."

He hitched her a little higher and carried her into the bedroom where he set her on her feet. "You're too short now," he grumbled.

She moved to kneel on the edge of the bed. "Better?"

"Much." He aligned himself against her and they kissed again, brushing each other's jackets away. "I could pet you for days in this," he said of her cashmere sweater, hands skimming deliciously over her shoulders and back and rib cage and breasts.

For a long time, that was all he did. He petted and kissed her until she was leaning off the edge of the mattress, trying to get closer to him. Seeking the ridge of flesh that she wanted to feel in the cradle of her thighs.

"Wait here." He steadied her before he walked into the bathroom.

She sat back on her heels, trying to blink herself out of the fog of arousal and the sudden denial of his touch. It could have been a moment to catch her bearings and rethink this, but he was already coming back.

He threw a strip of condoms onto the bed. "I presume I need those."

"You do." She was thrown by how little thought she'd given to protection, but she wasn't on the pill anymore.

He began undressing so she did the same, tilting up the edge of her sweater to ask, "May I? Or did you want me to keep it on?"

"You may." He granted his permission in a deep tone of authority that should have made her balk. He wasn't the boss of her, but that hint of dominance was kind of a turn-on.

He wanted to control this moment and she wanted to push back so she took her time peeling up the edge of the ultra-soft knit, revealing one centimeter of skin at a time, stretching tall and holding her arms up to give him a long look at the demicups made from blue-and-gold lace that she wore beneath it.

"You very much may," he said in a pleased rumble as he pulled the sweater free of her upraised arms and discarded it on the floor. "*Dios*, that's pretty." He traced the edge of the lace along the upper swell of her breast, tickling her skin.

Her nipple peaked against silk. He took care to reward her response with a lingering caress there.

"Take your hair down," he said as he brought both his hands into play against the bra cups.

He was shirtless now and her hands went to his naked shoulders, wanting to feel all of his satiny skin. Wanting to kiss him and taste the hot plane of his chest.

He dragged her hands from his neck and moved them to the back of her head. "Let me see how long it is," he insisted.

A helpless protest throbbed in her throat, but she did as he asked, pulling pins that fell willy-nilly to the floor.

As she did, he steadied her with his hands on her waist, watching intently. When the brunette waves fell around her shoulders, he ran his fingers through the length and held her head for a long, hot, ravenous kiss.

She was so lost in that dark, velvety space, she didn't realize the weight of his hand was tangled in her hair, tugging her head back until his lips moved into her throat and down. He brushed aside her locket and dislodged the cup of her bra, lifting her breast to capture her nipple with the pull of his mouth.

Lightning streaked into her loins. She clasped at his shoulders, thinking she was about to fall onto her back, but his arm slid to support her as he held her off balance and feasted on her breast, teasing and feeding those fingers of electric heat that lanced through her abdomen and detonated between her thighs.

When she thought she couldn't stand another moment of those intense sensations, of feeling suspended and helpless and consumed, he moved to her other breast.

"Joaquin," she panted, shaking with arousal. Her core was drowning in neglect.

He lifted his head. "Too hard? I want to eat you up."

"I want...*this*." She splayed her hand on his abdomen then slid her palm lower to cup the thick ridge behind his fly.

He yanked open his belt and unzipped. She slid her hand inside the heat, behind the waistband of his boxer briefs, and clasped the steely weight of his erection.

He groaned into her mouth as he kissed her again, letting her explore his shape, running his hands over her back and buttocks, nipping at her ear and tugging at her hair again until he made a rough noise of tested restraint and caught her wrist.

"Finish undressing."

She opened her trousers, then dropped onto her back to work them off her hips and down her legs. As she kicked them away, she arched to reach behind herself and release her bra.

She was still untangling herself from the bra straps when he pressed a hand to her hip, stilling her so he could study the panties that matched her bra.

"You have exquisite taste." He followed the lace across her hip and into the V it took over her mound.

She bit her lip. Dampness flooded into the flesh that he traced through silk.

"H-how would you know?" she asked in a wicked challenge that was pure audacity.

"Oh, I will find out. Trust me on that, *querida*." He peeled her panties down and away before he touched her again, this time letting his fingertip sink into the slippery folds that parted easily under his caress.

"Blond," he noted of the neatly trimmed thatch. His curious gaze came up to the hair she colored, but she wasn't capable of conversation. He had found her sweet spot and knew exactly how to incite the most delicious sensations.

She couldn't keep her eyes open. Climax gathered as tension in her abdomen. *Need*.

"I want to be inside you so badly, I can hardly breathe," he said in a rasp, gently invading with a wicked touch.

She stilled his hand. "I'm going to come," she gasped.

"Then you should." He pressed deeper and his thumb rolled across the knot of nerves that was already pulsing.

With a harsh groan, she pinned his hand with her own,

thighs clamping closed while her body twisted in the throes of acute pleasure.

It should have been embarrassing to lose control with him watching in the full light of day, but it felt *so good*. Wave after wave rolled through her, each one more gratifying than the last, until she was shaken and breathless and floating.

As the storm receded, he eased his hand away and nudged her thighs open, rolling her onto her back. Her heart was still galloping, her breasts quivering with her uneven breaths.

He finished stripping and kicked away his clothes, gloriously naked from powerful shoulders to defined abs to thrusting erection.

She blindly felt for the condoms and offered them.

"I have promises to keep, *querida*." His mouth slanted into a sinfully cruel smile and he bent to steal a wicked, intimate taste between her thighs.

She cried out. And shuddered with fresh longing. Then she moaned as he pulled her hips to the edge of the bed and mercilessly drew her back to a state of acute arousal. When her fists were in his hair and she was lifting her hips in a plea for the climax that hovered so elusively, he rose and reached for the condoms.

"As I said. Exquisite." His expression held carnal intent, but he said, "Now, tell me again what you want. Be specific."

"You. This." She caressed the naked column of heat as he moved her up the mattress and used his knee to spread her thighs. She squeezed and sought the places that made him twitch. She was completely stripped of inhibition. "I want to taste you." She licked her lips.

His breath huffed out as though he'd been punched.

"But I also want to feel you here." She ran her hand to her own sex, where she was soaked and aching.

"Then you shall have me," he said through his teeth and rolled on the condom.

As he loomed over her, she guided him into place. He filled her in one firm, perfect thrust that made her arch in glorious abandon.

When he kissed her, she tasted herself and it only made the experience more erotic. Profound. She wrapped her arms and legs around him and urged him to unleash his full power, propelling them both into the volcano.

Coated in sweat and still suffering aftershocks from his powerful orgasm, Joaquin dragged himself free of her. He discarded the condom, then dropped onto his back beside her. His chest continued to heave, striving to catch his breath.

What had started as a pleasant diversion had turned into something that bordered on cataclysmic. Sex was supposed to be just sex. It was a shared experience in which he gave more than he took. He was never as generous with his business partners as his intimate ones, but in bed it was a case of wanting the same thing: pleasure. Giving was as good as getting for him. They were two sides of the same coin. The encounter was delightful while it lasted and afterward, his appetite was sated. His desire to possess was gone.

So why did he have this prickling sense of loss?

It wasn't the grief of losing his brother. Not the reduction of assets due to stock market fluctuations or other business cycles. This was the sense of something being *taken*. Held out of reach.

Which didn't make sense because she was right here.

And he had no intention of keeping her.

This unsettled sensation was a belated reaction to his father's attempts to manipulate him, he decided. He was stuck in the confluence of two crashing forces: his desire to expunge his father from his life and his responsibility to his brother's wife and children. He'd taken brief refuge from that mental war in the fleshy paradise that was Siobhan. He didn't regret it, but he couldn't let this respite she'd offered him become more significant than it was.

He couldn't let desire for her dull him to his duty.

"You know when you get a really great massage and you never want to move again?" She rolled onto her stomach and hugged the pillow that she pulled under her head and chest. Her eyelids drooped heavily as she blinked at him. The corners of her lips tilted in libidinous pleasure. "That's how I feel right now," she purred.

"I don't get those kinds of massages, but no judgment."

"As if!" Her teeth flashed and she slid across the sheet to drape herself over his chest, making him delightfully aware of the way her breasts brushed his skin before settling warm and plump against him. "I thought you promised me dinner?"

"Are you hungry? Why on earth would that be?" Despite his decision to distance himself, he absently gathered her more fully atop him. "I can order something. Or would you rather dress and go out?" Leaving this room would be prudent.

"This is nice." She shifted in a full body caress, legs interlacing with his own in a way that was pure seduction.

"It is." He ran his hands down her back and over the cool cheeks of her ass, thinking the cashmere had been lovely, but he preferred her naked skin. Perhaps he would indulge himself, and her, a little longer.

But only a little.

She nuzzled his jaw and her hair fell across his mouth. He brushed it back behind her ear.

"Why do you color it?" Not that he was complaining. On the contrary, he was mildly turned on by the fact *he* knew her natural color and few others did.

"No one takes me seriously as a blonde." She slid off him and sat up, letting her dark hair fall forward to curtain her profile. "Do you mind if I pop down to my room? I need to take out my contacts." She blinked at him.

He kept getting the sense she was hiding something. It provoked his frustration that he wouldn't get the chance to learn all her secrets, but such was his life right now.

He kept a light tone as he said, "If you come back and your eyes aren't blue, I really will believe you work for the government."

"But which one?" she challenged with a cheeky grin.

He slid his fingers along her hip and thigh, unable to keep from enjoying the supple softness of her. She was a warm, glowing light that mesmerized him the way a candle flame drew a moth.

"My eyes are blue. I promise." Her expression altered as she noticed the scar on the side of his chest. She gently traced it. "Broken rib? That was a bad one."

"It was," he agreed impassively, not telling her the hospital stay had been a relief from worse.

Her mouth grew pensive and her touch on that sensitive scar began to burn.

He caught her hand and carried it to his lips so he could kiss her palm.

She let him, but looked deeply into his eyes. "You don't want to talk about it."

"I don't." He tried to soften his words with a caress of

her cheek, but he couldn't escape the fact he was setting hard, necessary boundaries. "If you're looking for someone you can truly share secrets with, I am not that man."

She blinked in a way that suggested his words had struck like a blow. She bit the corner of her mouth and looked toward the window as she sat up and withdrew her hand.

He fought the urge to drag her down into his arms again. To press her beneath him and make her his all over again. He'd never been possessive. He hadn't been allowed to be. Everything was Fernando's with very few crumbs left over for the spare.

Joaquin had taught himself *not* to want anything to be his. That had helped enormously when it came to gambling in tech manufacturing. He was willing to take risks that others weren't, simply because he didn't attach himself to material wealth or personal recognition. Losing a contract or a sum of money annoyed him, but he didn't let it affect him too deeply. The global company his father was now dangling like a carrot, pretending he had intentions of allowing Joaquin to run it? It meant absolutely nothing to him. He didn't want it. At all. Only his loyalty to his brother compelled him to take an interest in keeping it afloat.

Siobhan, though. He discovered he wanted Siobhan. It was visceral, this urge to grasp onto her and keep her by his side.

Which was disturbing enough to prevent him from giving in to that desire. Everything he possessed needed to be something he was willing to lose. It was the only way to stay sane. Fear of losing something he really wanted was the reason he coveted nothing.

He tucked his arm beneath his head to keep from

reaching for her, but his conscience pinched as he acknowledged she might not be as sophisticated as he'd judged her to be.

"I've hurt your feelings."

"No." He suspected she was saving face, adding with forced lightness, "Apparently, you're right about fate and free will. We're not meant to be. This was lovely, though. Thank you." Her hair spilled across his chest and cheek as she tapped his mouth with hers then flitted away just as quickly.

Was. He unwound his arm from behind his head, but she was already sliding off the bed. "You're not coming back?"

"You still want me to?" she asked over her shoulder, allowing him to glimpse a vulnerability in her gaze that kicked at his conscience again.

Let her go, he told himself, but his mouth said, "If you want to."

Her smile dawned in a way that expanded light inside him, promising a stay of execution from the mess that awaited in Madrid.

As she dressed, he rose to pull on his own trousers, then followed her into the lounge where she picked up her shoes, but didn't put them on.

"My walk of shame is only down the hall."

"Is that how you feel?" he asked with dismay. "Ashamed?"

"No. I'm actually feeling very smug." She slid him a heavy-lashed look that tightened his skin.

"Good. I'll order dinner and call someone to clean up the glass. Hurry back."

They kissed lightly. Too lightly. If he'd known it would be their last kiss, he would have made it count.

CHAPTER THREE

Two weeks later...

SIOBHAN HAD BARELY learned how her new boss, Oladele, liked her coffee when she came in to find the woman already at her desk, still wearing a raincoat speckled with the drizzle of Madrid's December morning. Among the handful of people who had also trickled in before nine, there was an air of alertness. Something was going on. Something big.

Oladele was VP of Legal here at LV Global. She'd risen in the ranks under the previous president, Fernando Valezquez, and still choked up when she spoke of him. He'd passed suddenly over a year ago. It had been an electrical accident of some kind. His father, Lorenzo, had since come out of retirement to retake the helm.

"We're in a state of transition," Oladele had told Siobhan on her first day. "Señor Valezquez will return to retirement once a decision is made on his successor." Her expression had been pleasant, but as deadpan as a high-stakes poker player's.

Siobhan's antennae had gone up, thinking there was a lot that Oladele was leaving unsaid, but she wasn't likely to be forthcoming until Siobhan had proven herself trustworthy. Oladele had hired Siobhan for her legal aspirations, her fluency in six languages, including Modern Standard Arabic, her stellar grades and the security abstract she had voluntarily attached to her CV.

Siobhan had a feeling that last item had been the clincher because there seemed to be ample staff here at LV Global who could have stepped into the shoes of Oladele's very pregnant EA.

After two days of orientation with that EA, Siobhan was on her own. She loved everything about the job and the new life she was starting. She had leased a gorgeous one-bedroom flat in the barrio de Chamberí and, so far, was still unrecognized as Dorry Whitley. She would ride that horse as long as it had legs.

The only stitch in her side was the memory of returning to Joaquin's hotel room in San Francisco to find the door propped open. A young woman from housekeeping had been sweeping up the broken glass.

"He said to tell you he had to leave, but to charge your dinner to this room and take the champagne." The woman had pointed at the bottle in the bucket of melted ice.

Siobhan had stood there in a hotel robe over fresh lingerie that she had put on for *him*. She had felt so cheap, so scorned, so *foolish*, she had wanted to die.

She should have celebrated her new job alone, she kept telling herself. But that thought was always followed by a slithery reminder of how delicious the sex had been—which she almost wished had been terrible because now the bar had been set so high, she feared she was spoiled for anyone else.

Why were men so awful? Why was she so terrible at seeing how awful they were?

"I'll be right up," she heard Oladele say. The phone landed hard in its cradle.

Siobhan snapped out of her funk and finished removing her coat. She dropped her bag into its drawer and rushed into Oladele's office.

"Did I miss a text about an early meeting?" It was a mortifying thought. She prided herself on being thorough and prepared.

"I only learned an hour ago that there was an emergency board meeting." Oladele started to remove her coat and Siobhan hurried to help her. Oladele was a diminutive woman of fifty-three with narrow shoulders and a very short haircut, which formed a cap of tight curls against her scalp.

"I'll make your coffee. What else do you need? Did you miss breakfast?"

"I did, and yes to the coffee, but we're needed upstairs. Bring your laptop."

"May I ask what happened?"

"We're merging with another firm." Oladele flicked her gaze to the open door. "That's the language you will use," she added quietly with a warning tilt of her brows. "I didn't expect it to happen like this, definitely not this quickly, but here we are."

Siobhan didn't have time to process what that might mean. Within moments, they were hurrying off the elevator onto the top floor, which was the company president's domain.

She hadn't been up here yet. It was ten times more luxurious and imposing than the offices they occupied two floors below. The entire building was tastefully updated from the original construction a hundred years ago. Everything she'd seen was sophisticated and refined.

She had barely taken in the beautiful inlay of the mahogany and oak in the parquet floor, or the oval-shaped wall that separated the empty receptionist's desk from the rest of the floor, when the sound of an age-graveled baritone struck her ears.

"You thief! You think you can do this to me? You vile piece of—" An ugly streak of insults was hurled, growing loud enough to send a spike of alarm through Siobhan.

Another male voice responded, low and cold, saying something about protecting *it* for the children.

Shock waves went through her as she heard the second voice. It wasn't just the lethal tone. He almost sounded like—

No. She was imagining things. Joaquin was Spanish, but he wouldn't be *here*. That was too much of a bizarre coincidence.

In front of her, Oladele checked her step. Siobhan copied her, moving to set her back to the wall as a man with iron-gray hair strode with purpose toward them. His navy suit was well tailored to accommodate his barrel chest and stocky frame. His jaw wore a frost of stubble, as though he'd missed shaving this morning. His hair was slicked back, but untidy. His face was purple with fury.

He glared at Oladele as he passed them.

"Lorenzo," Oladele murmured, offering a deferential nod.

"You helped him, didn't you?" He was so livid, spittle had collected in the corners of his mouth. He glared blame at both of them. "Judas. I should have fired you when I had the chance. This is not over." He moved past them to jab the button for the elevator.

Oladele looked shaken, but motioned for Siobhan to accompany her into a foyer where a chandelier in a recessed ceiling hung over a small arrangement of late nineteenth century furniture. Three tall windows looked onto Madrid's business district. On another wall, shelves of old books were fronted by doors with paned glass.

"Wait here while I step into the meeting room. The board may still be in discussions." Oladele moved through a pair of open doors into a corridor.

Siobhan shifted to read a few titles on the books, which gave her a view down the hallway. She wasn't trying to spy, but she heard a door open and a woman's voice said in Spanish, "I should get back. The children will be awake and looking for me."

"Of course," a male voice replied. *That* male voice, the one that sent a preternatural shiver through Siobhan, making her abdomen clench and her scalp tighten.

She watched in mesmerized horror as a stunning woman stepped from the office at the end of the hall. The elegant brunette wore a wool skirt in gray plaid with a black turtleneck and a camel-colored overcoat. She was tying a green silk scarf over her hair.

Then *he* stepped out. Joaquin.

Siobhan's heart stopped. He was even more handsome than when she'd last seen him. The image of him shirtless, wearing only his trousers and a half-lidded look of satisfaction was imprinted on her mind. Today he had the air of a man who'd taken care with his appearance. He was shaved and had a fresh haircut. His somber blue suit fit him like armor, giving an impression he had dressed for an important moment. A ceremony.

Or a burial.

Her jumble of sensual memories collided with harsh reality, sending a piercing sensation through her belly, one that was steely and sharp and locked her in place.

Her morbid inability to look away meant she watched

him bend his head to kiss both of the woman's cheeks with casual familiarity.

"My car should be waiting for you. I'll see you later—"

He spotted Siobhan and stood at attention. His glare of astonishment traveled down the length of the corridor like a quaking force, crashing into her and knocking her breath from her lungs.

"What are you doing here?" he demanded.

Her heart was already thudding in guilt and horror. Now adrenaline leaked into her blood, urging her to run, but she couldn't move. She was frozen in shock. In repulsion at him and herself.

He was *married*?

At that second, Oladele stepped from a door midway along the hall, arriving between them.

"Señor Valezquez," she said politely. "Señora. It's nice to see you." Oladele followed the stark glare Joaquin had pinned on Siobhan. "Ah. No need to be alarmed. Siobhan is covering my assistant's maternity leave. Siobhan, this is Joaquin Valezquez, our new president. Congratulations, señor."

Siobhan was probably expected to say something similar. Maybe, "It's nice to meet you." She couldn't speak. She wanted to die. She wanted to run from the building and never come back. She wanted to scream, *Married? You're married?*

"You have a busy day ahead. I'll leave you to it," the woman in the green scarf said. She offered Siobhan a curious smile as she left to go home to their *children*.

Oh, he was horrible. He was every bit as cold-blooded and manipulative as Gilbert in a completely different way. She was an *idiot*.

"Siobhan?" Oladele prompted. "I believe we're meeting in the president's office." She looked to Joaquin for confirmation.

"I just need..." She couldn't finish. Could barely speak. She dove through the door marked with the stenciled figure of a triangle with a dot on its point. Her behavior was deeply unprofessional, but this was a full-blown panic attack.

She had asked him if he was single and he had lied straight to her face before pulling her into an adulterous liaison.

Hot tears blinded her as she emptied her arms onto the vanity shelf beneath the mirror. She pushed into a stall where she leaned on the door, thinking she might throw up. She sat down, so lightheaded she was afraid she'd faint and knock herself cold on the porcelain.

"I—" Oladele sounded perplexed and took a step to follow Siobhan.

"When did you hire her?" Joaquin asked with acute suspicion, attention pinned to the lavatory door that had closed behind Siobhan.

"She started at the beginning of last week. Why? Do you know her?"

"I'm not sure," he lied. Hell, yes, he knew her. His body had recognized her with a pulse of animal lust the second he glimpsed her, roaring in a way that nearly overshadowed his astonishment at seeing her here of all places. "Can I see her file?"

"Her credentials are excellent. She's actually overqualified—"

He shot Oladele a look that had her pressing her lips into a line.

"But if that's something you would like to review yourself, I'll go to my desk and forward it," she said mildly. "I don't have access to those documents on my phone."

"Thank you."

At that moment, the board members began filing out of the meeting room.

Oladele moved into the sea of bodies flowing toward the elevator.

Still twitching with aggression from that volatile meeting, and now at this unexpected interloper, Joaquin kicked the stoppers out of the doors at the end of the corridor, closing it into privacy. Then he walked into the ladies' room, checked that there was only one pair of feet in the stalls, and turned the lock on the main door.

"Siobhan."

"What the hell?" The stall door clapped open. "You can't be in here."

She stepped out, pale face flushing red with high emotion, every bit as enticingly beautiful as he remembered.

He had to consciously keep his gaze from wandering to the open collar of her striped shirt and well-cut, single-button blazer. Her outfit was professional and conservative, exactly as it should be for her role as assistant to their head of legal.

He still found her entirely too sexy.

"I just acquired the building with the company." He leaned on the partition that separated the sink area from the vanity nook. "I can go anywhere I want. What are *you* doing here?"

"In this room?" She pointed to the floor. "Trying not to vomit over the fact that I slept with a married man. Who has *children*. You absolute disgusting scumbag. How *dare* you lie to me about something like that?"

Her anger was incendiary. Thrilling. She radiated the

energy of a typhoon, terrifying yet awe-inspiring. There was also something perversely gratifying in her temper. She wasn't merely offended. *How dare you lie to* me. It was personal. She was jealous.

He shouldn't like that. At all. But he did.

"You're referring to Zurina?" He lifted one patronizing brow. "She's my sister-in-law."

"Oh." Her hard boil of fury simmered down to an annoyed scowl. She narrowed her eyes on him, though. "You really aren't married? Because—"

"I am exactly as I presented to you when we met. You are the one with something to explain. How the hell do you come to be working for my father?" That was highly suspicious. *Highly.*

"I don't." She was taken aback. "I work for Oladele. Aside from when your father walked by us ten minutes ago, I'd never seen or spoken to him." She moved to the sink to wash her hands.

"You want me to believe your working here is a coincidence?"

"Unless *you* planned it, then yes. That's exactly what it is. I told you I was starting a new job covering a mat leave."

"You let me believe that was in Australia. Or San Francisco." He didn't know what he'd thought, but he sure as hell hadn't imagined she was coming *here.*

"You said you live on your *plane.* Maybe if you'd stuck around, instead of skittering away like a spider under a door, I would have told you I was coming to Madrid." She shook out a cloth hand towel and wet it under the tap. "You could have simply let me leave without asking me to come back. That second trip down the hall really was a walk of shame." She gave the wet towel a hard wring and dabbed a corner of it under her eyes, fixing her smudged makeup.

Tears? He might have been more disturbed by that if he wasn't seeing them here, amid an outright war with his father.

"Zurina called me with an emergency." He hadn't liked leaving without a word, but he hadn't relished knocking on doors to find her, then trying to explain.

He hadn't liked that there'd been a part of him that had leaped toward asking her to accompany him. For that reason, a clean break had seemed easier. Safer.

But the clean break hadn't happened.

"Go back to explaining how you're here," he demanded.

"You really think I'm here by design? Until Oladele said it a few minutes ago, I didn't know your last name." She pivoted to face him, forcing him to quit ogling the shape of her ass in her blue trousers.

"You didn't investigate the company you were applying at?" he asked skeptically.

"I used a placement agency. They gave me an abstract, but I wasn't told it was LV Global until I'd been offered the job. I spoke to Oladele at one point, but that was about my duties. When I did look it up, it said the president had passed away over a year ago and that his father had come out of retirement to run things." She threw the damp towel in the laundry basket. "Frankly, I didn't need to know more than that. My priority was to be closer to my sister and gain experience in legal. I've been meaning to read more about the company, but I've been busy moving continents and visiting with family."

This all seemed too tidy for him to believe. On the other hand, there was very little on line that linked him to his father. He certainly didn't take any pains to acknowledge his relationship to Lorenzo.

She waved at the door. "Is Oladele out there, wondering why you're accosting her EA in the toilet?"

"She's downstairs." He stole a quick glance at his phone. The file hadn't been forwarded yet so they had another minute. "You can't work for me."

"I don't. I work for Oladele."

"She works for LV Global, which I have just acquired. You work for me."

"So? Are you unable to be professional because we had a brief interaction in the past?"

"Interaction," he scoffed. In *the past*? It was two short weeks ago. Still a very vivid memory that he relived at least once a day. In the shower. It was all he could do not to think of other uses for that counter ledge right now.

Dios, her effect on him was as strong as it had been when he'd first glimpsed her. Stronger, now that he knew what a volatile match they were. Distracting.

"What do you want to call it?" She held her chin up, mouth tight, stare as cold as ice. "You made it clear it was nothing significant. I feel the same."

Liar. She was too angry for him to believe that. And, try as he had to diminish it into a pleasant but trivial memory, he couldn't.

"Blame fate. She's having a laugh, I suppose." Her lips stretched in a facetious smile before she added in a mutter, "But if you think I made a *choice* to see you again, you're wrong."

He narrowed his eyes, surprised how deeply that got under his skin.

His phone pinged, notifying him of Oladele's email.

"She's on her way back." He unlocked the door and peeked out, then held it open. "My office."

CHAPTER FOUR

"You don't really intend to fire me," Siobhan said as she entered a room that was full of heavy furniture and the embedded funk of cigarette smoke. "You can't."

"I absolutely can," he contradicted. "I don't even need a reason beyond the fact I'm restructuring."

"But that's not fair. No one needs to know anything happened between us." How could he be so casually ruthless? Standing there with all the mesmerizing confidence that had attracted her so inexorably in the first place while only giving her half his attention as he read his phone?

"Six languages? You were taking your degree in that, weren't you?" he recalled. "Why Arabic?" He lifted his gaze from his phone, scrambling her brain in a new way.

"What are you reading?" She hurried toward him, trying to see while feeling exposed.

"Is this security reference authentic?" He expanded the PDF. "I supply components to TecSec. I know the man who signed this. *Personally.*"

"So do I. Obviously." She was standing too close. She was acutely aware of his height and the faint scent of his aftershave. That particular fragrance had been all over her skin that night until she had skulked back to her room and furiously scrubbed it off in the shower.

"How?" he demanded.

"Pardon? Oh." How did she know the man who ran one of the most elite security companies in the world? "That's confidential." She looked to her nails.

"I'll check it," he warned.

"Go ahead. Call him right now." She held his stare, but it wasn't easy when she knew that delving into her security clearance risked dredging up her connections. Her past.

The sting of that old humiliation began to scorch her cheeks.

He noticed.

For a few seconds, they were locked in a long stare. The atmosphere shifted from animosity to something else. Awareness. Sensual memories. *Pull*.

There was a tap on the door and Oladele entered.

They both took a quick step back from each other.

Oladele faltered, clearly sensing the crackle of tension. "Should I come back?"

"No. Come in." Joaquin flashed Siobhan a stern look that said *this isn't over*, but waved them to take a seat. "My team is on their way from Barcelona. Siobhan, advise the LV Global executive we're meeting in the board room in thirty minutes. I want to finalize this acquisition before my father finds yet another way to damage the ship."

Siobhan hadn't eaten since her avocado toast first thing this morning. It was closing on seven o'clock, but she had one more meeting to schedule before she left for the day. She was both limp with exhaustion and wired with adrenaline as she typed out the blessedly short agenda.

After Joaquin had unceremoniously ghosted her in San Francisco, she had done her best to turn the page. Thankfully, she'd been running flat out with the move and starting her new job. That meant that, until today,

Joaquin had only intruded on her dreams, where he once again ran his hands and lips over her skin, setting her on fire with carnal need.

She always woke ashamed of herself, but now she was reeling at having seen him again. She was still reacting to the roller coaster of learning he was *not* married, but had definitely taken charge of her place of employment. Erotic spot fires shouldn't be cropping up at every turn, but they did, ambushing her with a flood of heated yearning followed by a cold bath of humiliation when she recalled the horrible way he'd left her.

Her heart kept stuttering with apprehension at the power he now had over her. It was bad enough he could axe her job with a word. Worse was the fact she was reacting to him as ferociously as she had that night. Her nerves were attuned to an awareness of him, ears pricked for the sound of his voice while a mortifying coal of sexual heat sat in the pit of her belly.

Work saved her to a point. It was a very busy day, but she stole one quick search of him online. It was another form of self-torture. She learned he'd been engaged at the time his brother had died eighteen months ago. The engagement had been broken off shortly after, but learning he'd been so close to another woman so recently made her feel…unsettled. He might not be married, but he'd been planning to marry. Knowing that added to the undercurrents between them as the day wore on.

After their altercation first thing this morning, she did everything she could to prove herself competent and reliable and professional. He only acknowledged her in a work capacity, which was to say, barely at all. She told herself that was a relief, but his brisk tone left a mark on her nerves. He'd spoken the same way to everyone, though.

Things were very tense on all sides. She knew better than to take his attitude personally, but it felt like a fresh rebuff.

Not that she wanted his attention. Did she?

She didn't know what she wanted. She hadn't had a chance to process any of this, including the awe she'd felt as she watched him seize the leadership role. She had a lot of really strong men in her life and Joaquin could hold his own with any of them.

In a series of rapid-fire orders, he had delegated various tasks to her and Oladele, then brought them in to witness a battle royale in the meeting room. Joaquin had outlined to the LVG executives that the board had voted to allow his company, ProFab Worldwide, to assume LVG's debt. In exchange, he had gained controlling interest in the company. Lorenzo had been ousted. Joaquin was the king of the castle and restructuring began now.

Some department heads had sighed in relief. Others had been as outraged as Lorenzo.

Joaquin knew what he wanted, though. He had stated it clearly and didn't flinch under pushback. The first man who refused to carry out his instructions was dispassionately invited to leave and not come back. *Does anyone else wish to waste my time?*

Through it all, he hadn't acknowledged her with so much as a glance while she'd been riveted by him.

After a few more highly charged meetings, Joaquin had left for the day, but the building had continued to reverberate as the news traveled to all corners and his own team began meeting with the department heads. Siobhan and Oladele were some of the few people who got any work done. The rest were gossiping or responding to media requests. Others were frantically putting the word out that they were seeking alternate employment.

"It was a big day," Oladele said, stopping by her desk and startling her out of her reverie. "Expect the rest of the week to be the same."

"I've been thrown into the deep end before." Siobhan smiled weakly. "I don't mind."

"I can tell. You handle pressure very well." She cocked her head to give her a more penetrating look. "Including the concerns around your security clearance."

"They were understandable, given all that's going on. I didn't take offense."

That wasn't what Oladele was asking. She knew darned well more than a security check had prompted Joaquin's interest in her new EA. Siobhan wasn't about to admit she'd slept with their new boss, though.

"I have a million questions," Siobhan said. "But I'm sure things will clarify as the merger completes."

That's the language you will use, Oladele had told her this morning, even as Joaquin had been swinging in here like a pirate with a cutlass clenched in his teeth, taking the ship by force.

"Don't stay too late," Oladele warned.

"I'm leaving right after I send this. I'll see you in the morning."

Ten minutes later, Siobhan hit Send and got a text from an unknown number before she had finished belting her coat.

Are you still at the office? We need to talk.

Her pulse skipped. She knew exactly who it was, but replied, New phone, who dis?

Her phone rang immediately.

"Hola." She glanced around to ensure she was the

only one in earshot. The floor was deserted, save for a janitor wiping down the break room. Even so, her nerves prickled as though she was doing something illicit yet titillating.

"I'm in my car." Joaquin's crisp voice abraded her nerves while fanning the heat in her middle. "I'm at least twenty minutes from the office. Traffic is a nightmare."

"That's why I take the metro." She forced a laissez-faire tone that was a complete fabrication.

"To where? Chamberí? That's where I was headed. I thought you would be home by now. I'll book you a car."

"You just said traffic is a nightmare."

"It is." He hissed out a curse. "I'll find a restaurant and text you the address."

"Why? No." There was a part of her that was…flattered? *Don't be stupid*, she quickly scolded herself. He didn't want to see her for romantic reasons. Today's acquisition had been very hostile. From what she'd gathered, Lorenzo had disowned Joaquin years ago. Joaquin probably still had doubts about her loyalty. "We've agreed nothing happened." It felt like a small victory to throw that in his face. "There's nothing else to say."

"We talk tonight or we don't talk at all," he said unequivocally.

He did want to fire her!

She looked at her phone, very tempted to tell him where he could shove this job and his arrogance, but she answered him anyway, "Oladele needs me, you know. This has been a very long day. I'm still in my work clothes. I want to go home, eat some instant noodles, then fall into bed. I'll see you tomorrow." So there.

"You're not eating instant noodles. I'll pick up takeout." He already ended the call.

What an annoying, domineering man. How had she ever found him attractive?

She knew how. *I'm interested. There's no improving on perfection.*

He had charmed her and she'd fallen for it. Duped again.

She shouldered her bag and left, wondering why he wanted to see her when it sounded as though he only wanted to dismiss her. He could do that with a memo from HR.

Losing her job was a distressing thought, but she didn't *need* to work the way some did. She had many fallback positions. She liked this job, though. She liked that she was supporting herself, building a relatively ordinary life where she was taken at face value, not seen as riding on nepotism or as a conduit to people who were more wealthy and powerful than she was.

What if he did want to see her for more personal reasons, though? The wicked, misguided trollop inside her gave a slither of glee, but she pushed her firmly back into her mental bedroom.

No. Nothing like that could happen between them. He might not be married, but he was her boss. And he'd walked out on her without a word in San Francisco, leaving her feeling discarded and devalued. She'd spent every day since trying to work out whether she was an idiot who didn't recognize a player when she met one, or trying to work out what she'd done in those last seconds that had been so horribly wrong he had run away the second she was out the door.

Her scorn carried her the rest of the way home, through the sea of commuters and holiday music.

She was genuinely exhausted as she walked from the

station to her building, barely taking note of the festive bower of street decorations and the bustle of Christmas shoppers.

Her weariness made sense. She'd been pushing herself for a long time. She had tutored to support herself in Australia, refusing to live off the nest egg she'd accumulated in her previous life. The day after exams, she flew to London to see her mother. That had been her first stop before she visited her sisters in America while prepping and interviewing for six very different jobs, including two in California.

By the time she returned to Sydney, she had circumnavigated the globe inside of two weeks and hadn't adjusted to the time zone before she'd been on a plane for her new life here in Madrid. She'd started work the day after landing and still hadn't finished unpacking.

Maybe she would skip eating and go straight to bed, she decided as she approached the front of her building. More than anything, she needed to catch up on her sleep.

A car arrived at the curb beside her. Joaquin smoothly exited the backseat. He'd changed from his suit into a more casual pair of dark trousers with a pullover and a raincoat that hung open as he slammed the car door.

The charge of masculine energy that came off him was so electric, she felt it like a snap of static grounding through her. She disguised it by nodding at the insulated takeout bag he held.

"Side hustle?"

"Considering what I paid to clear my father's debts, I need one." He nodded at the front door. "Let's eat. I'm starving."

CHAPTER FIVE

SHE WAS FAMISHED, too, which left little fight in her. Siobhan brought him into the building, vibrating with awareness of him and nearly wilting with hunger when the food aromas filled the elevator.

Inside her flat, he glanced around as he removed his coat and accepted the hanger she offered before she removed her own coat.

It was an older building. The rooms were small, but bright. Both the living room and bedroom had a thin balcony that looked onto an alley and an even more ornate and visually pleasing building across the way. The wall between the bedroom and living room had been partially removed and fitted with a pair of frosted glass doors that she left open to create a more spacious feel.

She was a tidy person. The bed was made and there was only a discarded scarf on it that she had decided not to wear at the last minute this morning. It still felt…intimate, heightening her jumpiness at having him in her personal space.

He doesn't want you, she reminded herself. She didn't know why he was here, but it wasn't that.

She took the food into the kitchen. It was a narrow galley that ended with a door into the minuscule bathroom, but the setup was efficient and it had a good-size pantry along with newish appliances.

Conscious of the impression he was gaining, she clarified, "It came furnished."

The sofa and chair were upholstered in a floral pattern that was too busy for her taste. She preferred contemporary styles and solid colors.

"I was lucky to find a sublet that I could get into right away. I love the location."

She never hung pictures of family so she would warm the space with paintings she'd purchased while living in Australia. They were on the floor, propped against the wall with framed, free-expression artwork made by her nieces and nephew.

She washed her hands, then set the table with the fragrant fideuà, which was a paella made with vermicelli noodles. It was piping hot and ready to serve in enameled cast-iron dishes with lids. Warm flatbread accompanied it along with tapenade, a salad and custard-filled buñuelos for dessert.

"Corkscrew?" he asked, showing her a bottle of white wine.

She handed it over with one glass. "None for me. If I have anything stronger than a glass of water, I'll be flat on the floor."

He set aside the bottle without opening it. "How hard has Oladele been working you?"

"It's not that." She refused to let him think she was anything but delighted by her job. "I haven't taken a proper break since before exams. Oladele said the office will close for Christmas on the nineteenth, though." That was only a week and a half away. "I'll catch up on my sleep then."

Oh, heck. She still had to finish her shopping for the children. Whether she joined her sister or not, she needed gifts for everyone.

"That's not the face of someone anticipating a break from work," he said, making her realize she'd revealed how daunted she was. And that he was watching her as closely as he had that night in San Francisco.

Disturbed, she explained, "I just remembered the Christmas shopping I have to finish."

"I wasn't sure if you celebrate. You don't have a tree." He flickered his gaze around her undecorated lounge.

"I haven't had time to get one." Truthfully, she hadn't made time. "My sister invited me to join them so there doesn't seem a point if I won't be here." That was her excuse for eschewing the wreaths and garlands she had once looked forward to hanging.

Last weekend, she had stayed with her nieces and nephew while Cinnia and Henri had flown to Paris for a function, hoping her weekend visit would excuse her from the holiday altogether, but the pressure had only increased.

You haven't had Christmas with us in five years, Cinnia had scolded. *Everyone wants you here. You know that.*

She did. And she wanted to see everyone. It wasn't the people she was avoiding. It was this time of year. She used to love all the joyful decor and festive traditions around Christmas, but these days they regressed her back to that heart-stopping moment when she'd realized how badly she'd messed up.

Pushing her dark thoughts aside, she waved an invitation for Joaquin to join her at the table. They both sat and tucked in without ceremony.

"You?" she asked, trying to make this extraordinary

situation feel normal when all she could think about was the way they'd flirted over drinks and fallen on each other with a different type of hunger.

This was the meal he had promised to order for them before he had dumped her.

Why did she let that continue to sting? He'd made it clear they were ships passing even before they'd slept together, then told her afterward that he wasn't someone to plan to share things with.

She had slept with him knowing they weren't likely to have a future and she'd been fine with it. It was only in the afterglow, when she'd been anticipating going back to him for the rest of the night, that she had indulged a few expectations, wondering if maybe there *could* be more between them.

She lifted her gaze and found him watching her with a pull of dismay in his brows.

He was even more aloof and unreadable than he'd been in San Francisco.

Her stomach curdled anew with the fear she'd done something wrong. Offended or disappointed or repelled him in some way.

"I was only asking what you do at this time of year. If that's a state secret you don't care to share…" She was trying to be ironic, but the joke fell flat. She looked hopelessly at her food, appetite evaporating.

He let the silence hang for an extra second before stabbing his dish as though it needed killing before eating.

"My brother used to invite me to join him and Zurina. I always refused because our father was also invited. Last year, I gave in for the children's sake. It was their first Christmas without Fernando and it turned into hell because my father was there. We despise each other, as you may have gathered." He closed his lip over a mouthful, pensive as he chewed and swallowed.

She had gotten that memo. It had slapped her in the face this morning in the form of Lorenzo's rage.

"This year, Zurina and her parents are spending a few weeks in the Canary Islands," he continued. "I put them on my plane this afternoon. She asked me to join them, but I'll work. Prepping for today pushed my own projects to the back burner. I need to catch up."

"I'm still trying to understand what happened today," she admitted wryly.

"Same," he said with pithy sarcasm, flickering his gaze over her face and shoulders in a way that made her feel off balance.

She dropped her eyes, hating herself for *liking* the feel of his gaze. For quietly willing something more visceral out of him.

"I called Killian about your security clearance. He said he knows you through clients. He declined to tell me who they are, but said you were at liberty to reveal that information if you chose to."

"I don't." Her heart clenched in a pulse of discomfort.

Out in the street, there was a faint jangle of sleigh bells. It was the only noise for a few seconds, amplifying his silence.

"My partnership with Killian is reciprocal," Joaquin said. "I supply some of his hardware. He ensures my proprietary designs are well protected. He wouldn't set me up for industrial espionage when it could compromise his own interests, but I still find your presence in my father's company too convenient."

"For who?" she snorted.

"See? It's problematic for both of us."

"You can't fire me just because I accidentally had sex with you! I didn't know you were buying the company I was coming to work at." Dismissing her would be worse than mean-spirited. It was a betrayal of how vulnerable and uninhibited she'd been that night. He had already tossed her away like trash once for it.

"I can't afford mistakes right now."

"I didn't know I was one." She quit the table abruptly. Angrily. "I told you I hadn't slept with anyone in ages and this is why." She pointed at the floor between them. "I didn't want a man derailing me from my aspirations again." She had sensed that he had the power to pull her off course, but had found him enthralling enough to risk it. "I never dreamed you were the sort to deliberately sabotage my career. Out of misguided spite."

"I'll help you find something else—"

"Oh, don't do me any favors," she snapped. "I know people if I want to get hired through nepotism. I don't."

She paced across her small lounge, but when she reached the door to the balcony, she was compelled to yank the drapes to block out the colored lights on the neighbor's balcony. They were another throbbing reminder of that other time she had been profoundly stupid where a man was concerned.

Maybe if Joaquin understood that she really was okay with keeping a firm distance between them, he would let her stay? A pang of humiliation wrenched behind her navel. She refused to beg leniency from a man who had already made it clear he didn't want her.

She would fight for her job, though. He didn't get to take her dignity *and* her nascent career.

"I won't tell you who Killian's clients are, but I'll tell you why I went to Australia to start over," she decided, turning to face him. "I was living with some of them in London. The man I was seeing used me to get information on them." She still felt sick when she thought of it. Her eyes grew hot with remorse. With a ferocious desire to reverse time. To go back and not be so caught up in romantic ideals. She'd been so naive. So *oblivious*.

"Killian didn't do a background check?" He turned in his chair to face her more fully.

"Sometimes people aren't bad until they decide to be bad." She gritted her teeth at the nausea rising in her throat. "I'm not sure if he dated me in a long game or realized after we started seeing each other that being close to me could be profitable. Either way, he fooled me into believing we were in love." Self-contempt clenched in her chest.

His expression seemed to harden as the silence thickened, growing potent. Maybe that was her imagination, though. Why would he care about her feelings for another man beyond seeing her as foolish for falling for him?

"I like to think I'm smart." She forced herself to keep talking. "I already knew people could be self-interested, but he seemed different. Keen and..." He didn't need to hear all the ways she'd fallen for Gilbert's charms. "It was coming up to Christmas. He wanted to meet the people who were close to me." She brushed at a tickle on her cheek. "I brought him into a world where I was entrusted to help keep the jackals out."

Still, Joaquin didn't say anything while remorse sat like a jagged rock in her throat. It stayed heavy and thorny in her chest.

"He put together an exposé on them," she said shakily. "Not a bad light, but it revealed a lot of personal information. He thought he could do it anonymously. He tried selling the story with photos of their children, even though he knew the family worked hard to keep their faces out of the public eye." She started to tear up, *so* ashamed. So angry at Gilbert and herself.

"Did they manage to quash it?" he asked grimly.

"Yes. Thankfully, they have the money and influence to buy stories like that before they're published. Then some of Killian's professionals paid him a visit to ensure he didn't have copies. He was a promising engineer, but as far as I know he now runs a fish-and-chip truck in a dodgy part of London. The whole thing sits in my gut like an ulcer."

She gripped her elbows, still stinging with the humiliation at allowing herself to be used. At knowing he hadn't wanted *her*.

"I realize that doesn't make me seem like a reliable person to have on your payroll, but the fact is, I know what it's like to be manipulated by sex and emotion. I would never do that to anyone. It's horrible."

His cheek ticked once before he swore and looked away, then scrubbed his hand over his face.

"It's not just you." He rose and took a few agitated steps. "It's *him*."

"Who?" Her pulse skipped at the way he was suddenly in motion. "Your father?"

"Yes. He's the reason I left San Francisco without speaking to you." The look he flashed her held something that relit the spark in her chest that she was trying very hard to smother.

She clenched a fist against the sensation. *Don't fall for it.*

"What happened?"

He pinched the bridge of his nose, sighing heavily before he dropped his hand to reveal a weary expression, one that sent a ring of empathy through her.

"The minute you left that night, I picked up a message from Zurina. My father was trying to force her to marry him. She was very upset."

The woman in the scarf? "She's far too young for him."

"He's seventy-two. She's twenty-eight," he agreed grimly. "She's also a very wealthy woman. She brought her own fortune to the marriage and inherited Fernando's shares in LV Global along with his very lucrative investment portfolio and other properties, including the family vineyard that Lorenzo gifted them on their wedding day."

"He needs the money?"

"Yes," he said bluntly. "I didn't know how deeply in debt he is because I don't care to know. When Fernando passed, he seized the chance to return to the helm and I didn't fight him because LVG isn't something I wanted. But he immediately used its cash reserves to pay down debts to cronies. He's been taking on more debt ever since, putting the company at risk. Market forces have played a part, but Lorenzo's incompetence is the bigger issue. Fernando spent a decade moving the organization into the modern age. Lorenzo wants to take it back to what was familiar to him. He brought in his yes-men. They're all dinosaurs. You met some of them today." He waved a disparaging hand.

Does anyone else care to waste my time?

"He's been pushing aggressively toward what was tried and true thirty years ago. The board has been watching the place capsize in real time and were pressuring him to bring me aboard. He was teasing me with it, but he had no intention of giving it to me so we were at an impasse. If not for Zurina and the children, I would have let him drown in his own red ink. But I can't do that."

She could feel the frustration and animosity coming off him in dangerous, radioactive waves. It wasn't directed at her, but it was still intimidating.

"So you bought up the debt to oust him."

"Yes. Zurina's support was vital to my takeover today. Also, now that I have control of her interest in LVG, she has less value to my father. He should leave her alone, but we'll see." He pushed his hand through his hair.

"Doesn't that put you in his line of fire instead?" she asked with concern.

He shrugged that off, expression remaining hard. "I long ago accepted that he will plague me until one of us dies. I expect him to use any means to sabotage me, my company and LVG, now that I've stolen it from him." His gaze swung to her, landing with a crash. "That includes you."

"Me?" A clunking sensation swept through her limbs. "How could he use me? *Why* would he?"

"Because he exploits anything he perceives as a weakness." His graveled tone made her heart roll to a halt in her chest. "If he learns we're personally involved, he'll use it."

"But...we aren't," she said faintly, realizing they *couldn't* be.

She had thought he was treating her with such coldness because he didn't like her. Because he had regrets about San Francisco. She'd been feeling very brushed off and hurt.

Now her brain was catching up to the fact he'd left her for a family emergency. One with higher stakes than she could have imagined. He hadn't owed any explanations to a woman he'd spent an hour with, no matter how intimately they'd spent that time. He had believed he would never see her again. That was why he hadn't come to her door to tell her all of this then.

As her shell of umbrage cracked and fell away, so did most of her defenses against him. A need to help rose like a force inside her.

"Keep me on," she urged. "I will be a valuable asset and no one will ever know we…" She swallowed whatever words might have described the way they'd knotted themselves together, wringing so much pleasure from a brief hour. "I promise."

She wasn't pleading for her job as much as a chance to keep seeing him, if only from afar.

His mouth tightened. The way he delved into her eyes with his narrowed gaze made her feel obvious. Naked. As though he read her motives as clearly as a neon sign.

His cheek ticked. Did he feel it, too? The temptation? The *want*?

A hot pressure of desperation arrived behind her breastbone. She looked away, blinking, trying to douse it with a measured breath.

"Fire me, then. I don't care," she lied while anguish slithered in her belly.

"You can stay," he said abruptly. "For now." He moved to the closet. "We won't talk of this again. San Francisco didn't happen."

She nodded jerkily while a flip-flopping sensation of relief and disappointment nearly pushed a whimper from her throat. This was what she wanted, wasn't it? She would keep her job. He wouldn't interfere in her life.

A weight sat on her chest as she came to the door and watched him shrug on his overcoat, though. A sense of lost potential. Deep in her fanciful brain, she had thought maybe destiny had brought them together again.

The reality was they hadn't had any sort of connection beyond sexual. She'd been a release valve for him at a time he was under a lot of pressure. Now that was firmly in the past.

"There's something I wished I'd done before you left my room that night," he said with a hard set to his jaw.

"What's that?" she asked, lifting her gaze with surprise.

"I should have said goodbye properly." His hand arrived at her waist and the other cradled the side of her neck, dragging her close.

Time turned to gelatin, making each movement slow and deliberate and profound. Her hands slid upward of their own accord, arriving at his shoulders to twine around his neck. She rose on tiptoe, offering her mouth without speaking another word, and dove her hand into the hair at the back of his head, urging him down.

Because she had longed for this, too. She had needed to know if it had been as good as she imagined.

It was.

As his lips sealed over hers, a sob left her, one of pain because the electric sensation of kissing him was too intense. It rang like a bell through her arms and across her chest, urging her grip to tighten around his neck. To cling. Because they couldn't *do* this.

For a long minute they did, though. They held fast to each other while they said *hello* and *I remember* and *goodbye* in the same long, poignant kiss. The thickness of his erection nudged against her aching mound and he could have easily taken her to her bed. She was ready to drag him there herself.

But he drew back abruptly, as though being wrenched from her by an invisible force.

It stung like a tear. Her heart pounded loud enough to deafen her ears. She kept her eyes closed, not wanting to face the inevitable. Not wanting him to see how utterly he owned her when he was, once again, the one pulling away.

She heard him take one shaken breath and the door closed behind him.

"See you tomorrow," she whispered.

CHAPTER SIX

Joaquin couldn't afford a single misstep. Lorenzo had retreated to his town house after the board overthrew him, but he was back at the office in the morning with a phalanx of lawyers, trying to retake his mantle.

Joaquin was no longer the teenaged boy with a black eye and nothing in his pockets, though. He had his own resources. He met his father inside the revolving door to the street with his own lawyers, a half dozen security guards and a "go quietly and this is yours" settlement offer.

After taking the envelope from Oladele, he held it out.

Lorenzo knocked it from his hand, berating him loudly for all the staff to hear as they hurried in from the street and headed to the elevator.

"You're making a fool of yourself." Joaquin cut through his tirade. "Take that offer. It includes a profit share in the estate in La Rioja and expires at midnight."

His father's hair nearly came off his head. "You can't take that from me! I gave it to your brother. It comes back to me."

"It will be secured in trust for your grandchildren." The sprawling vineyard was highly profitable and was another reason Lorenzo had pressured Zurina to marry him. "If you want a benefit from it, take that offer." Joaquin nodded at the floor, refusing to pick up the envelope.

"You think you're getting the better of me, don't you?" Lorenzo stepped forward to poke his chest.

"I've never seen anything but the worst of you." Joaquin curled his lip. "Touch me again and you'll see the worst of *me*."

As he stared down his father, his inner antennae prickled. Siobhan walked by in his periphery.

Joaquin didn't look, but he caught tall boots kicking a tweed skirt as she circled their group. Their kiss last night had tasted like champagne and hunger. Like the things they'd done when they had wrecked a hotel bed. Like the things he wanted to do with her again.

Leaving her last night had nearly pulled his soul from his body. He'd definitely left a piece of himself there with her.

But even though he felt her gaze on him, he didn't *allow* himself to look at her. It would betray his interest to Lorenzo.

Lorenzo looked at her, though. Among his thousands of faults, he was a lecher for young women, which was objectionable any day of the week. Today his attention on Siobhan was beyond galling. It was revolting.

"Leave now," Joaquin said in gritty warning.

Lorenzo swung his gaze back to Joaquin's, teeth bared in a sneer. He was trying to work out whether Joaquin's hostility was purely due to his presence here or if it had gone up a notch upon Siobhan's arrival.

Oladele picked up the envelope and handed it to one of Lorenzo's lawyers.

"This isn't a negotiation. It's that or nothing." Joaquin pointed at the envelope.

His father spit on Joaquin's shoes.

Joaquin spit right back and held his father's glare of outrage. He would not back down. Not anymore.

Siobhan stood transfixed as she watched Oladele set a hand on Joaquin's sleeve in a gentle signal to hold his temper in check.

"This isn't over," Lorenzo declared before storming out.

The elevator pinged next to her. Siobhan scrambled to grasp at the door, waiting while Joaquin strode toward her with his entourage of suits.

She had taken far too long deciding what to wear today, eventually choosing a short jacket in earthy brown over a tweed skirt with a fedora to protect her hair from the rain. She offered a hesitant smile as Joaquin approached, but his gaze skimmed past her, making her stomach clench in embarrassment at trying to engage him.

She looked to the floor, still confused by his kiss after making it so clear to her that they couldn't be anything but boss and employee.

Everyone stepped into the elevator. No one spoke as it rose, but the air was thick with undercurrents. She picked out Joaquin's aftershave among the other fragrances in the small space and drew it deep, filling her nostrils with the tangy, tangible feel of his cheek brushing her jaw. His hungry lips devouring hers.

Her face felt stiff with the effort of maintaining a neutral expression. It took all her effort not to glance at him as she departed with Oladele onto their floor.

She tried very hard not to betray her awareness of Joaquin, but within hours, they were called to the boardroom next to his office.

Others were already there, including Joaquin's assistant, a young man she'd met briefly yesterday. Siobhan sent him a friendly, "Good morning."

The other man returned her smile with a warm one of his own that quickly turned to a daunted look aimed beyond her shoulder.

She followed his line of sight to Joaquin.

He hit her with a cool stare of disapproval, one that peeled a layer from her composure, leaving her raw.

With an indignant lift of her chin, she took her seat behind Oladele while Joaquin shifted his attention to his laptop.

"Lorenzo has rejected the settlement offer and has begun a counterassault. He is claiming to still be CEO until the shareholders vote otherwise. He's also smearing my reputation and bringing ProFab into it." That was Joaquin's company in Barcelona. "Pursue defamation charges. He must have signed nondisclosure agreements that prevent him from discussing the inner workings of LVG. See if he's still bound by that."

Oladele nodded and glanced at Siobhan to make a note.

"I'll look into the D&O liability insurance, too," Siobhan said. "Directors and officers," she explained as everyone looked at her. "Its purpose is to cover unintentional negligence, but if he was the CEO, and deliberately causes the devaluation of his company, he could be exposing himself to legal consequences. There may be a means to pursue charges. Perhaps letting him know that would encourage him to back down."

Oladele made an approving noise and several heads nodded, but Joaquin only pinned her with an inscrutable look before turning his attention to the head of accounting, requesting an audit to prove that his father had been fabricating numbers during his tenure.

The meeting broke up and Joaquin walked out, leaving a wake of relieved exhales behind him.

As everyone rose, Oladele said, "Siobhan, will you ask Joaquin if he's had a chance to review the documents I sent this morning? I have to return this call."

"Of course." Overcoming a wave of trepidation, Siobhan went to his door, which was open. He was standing at his desk, tapping on the keyboard of his laptop. She knocked.

"Come in. Close the door," he said as he saw her.

"Oh. I'm only here to ask…" She slipped in and pressed the door closed behind her. "Oladele is wondering if you've had time to review the documents she sent?"

"I was about to do it. What's going on with you and my assistant? HR frowns on office romance."

She stood taller, insulted when his assistant was a virtual stranger and *San Francisco didn't happen.*

"Has the policy changed?" she asked archly. "Because I read all of them when I onboarded. HR asks to be informed of romantic relationships to mitigate liability. If necessary, they will transfer employees without penalty." She responded to his elevated brow with a sugary smile. "I do my homework."

"Is that the long way of saying *nothing*?"

"Yes." The heat of humiliation began climbing from her throat. "I know you think I'm fast, but I'm not frequent about it." She turned to yank on the door latch so she didn't have to stand here boiling in his ugly judgment of her.

"I didn't say that," he growled behind her.

"You implied it." She pulled on the door.

"Wait," he commanded.

She set her teeth and held the door open, forcing a bored expression onto her face as she turned back to him.

"That was a good idea about the D&O insurance," he said begrudgingly. "It won't work—"

"Is that a compliment? Because you've buried it," she mocked.

"Lorenzo doesn't scare easily," he continued without reacting to her sarcasm. "But I can see that you're looking for fresh angles of attack. That's the sort of ingenuity I appreciate in the people who work for me. Let me know if you find something with teeth."

Oh. He really was complimenting her.

Was she supposed to say thank you? You're welcome?

She definitely wasn't supposed to stand here gawking while he said impassively, "Anything else?"

"No." She left, flushed and disconcerted by the entire exchange.

The rest of the week passed in similar encounters where Joaquin largely ignored her unless she had the nerve to speak up. He never berated her for offering an opinion, but he didn't express overt appreciation again.

She kept reminding herself that they had both agreed—that she wanted as much as he did—to leave their one-night stand in the past.

But she still experienced a thrill of anticipation each time Oladele said, "We're needed upstairs."

Simply being in a room with Joaquin wired her with excitement.

"I know this has been a demanding time," Joaquin said on Friday afternoon, wrapping up a meeting in the boardroom where someone had brought homemade polvorónes, a shortbread-style cookie, and anise-flavored crumble cookies called mantecados. "You've earned your weekend. Rest up and give me your best for one more week. Then we can all relax through the Christmas break."

Rather than leave as he usually did, he hung back to answer a question from someone in PR.

"Gracias," Siobhan murmured as she moved past them.

"Oh, that's you, Ms. Upton," Joaquin said with an ironic quirk of his mouth. "I didn't recognize you in your glasses."

Her pulse tripped over the fact he had noticed her at all, let alone such a tiny detail. She touched the navy-blue frames.

"Is that a joke?" She couldn't believe he was making one, not that he had failed to recognize her.

"Yes." The corner of his mouth indented with self-deprecating amusement.

Someone said something about superhero disguises and conversation turned to the latest blockbuster scheduled to release over the holidays.

She followed the crowd to the elevators, not letting herself look back, but she was still replaying his remark, shyly gratified to have provoked his almost-smile.

"Siobhan." Oladele hurried out from her office as Siobhan arrived at her desk. "This was delivered by courier while we were upstairs." She handed over an envelope. "Joaquin needs to see it. See if you can catch him before he leaves."

Siobhan hurried back to the elevator, past his assistant at the reception desk, and found him locking his office door at the end of the empty corridor.

"Oh, good. I thought I might miss you." She strode toward him. "Oladele said this was left on her desk while we were in the meeting." She halted as she reached him, but had the strangest sensation of continuing forward. She slapped a hand on the wall, catching her balance, alarmed.

A firm hand wrapped around her arm. "Are you all right?"

"No," she said reflexively. "Yes. I'm not sure. Just a little dizzy. I think I caught a bug."

Heat suffused her at the way his grip eased, but his hand stayed on her arm. She looked at it, wondering if he could feel the way her muscles were melting and her blood was turning to honey.

He released her and his fingers rubbed into his palm.

She adjusted her glasses and cleared her throat. "I was with my sister's kids last weekend. I love them to death, but children are walking petri dishes."

"Reason number one million why I never plan to have them." He shook the pages from the opened envelope.

"Really? That surprises me."

He paused to lift his gaze, snagging hers without effort.

She didn't know how to interpret that and quickly babbled, "It's just that I read you were engaged last year. That suggests you were planning to start a family."

"Siobhan. This conversation is inappropriate." He used an even tone and he wasn't wrong, but she took his remark like a slap. One she deserved.

He had expressed a normal concern for a coworker and she had let it devolve into telling him her life history and admitted to looking him up. Bringing up his romantic history, asking him about his plans to have children, was totally offside. The fact that *they* had a history between them pushed her inquiry from nosy into the sort of thing one asked an intimate partner as a compatibility check.

While her cheeks flamed with chagrin, she glanced over her shoulder. The doors to the corridor were closed, but they might not be as alone as they thought. His assistant had still been at his desk by the elevators. There could be stragglers in the boardroom.

"I'm sorry," she said, stricken and unable to raise her eyes to see what was in his expression. "I'll go." She pivoted one foot.

"Let me see what this is first," he muttered and glanced over the cover letter then swore tiredly. "My father is taking LV Global to court. This is what sort of man he is." He fluttered the pages in impotent fury. "He would rather lock me into years of court appearances and legal fees, demonstrating to the entire world that he is no longer fit to run this company, than accept that irrefutable fact. Give this back to Oladele. Tell her we'll discuss it Monday. Then go home and get some rest."

She wordlessly took the papers, fighting to keep her chin up as he walked alongside her to the elevator. Did he *have* to step into it with her? The space felt so claustrophobic she could hardly breathe. She kept replaying her *inappropriate* words, feeling unbearably gauche.

"You could make this easier," he said as the elevator descended. "Wear ugly clothes. Stop showering."

They were both staring straight ahead. For a second, she wondered if she had heard him correctly. Then she thought about telling him *that* was inappropriate, but a tiny glow flickered to life in her chest and began to expand, warming her to her fingertips and toes.

Every day she came to work anticipating her moments with him, and every day she felt tortured by them. Let down, even. She thought about their kisses and their lovemaking far too often. She reminded herself constantly that they weren't going back to that.

But he seemed to be telling her that he still felt this awareness, too. This attraction.

As the elevator stopped on her floor, she said, "I'm probably carrying a deadly plague."

The doors opened.

"See? Was that hard?" he drawled.

She bit back her pleased smile as she walked away.

CHAPTER SEVEN

Siobhan ignored Joaquin's order to rest and spent the weekend Christmas shopping.

She even made a point of watching children who were blinking in wonderment at toys and pausing to listen to a choral group singing before a massive decorated tree, trying to remind herself why she used to love Christmas so much.

It cheered her a little, but she couldn't seem to shake a leaden feeling in her limbs. No actual sniffles or cough arrived, though. She wasn't running a fever or even feeling achy. She was merely tired and her stomach was a little unsettled so she stuck to bland foods and skipped coffee and wine, hoping to feel better by Monday.

She didn't, but she wasn't any worse so she didn't feel justified calling in sick. There was still so much to do and she didn't want to let Joaquin down.

She didn't want to miss a chance to see him. That was the real reason.

You could make this easier.

She'd been deeply stung when he had rebuffed her remark about his engagement. All she had been able to learn online was that it had been announced a few weeks before his brother passed and was called off shortly after.

But he was right. It was very personal and none of her business. She shouldn't have brought it up at work or anywhere else.

She had been deeply surprised by his *reason one million* for not wanting children, though. It had struck a pang of distress in her because she wanted children someday. She didn't really believe in fate, either, but the way she and Joaquin had come together so coincidentally after parting in San Francisco had made her secretly wonder if greater forces were conspiring to throw them together.

His aversion to children told her they weren't as sympatico as she'd hoped. Not that she should have any hopes where he was concerned. Even if he was physically attracted to her, his remark in the elevator told her he didn't want to be.

She wished she had his Teflon air of aloofness. It was taking all her effort to hide her crush on her boss while he looked through her half the time and, when he did acknowledge her, put up barriers so quickly afterward, it was like walking into a glass wall, halting her in her tracks.

Despite that, she inwardly jumped for joy when she picked up an email from him, addressed to her and Oladele.

I'll be meeting with investors all week. I don't want any delay in responding to my father's legal action. My assistant has instructions that I can be interrupted at any time if you need my signature or authorization to keep things moving.

Twice that day, Oladele handed Siobhan a folder and asked her to run upstairs. Twice Siobhan gave strangers an apologetic smile while she patiently waited for Joaquin to skim the paperwork and sign off.

"I'm confused," she told Oladele when she returned the second time. "Why is he meeting investors individually? It doesn't seem very efficient. Why doesn't he hold a conference call and be done with it?"

"My educated guess is that these are his own investors in ProFab. Lorenzo is trying to undermine him, suggesting Joaquin took on too much debt by purchasing LVG. Lorenzo wants them to pressure Joaquin to back off, but he's reassuring them instead, and doing it in Lorenzo's office, which is a nice touch." Oladele's mouth quirked.

Siobhan had to admire the power move. "I guess coming here shows them what he's purchased, too."

"The personal touch will have a ripple effect. Word will spread," Oladele added.

It was the sort of tactic Siobhan's brother-in-law would use. Why host a press conference if a whisper campaign was more effective?

She started back to her desk, then paused.

"Can I ask... How did you meet Joaquin?" That wasn't really what she wanted to know.

"Through Fernando. Joaquin sometimes came to the parties he and Zurina hosted." Oladele gave her a circumspect look. "If you're asking if I conspired with Joaquin to oust Lorenzo, I did not. I could tell the board was leaning toward handing things to Joaquin, but Zurina spearheaded that. Lorenzo left me a voice mail the morning it happened, asking why the board was meeting without him. I didn't know it was happening until it was."

"I'm sorry. I wasn't implying that you acted improperly. I know you wouldn't," Siobhan assured her.

"I don't think you would act improperly, either." Oladele held her gaze for an extra millisecond, allowing the significance of her statement to sink in before she switched back to work mode. "Can you get Señora Perez on the phone for me?"

"Of course."

Oladele knew, *knew* there was more to Siobhan's relationship with Joaquin than either of them admitted to. Should she confess that their romance had lived and died before she got here?

Tuesday was more of the same. As Siobhan was searching through old records, Oladele handed her a folder.

"Upstairs?" Siobhan guessed.

"Sí, por favor."

Siobhan hurried to the elevator with too much eagerness. She waved the folder at Joaquin's assistant, who nodded at her to approach the inner sanctum. She moved down the hall, past the empty boardroom and paused when she found a bodyguard stationed at Joaquin's door.

It was the first time she'd seen one here, but it was a fairly normal sight to her because Cinnia and all of her in-laws employed them. That was how Siobhan knew Killian. He handled all the security for her sister's family. Siobhan had taken self-defense classes with one of his instructors when she'd been a teenager and still practiced on a regular basis.

She showed her work badge to the man, but before she could knock, the door was pulled inward.

Joaquin's voice was saying, "—appreciate your making time—"

He cut himself off as he noticed her.

"¿Firma, por favor?" She waved the folder as an explanation and stepped back to allow his guest to exit. Her

cheeks warmed with pleasure at how arrested Joaquin had seemed by the sight of her, though.

"Give my best to your family," Joaquin said absently.

"I will," promised a male voice as a strange man stepped out.

Siobhan had conjured a polite smile for Joaquin's guest, but it fell off her face. He wasn't a stranger at all. The handsome man in his forties was very well-known to her.

"Dorry," he said with surprise.

"Ramon." Siobhan breathed the name with shock and enough familiarity to raise Joaquin's hackles.

He'd started to open the door and found her unexpectedly outside it. In that millisecond of being hit by the sight of her, he'd been taken aback by how beautiful she was. By how *pleased* he was to see her.

Today she wore a thick gray knit dress that fell to the tops of her knee-high boots. A chunky belt of square silver links nipped at her waist, and its neckline draped like a scarf. Nothing about it was particularly sexy or daring, but she made it look runway chic.

Then Ramon Sauveterre stepped out and *hugged* her.

A deeply regressive emotion exploded through Joaquin. He clamped down on it, but the atavistic taste for blood stayed on his tongue.

Because Siobhan hugged Ramon back. And she offered the other man a bemused, untampered laugh. Not the kind she muted as quickly as it formed, the way she'd been doing around here, if she suddenly realized he was watching her. This was natural and lovely and full of genuine affection.

"It's good to see you." Ramon hung on to her arms,

continuing to smile fondly at her. "I knew you'd taken a job in Madrid. I didn't know it was here. I've already sent the family south, but I wanted to take this meeting." He glanced at Joaquin with bemusement.

Whatever was in Joaquin's face erased Ramon's good-natured humor. He pulled his brows together. The temperature in the corridor dropped several degrees.

"I do work here." Siobhan's tone grew reproachful. "And everyone here knows me as Siobhan."

"Oh, hell." Ramon gave his jaw a rub then held out his palm. "My bad, but when have I ever had to call you that?"

"Today. Right now. This is the moment you were supposed to call me that."

They shared a look of laughter and apology and history. So much history it made Joaquin want to pull Siobhan into his office and lock out everyone else, most especially his too-suave business partner.

Joaquin had never been a jealous person. He hadn't been allowed to be. He'd had a taste of it with his assistant last week and learned the emotion didn't sit well with him. At all.

"*How* are you two acquainted?" he asked coolly.

"Oh. Um." Siobhan folded her arms and flickered a look between them.

"I'll let you fill him in." Ramon gave her shoulder a squeeze. "My plane is waiting. Do you need a lift? Should I wait for you?"

"No, I need to work, but thank you. I'll see you again soon."

Ramon kissed both her cheeks, needling the green monster within Joaquin before he gave Joaquin a last thoughtful look and left with his bodyguard.

Joaquin opened his door wider and jerked his head at Siobhan to enter.

"What—" he said as he pushed the door closed with a hard click "—was that?"

"Someone I know." She shrugged it off, avoiding his gaze as she set the folder on his desk. "Oladele is waiting for this. Do you mind? I have a lot of work that needs to be finished by end of day, and the big boss is looking for any excuse to fire me." She delivered the facetious remark with a distant smile that could have come from his own arsenal.

He hated it.

"Tell me." He approached the desk and closed his hand over the pen she held out, capturing her fingers in his grip. Not tightly. Just enough to hold her full attention. Just enough to hold *her* and convince himself she was, in some small way, his. For now.

"You're asking me to share something highly personal." She could have pulled her hand away, but she didn't. Her chin went up a notch. Her lashes flickered and he thought her breath stuttered. "Too personal for the workplace." *Inappropriate*, her defiant glare said as she slid a pointed glance to his grip on her hand.

She was getting back at him for that day in the corridor, when he'd told her she was out of line with her personal question about children. He'd felt small when he'd slapped it down, but every moment around her was a struggle. Even as he commuted to the office, before he saw her, he would wonder what she would be wearing today. Hair up or down? Glasses or contacts? Heels or boots? Did he have a meeting scheduled that would bring her up to his floor? Or did he have to engineer a glimpse of her from afar?

Then, when he did see her, he had to fight the urge to fall into bantering with her. He fought standing too close. Fought asking her to dinner. Fought pulling her near—

He wanted to yank her into his arms right now.

He let go of her hand.

The pen dropped to the desktop.

"Tell me how you know him or I'll imagine you were lovers." He drew the folder closer, pretending disinterest even though his vision was still violent green.

She made a choked noise. "Why would you care if we were?"

"I care," he ground out and jerked up his head.

Her breath cut in and her eyes flared wide at whatever she read in his face. Her mouth softened and her jaw went slack.

Angry with himself for revealing so much, frustrated at this sensation of being eaten alive, he said bitingly, "I thought you had hard boundaries around adultery. He's been married for years. They have children."

"I know that," she said with a flash of her own temper. "My sister is married to his brother."

"Henri?" Joaquin had met Ramon's identical twin on more than one occasion along with both their wives. "Your sister is Cinnia?" The resemblance seemed obvious now as he looked past Siobhan's dark hair. "This is the wealthy family you're related to?"

"Yes." She folded her arms and radiated defensiveness. "Why does it matter?"

Because *wealthy* was a gross understatement. Joaquin was wealthy. The Sauveterre family, two pairs of identical twins, were celebrities. The younger pair of girls was *royalty*. The family's wealth and fame had made them targets, though. When Ramon and Henri had been teenagers, one of their sisters had been kidnapped. She'd been recovered and all the siblings were married with children of their own now, but they still maintained a heavy security presence as a precaution.

"When your boyfriend took those unauthorized photos, it was them?"

"Ex," she corrected tightly. "Yes. Ramon's children. I was staying with them while I went to Cambridge."

"Why?"

"I was working on my language degree."

"Why were you staying with them?" he spelled out.

"Because I was going to Cambridge," she said with exasperation. "Ramon was working out of the London office. Izzy had just had their twins. They had nannies, but I had already helped Cinnia with their twins and Izzy doesn't have siblings. She didn't have a network in London and needed someone she..." She cleared her throat. "Someone she could trust. It seemed like a win-win for me to stay with them."

"But it wasn't? Because of what your ex did?"

"I don't want to talk about it." Her shoulders hunched in disgrace.

"Why did Ramon call you Dorry?" he asked in confusion.

"I told you I changed my name."

"Yes, but why?"

"Why do you want to know?" Her voice thinned with persecution.

"Because you don't need this job." He stabbed at his desktop. "Which makes me wonder why you fought so hard to keep it."

"Oh, my *gawd*," she muttered, striding toward the pair of sofas that faced each other over a coffee table. "You're right. I don't need to work. Henri has been paying me an outrageous allowance since I went to live with him and Cinnia at fourteen, when she had *their* twins."

"They didn't have nannies?"

"Yes, but Cin was actually very sick when she delivered them and they were taken by C-section. Plus, she and Henri had just got back together. He thought she would feel isolated if she didn't have family around. I was already homeschooling and helping Cin with her estate practice so it made sense. I stayed because I liked being part of their family." Her voice softened and she traced the seam on the back of the sofa. "Henri's siblings all treated me like I was one of them. It was nice."

"He still supports you?"

"No." She crinkled her brow at him. "You must know their family history, that Henri's sister was kidnapped when they were young?"

"Of course." It had dominated the headlines, especially here in Spain.

"Henri is very careful about security because of that. He wanted me to live with them because he knew I was safe there. He put me through the self-defense courses that Cin and his sisters took and I was drilled on all the security protocols. I knew what was at stake and didn't make social profiles, but Dorry Whitley was well-known enough that if people heard my name, they would ask me about them. I learned to spot when I was being befriended because someone wanted access to them. Then I missed one."

"What's his name?"

"Putrid McDogmeat." She stood with her arms folded, back stiff. "I had always felt wrong about accepting Henri's support. It felt as though I was being paid to be Auntie Dorry. When I put Ramon's children at risk..." She shuddered. "I couldn't be on the family payroll after that."

"Did Henri blame you? Because Ramon doesn't seem to be holding any grudges."

"No. They've always been very magnanimous. Ramon says it was his mistake because he allowed me to introduce Gilbert to his children. But it was *my* mistake. *I* dated the man. *I* vouched for him." She turned to stab between her breasts. "I couldn't stay with them after that. And I didn't want any footprints leading back to them, either. I moved to Australia and asked Killian to give me a new ID and school records, so I wasn't Dorry Whitley anymore. I kept a low profile, worked my butt off for top grades and got this job on my own merit. That actually means a lot to me. I *like* being Siobhan Upton."

Joaquin leaned his hip on the desk. "That's not the only reason, though, is it?"

"For what?"

"For changing your name. You don't want to be Dorry because you're mad at her. You're punishing her."

"No." She scowled into the middle distance, mouth twitching sullenly. "Maybe. I deserve to be punished. It was a horrible, dangerous mistake."

"You're being too hard on yourself."

"You're entitled to your opinion even if you're wrong." She looked to the side.

He snorted and moved close enough to catch her gaze. "I'm never wrong. Like you, I'm perfect. Never make mistakes."

She frowned, mouth pouting. "Can you please—" she cleared her throat "—not tell anyone who I am?"

"I won't say a word," he assured her.

"Thank you." Her shoulders relaxed. "I just don't want people to..."

"I understand." It was a lot to carry. He was annoyed that Henri had put that much pressure on her, but he also had the impression she put a lot on herself.

Dios, her scent went to his head when he stood this close. It wasn't bold enough to be perfume. It was a subtle combination of shampoo and hand cream and the summer peach fragrance of *her*. He searched for its source, gaze tracking into her throat then back to her cheeks.

She tilted her head back and her gaze tangled with his. She licked her lips.

He was a man, not a machine. With temptation this close and the nip of jealousy still in his blood, his resistance to her all but vanished. He hooked his finger in her belt and tugged, inviting her closer.

She flowed into him so he was able to slide his arms around the soft column of her. His mouth found hers and her taste washed through him. Lust flexed its claws deep into his skin, fueling his hands in their quest to map her shape and meld her to his front.

"Joaquin," she moaned as he sought the fragrant skin of her throat. Her arms climbed behind his neck so it was no effort at all to hitch her hips onto the back of the sofa and push her skirt up, exposing her thighs in thin black leggings to his restless hands.

This was where he had longed to be again. He pushed deeper into the V of her thighs until he felt the heat of her against the ridge of his erection. Until her mouth was firmly under his again so he could devour her.

The wrinkled suede of her boots pressed erotically against the backs of his legs, urging him to press harder. The gorgeous weight of her breast filled his hand, her nipple pebbled firmly enough he could feel it through the knit. He set his other hand on her tailbone, the bar of his arm keeping her from falling to the cushions while he ground himself against her.

She said something. It could have been a demand or a plea. He didn't know. All he knew was that he was starving and needed this. *Her.*

As lust began to overwhelm him, compelling him to claim her, he drew her back onto her feet and turned her to face the back of the sofa.

She gasped and thrust her ass against his fly, crushing the ridge of his erection in the most delicious way. He dragged her skirt up and caught the waistband of her leggings, starting to drag them down, revealing her round ass and the midnight-blue lace that cut across her cheeks.

He followed the dark line of color with his fingertips into the crevice of her thighs, seeking the heat. The dampness. The welcoming clasp of her sheath as he delved into paradise.

She moaned in a way that stroked him like velvet and arched her back. Inviting him to explore deeper. To take.

Condom, he thought and glanced around, only then seeing where he was.

He cursed crudely and pulled his touch away too roughly, pulling back from her so abruptly, she gasped in shock and clung to the sofa while she sent him a wild look over her shoulder.

"What's wrong?"

She was nearly irresistible with that sensual flush and her heavy eyelids and her pupils shot wide with passion.

"I didn't lock the door. *This* is a dangerous mistake, Siobhan." She *worked* for him.

She gasped and yanked her clothes back into order,

mouth taking on a bruised pout, eyes wide with speechless hurt. Her ankle wobbled and he tried to steady her, but she disdainfully pulled from his touch.

"Leave the folder with your assistant," she said in a hollow voice. "I need the ladies' room."

"Siobhan." He took a step to go after her, then stopped himself. *Damn it.*

He was her employer. He couldn't *do* this.

How had this even happened. He had been succeeding at treating her like any other employee until— No. He hadn't. If he was brutally honest with himself, he would recognize that even when he wasn't overstepping boundaries, he was a little harder on her, a little slower to offer praise, taking care not to reveal so much as a hint of favoritism toward her.

He was trying to *protect* her, though. She saw every day the lengths Lorenzo would go to strike at him. Surely, she understood why this couldn't happen?

Who could comprehend it, though? Really? He didn't fully understand Lorenzo's hatred of him. Lorenzo had been equally hard on Fernando, but had at least acknowledged Fernando's position as his heir and groomed him accordingly. For years it had merely been favoritism of one son over the other, but once Lorenzo had been back here at LVG, it had become outright efforts to sabotage Joaquin. Why?

Yes, he'd been a boisterous child, always getting into things. He saw the same energy and curiosity in his nephew and knew it was easy to see that behavior as defiance.

We caught him putting his dinosaurs in the toaster, Fernando had said of the boy during one of their last conversations. *Pulled a chair over to reach it. He wanted to know what would happen.*

Fernando had been nonplussed, but proud of the boy's ingenuity and desire to experiment.

Lorenzo had never been proud of Joaquin, though. He'd saved his praise for Fernando, who'd been smart and athletic, but also deferential and disciplined. Lorenzo had blamed his wife for Joaquin's strongmindedness. *Teach him his place*, Lorenzo had told her many times.

Then his mother had left and Lorenzo had taken on putting Joaquin in his place with his own firm hand. Fernando had intervened as often as he could, but Lorenzo had swung enough at both of them that it made little difference. He preferred to punish his youngest, though. The one who didn't matter.

There were times Joaquin had kept himself on a tight leash, thinking maybe, if he was good enough, his mother would come back. She had sworn to him that Lorenzo had driven her away, not him, but he still blamed himself. He was too quick to speak out, always determined to find a way to whatever he wanted even if he would be punished for it.

He knew now that his mother had taken the brunt of Lorenzo's anger until she feared for her life, never dreaming her husband would turn on their sons. Then Lorenzo had undermined her financially and socially, making it impossible for her to gain custody of them.

Eventually, Joaquin had realized how much abuse she had taken on his behalf and, in a twisted way, was glad she had left so he didn't have to worry about her.

Then there was Esperanza. Joaquin never would have engaged himself to her if he had known he would wind up back in his father's sphere. From the moment Lorenzo was introduced to her at Fernando's wake, Lorenzo had behaved intolerably toward her. When she broke their engagement a few weeks later, Joaquin knew it was for the best that she distance herself from him.

Women didn't fare well when they were attached to him. Even his brief liaisons were fraught with the same thing that was plaguing Siobhan right now—he was aloof. Inaccessible. Not outwardly cruel, but carrying a history that left him stunted. Unable to attach.

Women left him and he let them go for their sake and his own.

He wasn't letting Siobhan go, though. He kept trying to make himself relegate her to his past, but every time he pushed her away, he felt as though he was peeling away his own skin.

Even so, this obsession with her *had* to stop.

CHAPTER EIGHT

SIOBHAN HAD A restless night. She tossed and turned, reliving how Joaquin had been so antagonistic about Ramon. Jealous?

That was what she'd thought when he'd declared so angrily, *I care*.

He had startled her enough that she'd spilled her guts over how badly she'd misjudged Gilbert and his feelings toward her.

Joaquin had seemed so kind, then. He'd sounded as though he really did care.

Flowing into his embrace had felt as natural as it had every other time. And she ought to know by now that an explosion of passion would happen, but it had caught her off guard, being even more powerful than she expected. She would have made love with him in his office! Anyone could have walked in on them.

She covered her hot face thinking of her abandonment and the way that he had put such a cold stop to it, as though he was barely affected at all.

He didn't care. Not really. Not the way she longed for someone to care about her.

Once again, she was fooling herself into seeing what she wanted to see.

To hell with him, she resolved as she dressed for work.

She had tried to make it clear to him that she needed to support herself financially because she didn't feel right leaning on people she'd let down. She resented how he was making her ability to do so seem *impossible*.

She jerked her brush through her hair hard enough to bring tears to her eyes, gathering it in a low ponytail as if it was Casual Friday when it was only Tuesday.

She had a *plan*. A few weeks from the end of this mat cover, she would start looking for an entry-level management position. Maybe in Miami, she thought spitefully, even though her sister's life there was very WAG-centric with lots of hours devoted to hair and nails and parties as she kept up with the trends set by the other wives and girlfriends of the athletes.

Those athletes had a lot of money, though, and there were a lot of contracts for sponsorships that needed a sharp eye to dot i's and cross t's.

Alternately, she could move back to London and find something in banking or insurance. Or try San Francisco again. Programmers were a dime a dozen, but a lot of them worked on contract. There was a ton of opportunity for her there.

Now that she was gaining experience in acquisition at this tech company, she would be an even stronger candidate there.

So yes, Joaquin, I need this job, she silently shouted across the city at him.

She refused, absolutely refused, to let him jeopardize it.

Not that she brought her best game to the office when she finally got there. She felt hungover, nursing a vague nausea that she blamed on her lack of sleep.

When are you arriving? her sister texted midmorning. *The children are asking.*

She ignored Cinnia's message, feeling too overwhelmed to think about Christmas when she still needed to get through the week.

And the staff party, she was reminded when someone came around collecting final numbers.

"Are you bringing a date?" they asked.

A wicked vision of Joaquin flashed in her mind. Would he ask her to dance? *Oh, stop it*, she scolded herself. What was she? Twelve? Ugh.

"I haven't even found something to wear," she replied, wishing she could bow out altogether, but these sorts of events were valuable networking opportunities. She would push through.

"We're needed upstairs," Oladele said, arriving at her desk to interrupt them.

Siobhan smiled a weak apology and gathered her things, accompanying Oladele to the elevator.

"You seem pale today," Oladele noted. "Are you unwell?"

"It's this color." She plucked at the mustard-toned pullover. "I should give it away because it washes me out, but it's one of my comfort wears." The thick, soft knit felt like a hug.

"I have a cardigan like that. It's full of holes. I can't leave the house in it, but I refuse to throw it away."

They continued joking about their reluctance to break up with favorite clothing until they walked into the boardroom.

Joaquin was already there with several other people. His gaze swept over her in a way that scraped at her composure.

Siobhan sobered and averted her eyes, heart squeezed by the vise of her behavior yesterday.

No more, she resolved as she took her seat behind Oladele and opened her laptop, preparing to take notes. She might respond to him physically, but that was a trick of chemistry that meant nothing. She was setting higher standards for herself.

They were *over*.

Joaquin had steeled himself against so much as looking at Siobhan when she arrived for the meeting, but his damned inner radar had heard her voice approaching and turned his head.

Now, as he quickly ran through the agenda, making swift decisions around reallocating resources, all he could see was lipstick the color of pink gelato against a pale complexion, a chunky yellow knit clinging to narrow shoulders, and breasts he'd caressed as recently as yesterday.

The tension in his abdomen, and lower, came out in his voice.

"Where are we at with the defamation charges?" he asked Oladele, stubbornly keeping his gaze on her, not the stony, downcast face behind her.

"I was going to chase that this morning, but was sidetracked by a complaint lodged against me at the General Council's office," Oladele said.

"By who?" he bit out.

"It was anonymous," Oladele said with an annoyed shake of her head. "But I'm sure we can guess who's behind it."

"He does not come after my staff," Joaquin gritted out, infuriated by how petty Lorenzo was. He had no compunction against destroying innocent people if he could score a point against his son.

See? he wanted to say to Siobhan. *This is what I'm shielding you from.*

"Stay behind after this," he ordered Oladele and quickly wrapped up the rest.

"Do you need me?" Siobhan asked Oladele, gathering her laptop and notebook into her arms as everyone else filed out.

"No," Joaquin answered.

Siobhan flinched at his tone and flashed him a glance then haughtily turned her gaze on Oladele.

He kicked himself, especially when Oladele sent him a look of surprise as well before she answered Siobhan. "Head back to your desk. I'll be down shortly."

Siobhan nodded and moved to the door.

Joaquin took a single long stride to get it for her, feeling like a heel, wanting to at least catch her eye and let her know he hadn't meant to be so rude.

If he hadn't been right there, staring at her profile, he would have missed the way the rigidity left it and her eyelashes fluttered. He would have missed how her color leached away and her knees buckled. He wouldn't have been close enough to catch her before she hit the floor.

"Wha—?" His heart lodged itself in his mouth as her dead weight slumped in his arms. Her laptop hit the carpet and her notebook splashed open.

Oladele gasped.

"Call first aid," he barked.

Since he'd caught her and knew she wasn't injured, Joaquin gathered Siobhan against his chest. "Get the door. I'll put her on the sofa in my office."

Seconds later, he eased her onto the cushions, heart

crashing against the walls of his rib cage. Her eyes were already blinking open.

"What—?"

"You fainted." He had rudimentary first aid knowledge and pulled her eyelids up to ensure her pupils were even, then pressed his fingertips to the pulse in her throat.

"First aid is on their way," Oladele said from the door. "Do we need an ambulance?"

"*No*. I just stood up too fast." Siobhan brushed his hands off her and sat up, forcing him to rise so she could set her feet on the floor.

He touched her shoulder to keep her seated, ready to catch her if she slumped forward.

"I don't need first aid," she said impatiently. "That's embarrassing. I'm fine."

"You are not. You were dizzy the other day." Joaquin had let himself believe her when she had said it was a bug, even though a tiny seed of suspicion had arrived in his brain at the time, one he had dismissed before he allowed it to take root. It was too perilous. It would consume his thoughts if he let it, so he had brushed it away.

It was quickly growing too big to ignore, though. Or would. Over the next nine months.

No. He pinched the bridge of his nose, still wanting to believe it was something else.

"Do you have a headache?" He didn't want her to be genuinely ill, but it was the only other explanation. "A cough? Other symptoms?"

"No."

"I wish you had told me you weren't feeling well." Oladele flicked Joaquin a look of speculation that only landed on him long enough to blow up his shell of denial before she returned her concerned frown on Siobhan. She suspected the same thing, but she was too circumspect to say it aloud. "I don't fire people for being ill, even if they're new on the job."

"I didn't think you would. But I'm not sick," Siobhan insisted. "This is self-induced. I've been burning the candle at both ends."

"Did you miss lunch again?" Oladele asked.

"You've been skipping lunch?" Joaquin snapped before she could answer.

"A couple of times on those first days. Things were busy. You're both overreacting."

On the contrary, he'd been underreacting. Refusing to see what was blatantly obvious.

Damn it, *he* was starting to feel faint. There was a buzz in his ears and he couldn't find any oxygen in this damned dungeon of an office.

"I insist you take better care of yourself," Oladele was saying. "I'll fetch your things. I want you to start your Christmas break immediately. See a doctor as soon as you can, then let me know if you need more time off. Otherwise, I'll see you in the New Year, back in fighting form." Oladele opened the door. "Ah. Here's first aid." She let in a young man wearing a red cross on his sleeve. "I'll be back in a moment."

Oladele left and the young man asked permission to check Siobhan's vitals before he applied a blood pressure cuff to her arm and used a stethoscope against her inner elbow.

"This is very unnecessary," she complained to Joaquin.

He pointed at the phone against his ear. The receptionist at the clinic had just picked up. He advised her that he was bringing his colleague for an assessment.

"We'll be there in thirty minutes," he said before ending the call.

"I can book my own doctor," Siobhan said with annoyance. "No, I'm not diabetic," she replied to the first aid attendant who was running through a checklist. "No, no, no," she continued.

"Pregnant?"

"N—*oh*." Her reply came out a lot less certain. Her voice actually cracked. She began to blush. Deeply. She shot a stark look at Joaquin.

She really hadn't suspected? Because in his mind it had become as impossible to miss as a five-alarm fire. He was already down the road of how he would shield her from his father's machinations while questioning his own fitness as a father. He had never wanted to face these sorts of dilemmas. That was why he used common sense and condoms.

"I apologize." The attendant misinterpreted her embarrassment. "These are personal questions. I shouldn't be asking them in front of anyone else. Would you excuse us, señor?"

"The clinic is holding a spot for her," Joaquin said crisply. "You can cut this short. I'll take her there myself."

"I can do that if—" the young man started to offer.

"No," Joaquin said.

"Of course." The young man kept his speculations to himself as he repacked his bag, telling Siobhan, "Your vitals are normal, but shall I bring the wheelchair?"

"No. Thank you." She still sounded strangled.

She refused to look at Joaquin, remaining stoic as Oladele arrived with her things.

Joaquin helped her put on her coat, then took her bag.

Her expression remained stiff and unreadable as they left his office.

He heard her thoughts all the same. They echoed his own.

This can't happen.

No, no, no. There were a million reasons she couldn't be pregnant, especially by Joaquin. He was her *boss*. They barely knew each other. They had only had sex once. He had worn a condom.

There was no way she could be pregnant.

She accompanied him to the elevator anyway, blaming the roil in her stomach on nerves. It had to be nerves. But why was she nervous if there was nothing to worry about?

"Have you been with anyone else?" he asked when the doors of the elevator enclosed them into privacy.

"No." Her heart lurched as though the car was freefalling. "Have *you*?"

"No," he said coolly. "And I didn't think you had, but I thought I should ask."

For some reason, his question made it more real. More likely. Her eyes grew hot. It became impossible to draw a full breath.

"What will we do if—" Her voice broke.

"Let's wait to see if there's anything to talk about before we talk," he said in that same grave, detached tone.

She caught back a panicked sob and nodded, for once bolstered by his air of cool command. She let him escort her across the lobby, ignoring the stares from the handful of employees who recognized them. She must look like death. She felt as though she walked through sticky molasses.

They were both quiet in the car. She didn't know what

he might be thinking behind his remote expression. She didn't have room in her turmoiled thoughts to imagine it. She just kept trying to blame these symptoms on all the stress she'd been under. It was flu season. Sometimes she felt off when she was expecting her cycle. That was all this was. It had to be!

She knew it wasn't, though. She knew.

The moment they entered the reception lounge, before she even saw the doctor, she asked for a sample cup and took it to the toilet.

She went into the examination room alone and the doctor came in a few minutes later to introduce himself.

"Your suspicion is correct," he said with calm professionalism.

"But I had a period." She barely got the words out, her mouth was so dry.

"Typical? Or lighter than normal?"

"Light." Barely spotting, but it had been right on time. She had blamed all the travel and time changes for it finishing before it had properly started.

She wanted to fold in on herself for being so naive. For not understanding that was why she was so tired. She'd been around dozens of pregnancies over the years. She should have recognized when it happened to her.

It hadn't occurred to her because she wasn't ready to be a mother. She didn't even have the sense to notice she was about to become one!

Was she really going to be a mother? Her heart was beating so fast, she had to wonder if she was going to make it through the end of the day. She tried to imagine what her life would look like with a baby and all she saw was a white void where her job and apartment and career ambitions had been.

Distantly, she heard the doctor prescribe prenatal vitamins and mention the need for a physical and a scan and ongoing prenatal checkups "if you choose to continue to term."

Her heart lurched. She had always planned to have a family, just not yet. Not alone.

What would Joaquin even say?

Let's wait to see if there's anything to talk about before we talk.

Reason one million that I don't want children.

Her hands were icy as she gathered her handbag and returned to the waiting area.

Joaquin was still on his feet and turned from the window. He flinched when he saw her expression and wordlessly held her coat.

In the elevator, she said, "We have something to talk about."

He nodded curtly and escorted her into his car.

She didn't pay attention to where he took her, not until they arrived at an unfamiliar building.

"Where are we?" she asked numbly as he helped her step onto the sidewalk.

"My apartment. The security is excellent and my father has a town house in Salamanca. You don't have to worry he'll turn up here."

Lorenzo was the last thing she was worried about. Joaquin hadn't beamed with joy and hugged her when she gave him the news. He had retreated another thousand miles inside himself.

She had an impression of marble columns and a polite door staff as they entered. Like many public spaces this time of year, the lobby was decked with twinkling lights and scalloped ribbons interspersed with bells. A beautiful nativity scene with hand-painted figurines stood on a table between a pair of elevators.

Joaquin used his thumbprint to access a panel. Seconds later, they entered a penthouse that had been modernized while keeping much of the building's heritage charm.

He waved her into the living room where a tree sparkled with white lights. Flames danced in the gas fireplace.

"This is Marta, my housekeeper," he said of the middle-aged woman who emerged from the kitchen to smile in greeting. "Thank you for staying late, Marta. This is Ms. Upton."

"*Buenas*—um, *noches*?" Siobhan had lost track of time. There was still a glimmer of fading dusk beyond the windows, but she felt as though a week had passed since she'd fainted at work.

"Welcome," Marta said in warm Spanish. "May I take your coats? I've prepared a light meal if you'd like me to serve it?"

"I texted her that you missed lunch." Joaquin seated her at the dining table where freshly baked buns gave off a heavenly aroma. Candles wreathed in holly sat on the table, lending a gentle festive atmosphere.

"That's not why I fainted," Siobhan said when Marta was in the kitchen. "The doctor said it's not uncommon for blood pressure to fall in—" she had to clear her throat, still wrapping her head around it. "—in early pregnancy. He said he'd test my iron levels when I go back for bloodwork, to be sure I'm not anemic."

Marta brought out bowls of *pescado en blanco*. It was a light soup that Siobhan already knew would sit gently in her unsettled stomach.

"I've kept you late enough," Joaquin said when Marta

asked if she could bring them anything else. "We'll manage. Enjoy your evening."

"*Gracias, señor.* I'll clean the dishes in the morning." Marta wished them good-night and left.

"I feel like all you do is feed me," Siobhan said as she tucked into her soup.

"If you would feed yourself, I wouldn't have to, would I?"

She was so on edge, she flinched.

They ate in subdued silence.

"So, um…" Siobhan couldn't stand the suspense any longer. "Still a skeptic about fate?"

It was a terrible joke. He didn't reveal one glimmer of amusement.

"We both have free will here. Your choices will affect mine so, ladies first."

Her veins stung with heightened emotion. This was sooner than she had planned to start her family and she had always imagined she would be in a loving, committed relationship when she did, but "I'm having the baby."

CHAPTER NINE

HER VOICE WAS QUIET, the words simple, but they hit Joaquin with the force of a hurricane wind, nearly knocking him from his chair.

She was having the baby. *They* were having a baby.

The world titled on its axis. He resisted the urge to grip the table as he felt himself falling into empty space.

Conflicting responses warred within him. A desire to backtrack. If he could return to that elevator in San Francisco, he would go to his room alone— But no. A resistance rose in him even as he considered giving up that memory. It was too good.

Let the doctor be mistaken and I'll... What? What could he do to atone for getting a woman pregnant?

"You're not happy." She pushed aside her empty bowl and walked to the fireplace where she stood with her back to him, hunched, hugging herself. "It's okay. I'm making this decision for me. I want to be a mother. I'm not doing it lightly, either." She turned her head to speak over her shoulder, offering him the curve of a cheek carved from ivory. "I've been around a lot of pregnant women and their children. I know what I'm in for more than most first-time mothers. I have a ton of support and resources. You don't have to be involved."

"Stop." He left his own chair and walked around the

sofa toward her. "I've never wanted to be a parent, that's true. It doesn't mean I intend to ignore the fact I'm about to become one." *I am one.* The fist around his lungs clenched tighter.

"But no one needs to know that. Most couples don't tell anyone about their pregnancy in the first trimester anyway, in case something goes wrong. We can keep pretending we're merely acquainted—"

"No." He didn't let her finish, offended on a very primal level that she would even suggest he turn his back on both of them.

Something very visceral was springing to life in him that he didn't want to examine too closely. It was greedy and atavistic and protective and it wouldn't be pushed to the margins where his actions would be ineffective.

"Why have you never wanted children?" She pleated her brow in anxious incomprehension.

He winced and reached for the most obvious explanation.

"I travel too much. They're a level of responsibility that always seemed inconvenient." He loosened his tie, feeling constricted by it. "One of the reasons my brother and I struggled to reconnect was the fact he had young children. His family was his priority. Which was as it should be, but I saw how much of his time they monopolized."

He pushed his hands into his pockets, still trying to wrap his head around this news while that belief, that personal *standard* of his brother's, settled into him as his own. His priorities had been shuffled. New ones had arrived at the top in the form of Siobhan and their child.

"I am responsible for this baby, though. I refuse to shirk that."

"That's admirable, Joaquin, but a child needs to feel

like more than an obligation." Her chin stayed low with admonishment as she lifted her lashes. "You need to *want* to be a parent. With me." Her voice wavered toward hysterical laughter. "For twenty years. This is a big decision for you, too. *You* can take more time to think on it."

Her pregnancy wasn't even visible. The idea they would be linked by this unformed person for the rest of their lives was something too big to grasp. The profound weakness a baby would create for him was terrifying to comprehend, but there was also a strange allure in this news.

A glimmer of something arrived in him. It was akin to what he'd seen in Fernando when his brother had introduced him to his firstborn, looping his arm around Zurina, who had been holding the baby. The pride in his brother's expression had been so blatant, Joaquin had been embarrassed for him, but he could feel emotion dawning in his chest.

"The deed is done," he said. "I *am* a father. If you're asking how I intend to behave as one, the answer is, *better than the example that was set for me.*"

As he made that decision, and this new reality began to settle on him, his mind raced ahead to reconfigure his future around both of them.

"I appreciate you saying that." Siobhan sank with profound relief onto the edge of the sofa cushion, elbows on her knees, fingers laced before her unsteady lips.

The truth was she was moved by how quickly and firmly he was committing to their baby. It meant a lot to her.

"I was raised by a single mom. I don't have qualms about being one. I know the part that really matters is having someone who loves you." Even if she had faced raising their baby alone, she would have had a ton of help from her mother and sisters. "All of my sisters remember our father except me. I was a toddler when he died. It left a blank space that Henri did his best to fill, but he didn't come into my life until I was in my teens. Then I saw what a loving, involved father he is to their children and I've always known I wanted that for my own. So thank you."

"For not leaving a blank space in our own baby's life? You're welcome, I guess?"

Our own baby.

Her shock was wearing off. Anticipation gathered in her chest and thickened in her throat. Joy expanded through her, creating room for the new love that was blooming inside her. What would their child be like? Moody and watchful like Joaquin? Aloof? Or affectionate and cheeky like her?

She let herself picture Joaquin with an infant against his heart and was nearly overwhelmed by longing. Would their baby bring out a warmth in him he didn't otherwise reveal? Or was she conjuring a romantic illusion?

Henri hadn't wanted children when he and Cinnia had started their affair. Cinnia had broken things off with him when she discovered her pregnancy, then hid it from him for months, even though they'd been in a relationship for two years. Even though they'd been in love, whether they had admitted it to themselves or not.

Her situation with Joaquin was very different, Siobhan acknowledged with a pang of chilling clarity. She and Joaquin were essentially strangers. They had slept together once. They had a few conversations between them that had been very personal on her side, but there was a lot she didn't know about him. She didn't have any of the confidence in his feelings that Cinnia had had about Henri's. In fact, all he'd done was shut her down.

For all she knew, Joaquin was only stepping up because of her relationship to Henri and the rest of the Sauveterres. He was a practical, tactical man. He had to recognize that, on a social level, having a baby with her would tie him into their circles forever.

And she was liable to let him! From the moment she had seen him again, she had been fighting her desire to be physically intimate with him again. To feel once more his masterful stroking of her body, the exquisite spikes of pleasure he brought forth, the culmination and blissful aftermath.

He didn't truly care for her, though. He might be decent enough to catch her when she fainted and show concern over the baby he'd put in her, but he wasn't as affected by her as she was by him. His ability to cool things off between them again and again proved it.

Which made her worry she would fall further under his spell if she didn't keep a firm distance.

"Okay, so, um, that's good to know that you're, you know, committed. I'll keep you posted as I make decisions." She rose and found her handbag. "Is your driver still on the clock? Or should I order my own car?"

His dark brows quirked in astonished puzzlement. "To where?"

"Home. Wait. Is it still rush hour?" She glanced toward the windows where city lights were sprinkled against the dark night. "Maybe I'll take the metro."

"You fainted today." His tone said, *remember?*

"Right. Car, then." She brought her phone from her purse.

"Siobhan. You're not going home. You'll stay here where I can keep an eye on you."

"I'm not going home to paint the ceiling. I'll put my feet up, have an early night. But I *have* to go home to take out these contacts. They feel like sandpaper." She blinked as she tried to read her screen, growing desperate for time alone to regroup and come to terms with all of this.

"Don't order a car," he said with impatience. "I'll take you home." He came to hold her coat for her. "You can pack what you need to move in with me."

CHAPTER TEN

"What? I can't move in with you!"

"Why not?" Joaquin asked the question, but then held up a finger as he brought his phone to his ear.

She stewed while he spoke to his driver.

"He's happy to collect overtime." He ended the call. "He'll meet us downstairs in a few minutes."

"What on earth makes you think I want to move in with you?" she cried.

"Your tone?" he suggested drily as he pulled on his own overcoat.

"Why would you even want me to?" she demanded. The belt on her coat felt too tight.

"Half the building saw us leave together today. I would love to believe I've ferreted out all the moles, but rumors are liable to get back to my father. I won't underestimate what he might do with that information. You can't work there, not while he's still trying to reclaim it."

"You're not firing me." She put her foot down.

"No, I'm protecting you," he said in his most implacable tone. "You heard today how he's going after Oladele." He muttered a distracted curse and rubbed his jaw. "I still have to deal with that. But he could target you just as ruthlessly."

"So I should lie down and let him quash my career before I've properly got it off the ground?"

He glowered at her.

She lifted her chin and gave him a too-sweet smile. "Yeah. It turns out I'm smart enough to see the holes in your logic."

"As your employer," he said very patronizingly, "and the father of your unborn child, I *insist* you stay off work until you have your health in order. *Then* we will discuss if and where you can work." Oh, he was smug over that.

"I'll make my own decisions, thank you very much."

"Then make smart ones!" He opened the door.

"How does quitting my job and moving in with you serve me in any way?"

"We just agreed we're doing this together." He nodded at her middle. "How does that happen if I'm in Barcelona and you're here? Because as soon as this acquisition is finalized, I'm finding a new CEO for LVG and will only be here quarterly."

"And you expect me to pick up sticks and go to Barcelona with you? For how long?"

"Twenty years?" he replied, shrugging.

"You're unbelievable."

The driver arrived at the curb as they exited the building. Siobhan got into the car because she had a feeling Joaquin would have the driver take him to her building regardless.

After ten minutes of stewing in bumper-to-bumper traffic, she leaned forward to ask the driver if he spoke English.

"No, señora," he said with an apologetic shake of his head.

"No problem," she assured him in Spanish. "Please

disregard any raised voices you hear in the next few minutes."

The driver chuckled and Siobhan switched to English.

"You don't get to order me to quit my job and move in with you," she hissed.

"What are you? A vampire? You're *invited*."

"To be what?" she challenged. "Your houseguest? Are we going from pretending *not* to be a couple to pretending to *be* a couple? Will we be roommates who coparent or are you *inviting* me—" she wrapped the word in a layer of sarcasm "—to start a relationship with you?"

He seemed to retreat a little more into the shadowed backseat. "We're already in a relationship."

"Hardly." He ignored her more often than he spoke to her.

"You're asking if I want to have sex with you?" he growled. "I think I proved that yesterday."

A choked noise of embarrassed skepticism left her.

"Again, I was protecting *you*. The door wasn't locked," he reminded her through his teeth. "I don't care who sees my ass. I'd happily finish what we started right here, right now, but you fainted today so sex is off the table."

Her pulse skipped at the lewd image he painted. She almost told him the doctor hadn't said she couldn't have sex, but she refused to beg for crumbs from him.

"What I'm hearing is you want me to move in with you, be a mother to your child and conveniently sleep with you. Essentially, be a wife without being your wife."

"We can talk about marriage," he said with a note of surprise. "I'm open to it."

"We don't even know each other! A few weeks ago, you made it clear you weren't interested in sharing anything more than one night. Not even that," she reminded hotly. "So excuse me if I don't rush to move in with a man who might want his baby, but doesn't really want *me*."

He did want her, though. It was torturing him how much he wanted her because he had learned to only care about the things he needed. He would battle to the death over food and air. Sleep was a necessity, but a comfortable bed was a want. Sharing a bed with *her* was...

An old, twisting sensation went through him, the one that reminded him not to reveal his wants. Wanting her meant exposing a flank. It meant putting her in the line of fire. And their baby? He could hardly stand how vulnerable that made him.

Yet, a dark part of him was pleased her pregnancy forced him to bring her more fully into his life.

"I wasn't prepared to start something long-term when I met you. Not with all of this going on with my father. A relationship would have been a distraction. But now..."

He sensed her head turn. She was listening attentively.

"I know I'm difficult to read. You're not the first woman to say so, but I don't like people to know what I'm thinking or feeling. That's not comfortable for me."

"It's not comfortable for anyone," she said impatiently, tucking her chin on her palm and her elbow on the armrest as she looked out her side window. "But at least tell me..." She dropped her hands into her lap. "Is that the only reason you gave me the brush-off that night? Or..."

"What?" he prompted.

"It's not that long since you were engaged. Was I a rebound from that?"

"No." The car stopped. He stepped out to put an end to the conversation.

His driver opened her door and Joaquin arrived on the sidewalk in time to offer his hand as she rose from the car.

"Thank you," she said stiffly. "But you don't have to walk me in. We can talk tomorrow." She nodded at the car as though dismissing him.

Did she really think she could out-stubborn him? "You're not spending the night alone. Not until you've had all the bloodwork and whatnot from the doctor."

"What are you going to do? Stare at me while I sleep? Because I don't see a point in spending time with you if you refuse to talk to me."

"I'm not refusing." Just avoiding certain uncomfortable topics. "We're staying here tonight," he told his driver. "Come back for me at seven tomorrow morning."

Siobhan huffed a noise of muted outrage and started toward the front doors.

"What exactly do you want to know?" he asked reluctantly as he caught up to her.

She paused with her key fob in her hand, surprise in her expression. "About your engagement? What was her name? How did you meet her?"

"Esperanza. She works in real estate. She found my penthouse in Barcelona for me."

"Why did you break up?"

"My father." He took the fob from her loose grip and waved it at the sensor, then held the door. "I wasn't involved in LVG when I proposed, but after Fernando passed, I came here to support Zurina through the funeral. My father assumed I was here to fight him for LVG and turned his spite onto Esperanza."

"In what way?" She wasn't watching where she was going. She was looking at him so he took her elbow as he led her to the elevator.

"Insults. Tantrums," he said tiredly. "Veiled threats. Nothing illegal. He's very clever that way. And manipulative. When I called him out on his behavior and ordered him from Zurina's home, he accused me of trying to prevent him from seeing his grandchildren. I couldn't be around him without wanting to strangle him. That's how he got Zurina to allow him to take over at LVG. She was trying to keep the peace and lived to regret it. He still saw me as a threat, though, and began interfering in Esperanza's real estate deals. She said she couldn't marry me if it meant losing her livelihood. I couldn't abandon Zurina so I agreed we should break it off."

"I think *I* mentioned not wanting to lose my livelihood," she muttered as they stepped into the elevator. "Are you...still in love with her?"

"No."

"*Were* you?"

"No."

"Really?" Her eyes flared wide with surprise. "Then why were you planning to spend your life with her?"

"Compatibility?" He shrugged.

"You mean...in bed?" she asked warily.

Dios, she was persistent.

"She didn't want children," he said flatly.

Siobhan took a sharp breath, staggering back a step.

"I'm being frank so you don't think I'm harboring secrets." The doors opened and he held them for her. "Esperanza has a likable personality and she's very career focused. Marriage was never a goal for me, but after we'd been seeing each other for a year, she asked if I intended to propose. We were comfortable, so I did."

"She wasn't in love, either?"

Here he vacillated before telling the truth. "She said

she was," he admitted. "That's another reason I didn't fight her leaving. I didn't want to lead her on."

Siobhan stopped at her door, expression deeply vulnerable.

"I'm not built for that sort of depth," he admitted with a wince, feeling as though he stood on quicksand. He felt *inadequate*. But it was best to make that clear to her now. "I promise to be a good partner to you, though. I will support you. I will protect you."

Her brows pulled with uncertainty as she took back her fob and opened her door, striding in ahead of him.

He followed, coming up short as he saw her flat had been overturned.

As she reached for the door on the closet, Joaquin caught her arm and scooped her behind him, corralling her against the door to the hall.

"What—?"

"Leave. Go to your neighbor's. He might still be here."

"Who?" Her fists instinctively closed in the folds of his coat.

"Whoever searched the place. I'm calling the police!" he called out, reaching into his pocket. "He's gone too far this time," he added in a mutter of barely contained rage.

She peered around him into her silent flat, glimpsing the chaos of wrapping paper, ribbons and unwrapped toys. Nothing else looked amiss.

"Wait," she said sheepishly. "I left it like this."

His shoulders dropped. He angled to look down on her, astounded.

"I've been trying to do the wrapping all week." Acute embarrassment rose in her. She walked into the mess and discarded her coat over a chair, kicking off her shoes. "I told you it was Christmas when Ramon told me what Gilbert had done. I was actually wrapping gifts." She waved hopelessly at the wrapping paper she had unrolled across her dining table. A train set was centered on it. Tape, scissors, ribbons and labels were scattered next to it. "I used to love this time of year. Now it stresses me out. That's the real reason I don't have a tree. Christmas is ruined for me."

He frowned. "What have you been doing since it happened?"

"Asking Mom and my sisters to join me in Australia." She pulled her shoulders up defensively. "It feels different there. It's summer. We kept it no gifts and went snorkeling or had a barbecue. I didn't have to face it. But Cinnia will have all the children there this year. I couldn't say no. I *want* to be there, but also…" She clutched her stomach. Her chest felt tight.

"This is genuinely difficult for you." He came across to rub her arms and frown at her.

"It is." She grimaced at the sheer volume of the task ahead. "I feel so silly for reacting like this, but each time I try to do it, I just *can't*."

"I'll do it." He wasn't laughing at her, which kind of made her feel extra wobbly inside. "Remove your contacts or whatever it was you needed to do."

"*You're* not going to wrap all these gifts," she said with disbelief.

"I am." He released her and shifted the train set on the paper. He lifted the roll to better estimate how much was needed then picked up the scissors and slid them in a smooth hiss, cutting a precise line.

"Do you like it?"

"I don't mind it." He knew what he was doing, too.

He was economical and very tidy, keeping everything square, folding edges for clean lines, tucking and taping with smooth expertise. "The first component I manufactured was a type of gaming goggles. My initial order was two thousand. I sold out in three days, partly because I promised to gift wrap them. Do you know how many employees I had at the time?"

She shook her head, bemused.

"One. Me."

"Really?" A smile tugged at her lips, picturing him both proud and overwhelmed by his own success.

"I had to become very good, very fast." He pulled a stretch of ribbon from the roll and wrapped it in jaunty angles around the corners of the gift. He tied it off and, with a quick zip-zip of the scissor blades, bounced a few curlicues into the tails. He topped it with a bow and offered it to her. "Santa's helper unlocked."

It was beautiful.

And it was such a kind gesture, she thought she might cry.

CHAPTER ELEVEN

Joaquin hadn't done anything so menial in years, but it was worth it for the bright smile it put on Siobhan's face. It felt good to do something concrete for her, especially when she kept yawning so hard.

"Go to bed," he urged. "I'll join you when I'm done."

"I love how you assume you're invited to sleep with me."

"If you want to go back to my place, I have a guest room," he said mildly.

"Tsk." She stood in the opening to her bedroom, a truculent look on her face. She had changed into yoga pants and a tunic and adjusted her glasses before catching another yawn in her cupped hand.

"I would offer to tuck you in, but you're too tired for sex. Go to sleep. We can argue as much as you want tomorrow. Promise."

"Generous of you," she muttered, but a few minutes later she closed the bedroom doors and the lights went out.

Two hours later, he stripped to his briefs and carefully settled beside her. Her bed was only a queen so he was close enough to feel her body heat.

"Joaquin?" she murmured sleepily as she rolled toward him.

"Are you expecting someone else?"

She gave a muted hum of amusement. "Thank you for doing the wrapping. I really appreciate it." Her warm, silky hand found his upper arm, waking the animal in him.

"De nada." He rolled to face her, tucking his arm under his pillow while catching her hand and bringing it to his lips. "Are you awake or going back to sleep?"

"I—" She drew her hand out of his. "I'm afraid to move in with you," she admitted in a whisper.

His heart swerved. "Why?"

"Because then we'll do that. And I might fall in love with you. I don't want you to propose one day because I make you feel like you have to and you only do it because we're comfortable."

Ouch. He fell onto his back again.

"I'm sorry. That came out harsher than I meant it to."

"It's fine." Fair. "Go to sleep."

"You're angry."

"No." Not at her. He was angry at himself and his own limitations.

She rolled away and exhaled.

He stared at the ceiling, trying to see his way through this because the irony was, if he ever proposed, it would be *in spite of the fact* he wasn't comfortable with her. Siobhan had been disrupting his life and his peace of mind from the beginning. Even before learning about the baby, he'd been unable to forget her. He found her interesting and smart and funny.

Now the baby was upending his entire existence and he ought to be furious, but he couldn't find it in him to be sorry. That was what he was thinking as he closed his eyes. *I'm not sorry.*

His subconscious reminded him why he should be, though. As reality folded into the dream world, Lorenzo's true nature lurched into his psyche.

That's not for you. Only Fernando may have that.

In the way of muddled dreams, an old memory was rewritten. Siobhan was *there*. Lorenzo's arm was swinging, but not toward Joaquin.

"Siobhan!" he shouted, waking with a jolt to an unfamiliar place and movement beside him as she sat up, gasping.

"It's okay." He searched out her wrist, keeping her on the bed so she wouldn't flee into the shadows and trip.

His throat was still rasped by his shout, his chest tight with adrenaline, his skin clammy. The disturbing images of his dream stuck like cobwebs that he mentally had to brush away.

"Did you have a nightmare?" She sank onto the mattress beside him. Her hand arrived on his chest while the rest of her aligned along his side. "Your heart is racing. Are you okay?"

"Fine," he lied while he fought the urge to loop his arm around her and hug her against his tacky skin.

He was too raw for that. Too involved, if he was reacting with this much terror to his own imagined threats.

"I didn't mean to wake you." He pressed her away. "Go back to sleep."

"But—" She sat up again as he left the bed. "It's still early. You need to sleep, too."

"I'll check email. There will be some from overseas that need answering." It was a fib, but he needed to regroup. He picked up his trousers and stepped into them.

In the lounge, he looked at his phone, but his mind wouldn't focus.

Work had always been a productive coping mechanism. As a child, he had used homework and invention to avoid his father's criticism and attempt to earn his recognition. Later, he had labored to afford food and a place to sleep, but it had kept him from dwelling on how alone he felt. Once he had had more of a financial toehold, he had toiled feverishly to surpass his father's level of success, so he could no longer be victimized by Lorenzo. When that was achieved, he continued to strive as a point of pride. Out of spite, even, so he could look down on Lorenzo.

I won, was the silent message he had conveyed with the rise of ProFab into worldwide acclaim.

But had he? Lorenzo was still able to invade his dreams and leave the bitter taste of copper on the back of his tongue.

"Joaquin?"

Her voice pierced between his shoulder blades. He turned to see her in a blue robe wearing a worried expression.

"You said you'd start looking after yourself," he chided.

"I can't sleep. Not when you're having nightmares about..." She waved toward the knotted belt on the robe.

"That wasn't what it was about."

"What, then?"

"It doesn't matter."

She came closer and searched his expression in the dim light. "The stress of becoming a father brought it on, though. Are you having second thoughts?"

He wanted to deflect, walk away, close off. Anything to avoid this, but he answered her. "I'm not afraid to be a father," he blurted. "I'm afraid for *you*."

"Why?"

He scrubbed his stubble with his palm. The nightmare had been an icy, subliminal warning of what could happen if Joaquin wasn't vigilant.

"The dream was about my father."

"And me?" She closed the robe tighter across her chest with her fist. "But it was just a dream, Joaquin. Wasn't it? Joaquin, was he…abusive?" she asked in a whisper.

"Yes."

Her breath hissed in. "Physically? Your ribs?"

"Yes."

"Where were the authorities?" she asked with anguish. "Why wasn't he stopped?"

"He told the doctors I'd jumped from the hayloft. Boys will be boys."

"Your mother?"

"She had already left."

"And left you with him?" She started toward him.

He put up a hand, holding her off. He couldn't bear her tenderness right now.

"She didn't know. Not until later. Don't blame her. I was questioned, but I was worried I'd be separated from Fernando so I didn't tell them the truth."

"I don't understand how people can be like that. Especially to a child." She covered her mouth with her hand.

"I asked my mother once if I was the product of an affair, thinking that might explain why he was so petty toward me. I was barely old enough to understand that people could have affairs, but I wanted my father to be someone else. Desperately," he said on a scuff of a laugh. "She said he was just a mean, small, jealous man. He was," he said with contempt. "He was horribly jealous of his own brother. LVG was bequeathed to both of them and they fought over it until my uncle died. That's one of the reasons Lorenzo always made sure I knew Fernando was the heir and I the spare."

"But when Fernando died...?" Her brow was knotted with incomprehension, her chin crinkled.

"Jealous again. Of me." He lifted a hand and a defeated breath left him. "I think that's part of it. He's always seen me as a threat on some level, stealing attention or questioning him or pushing back on his bad ideas. Fernando and I were close growing up, despite his efforts to divide us. Maybe I just reminded him of his brother. I don't know, but it came to a head when I was fourteen and designed a relay component. We lived and breathed electronics growing up. In that way, I had a very privileged life."

"Not if he was abusive."

He looked away, trying to ignore the slash of pain that went through his chest. The wave of old helplessness that wanted to swallow him.

"In any case, I had the brain of an engineer and handed my father the schematic. I guess I thought if I earned his respect, things would change. It was the logic of a child. Of..." Wanting to be loved. Or at least accepted.

Siobhan was listening closely, searching his expression.

He swallowed. "It allowed LVG to become a leader in that pocket of the market. Two years later, I could see that it was a success. I wanted him to acknowledge that I had done something useful for LVG. That I was an asset. That's all." He was still baffled by his father's reaction. "I wasn't asking for money, only for him to say I had done a good job. He called me a liar, claimed he had designed it himself and threw me from the house." He could still feel his father's fist in his hair. The propulsion out the door. The gravel hitting his knees and palms. He could still hear the door slam behind him and the chill as rain began to penetrate his clothes.

"You were sixteen?" she asked in an appalled voice. "What did you do? Where did you go? Your mother?"

"She was in South America, losing her battle with breast cancer." Not that she'd told her sons of her ill health. "We rarely saw her. Fernando was away with friends. The staff was forbidden to open a door to me. I didn't have shoes or a phone. I started walking and, honestly, the farther I got from him, the better I felt."

"Where did you sleep? How did you survive?"

He almost smiled at how maternal she already sounded.

"Someone picked me up, took me to a shelter for teens. A few weeks later, Fernando brought me some things—my clothes and my ID. He gave me money. By then, I had a job selling souvenirs from a kiosk at festivals and cleaning up the site after the concerts were over. I was living in a house with ten other people, all of us down on our luck. Half of them were doing hard drugs. Others were hiding from immigration authorities or the law. The place was full of mold and infested with fleas, but I was so damned happy."

"Joaquin."

"Don't pity me," he said sharply. "It was the most agency I'd ever had. The most peace. I already knew what hell looked like. That was merely inconvenience."

"You didn't go to the police?"

"And say what? We'd had an argument and he told Fernando that I ran away. What if they sent me back to him?"

"Was Fernando safe with him?"

"He was old enough that Lorenzo thought twice about raising his hand to him."

"Is that why you were estranged from Fernando? Because he stayed with your father?"

"I don't blame him for that." He blamed himself for failing to spend more time with his brother when he had the chance. "I wanted him to join me on the outside, but he had put in the time and suffered in his own way. He felt he had earned his place at LVG."

"Even though it cost him *you*?" she choked.

"In his mind, he was claiming it for both of us. When Lorenzo had his heart attack, Fernando took charge and asked me to come aboard there. I was firmly estranged from Lorenzo by then. I didn't want anything of his. I was in Barcelona, scraping up financing for that gaming headset I told you about. Fernando persuaded Zurina's father to invest in me, giving me my start."

"That's another reason you left at the drop of a hat to help her," Siobhan said in a tone of hollow discovery.

"*Sí*. I would have kept my father out of my life forever, but when Fernando died, I had to come back into all of this." He waved abstractedly. "Fernando put up with his abuse for a legacy that means nothing, then died because he thought he could change out an electrical switch in a barn that should have been burned to the ground long ago. *Estúpida*!" He sliced his hand through the air. "But I won't let his suffering be in vain. He wanted his children to inherit LVG. So be it. I'll keep our father from destroying it with his pride and negligence. He's angrier than ever that I've usurped him, though. He'll come after me in whatever way he can. That's what my nightmare was about. He was coming for you."

"You think he'll be violent toward me?" She touched her chest, then her hand drifted lower, as though she wasn't aware of letting it settle on her abdomen. Her eyes widened in horror.

"I don't know." His stomach knotted. "But I can't afford to let down my guard. I *won't*. That's why I'm so adamant that you live with me."

She absorbed all of that with a frown of grave consternation.

"But I could…" Her brow flexed with anguish. "If you're that worried about my safety, I could stay with my sister after Christmas. And not tell anyone you're the baby's father."

Frost spread through his chest as he saw that, once again, his father was about to take something from him. Two people he wanted in his life very, very badly.

The harp strings of his phone's wake alarm began to play.

He hit Stop.

"I need to shower. My driver will be here soon."

Siobhan had wanted to know why he was so aloof. Now she did. Joaquin had been denied the security he was meant to feel within his family so he played his cards close to his chest. In fact, he'd been actively harmed by someone he ought to have been able to trust. Even his relatively good relationship with his brother had been twisted and cut short before it had had a chance to heal.

She couldn't be someone who hurt him, too. She couldn't isolate him from his baby, not when she knew what wellsprings of love they were. She had to give him an opportunity to be a father. For his sake and their child's.

Even if it tipped her equilibrium toward falling for him.

She was trying to be so careful with her feelings! But

they were sliding like quicksilver, leaking and seeping out of her toward him, refusing to be caught back.

What would happen when he realized that?

That's another reason I didn't fight her leaving. I didn't want to lead her on.

He came into the bedroom a few minutes later. He was in his trousers again, but his hair was damp and his chest gleaming. He picked up his shirt from the chair and shook it out.

"I *will* keep you safe, Siobhan. I swear it," he said in a voice so vehement, her pulse skipped hard in her veins. "I wasn't trying to frighten you. I only want you to recognize the danger is real. But this situation won't go on forever. I won't allow it to."

"I believe you." She took another pair of slacks from the wardrobe and folded them into her suitcase. "But if I learned nothing else from the Sauveterres, it's that you can't live your life in fear. Take sensible precautions and go about your business, which is what I'll do. I'll move in with you if it makes you feel better, but I intend to keep working. At LVG."

The tension eased from his expression as he smoothly buttoned his shirt. "Those are your terms?"

"Yes."

"Provided your doctor agrees, I accept. But I live in Barcelona," he reminded.

"I know. I'll talk to Oladele about working remotely." She took the small win and continued packing, but paused when her phone vibrated on the night table.

She turned it over to see Cinnia was calling. A pained noise escaped her.

"What's wrong?"

"Nothing," she said heavily. "Just my sister. She tried

me twice yesterday and I ignored her because..." The pregnancy news had consumed her. "She wants my ETA, but..." She looked to the gifts he'd wrapped and stacked so neatly. "What do I do about Christmas?"

"Spend it with your family." His face smoothed into those unreadable lines that she found so frustrating. "I know you'll be safe there. I plan to work anyway."

"But..." She couldn't leave the father of her baby alone on Christmas mere days after they learned she was pregnant. What if something happened and she went into hospital? She would want him with her.

If she was only going to visit Cinnia, she might have confided her happy news, but everyone would be there and it was too soon to tell the world. The magnitude of holding on to her secret while fighting her anxiety over the holiday began to balloon in her mind. Tears welled in her eyes.

"Would you come?" she asked over the insistent buzz of her phone. "If I ask her...?"

Cortisol poured through her bloodstream as she recalled what had happened the last time she brought someone home for Christmas. Why was this so messy and *hard*?

Joaquin wouldn't betray her the way Gilbert had. Would he?

"If you want me to be there, yes." His dark eyes were fathomless. Some emotion flickered across his expression too quickly for her to interpret it. Wariness? Something warmer?

Relief eased the pressure in her chest. She pressed the quivering sensation from her lips and answered the video call, propping the phone against the bottom of her lamp so she was in the frame and Joaquin remained off camera.

"Hi, what's up?" she asked.

"Ramon said he offered to fly you down with him and you said no." Cinnia had her blond hair pulled back with a headband and was working moisturizer into her clean face. She was fourteen years older than Siobhan, but looked closer to thirty than forty. "Do *not* tell me you're backing out."

"No. Work's been busy. They can't spare me." That wasn't entirely true if she was taking a few days of medical leave, but Cinnia didn't need to know about that. "I was planning to take the train Saturday—"

Joaquin shook his head.

"Sunday?" she asked.

"Is someone there with you?" Her sister's tone grew pointed and she stared hard through the screen. "On a workday? This early in the morning?"

"I was about to tell you," Siobhan grumbled. "I'm seeing someone. Ramon didn't say anything?"

"Should he have? Is it serious? Do you want to bring him to Christmas?"

"Just like that?" Despite her history? "You don't even know who he is."

"Of course, I do." Cinnia began brushing out her hair. "Ramon told Henri he thought something was going on between you. Henri told me. Why do you think I'm calling? Henri said he doesn't see any issue in having Joaquin join us so why don't you put me on to him and I'll invite him."

With a roll of her eyes, Siobhan handed the phone to Joaquin.

CHAPTER TWELVE

Joaquin discovered the only reason he had tolerated going into LVG was the opportunity to see Siobhan. Now that she was taking the week off for doctor visits and rest, being here felt more oppressive than ever.

Sleeplessness had something to do with his poor mood. And worry. Morning sickness had arrived the day she moved in and was hitting her at all hours. She had tried to sleep in the guest room, but he'd persuaded her to sleep with him so he could help her in the night if she needed it, fetching ice water and ginger tea and wringing out damp facecloths.

He hated seeing her miserable, and lying beside her while she slept was a delightful form of torture. He listened to her breathe, not touching her, afraid to move lest he wake her. Feeling her so close couldn't help but turn his mind to intimate acts, but he savored that time, too, feeling like an anchor coming to rest on the sea floor. *I'm not alone anymore.*

At the same time, he ached. *Ached.*

Trying to distract himself by thinking of what sort of father he'd make wasn't effective. It was too puzzling. And big. He kept trying to imagine knowing what to do with a crying baby, what to say as the baby grew old enough to talk. He'd never even held his brother's children, certain he'd break them. How would he become what his own child needed him to be?

When he finally did drift off, dark scenes from his past arrived. They always had Siobhan in them. His father would turn on her and Joaquin would be paralyzed, held back from protecting her. It was suffocating. Blood chilling.

Thankfully, today was his last in his father's office until the New Year. He left midmorning to meet Siobhan at the clinic where she was having her first scan, to confirm her due date. She had lined up a specialist in Barcelona where they would station themselves through her pregnancy, but they both wanted the peace of mind that this initial scan would hopefully provide.

She was already in a gown on the table when he was shown into a dimly lit room.

"How are you?" He took the hand she reached out, noting the bandage inside her elbow where she'd had blood drawn.

"Feeling like a captured alien being dissected for science. Oh! The nurse said my prenatal vitamins could be making me sick and gave me a different brand to try."

"That's good."

"Ready?" The technician cautioned, "Don't worry if we can't hear the heartbeat yet. At this stage, the heart isn't fully formed, but… Ah." As she began the scan, she brought up a grainy image of a kidney bean. The image wobbled then steadied. Something flickered. "That's the cardiac pulse."

All the air rushed out of Joaquin's lungs.

Siobhan turned her head, mouth trembling with a smile of wonder.

Such want rose in him then, he could hardly withstand

it. He wanted this. He wanted the baby and the woman. He wanted a future he could believe in.

It was terrifying to want this hard. Especially when the level of responsibility a child represented threatened to crush him. He had somehow convinced himself this was no different than his duty to look out for Zurina and Fernando's children, but no. This was *his* baby. Conceived with a woman who was taking up increasing space in his life. Not just physically, but in the way she occupied his thoughts and stoked his emotions and held a spark of himself inside her.

The idea of her carrying a new life was like trying to contemplate the breadth of the universe. He had to shut his thoughts down before his skull cracked. He had to lock the greedy, hungry, possessive groaning beast within him behind a wall of reserve.

He had to consciously loosen his grip on Siobhan's hand so he wouldn't crush her bones and watched as the technician finished taking various measurements, studying the woman's face to be sure there were no flickers of concern.

A short time later, Siobhan was dressed and sitting beside him, waiting for the doctor to return to the consultation room.

"Are you okay?" Siobhan asked him warily.

"Yes," he said with surprise. "Are you?"

"Yes. But you went so quiet."

Because he was astonished. The full magnitude of her pregnancy was hitting him.

"Until now, my thoughts have all been around you, how I can support and protect you. Now I'm realizing there will soon be another person in my life. I'm trying to imagine what sort of father I'll make. I know I won't be abusive," he hurried to say, needing her to know that.

"I know," she said swiftly. Earnestly. "I think you'll be a wonderful father."

He winced and shook his head.

"I don't know if I'll be generous enough with myself." He kept thinking about her reservations about sleeping with him. About her fears that he would disappoint her by inciting feelings he couldn't return. "I've taught myself not to want things, so losing them doesn't matter. That's why I don't attach to people. The way my mother left... She had to. I understand that, but she got sick before I was able to spend more time with her. I lost her twice. Then Fernando..." He swallowed the ache in his throat. "It's easier to hold everyone at a distance. You can't do that to a child, though. You have to be open. Loving. I don't know if I can be." That was what he had tried to tell her the other night when he'd told her about Esperanza. That deep inadequacy tortured him as he thought about becoming a father.

"Trying is the first step and I know you'll do that." She reached across to squeeze his hand. "You're already trying to be there for your brother's children, even though it's difficult. That counts."

"It's not enough. I know that." It was frustrating to feel so locked up inside. Not just broken, but like a bone that had healed wrong and couldn't change.

"Joaquin. Please trust me when I say this..."

Dios, she had the ability to sound tender and sweet. Her expression softened and he felt those wrongly healed bones inside him shift anyway, trying to straighten.

"Because I have been around a lot of babies. They are medically designed to latch on to your heart and pull it from your chest." Her tone turned rueful, her smile playful. "The big eyes? The pure, unconditional love they drool all over you? You won't stand a chance."

He snorted.

"You're really selling it," he said drily, but found her words irrationally reassuring.

The door opened and Joaquin reflexively closed his hand tighter on hers, holding his breath until he saw the doctor's smile.

"Everything looks as it should," the doctor said. He reviewed Siobhan's bloodwork with her and promised to send the results to her new doctor in Barcelona.

"Do you have any questions? Partners usually want to know about lovemaking." He sent a wink in Joaquin's direction before saying to Siobhan, "Provided you feel up for it, you may continue with your normal activities."

CHAPTER THIRTEEN

JOAQUIN HAD GONE back to the office after her scan, dropping Siobhan at the spa so she could have her hair done for the LVG Christmas party tonight.

After an afternoon of pampering that included a nap on the massage table, she arrived home to find him asleep on the bed, ankles crossed, arms folded, still dressed in his shirt and trousers from the office.

She softened her step as she crossed to the closet, not wanting to wake him when neither of them had been sleeping well since she'd moved in, but he'd shown her such concern, she'd melted every time.

More tender feelings had accosted her today when he'd revealed so much of himself. He'd pulled *her* heart from her chest as she recognized how much loss he'd suffered and how very hard it was for him to open himself as a result. It made her want to show him it was safe to let down his guard.

Even though letting her own guard down meant risking her heart even further.

"Siobhan?" He cleared the gruffness from his voice.

"Yes. I'm here." She poked her head out of the closet.

"Blond." He turned his head on the pillow, mouth quirking in a hint of a smile.

"Yes." She pulled a kimono over the bra and underwear

she'd just changed into and came out to do a small twirl, showing him the way her hair had been styled half-up, half-down. "When I made the appointment, I was planning to have my roots touched up, but now that I'm pregnant, I don't want the chemicals on my scalp. This was foils and won't be so obvious when the color grows out."

"It's pretty. You are."

"You haven't seen my dress yet."

"I'm enjoying the lack of one, if I'm honest." He tucked his arm beneath his head and let his gaze track to where her legs were revealed by her short robe.

They hadn't talked about sex since the night he'd slept at her flat. She'd been sick and he'd been very chivalrous. It was all very Victorian.

But the doctor's endorsement had been heavy on her mind all afternoon, intertwining with her desire to feel closer to him. She did feel a lot better today, having skipped the troublesome vitamin.

Very tentatively, she slid one lapel of the robe off her shoulder, revealing the strap of her cranberry-red bra. "Any chance you're feeling festive?"

"Are you?" He didn't move, but his voice deepened. A watchful tension came over him. "I thought you preferred we keep things platonic."

She had been sincere when she said she was afraid she would fall in love with him, but she was already halfway there. And how could she convince him it was safe to love if she wasn't willing to let it happen to her?

"I also said sex would probably happen if I moved in," she said wryly, drawing the robe back onto her shoulder. "But if you don't want to…"

"I do," he said firmly. "Badly. I think about it a lot. But once we're down that road, it will be hard to go back."

"I know." She moved a little closer to the edge of the bed. "But I keep thinking that we're living together and starting a family and presenting ourselves as a couple. Shouldn't we try to be one? I mean..." Her smile turned itself upside down. "Fate must be wondering how many more messages it has to send."

"If we do this, it's because we're making that choice. You know that, right?"

"Yes. Sound mind and body," she said with a small eye roll.

"And you want to make that choice?" He held out his hand.

Very much.

Her heart turned over as she walked closer to the bed, shedding the kimono as she went.

His breath hissed in and his laser-focused gaze practically seared her skin as he took in the underwear that formed a V across her hips.

"But can you make love to me without ruining my hair and makeup?" she challenged as he guided her to sling one leg over his hips. She pinched her elbows together, using her upper arms to mash her breasts together, leaning forward so he had a good view of them threatening to spill from the tops of her bra cups. "Because I paid a lot of money to look this good."

"Worth every centimos," he said in a thick voice. His hands bracketed her hips. He dragged his gaze up to hers. "*Mi cielo*, I am certain you are about to ruin me. I'm looking forward to it."

She smiled, wallowing in a sense of feminine power as she opened his shirt buttons, starting at his waist and working her way up. As she shifted, his erection pressed beneath her.

He pushed his hand between them, adjusting himself. His knuckles brushed her mound, intimate and sending a flare of heat through her abdomen.

"You think about it a lot, too, hmm?" His mouth curled with wicked triumph. "That day in my office?" He turned his hand to cup her there, flexing his grip while his other hand skimmed her thigh then pressed her tailbone, encouraging her to press deeper into his palm. "Have you been aching for this?"

"Yes." Shattering tingles washed through her. She bit her lip, whimpering. Pressing. Struggling to finish spreading his shirt when her spine was beginning to melt.

She flowed down onto him, seeking the warm brush of his skin against her own. A kiss.

"Careful." He pushed his head into the pillow and set his hand against her collarbone, holding her off from pressing her mouth to his. "I have orders not to smudge. Which is going to happen if you're wet…"

He caressed her nape beneath the fall of her hair while he ran his amused, nibbling lips into her throat, sending shivers down her front so her breasts grew full and heavy. His other hand was still cradling the heat at her core, holding her in a delicious trap of sensuality.

Everything in her tightened, seeking *more*. She wanted him to roll her beneath him, but this was a game for him now, seducing her by delicate degrees—a scrape of his teeth at the edge of her jaw, the shift of his strong thighs pushing her legs wider so she sat deeper on his palm. The slide of his finger beneath the placket of silk to search out slick, slippery flesh that welcomed his exploring touch.

She moaned. For a long few minutes it was just that, her braced on shaking arms, enjoying the nibble of his lips in her throat and the caress of his touch.

"Bring this up to me," he said in a rasp when she began to dance her hips.

"What?" She blinked at him, dazed with lust.

He caught the lace against her hip and tugged. "Hold on to the headboard. Let me taste you."

It was utter debauchery, but the glitter of carnality in his eyes matched the needy hunger that gripped her. She shifted, allowing him to guide her into position and brush the silk placket aside and lick into the heart of her.

A guttural groan of pure wantonness left her.

His wicked hands moved over her, brushing her thighs and cradling her buttocks, shaping her breasts and holding her hips to encourage her to rock and seek and take her pleasure to the fullest.

In a sudden rush, a wave lifted her and crested, throwing her into a glorious maelstrom of pleasure, one that had her crying out in abandon.

Then, as she was still trembling and tingling and trying to catch her breath, he slid from beneath her and rose behind her.

"Don't move." She heard his zip and the rustle of his clothes. "Stay right there," he growled. His hand joined hers on the headboard, pinning one in place.

The rough fabric of his trousers arrived between her thighs. The cool teeth of his fly scored the underside of her buttock and she felt the graze of his knuckle as he guided his swollen tip against the pulsing, exposed flesh between her thighs.

She arched in welcome, moving her knees, offering. Inviting.

"Hold still, *mi reina*. I don't want to move a hair out of place—" His voice was lost in a ragged groan as he filled her with one slow thrust.

A fresh moan of joy left her, one of pleasure and luxury and homecoming.

"Gently, now," he whispered, palm splaying on her stomach then sliding downward. "Hold tight. Stay still."

He moved with disciplined power. While one hand slipped her bra strap off her shoulder, and his mouth branded her skin, his other hand caressed the soaked flesh clinging to the pistoning thickness of his. Within moments, she was sobbing in renewed joy, close, so close to breaking again.

"Wait for me." He slowed his touch. His strokes. "Wait. I'll tell you when."

She clenched the headboard in her hands. Clenched her eyes tight and clenched on him as she arched, held on the pinnacle in the most exquisitely fiendish way.

"Please, Joaquin," she sobbed. "Please now."

"Now." He clasped her hips and drove deep, shouting in triumph behind her.

CHAPTER FOURTEEN

After two whirlwind parties, one at LVG and another in Barcelona for ProFab, they flew to Marbella in the south of Spain.

Joaquin had been ridiculously proud to have been seen with Siobhan's fingers laced between his own. She was beautiful, charming and graceful on the dance floor, making such evenings far more pleasant than they'd been in the past. He had anticipated some side-eye over the fact he was dating his employee, but an HR memo had circulated, explaining they had had a "brief relationship prior to the takeover." It was enough that any gossip about them had fizzled quickly.

After a lazy morning, they ate lunch on his plane. He was still stoned from their lovemaking, but Siobhan was unexpectedly quiet in a way that struck him as tense, especially on the drive into the hills from the Marbella airport.

"Are you feeling off?" he asked with concern.

"No. The new vitamins seem to be sitting better." She looked up from fiddling with the bracelet he'd won for her at his company's silent auction. It was an artistic blend of mismatched gold and silver links that she had seemed to love, but she looked on the verge of tears. "I'm nervous about bringing you here."

"You think I'll betray you or your family?" He captured her hand to still it, but was deeply unsettled. "You don't trust me?"

"No, I do." Her smile didn't stick, though. "I'm being silly."

He didn't get a chance to delve deeper. They stopped at a gate that read, *Sus Brazos*. Their driver greeted the guard who angled to send a smile at Siobhan.

"Welcome home, señora."

"Thank you, Baron." She found a smile for him. "Joaquin is my guest. He should be on the list."

"He is." The guard glanced between a screen and Joaquin, ensuring his identity, then waved them through.

"Do you mind taking the lower drive?" Siobhan asked the driver, who turned in to a winding lane that took them through olive and orange groves. They circled a pond and some gardens. She pointed through an orchard and down paths. "Stables. Staff housing. That's just a garden shed. There's a playhouse for the children. You can't see the tennis courts, but they're behind those trees."

Joaquin would have thought she was eagerly showing off the place she considered home if her nails hadn't been digging into the back of his hand. She was putting off their arrival as long as possible.

"Siobhan." He gently squashed her hand. "It will be okay. Nothing bad will happen."

Her lip briefly quivered and he read the message in her eyes. *You don't know that*.

They arrived in a cobbled courtyard with a fountain. Wide steps led up to a pair of huge doors on a Spanish colonial mansion.

Cinnia trotted out with a handful of staff behind her. She was even more like Siobhan in person. They had similar figures, both slender yet curvy. They were the same height, had the same profile and sounded the same as they greeted each other with equally effusive hugs.

"You've made me so happy!" Cinnia declared, pressing her baby sister back to blink her wet lashes at her. "And you've gone back to blond. *Much* better, but I may be biased." She flicked at her bobbed hair, then hugged Joaquin. "Thank you for bringing her. You have single-handedly saved Christmas."

"My work here is done, then," he drawled, thinking for Cinnia, perhaps, but what about for Siobhan?

They entered an empty foyer with a curved staircase that swept up to a gallery. A huge, unlit crystal chandelier hung in the dome of colored glass that poured stains of red and purple and green onto the marble floor.

"Where is everyone?" Siobhan asked.

"Tennis tourney. I said I'd bring you down once you arrived, but the nannies have the children in the movie room, waiting for you."

A gasp from the top of the stairs lifted all their eyes.

"You're here!" The voice of wonder belonged to a girl of ten or so. She gripped the rail and beamed with joy over it. She turned her head and started to yell, "She's he—"

"Wait!" Siobhan hurried up the stairs. "Hugs first. Come here."

The girl hurried to meet her on the stairs and they hugged tight. Siobhan kissed her a dozen times all over her face, making the girl giggle, then Siobhan pointed down at Joaquin.

"Look. I brought someone and I don't want to scare him. Your special job is to gather all the children and tell them to queue oldest to youngest. Bring them here so I can introduce them and we can all get our hugs. Can you do that for me?" She kept herself at eye level and tucked the girl's hair behind her ear.

"I'll tell Lettie to do it. She's the bossiest." The girl spun to race away.

"That's the real reason Cin begged me to come," Siobhan said as she came back to the bottom of the stairs. She flicked a teasing look at her sister. "I'm the only one who can literally keep these pelicans in a line."

"True story," Cinnia confided to Joaquin. "Bear with us. They're very excited. Once we get this greeting out of the way, you can take cover in your room. Oh. Here we go."

Giggles and stifled squeals accompanied the shuffle of footsteps as children appeared on the landing, dutifully walking in a line. They wore a range of outfits from jeans and pullovers to frilly dresses to a superhero costume and a pair of pajamas. They broke into big smiles and waved energetically through the rail when they saw her, but the girl at the front sent a stern look that kept them from breaking rank.

"Look at you all so well behaved. Thank you," Siobhan said. "Lead them down here, Lettie."

The girl who had hugged Siobhan on the stairs came to the bottom step, so she was standing right in front of Siobhan.

No. That wasn't the same girl. Twins, Joaquin recalled as he looked between her and the girl behind her. Identical blue eyes blinked at him with curiosity. In fact, as he looked up the stairs, he saw more twins.

"Señor Joaquin Valezquez is my guest. You may call him Tío Joaquin. And he prefers Spanish?" she asked.

"French and English work, too."

"Good. Okay. Pay attention," she warned him over her shoulder. "There will be a quiz later." Siobhan set her hands on the first girl's shoulders. "This is Colette, Cinnia and Henri's daughter and Rosie's twin."

Rosie leaned out to wave at him. "You can tell us apart because I like to wear pink and Lettie only sometimes does."

Lettie did not introduce herself as the bossy one, but she did stick out her hand in a way that reminded him of her father and uncle. Very sure of herself. "It's nice to meet you."

"The pleasure is mine," Joaquin said sincerely as he shook her hand.

"Very nice." Siobhan hugged Colette and kissed her cheek, earning a wrinkled nose and a happy smile before Colette moved to the other side of the stairs and sat down.

Rosie led everyone down a step. "Are you Auntie Dorry's boyfriend?" she asked.

"I am," Joaquin said.

"Hmm." Her little brows went up in speculation as she moved to sit behind her sister.

A boy came next, tall with dirty blond hair and ice-blue eyes.

"Prince Tyrol of Elazar," Siobhan said. "King Xavier and Queen Trella's eldest."

Right. They were spending Christmas with royalty. Two pair of monarchs, in fact.

Siobhan hugged Tyrol with all the enthusiasm and familiarity she had shown her sister's children, kissing his cheeks until he chuckled and pushed her away.

"Please call me Tyrol," the boy said when Siobhan released him to shake Joaquin's hand. "We don't use titles when we're with family."

"Tyrol is only a few weeks younger than the girls," Siobhan said. "This is Malik, Prince of Zhamair. His parents are King Kasim and Queen Angelique." Siobhan warmly embraced the boy who came next. "Play chess against him if you like to lose."

He flashed a grin. He was perhaps a year younger than the other children with light brown skin and black hair. His intense brown eyes were surrounded by the sort of thick eyelashes women coveted.

The next boy led the group down another step.

"This reminds me of that old movie where the children sing on the stairs at their parents' party," Joaquin said with a smirk.

Rosie gasped. "*We* should do that."

Siobhan touched her lips, urging her to silence as she introduced, "Miguel, Ramon and Izzy's eldest."

Did her voice shake a tiny bit? Did she hug this boy a little longer and harder and look a little more distressed as she did it?

Her love for all of these children was very obvious in how well she knew each of them and how much affection they were showing her. It drove home for Joaquin how truly devastated she must have been to have caused any sort of peril for them. He instantly wanted to find this man who had broken her faith in herself and find a way to make him sorry.

She released Miguel and greeted the next boy with an affectionate smooth of his sandy blond hair. "Remy is Henri and Cinnia's son. He's turning seven on my birthday."

"We're birthday twins," he said and moved to sit with the others.

"Do us together. *Please*, Auntie Dorry?" A girl of

about five stepped down so she was on the same step as the one ahead of her. The pair of girls had strikingly similar features, but distinctly different hair and skin colors.

"This is Genevieve, Princess of Zhamair." Siobhan bent to squash the girls together, making them giggle before she released them to cup the other girl's beaming face. "And Vivien, Princess of Elazar. Our cousin-twins."

"Oh? Same birthday?"

"Uh-uh. My mama couldn't hold me in her womb so Tía Gili did it," Vivien explained. "We have different mommies and daddies so we're cousins, but we're still twins because we grew together and were born together."

Joaquin was impressed by the science, the startlingly selfless act by one sister for another, and the fact these girls had a grasp on what made them unique.

"Finally, Maya and Sofia, Ramon and Izzy's twins." Siobhan stretched her arms to hug the last pair together, too, eyes sheening with fresh tears before she closed them. "Maya and Sofia are five, same as the cousin-twins."

"We thought they were the last batch in the oven, then we got the big news," Cinnia said.

Joaquin snapped a look to Siobhan. Had she told her sister?

"That's right. Two are missing!" Siobhan tucked her fists on her hips and pretended to search around her feet. "Lettie?"

"I tried to take them yesterday, to play house," Colette said. "Mama said no."

"Aren't you the killjoy," Siobhan teased Cinnia.

"I know, right?"

"We'll meet Gili and Kasim's twins later. Thank you for using your best manners." Siobhan clapped her hands.

"Go back to what you were doing. We'll play hide-and-seek after dinner if you want to."

"Yes!" The children raced up the stairs.

Siobhan kept a smile on her face as they left, but it hardened and cracked when Cinnia wrapped her arm around her waist.

"See? They just wanted you here. We all do. You're shaking." Cinnia drew back to look at her, gaze widening in alarm.

"I'm fine." Siobhan brushed her off.

Joaquin saw how pale she was and clasped her cold hand.

"We had a late night at my company Christmas party," he lied. They'd actually left early, but Cinnia didn't need to know that. "Do you mind if we freshen up before we meet everyone else?"

Siobhan thought she was doing a credible job of keeping her emotions in check. She wasn't even sure why she was having such a rattled reaction. The children were all safe and healthy and happy. Their hugs always filled up spaces inside her that she wasn't aware had run empty.

But the whole time she'd been greeting them, she'd been suffering a growing sense of doom. Of failure. Guilt.

She brought Joaquin into the mini-suite that had been hers since moving here ten years ago. Cinnia had had it freshened up when Siobhan had left for London to live with Ramon and Izzy, so it was now a more neutral green instead of mauve. The hard-used computer desk and worn-in love seat had been replaced with sleek, comfortable new ones. The top quilt on the bed was no longer printed with periodic symbols. The bedding had been converted to the standard Sauveterre issue of blue with a yellow stripe.

It was still "Dorry's room," though. The shelves around the parlor area were stuffed with her old textbooks. The photo of herself with glasses, braces and a big smile, holding the newborn Rosie and Lettie, was still on the night table. The bathroom and walk-in closet were stocked with a selection of her favorite cosmetics and clothes.

Joaquin's things were already hanging in there, she noticed with a small double-take. That was weird, but nice.

"If you need anything, the house phone connects to the kitchen." She pointed to the cordless extension on the desk. "They relay messages to the drivers or security or whoever you're looking for. The doors to the balcony stick in winter. I'll show you how to do it." She swept the drapes away from the glass and unlatched the lock.

"Siobhan." Joaquin turned her and wrapped his arms around her in a hug that was tight enough to immobilize her. He ran his hands over her, smoothing all the fraying threads coming off her. "Catch your breath."

A tiny sob escaped her. She clutched at him. How had he known?

"I don't know why I'm upset," she said in frustration. "I love them so much and I want to be here, but..."

He didn't say anything, only closed his arms tighter around her, tucking her head into the hollow of his shoulder as though sheltering her from danger.

"You're right," she admitted in a strained voice as angry heat rose behind her breastbone. "I hate her."

"Who?" He lifted his head to look down on her, gaze sparking with battle readiness.

"Dorry." The scalding sensation traveled from behind her heart up to her throat. "I don't want to be her. She's thoughtless and naive and stupid. She doesn't deserve to be loved by all of those children who trust her. But I have to be her to be *here*." She brushed at a tickle on her cheek and realized it was a tear. "God, I'm pathetic."

She tried to turn away, but he kept her in the cage of his arms, holding her before him, unable to hide from herself or him.

"Why can't you forgive yourself and let it go?" he asked.

"Because they're innocent children!" She flicked her fingers toward the door. "I walked a wolf right into their home."

"Did you sneak him in? I thought you said Ramon allowed you to bring him into their home."

"Yes, but they all spoil me." She'd been a child herself when she came here. Henri and his family had indulged her at every turn. "Ramon trusted me to have a gauge on someone I was *sleeping* with. Someone I claimed to love."

He flinched, but only said, "You didn't *let* him betray you, Siobhan. He just did it." There was a ragged edge in his voice that told her he understood that type of pain at a soul-deep level. "Is it really Dorry you hate? Or how badly she got hurt? Is turning your back on her your way of hiding from *that*?"

A pulse of anguished discovery shot through her. It was the jump-scare of catching her own reflection in a mirror. More of those stupid, stupid tears rose in her eyes because one word was lighting up her brain. *Yes*.

She was deeply hurt and deeply angry that she'd been hurt. Her life had been one where she had been smothered in love. She had opened her heart to Gilbert as innocently as those children opened theirs to her. Having her heart stomped on and tossed away had been shocking. Unbearable.

"You're not the villain here." His graveled voice stirred her hair.

"I know, but..." She had to bite her lips to keep them from trembling. Her chest felt full of pins. "How could I love someone so awful? I feel foolish. I thought we were going to get married and... I keep thinking that I let it happen because I was in a hurry for this." She drew back to wave a hand at the room around them. The house and the family within it.

She began to shake again because she was laying bare more than her hurt and her heart. She was telling him what she wanted from *him*. And she already knew he might not be able to give it to her.

"I want a partner in life. I want children. Not just this baby." She touched her abdomen. "But siblings. A family. I want big gatherings and silly arguments over holidays and all the love—"

This wasn't supposed to be a test, but she sensed the way he withdrew a little, hiding his thoughts while she cleared her throat and continued to speak.

"—that I see when everyone is together like this. I always envied Cin for having this when I lived here. That's what I feel like I don't deserve after bringing Gilbert into their lives. I thought he was going to give me this and he *didn't*." The scored sensation behind her sternum deepened. "He showed me why I couldn't have it."

"Do you still love him?" Tension entered his body, as though bracing for a blow.

"No." The irony was she had hated Gilbert for so long, she couldn't remember why she had thought she loved him. He'd been a master at witty observations and charming compliments. He had claimed to want what she wanted—travel and a concentration on career, then a family. It had all been a lie, though. He hadn't even been good in bed! Not like…

Don't. The fact that Joaquin gave her orgasms didn't mean she ought to fall for him. *Don't fall in love again*, she warned herself, but the layers of her defenses were peeling away like broken eggshells. Joaquin wasn't even trying to get under her skin! He was only being himself: honest and honorable and protective. Holding her when she was upset. He didn't see through her. He *saw* her.

It was deeply perturbing, not because she didn't feel safe with him, but because she did. What if she was setting herself up for another grave disappointment?

The more time she spent with him, however, the more her turmoiled emotions around Gilbert became flaky remnants she was happy to discard. Letting go of her hurt and anger and guilt made room for this: for Joaquin and the things she felt for him that were already far stronger and sweeter and hotter and more enduring than she'd felt for anyone else ever.

She was falling in love with him, she realized with a lurch in her heart. And she wanted him to love her back.

Was it even possible for him to love, though? Was it possible for him to love *her*?

The yearning in her was so strong, she could only stare at the tab on his quarter-zip pullover, trying to hold back the burst of emotion that was threatening to crest again and spill over in fresh tears.

"You were young, Siobhan. You made a mistake. We all do that." He smoothed her hair and pressed it against her skin as he tucked his hand against her neck. "But the way you're punishing yourself puts me in an impossible position."

She frowned up at him. "How?"

"I won't tolerate anyone being cruel to the mother of my child." His thumb caressed the edge of her jaw. "So I must insist you set your anger aside, *cariño*. Be kind to yourself."

"Or you'll do what?" she asked on a chuckle of reluctant humor.

"Distract you. Coax you into a better mood." He dipped his head to graze a light kiss against her lips. "Remind you that you deserve to be treated well."

A spark of sensuality flew directly into her center and began to burn. He *was* distracting her. He was making her feel cossetted and appreciated and understood. He was making her feel *hope*.

And maybe, just maybe, she was lucky that Gilbert had disappointed her so badly. Otherwise, she wouldn't be here in this moment with this man. Maybe fate really had had a plan.

That thought was a jostling turn of a kaleidoscope, rearranging all her dark, jagged thoughts into new, colorful patterns. Something that dazzled.

"How well?" she asked as she stole her fingers into his hair. "Teach me a lesson."

"That would be my pleasure." He claimed her mouth with his own and reached past her to yank the curtain back into place.

CHAPTER FIFTEEN

I WANT THIS, Siobhan had said of the big family and the endearing chaos they created.

As the day wore on, Joaquin began to see the appeal. There was a lot of laughter and teasing and children scooped up by loving arms that belonged to the nearest adult.

He also caught a glimpse of the indulgent mother Siobhan would become. It did something to his heart when he saw her with the youngest princes of Zhamair, cooing and cradling the identical twins. It caused a stretching sensation in his chest that stole his breath.

The princes were five months, he was told. Both were strong, determined little wrestlers. They smiled at her, chewed their fists, batted clumsily at each other, then dug their toes into her while trying to scale her shoulders.

"Do you need me to hold one of them?" Joaquin was compelled to ask, experiencing the strangest impatience to see her cradle their own baby. To hold it himself.

"Don't you dare." She expertly firmed her arms around them. "The only thing better than holding one baby is holding two."

"Auntie Dorry is our baby whisperer," their father, Kasim, told him. "That's why Gili and I had twins. I was assured Dorry could be persuaded to come live with us."

"Oy, you did this on purpose, did you?" she teased. "Well, I'm tempted." She dipped her chin to nuzzle one round cheek, expression tender. "Maybe I'll take them home with me. You wouldn't mind, would you?"

"I think you're finally old enough for me to say this to you, little one, but *make your own*." Kasim stole one of his sons and held him over his head, pretending to eat the boy's guts and making the boy giggle.

Siobhan sent Joaquin a look of amusement at their shared secret. Job done.

An electric sensation struck Joaquin. It was a primal desire that went far beyond sexual want. Beyond his desire for her and their baby to be safe and comfortable. Beyond anything he had ever wanted for himself. He wanted this for *her*.

Which made it imperative to remove any threat from his father, once and for all.

He brought that up when he finished battling Henri on the tennis court the following morning.

Joaquin had won, but not easily. They sat down to orange juice and toasted bread smeared with olive oil, crushed tomatoes and slices of dry-cured jamón, watching Ramon and Isabella play Trella and Xavier.

"I presume Ramon relayed everything I told him in Madrid about my conflict with my father over LVG?" Joaquin asked.

"He did." Henri brushed his fingers on his napkin.

"I'm taking off the gloves with him. There could be blowback against Siobhan. And your family, once her connection to you is known."

"Then stop seeing her," Henri said.

I can't, Joaquin almost said, thinking of the baby, but

that was Siobhan's news to share when she was ready and the truth was, "I don't want to."

"This is serious, then?" Henri pressed. "You're in love with her?"

With Henri's astute gaze pinned on him, Joaquin felt as though he had his neck fully exposed, but he hated to show his hand—or his heart. Especially when he was so unsure of his ability to give it.

"My intentions are honorable, yes." He wanted to spend his life with her. He had known that from the moment he'd seen the pulse of their baby's heartbeat on the screen. No, the glimmer of a future with her had first flickered to life within him when she'd asked, *What will we do if...* Before that, even, when he had wished for more time than a single night in San Francisco.

"Having said that," Joaquin continued gravely, "I'd like to prevail on you for a favor, in the interest of time. I know how this request looks, or would in Siobhan's eyes. Hear me out."

Henri nodded curtly.

"I'm working at buying up my father's debts. Some of his creditors feel enough loyalty to him that they're refusing to sell to me, but if you were to approach them through your channels, he wouldn't know I was pulling the strings. I'm not asking you to be out of pocket. I'll cover everything."

Henri waved off that detail, even though they both knew they were talking eight and nine figures.

"It's a delicate situation. I need to keep Siobhan's true identity off my father's radar until I've crippled him. Otherwise, he has a fresh and effective avenue to attack me."

"Us," Henri said with a grimace.

"Exactly. I would call him ruthless, but *reckless* is the

better word. This favor isn't without risk for you. Say the word and I'll look at other options."

"The day he comes for my family is the day *I* cripple him," Henri said. "Does she need extra security?"

"I'm arranging that."

Henri nodded thoughtfully. "Have you discussed this with her?"

"Not yet." Joaquin grimaced again. "She would be devastated if she thought she was the reason my father came after any of you. I don't even want to put the potential of it into her head."

"Don't. She puts too much pressure on herself for our safety. That's my job, not hers. And she can't hide her connection to us forever. It sounds as though your father will become a problem to me eventually. I'm making the decision to deal with it now, while it's easily contained. Do you have a list of targets and timelines?"

"I do."

Christmas Day was utter perfection, filled with food and torn paper and nonstop laughter—especially when Malik discovered that all the gifts Joaquin had wrapped were missing name tags.

She and Joaquin looked at each other, perplexed.

"You said you'd do it," he reminded her.

"I did!" She burst out laughing.

Everyone groaned, but she recovered by having each child find a gift that was missing a tag. It turned into a game to open it and give it to whoever was the intended recipient. The children loved it.

Her gift for Joaquin *was* labeled. He looked uncomfortable accepting it, saying, "You didn't have to get me anything."

"I wanted to," she insisted and had to wonder whether he was given gifts very often. By his reaction, she suspected not.

He frowned with curiosity as he unwrapped the framed photo. He read the accompanying certificate. "You bought me a race car?"

"A share in the team Ramon is buying. You seemed interested when I mentioned it last week."

"I can honestly say this is something I didn't know I wanted, but I'm delighted to have. Thank you." He kissed her then dropped a gift in her lap that contained a pair of earrings he "thought would suit her."

The large, pear-shaped aquamarines were suspended from a shimmering row of brilliant-cut diamonds. When she joined him in bed that evening, she wore only them and thanked him by kissing her way down his torso, eventually making her way back to his lips.

"Not just for the jewelry," she whispered when his heart was still pounding and all the tension had left his body. "Thank you for being here with me. You helped me remember why I love this time of year."

She was in love with him, she realized in a rush of clarity. It was a wide, glorious light inside her, one that felt so distinctly *right* she didn't know why she'd fought it. Joaquin might still be reticent at times, but he was a fiercely protective, caring, indulgent man.

Her love was so fresh and new and perfect, she almost said it aloud.

But he was twisting to roll her beneath him, kissing her with ravenous passion.

"My turn to have a peek under the tree. I think there's one more gift for me." He parted her legs and slid down.

CHAPTER SIXTEEN

THEY LEFT THE next day, amid pleas to stay longer. Ramon and Izzy were staying through the end of the year, but both royal families were needed at home.

"Joaquin has work and we're attending a New Year's Eve gala. But I'm not so far away anymore," Siobhan reminded Cinnia. "Come see us anytime."

They hugged it out and Siobhan was still floating in warm, happy vibes when they arrived back in Barcelona.

She *loved* his home here. It was two stories in an older building and managed to be both spacious and cozy at the same time. There was a comfortable breakfast nook in a sunny corner of the kitchen and a wraparound terrace that looked onto the sea. A Jacuzzi tub stood on the balcony off the primary suite surrounded by wintering shrubs strung with fairy lights. Empty flowerboxes promised a riot of color in the spring.

After all the drama at LVG and the shock of her pregnancy and the busy-ness that had led up to Christmas, she needed the pleasant bubble of contentment that encased them between Christmas and New Year's. Joaquin mostly worked from home while she read a book on pregnancy and combed through a contract for him, making notes that had him saying, "Good catch." They cuddled in the evening while watching movies, slept late and made love midday because *why not*?

It was a life she could get used to. It was the life she wanted. With him.

But it only lasted until the last day of the year.

Neither of them had left the penthouse much and, now that they were away from Madrid and LVG, Siobhan had begun to believe Lorenzo no longer posed a threat. It was the sort of complacency she should have known better than to fall into, but she did.

She booked herself into a spa for the day, one where she knew the massage would put her to sleep. She needed a nap if she was going to stay awake until midnight tonight.

Toward the end of her pampering, when her makeup was done and the stylist was finishing her hair for the party, the woman in the chair next to her looked up from her phone.

"Are you Dorry Whitley?"

The bottom fell out of her stomach. Siobhan reached for her phone while playing it off with a confused, "Why do you ask?"

"This is you, isn't it?" The woman angled her screen to show Siobhan her own face.

Her phone rang in her hand. It was Joaquin.

"Are you safe?" he asked tightly.

"I think so." Ripples were traveling through the salon. She was getting surreptitious looks. "Qahira is here." As a precaution, Joaquin had hired her a bodyguard, one who had so far had precious little to do since she left the house so rarely. "What happened?"

"My father must have discovered your identity. The gossip sites are showing photos of us in Madrid with headlines about Dorry Whitley surfacing after being missing for years."

As though she was some sort of criminal who'd gone into hiding and had suddenly been spotted? Yuck. But it didn't surprise her. It was exactly the type of made-up scandal the press had pinned on the Sauveterres for years.

"I'll call Cin and warn her."

"Stay there. I'm coming to get you."

"No, I'm almost done. I'll leave in a moment." She glanced at the woman doing her hair. The woman nodded.

In the few minutes it took for her to put on her coat, someone from inside the spa had sold the tip. A number of photographers were gathered outside the spa in the courtyard entrance of potted trees that surrounded a reflecting pool.

Siobhan's driver pulled the SUV up as closely as he could, but there was no straight path to it. She had to walk around the water into one of the lines of photographers.

As she stepped outside with Qahira, the piranhas closed in, snapping their cameras. That caught the attention of several passersby who halted to record her with their phones. Someone shoved a microphone toward her face and asked a question in Spanish.

Qahira blocked him and shouted for everyone to "Move back!"

Siobhan saw an opening and tried to dart through, but was yanked to a stop when someone grabbed her arm.

She reacted on instinct, surprising her attacker by flowing into the force of his tug on her arm. She continued into a pivot, pulling the photographer off balance. As she did that, she ducked low and threw her hip into his groin. She heard his breath leave him as she reached behind her shoulder, grabbed behind his neck, got her back into his stomach and used his own momentum and the strength in her thighs to lift him off his feet.

She flipped him into the pool of water. His camera clattered to the bricks and the splatter of drops hitting the pavement was overloud. Everyone froze in shock.

"That's what you get when you touch someone without their permission," Siobhan said. "Who's next?" She took a threatening stomp toward the nearest person holding a cell phone.

Everyone stumbled backward.

"Señora." Qahira opened her long arms, forming a barrier while the driver opened the back door of the SUV.

Siobhan dove in.

Joaquin was livid when he saw the footage. *Livid*.

Siobhan's altercation with the photographer was posting on all the social media channels and entertainment sites, all from different angles, all showing her defending herself from the attack.

She called him from the car to reassure him she was safe. Then Killian called him as Joaquin was watching it. Then Henri called him. Siobhan's phone was pinging like popcorn as he met her in the lobby of his building.

"I'm taking you to the hospital," he said as he tried to keep himself from crushing her in his twitching, battle-ready arms.

"I'm fine," she insisted. "Shaken up, but that photographer will be the one wearing bruises." She pulled away and stalked into the elevator.

Joaquin waited until they were in the apartment to say, "The baby?"

"Fine, I think." Her profile turned stiff and wan. "I wasn't hurt and I was moving furniture before I knew I was pregnant. Nothing happened. I'll see a doctor if it becomes necessary, but for now, I'd rather be here where I'm safe and comfortable."

If it became necessary. The mere thought of her losing the baby made him sick. If she went through anything more because of his father—

Joaquin closed his eyes. He couldn't let himself think of it. It made him too murderous. This had to end. *Today.*

"No, you don't have to come," Siobhan was telling her mother over video chat. "I promise I'm fine. This will blow over in a few days— Yes, I know, but now that I know I'm doxxed, I'll take precautions. Yes. Cup of tea. Feet up. I'm doing it now. Tell the girls I'm fine, but I'm turning off my phone for a while. Thank you. I love you, too." She sank onto the sofa and blew out a long breath.

"Will you put the kettle on for me?" Siobhan called while she watched the video. "Oh, come on," she couldn't help exclaiming.

"What?" Joaquin asked shortly. "I thought you were turning that off."

"I was on the phone the whole way here. I hadn't seen the video." She sent him a bright grin, then looked back at the screen. "Whenever I took those self-defense classes, they would warn me that it's different in real life, that I might freeze in shock, but muscle memory works. I look like a freaking action star. And could I have been more camera ready?" She pointed at the hair and makeup that had withstood her tussle and was still on point and tapped Watch Again. "I'm so glad I wore those boots today."

"It's not funny, Siobhan," he near shouted.

"It kind of is." She couldn't help her smirk. "The guy looks like a cat that fell in the toilet."

"Nothing about this is funny."

She sobered as she took in his hair standing in spikes from his agitated fingers, his grim expression and the light of torment in his eyes.

"You're right. I'm sorry." She dropped her phone onto the cushions and rose to hug his waist, finding his body had turned to concrete, but his arms locked tightly around her. "I'm sorry you were worried about me." She rubbed her cheek on his chest then tilted her head back. "But don't you find it a little bit reassuring that I can take care of myself?"

"You shouldn't have to!" He pulled away and shot his hand into his hair again.

"I know, but this isn't your fault. We don't even know if your father is behind it. Someone else may have recognized me."

"No, it was my father," he said grimly, pacing a few steps. "Henri called me just before you arrived. I've been using him as a go-between to buy up some of Lorenzo's debts. One of the creditors put it together and tipped off my father to my plan."

"Wait, what? You were using Henri?" Her heart juddered to a stop in her chest. Her whole body went cold.

Joaquin held up a hand. "That was a poor choice of word. I asked Henri at Christmas to let me use his channels, so my father wouldn't know I was behind the buying of his debts. We were trying to stay ahead of my father learning of your connection to the Sauveterres. I knew he would exploit it once he found out."

"Why didn't you tell me?" She waved an agitated hand.

"I didn't want to upset you."

"And you knew I would be upset," she said, growing worse than upset. "You knew this was a red line for me.

I thought you wanted *me*. Not Henri and his resources. I thought you and I were growing closer. I thought I could trust you." She had fallen in *love* with him.

"You can," he swore, but the shadows of betrayal stayed heavy over her heart.

She shook her head, wondering how she could have been so stupid. Again.

"For God's sake, Siobhan. This is what he does." Joaquin's voice shook. "If he can't take what I have, he destroys it. Don't let him do that to *us*."

"What *us*? I'm here because I thought we were a team. A partnership." She had to blink fast because her eyes were welling. "I trusted you so *you* would trust *me*. I took a chance for our baby. For *you*. I wanted to show you it was safe to love me so I—" Her throat flexed, nearly closing over the words. "I let myself fall in love with you."

He drew a rough breath and held out a hand, but she brushed it away.

"Don't act like that's news to you. I told you it could happen! I thought at the very least it was *safe* to love you, but it's not."

A number of emotions flashed across his face before he shuttered his expression, brick by brick.

"It's not safe, no," he said in a tone that was so grim, it lifted the hairs on the back of her neck. "Not until I've dealt with him once and for all." He picked up his phone and walked to the door.

Her blood was congealing in her veins at how murderous he sounded. "What are you going to do?"

"Whatever I have to."

"Joaquin, stop," she cried, truly afraid he would do something he couldn't undo. "How does leaving like this reassure me you're in this relationship for *me*? I need to feel like I'm more than a means to an end, but you're choosing hating him over loving me. Do you see that? He is not the one tearing us apart. *You* are."

"What do you want me to do?" His voice was tortured. "Tell you I love you and beg you to stay here until I get back?" He shook his head in a way that negated his thrown-away words. "You're better off as far away from me as you can get."

Her brittle heart cracked. "Then I won't be here when you get back," she warned.

His breath cut in as though her words had been a knife into his chest, but he only asked, "Where will you go? Your sister's?"

"What do you care where I go?"

He didn't even say, *I care*. He just left.

CHAPTER SEVENTEEN

SIOBHAN DIDN'T LET herself agonize over whether to leave. She knew she would always have doubts about Joaquin and his motives if she stayed.

So she left.

The safest thing would have been to go south, back to her sister's, but she didn't want to pretend for the children and everyone else that she was fine. She wasn't fine. She was devastated. Brokenhearted.

She wanted to be alone. She felt foolish, exactly as she had after she had trusted Gilbert, so she went north. Home. To her mother's empty house in London. Where she had gone the last time.

Her eyes stung the whole way, but she fought back the tears. She could accept that Joaquin wanted to vanquish his father, but why hadn't he told her what he planned? She felt used again. Betrayed again.

And shut out. Why didn't he ask *her* to help? She was actually a very spicy bitch when crossed. Had he not seen how she had treated that man who had grabbed her?

That gauntlet of photographers had actually been really frightening. Once she was in the car, all she had wanted was to be home with Joaquin. Safe in his arms.

He *had* made her feel safe. Until this.

Four hours after hastily packing, she arrived in Hertfordshire.

The house she had grown up in was an older home on a property of mature trees and well-tended flowerbeds. It had been bordering on shabby when she'd been young. Their mother had barely been hanging on to it. They had all worked to keep things afloat. Cinnia had had her estate practice, the middle girls had worked in pubs and shops. Siobhan had shared a room with Cin so her mother could rent hers out. Aside from earning a few pounds babysitting, Siobhan had been too young to contribute, which had always made her feel like a liability.

Once Cinnia married Henri, everything changed, insisting the house receive a complete upgrade so it had top-notch security and a twelve-foot wall around the garden.

As she entered the code for the door, and Qahira moved into the shadows to ensure the house was empty, Siobhan thought of that old song that began, *Hello, darkness*. Except it wasn't her friend. It just made her feel melancholy.

"Clear," Qahira reported.

Siobhan thanked her and moved through the house, turning up the heat and putting on some lights.

The decor had also been refreshed in recent years. The floor was now a posh golden hardwood. There was a piano beneath the floating staircase, and the potting shed was a proper guest cottage where Qahira would stay.

Siobhan went upstairs to unpack, almost turning out of habit into the room she had once shared with Cinnia. Rather than two singles, it now held bunk beds for the twins to use when Cinnia visited their mother here.

That had Siobhan remembering Christmas and the fact Joaquin had attended the festivities with her. At the time, she had thought he had gone for *her*. Now she was questioning his motives. Had he been wanting to speak to Henri all along?

No. He could have talked to Ramon when Ramon was in Madrid. The fact was he didn't *need* her to use the Sauveterres. And Henri wasn't stupid. He wouldn't allow himself to be used. He would have had his own reasons for helping Joaquin.

Even if Joaquin had gone there specifically to ask Henri for a favor, he had still helped her work through her anger at herself. He had helped her build memories she would cherish for a lifetime. He had restored her joy in the holiday.

She closed her eyes against emotive tears as she remembered the way he had brushed off Maya's palm when she had stumbled.

"You need to kiss it," Maya had insisted. So he had.

He was going to be a magnificent father. She knew that deep in her bruised heart.

She believed he wanted to be a supportive husband, too. That was why he was trying to keep her safe. He did care about her. He had demonstrated that in countless ways, but she had let her insecurities get in the way. She had jumped straight to being used because it was easier to believe that was where her worth to him lay than that he valued *her*.

She was still devaluing *herself*. Acting as though she was silly Dorry Whitley, whom people saw as a conduit to power and money, when Dorry Whitley was actually a powerful badass in her own right. Everyone online was saying so.

Joaquin had let her go, though. The same way he had let Esperanza go when her feelings grew deeper than he was comfortable accepting.

He didn't love her.

Or did he?

What do you want me to do? Tell you I love you and beg you to stay here until I get back. You're better off as far away from me as you can get.

Had he *wanted* to beg her to stay? And only pushed her away and left because he felt such an urgent need to protect her from his father? She knew what that man was capable of. She had kissed the scars on Joaquin's skin.

Was she going to make him beg for her to come back? She should have stayed and showed him love really was a healing force. That it was safe to love her because she would stand by him no matter what.

Oh, God. She had made a terrible mistake.

Joaquin brushed past the tired-looking maid who opened the door of Lorenzo's Madrid town house and walked straight into his father's den.

Lorenzo was in his recliner, holding a cigarette and glass of brandy. He didn't lower the footrest, only squinted at Joaquin through the smoke.

The smell was both pungent and stale. Sickeningly familiar, bringing back too many memories of being called on the carpet for beratement or punishment.

Joaquin refused to think of that now. He was as cold and detached as the man before him.

"I wondered why you were diddling your assistant. Do you really think threats from her family will scare me?"

"They should." Joaquin set his phone next to the ashtray and sat on the chair beside his father's. "You're threatening an innocent woman who has nothing to do with you or me."

"She left you? That's too bad." His father puffed smugly on his cigarette.

A deep, aching emptiness had opened in his chest on his way here. Joaquin had never been so terrified in his life as when he had watched Siobhan flip that man into the water. Then he had seen her pulling away from him because she believed he had betrayed her.

I thought it was safe to love you, but it's not.

When she had said those words, they had lashed the back of his heart in the most painfully sweet way. All of him had stung as he absorbed something that ought to feel foreign. Threatening, even. Instead, his response had borne a strong resemblance to a soft, new tenderness that had been germinating inside him. He had wanted to catch her close and explore that, but no, loving him was not safe.

Until he left his father in a pile of his own ruin, Siobhan would never be safe.

So he had let her go, even though he had thought it might kill him. Even though walking out on her could break all those tiny threads that had begun to bind them together.

This had to be done. This bully would not rest until his ass was in the dirt and that was where Joaquin would put him, once and for all.

"I want the proceeds off the patent for the relay I designed."

Lorenzo snorted. "Cash running low now you don't have the backing of the Sauveterres?"

Joaquin didn't bother correcting him on his very healthy bank balance. "Would you rather I sued you to prove I'm the rightful owner? That you stole that design from me?"

"Who would believe you? You were a child."

"And yet I did it."

"With the education I paid for."

"And that gave you the right to take it as your own? I have since built up credibility in that field, in case you haven't noticed. Meanwhile, everything you released after my design was a second-rate knockoff of a competitor's design. Have you ever wished you'd kept me around to continue working for LVG?"

"No. I don't like you. I never have." He jabbed his cigarette stub into the pile of them in the ashtray.

"And why is that?" Joaquin asked, so filled with cold hatred, he no longer cared, but he made himself ask, "What did I ever do to you that I deserved to be put in hospital at eleven?"

"You're too much like your mother. Fernando looked like me, at least. You..." Lorenzo curled his lip. "And you never knew your place."

"You disgust me." He really did. Joaquin's stomach was turning. "I should have you up on charges for attempted murder. I was a child."

"A clumsy one." His father lit another cigarette.

"So you claimed. We both know what happened."

"I know that you wouldn't shut up about visiting your mother."

"Why didn't you let me live with her if you hated us both so much?" Joaquin was lancing a boil that had sat in him for too long, simply because he couldn't stand to be in the same room. Tonight, however, he would get the answers he needed, no matter how unpleasant or painful.

"Because that's what she wanted," his father said with a cruel curl of his lip. "And so did you."

"You put me in the hospital so I couldn't go to her. And refused to let her visit."

"It shut you up, didn't it?"

"Do you revel in making people suffer? Is that it?"

"I like to win. It's not my fault you've always been too weak to fight back."

"I was a child," he scoffed. "And I've never seen decency as a weakness. Another way I was like my mother, I suppose." He twisted his lips with contempt. "But you're right. I've always deluded myself into believing I could reason with you, but that's not possible, is it? I thought cutting you from my life would be enough, but you can't stand that I have succeeded in spite of you. In spite of your *theft*."

"That really sticks in your craw, doesn't it? Fine. I'll trade the proceeds on what remains of the patent in exchange for your shares in LVG."

"There are only a few years left on the patent. No. Go back to when I handed you the drawing and I'll consider it, since that's when the real money was made."

"It doesn't matter that you designed it. *I* funded the development of it."

"LVG funded the development. Which is why I'm keeping the company, by the way."

"I'll burn it to the ground before I let you keep it."

"Arson?" Joaquin rose and picked up his phone. "This is a useless conversation. As usual."

"See?" His father lowered the footrest and hitched forward on his chair. "This is why I treated you the way I did. It's so easy to best you. You never fight back. You don't *deserve* to be my son and have what I have. You give in too easily."

"I don't want to be your son. And I haven't given in." Joaquin glanced up from tapping the screen on his phone. He waited until the whooshing sound confirmed the file had sent. "I'm playing your game. Doing whatever it takes. You lie and cheat and threaten and steal. So that's what I've done." He tilted his phone. "Our conversation is with my lawyer. You'll be hearing from him on the stolen patent and the attempted murder that you just confessed to. And the arson you've threatened."

Lorenzo made a scoffing noise and threw his head back, but his gaze followed the phone as Joaquin pushed it back into his pocket.

"How does it feel? Never mind. I don't care," Joaquin derided. "Your debts are being called. By me. You might hang on to this house, but you'll lose everything in it. I've also decided to claim the artwork that was Mother's. Her will stated one third to her spouse, two-thirds to her children. You didn't know I knew that, did you?" He hadn't wanted the hassle of going after it, but all bets were off now.

"I've put a lien on the yacht until the audit at LVG completes. There are a lot of unanswered questions around misappropriation of funds." He started to leave then turned back. "The woman you keep in the pied-a-terre in Paris? She's been informed that the money tree has been cut down. She'll be gone by morning with whatever you might have squirreled in the safe there."

Lorenzo was turning purple, eyes sparking with outrage, but all Joaquin could think was how pathetic he looked.

"I'm not throwing you into the street the way you did me. Not because I'm too weak to do it, but because I don't need to. You'll be there soon enough." He started for the door.

The ashtray struck the wall beside the door, puffing ashes across Joaquin's sleeve.

"You're losing your aim, old man. I'm having restraining orders prepared. Zurina, the children, Siobhan. *Me*. We're all off-limits. Never speak to any of us again."

He walked out.

It was dawn on the first day of the New Year when Joaquin entered his empty penthouse in Barcelona.

He was exhausted, but he didn't stop to sleep. He only confirmed that Siobhan had actually left him, retrieved a box from the safe, then headed back to the airport.

He had the sense to check the security log before he filed his flight plan and learned Siobhan hadn't flown to Marbella as he'd thought. She had gone north, to London, so that was where he told the pilot to aim his plane.

It should have been a straight shot. New Year's Day was a slow day for travel. Half the world was sleeping off their celebrations from the night before, but a freak snowstorm over France forced his plane to land at the private airfield in Paris.

Swearing wearily, he disembarked and had the concierge book him into the onsite hotel. It catered to traveling VIPs like himself so his luggage was handled for him and his room details were sent to his phone. He would catch a few winks until the skies cleared then finish his trip.

As he walked into the lobby, he texted Siobhan.

I'm on my way to London to see you.

No. Don't come, she replied.

He stopped in his tracks, immediately swamped by grief. Not the grief that accompanied death, like Fernando. Not the loss of something taken, either. It was the loss of giving up something within himself, making himself vulnerable. Making his needs known. It was the grief of offering himself and knowing he would never be whole again because a piece of himself was hers now.

And she didn't want him. He was being discarded.

His phone pinged. He almost didn't look at it. It was all he could do to stay on his feet.

I'm on my way back, her text read.

To him?

For one second, he experienced that old feeling of desire. The one he tempered out of fear. What if he only lost her again a different way?

Hell, he might, he realized.

Don't go to Barcelona, he quickly texted. I'm grounded in Paris.

In the same second that he heard a distant ping, he heard a feminine voice say a confused, "What?" It came from around the corner. "So am I," she murmured. "Where in Paris?"

He took three long steps forward. His phone dinged in his hand, but he didn't have to read the message because there she was, standing in front of the elevators, staring at her phone. She wore a pink puffer jacket and jeans stuffed into boots rimmed in faux fur. Her hair was sparkling where snowflakes had landed and melted.

"Are you at Charles de Gaulle?" he asked her, voice rasped by disbelief.

She picked up her head and her eyes welled as she stared at him. Her lips began to quiver and her voice hitched. "No. I'm here."

He walked forward and snatched her into his arms.

They kissed forever. Hard enough to hurt, but it was a good hurt. It was the kind of hurt that uncramped muscle and knitted bone. It was the hurt of thawed flesh warming and prickling back to life.

It was the agony of apology and remorse and forgiveness.

"Um. Excuse me?"

They broke apart to see the doors had opened and a pair of well-dressed older women were trying to step out.

"We have a flight," one said.

"Of course." Joaquin steadied Siobhan as they stepped out of the way, then they both stepped into the empty elevator. "Have you been to your room? Come to mine."

"Heard that before," she said under her breath, then gave him a helpless, befuddled look. "I can't believe we're both *here*."

"No? I'm not surprised."

Fate? Did he really believe that?

He took her hand and led her to the room he'd been assigned, using his phone to access it then pulling her inside.

"I would have chosen to ground you here if I'd thought you'd be in the air. Were you really coming back to me?" He trapped her against the door. "Are you okay?" He ran his hands over her beneath her open coat, sparking need within her to be close, close, close. "Is the baby okay?"

"We're both fine. And yes. I just..." She cupped his face and brought his mouth back to hers. "Can we—?"

"Yes." He pushed her jacket off her shoulders and they stripped on their way to the bed.

Was it the most tender, prolonged lovemaking in history? Not at all. It bordered on frantic and stung a little because she wasn't quite ready, but she needed this connection *now*.

She gasped and he froze.

"Hurt?" He cupped her jaw and started to withdraw.

"No. Stay." She wrapped arms and legs around him. The sands in the hourglass stopped falling. Time itself halted as she kneaded her fingers into his hair and skimmed her thighs over his flanks and scraped her teeth against his whiskered chin.

"I shouldn't have left you like that," he groaned, burying his mouth in her throat.

"Shh. I don't want to talk about him. I just want to feel you."

"But I should have said it back, Siobhan. I love you. I love you so much…" His eyes misted. "Saying it aloud felt too dangerous. You wouldn't have left and I was scared for you. You are very, very precious to me, *mi amor*." He traced her eyebrow and followed an invisible line to the corner of her mouth. "You're everything I want. You've become someone I *need. You*. I don't know how to make you believe that."

"I do believe you," she said, letting the glow of it seep into the old fractures in her heart and heal them. Letting herself feel his love as the acceptance and celebration of her that it was. "I love you, too."

She set about making sure he felt it, just as he imbued every kiss and caress with tenderness and worship. They sighed and whispered endearments and groaned with sweet torture. The feelings intensified as they ascended toward a heavenly peak, until they were both caught there, clinging and sweaty and joyous. Drunk on each other. On love.

"I want to stay here forever," she gasped.

"We will," he said. Then held her tight as they fell.

They did what they had wanted to do in San Francisco. They stayed in bed, dozing between making love and ordering food.

Their luggage turned up eventually, not that they used more than a toothbrush.

"Should we go into the city?" he asked at one point.

"Cinnia would give me the code for their penthouse. It overlooks the Eiffel Tower."

It was already dark and they were comfortable in bed so they turned on a movie and fell asleep before it was finished.

She woke to find Joaquin wearing a frown as he read his phone.

"What's wrong?" she asked.

"Killian wanted me to know my father is catching a flight to Saint Lucia. They don't extradite to Spain."

"Will you have him stopped?"

"No." He had told her about his conversation with his father. "As evidence goes, his confession was incriminating, but it still would mean years in court. That's why I didn't try something like it sooner. That, and I didn't want to sink to his level."

She shifted so she could see the scar on his ribs and bent to set a kiss there. "Do you want to tell me about that?"

"Do you really love me?" He tucked his hand at the side of her neck, expression grave.

She was shocked and a little hurt that he would question it. "With my whole heart."

"Then no. I don't want to tell you. It will hurt you. I don't want to do that."

And somehow, that hurt more. Because it was a kindness at his own expense.

She pressed herself half over him, pulling him under the shelter of her slender arm and leg, wanting to cry for him. For the boy he'd been.

"The one thing I have never wanted to be is like him." He stroked her hair as he spoke. "But there was no other way to deal with him except to double-cross him. It felt wrong to do it. It's not the sort of person I want to be, but when he caused you to be attacked, I wanted to kill him. I really did. That is not the sort of husband and father you and the baby need. The kind you deserve. I questioned whether I should come after you."

She picked up her head, alarmed. "What changed your mind?"

"I thought of Fernando," he said simply. "He was equally cold-blooded when he took over at LVG after Lorenzo's heart attack. It was underhanded, the way he moved with the board to unseat him, but he had to do it. And he bore the consequences for years." He ran his thumb over her bottom lip. "Zurina still loved him. Which gave me hope that you would love me, too."

She ran her teeth across the tingle he'd left in her lip. "I wasn't sure if you loved me, but I thought you might, if I gave you a chance."

"Of course, I love you. It sits like a beacon inside me. That's what scared me. I had trained myself not to hope. I tried to hold back from you, but it's there all the same. Hope and want and a craving for you like I crave air. Maybe you're right. Maybe fate does want us to be together, but I need you to know that I'm *choosing* you, Siobhan. I'm choosing to love. To believe I can have you in my life. I'm doing this badly." He scraped his hand over his face.

"No. You're doing it right." She spilled her naked body over his. Her own chest full of hope and joy and gleaming love.

"Okay, then. Will you… Wait one sec." He rolled her

off him and stretched to reach the sleeve of his coat, dragging it from the chair to the bed. He fished through the pockets. "Will you wear this?" He opened the ring box to reveal a square diamond on a split band encrusted with smaller diamonds. It sparkled and shot prisms into the backs of her eyes, dazzling her.

"Are you asking me to marry you?" A smile was taking over her whole face.

"Because I love you, yes. Because I can't imagine my life without you. Because we're having a baby and I want to give you the family that you long for."

Oh. She blinked away fresh, emotive tears.

"Well." She cleared her throat. "Since it would be very comfortable and convenient to have the person I love and want to make babies with be my husband, I accept." She held her finger for him to put it on her.

"Brat." He brought her hand to his lips and kissed her fingertips. "Never leave me again. That was among the worst moments of my life."

"I never will," she promised with a press of her quivering lips to his.

EPILOGUE

One year later...

IT WAS THEIR wedding day. They were keeping it small, family only, and marrying at *Sus Brazos*. Siobhan's mother and sisters were here along with Zurina and her children and, of course, all the Sauveterres and their children.

It was the delightful madhouse of her dreams.

Siobhan should already be on her way to the suite that had been set aside for primping and setting hair and dressing her in her simple, seed-pearl encrusted gown.

Her groom had his own places to be, but he hadn't left their rooms yet, either. They had slept together last night and made love this morning.

A few minutes ago, Siobhan had finished feeding Rogelio, their four-month-old son. Joaquin had lingered instead of leaving, then took Rogelio while Siobhan stepped into the shower.

Along with nannies, there was a grandmother and countless aunties dying to hold him. All the other children wanted a turn giving him a cuddle and having photos with him, but as Siobhan came out of the bathroom in her robe, she found Rogelio was still here, playing with his father.

Joaquin sat in the armchair with Rogelio clasped in one arm. Rogelio was still in his jammies. He was strengthening his wobbly legs against Joaquin's thigh, one hand curled into the soft T-shirt Joaquin wore.

He chewed his fist as he watched the small teddy bear that Joaquin slowly swooped toward him. "He's going to tickle your belly."

As the plush bear arrived in Rogelio's middle, the baby let out infectious baby chortles. Joaquin laughed right along with him.

"Now he's going to get your neck."

Siobhan stood struck with wonder as she watched them. It wasn't the first time she'd seen Joaquin be so tender with their son. It happened many times a day, but it filled her with awe and tenderness and pure happiness every time. In this moment, the sight of Joaquin's defenses completely down as he allowed his naked love for his son to shine in his face, brought a squeeze of adoration to her chest and made her eyes sting with joy.

He noticed her. "You're ready to go up with him? I'm sorry, little man. If the adoration of all those women gets to be too much, call me and I'll take you to the barber with me." Joaquin dropped the teddy bear so he could pinch a lock of fine strands in two fingers to measure it. "You could use a shave and a cut, no? While we talk politics and the economy?"

"Do you want to take him to the barber with you?" Siobhan asked with amusement.

"I do." Joaquin looked at their son's big blinking eyes and swiped his thumb beneath his drooling mouth. "But your family will be disappointed if I take him so I will share him."

Rogelio caught his finger and brought his knuckle to

his mouth, using it as a teething toy, then kicked with excitement when she came close enough to reach for him.

"We'll have him to ourselves on the honeymoon," she reminded Joaquin as she took the baby and he rose to kiss her.

His wide hand splayed itself on her ass through the thin silk of her robe. "I'm looking forward to having *you* to myself on the honeymoon," he said in a low, sexy voice.

"Then we should get married, shouldn't we?"

"Details, details," he chided, cupping their son's head to press a kiss to his temple, then kissing her once more. "I'll see you soon."

A few hours later, Henri escorted Siobhan down the aisle to where Joaquin waited for her. Zurina stood up for him in Fernando's place. Cinnia was Siobhan's matron of honor. She held Rogelio, their ring bearer in an adorable baby tuxedo.

Siobhan teared up as they spoke their vows and pure love radiated from Joaquin's eyes. Her voice shook with emotion as she devoted herself to him, and he promised himself to her.

Later, after photographs and speeches, a song performed by the chorus of children and a wonderful dinner, Joaquin took her into his arms for their first dance.

Siobhan had requested "At Last", but for some reason, the band began to sing about Paris and Rome.

As wedding glitches went, it was nothing so Siobhan didn't make a fuss. The song was pretty and danceable. It seemed familiar, but Siobhan didn't place it until the crooner lamented that he had left his heart in San Francisco.

"Did you do this?" she asked, tilting her head back with amusement.

"What?"

"Change the song?"

"Is this not the song you wanted?" He was wearing a relaxed expression, not the one that hid his thoughts. He wasn't laughing at her and only looked mildly curious as he met her gaze.

"You're teasing me," she accused. "*This* song?"

"I didn't do anything. I swear. Do you not like it? It seems appropriate." His mouth twitched wryly at the lyrics.

"You really didn't ask them to sing this?"

"I really didn't." He touched his mouth to hers. "It must be kismet."

It must have been.

* * * * *

MILLS & BOON®

Coming next month

GREEK BOSS TO HATE
Michelle Smart

Footsteps approached.

Draco dragged a breath in through his nose, inhaling the soft scent of her perfume, and braced himself before turning to face her.

'You've tidied up,' Athena said brightly, as if nothing had happened, as if she hadn't just cruelly insulted his mother and he hadn't cruelly rammed some home truths down her throat.

'Someone had to.'

She shrugged. 'Not much point in keeping it tidy or unpacking. I'll be out of here soon.'

His mind unwittingly zipped to her bedroom. If he'd had to imagine it, he'd have pictured it like a witch's coven, not the soft, feminine, spotlessly clean room that it was. 'Not for another two months.'

'You'll have sacked me by then.'

'No.' He drilled his stare into her. 'That is not going to happen. You are going to spend the next two months tied to my side. By the time you're released from the contract, you'll be as sick of me as I am of you. Now, drink your coffee. We need to get going—we've got a long day of work to do.'

Continue reading

GREEK BOSS TO HATE
Michelle Smart

Available next month
millsandboon.co.uk

Copyright ©2025 by Michelle Smart

COMING SOON!

We really hope you enjoyed reading this book. If you're looking for more romance be sure to head to the shops when new books are available on

Thursday 18th December

To see which titles are coming soon, please visit
millsandboon.co.uk/nextmonth

MILLS & BOON

FOUR BRAND NEW BOOKS FROM
MILLS & BOON MODERN

Indulge in desire, drama, and breathtaking romance – where passion knows no bounds!

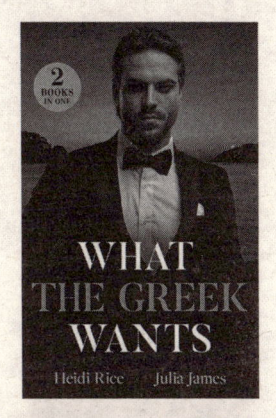

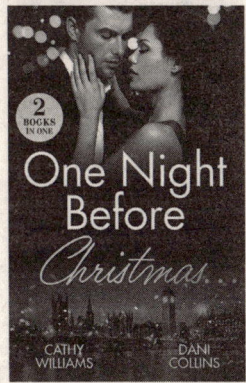

Royally His – LaQuette & Maya Blake

What the Greek Wants – Heidi Rice & Julia James

Seduced by the Enemy – Abby Green & Emmy Grayson

One Night Before Christmas – Cathy Williams & Dani Collins

OUT NOW

Eight Modern stories published every month, find them all at:

millsandboon.co.uk

TWO BRAND NEW BOOKS FROM
Love Always

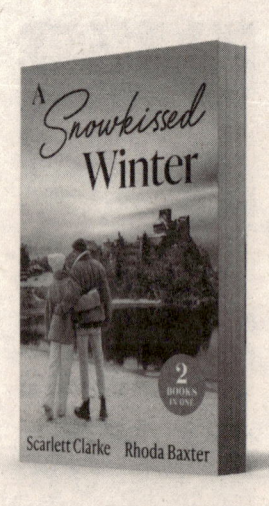

Be prepared to be swept away to incredible worldwide destinations along with our strong, relatable heroines and intensely desirable heroes.

OUT NOW

Four Love Always stories published every month, find them all at:

millsandboon.co.uk

OUT NOW!

SNOWBOUND Christmas Nights

3 BOOKS IN ONE

SHARON KENDRICK CAROLINE ANDERSON SUSAN STEPHENS

Available at
millsandboon.co.uk

MILLS & BOON

OUT NOW!

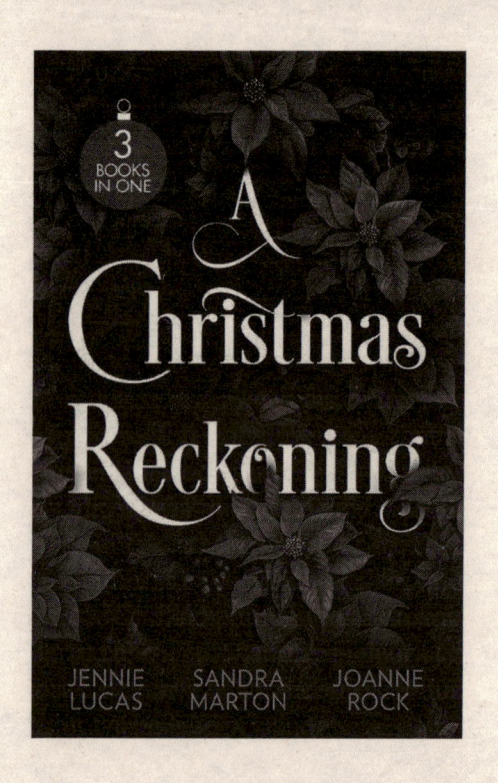

3 BOOKS IN ONE

A Christmas Reckoning

JENNIE LUCAS SANDRA MARTON JOANNE ROCK

Available at
millsandboon.co.uk

MILLS & BOON

OUT NOW!

The Christmas we almost lost

DANI COLLINS   **KATE HARDY**   **SASHA SUMMERS**

3 BOOKS IN ONE

Available at
millsandboon.co.uk

MILLS & BOON

LET'S TALK
Romance

For exclusive extracts, competitions and special offers, find us online:

- **MillsandBoon**
- **@MillsandBoon**
- **@MillsandBoonUK**
- **@MillsandBoonUK**

Get in touch on 01413 063 232

> For all the latest titles coming soon, visit
> millsandboon.co.uk/nextmonth